The
GREAT
WHEEL

The GREAT WHEEL

BY IAN R. MACLEOD

HARCOURT BRACE & COMPANY

New York   San Diego   London

Requests for permission to make copies of any
part of the work should be mailed to:
Permissions Department, Harcourt Brace & Company,
6277 Sea Harbor Drive, Orlando, Florida 32887-6777.

Library of Congress Cataloging-in-Publication Data
MacLeod, Ian R., 1956–
The great wheel / Ian R. MacLeod.—1st ed.
p. cm.
ISBN 0-15-100293-2
I. Title.
PR6063.A24996G73 1997
823'.914—dc21 96-53365

Text set in Stempel Garamond
Designed by Trina Stahl
Printed in the United States of America
First edition
ACEDB

For Gillian

EVERY YEAR AT the time of the harvest carnival, the Borderers came to Hemhill. They came in trucks with darkened windows, came fast down the highway through the ruins of the old city, past the low white houses and on into the big compound at the far end of the valley. For most of the year the warehouses behind the shockwire lay silent, the avenues and huts and wide concrete spaces were empty. But the Borderers rolled back the gates and powered up the shockwire. They filled the doors and windows with light. They fixed and they tested. They set to work.

On clear autumn nights after his bath and his storybook, John would lie in bed and listen as the hum of the compound carried across the fields. When his mother's kiss and his father's smile had faded, he liked to think of the Borderers down in the valley, those faceless people working shift upon shift through to morning.

Later, on the best nights, Hal would sometimes look in, sliding the door open to check for a wakeful glint in his little brother's eyes. It was Hal, sitting at the edge of the bed with his broad figure outlined against the glimmering room, who first told John about the Borderers. He explained how the harvest—the reducing of the hoppers of jelt to fibrous bricks, winnowing the wheat, pressing the oilnuts, draining chloroethane from the treetappers netted in the late summer hills—created conditions that were too dirty and dangerous for machines or Europeans.

"I've seen the Borderers working," he once said to John. "And I've been in the fields and watched them go by. They're skilled in ways that we aren't, Skiddle, and they work hard to earn the money they send back to their homes in the Endless City. Don't ever believe anyone who says otherwise. Really, if it wasn't for the color of their eyes, they'd be the same as you and I . . ."

Hal's voice rose and then faded as he leaned down to kiss John goodnight. He stood up from the bed and the door closed and his footsteps passed into silence along the landing, and gravity shifted as once again the room filled with the hum of the compound riding on the darkness down the valley. John thought of the Borderers working and of the city from which they came, of the Endless City, dark and empty as he now saw it, abandoned like the compound in the times between the harvests, yet infinitely vast. In his dreams, he wandered those soundless streets alone, was swallowed in the loneliness of black windows and untenanted doors, of turns and alleys and avenues unfolding forever into vacant squares beneath a sky without moon or stars.

THE SACRIFICIAL GOAT, with polished hooves, horns dyed red, coat washed pearly white, was tethered to the back of a ribbon-draped truck. The crowds along Gran Vía were cheering as it passed, shaking their fists, throwing scoops of mud and dung, spitting chewed reddish wads of the local leaf, shouting words of anger and encouragement.

Father John wiped the sweat from his face and pressed the cloth until it dissolved, then rested his gloved hands back on the sash frame of the top window at the Pandera presbytery, leaning out to watch the procession pass five stories below him. Behind the goat truck came witchwomen clattering teeth and beads, a gamboling clown, skull-faced conjurmen, jostling flags. Then the firefly glitter of excited children waving chemlights. Then the women, widow-black and keening like gulls. Here and there, he recognized the faces of some of his own parishioners.

A voice behind him said: "These people aren't like us, John. Sit down, sit down. What's the point in watching them if it bothers you so? Bella will be bringing the tea up in a minute..."

The procession flowed on between the houses. Colors ran like an oil-rainbowed river, red, silver, and gold from luminous fabrics; then came shimmering images from screens slung over donkeys trailing wires and powerpacks. Cartoon monsters and coupling bodies soared, half-solid, into the air. And what were the people singing? John strained his ears to catch the words accented with the guttural Magulf dialect. But even with the translat he always kept hooked to the belt of his cassock, he found the Borderers hard to understand, and the translat would be worthless now: the voices that drifted up with the seaweed smell of massed Borderer humanity ebbed and pulsed like static. The sound was formless, the yawning breath of a mouth surrounded by the clattering heartbeat of bells and drums.

He turned away from the window.

Amply seated, his feet propped on a soiled cushion, Father Felipe studied John though silver half-lidded eyes. "You've upset them," he said. "You know that, don't you? Upset them by refusing to get involved in their carnival. A lad came to the door here only the other day and asked—"

"It's not my duty to please these people."

"Ah, duty!" Felipe rumbled gently with laughter.

John pulled a chair across the gritty floor and sat down. Outside, he could still hear the rumble of the procession. "Animal sacrifice is pointless...wasteful. You think I should misrepresent the Church by seeming to approve of it?"

Felipe scratched absently at a food stain on his cassock. The room was half dark already, and the tiny glowing spines that

4

ran along the fingers of his gloves made a reddish blur. John glanced down at his own gloves, which were still veined a leafy green; he had several more hours before he'd need to pull the thread along the cuff and incinerate them.

"I'll tell you a little secret," Felipe said. "I used to join in that procession—when these legs here would let me. Wave that big censer from the back cupboard in Santa Cristina's chancelry." He chuckled at the memory. "I'm sure the children used to put some sort of drug in it."

It was no secret. The children had told John about it when they came up Santa Cristina's hill in the smoky dusk one evening as he was closing the church and asked him to bless the goat. The old priest was just playing games—or perhaps even acknowledging in a roundabout way that his precedent had put the new and younger man in a difficult position.

"Ah!" Felipe cocked his head and beamed. "Here comes tea." All John could hear was the sound of the procession drumming like rain, but Felipe had somehow got hold of an expensive ear implant to counter his deafness. He heard everything.

After a long moment, the door from the stairs creaked open and Bella backed into the room with a jingle of china.

"Bless you, my girl. *Gunafana...*"

The presbytery maid lowered her head. She had on a thin blue housecoat stained with sweat across the back, arms, and shoulders, and long-sleeved gloves of cheap cotton. Now that winter had ended, she'd also taken to wearing the impregnated facemasks they sold down at the Alcalá souk.

"And spicecake, I see. I really don't know how you do it. Bella, my dear, you're a marvel."

"Thank you, Fatoo."

"And I suppose you'd rather be out there, eh, my child? Joining in the fun?"

"No, Fatoo. This is my work."

"Of course! You see, John—here's another one who understands duty..."

John saw the attentiveness that came into Felipe's eyes as the young Borderer woman leaned to place the teatray on the low table. Every day those rheumy silver irises sparkled with sudden life as they studied the curves of her breasts.

Bella stepped quickly back. She crossed her arms. Her facemask sucked in, blew out. Framed by it and a fringe of black hair, her big chestnut eyes remained blank. Felipe liked her to wait here with them each afternoon as they took tea, but John hadn't grown used to having human servants.

"*Tak*," Felipe said. "You might as well get on with whatever it is you're doing, Bella."

Bella lowered her head again. "Yes, Fatoo."

Felipe watched the sway of her rump as she turned and left the room. The door closed. Her footsteps faded down the stairs as, outside, the carnival procession was now also fading, giving way to the sigh of the hot, ever-present wind. The ceiling fan ticked slowly overhead, circling shadows across Felipe's face, stirring the strands of hair that he smoothed across his bald pate.

"You're not the first one, John," he said, "to come here, to disapprove of these carnivals."

"I can imagine."

"I remember there was a blond-haired lad..." Felipe knotted his hands as he searched for and failed to find a name. His fingers squealed faintly, damp with condensation and sweat. "Anyway, *he* thought he could change things."

6

"Didn't you ever want to do that?" John asked. "Change things?"

"Of course." Felipe took the teacup, blew at the steam, then propped the cup on his belly. "In my youth, I thought I could be anyone, do anything. Of course, I've lost that feeling now."

"And doesn't that bother you?"

"Of course it does. The Endless City shakes so many of our safe European conceptions. Life here is put to chance in a way that we barely understand. How many funeral rites do you think I've performed down at El Teuf? Little scraps of flesh that hardly had a chance at life gobbled up by the mouth of that big incinerator..."

"Don't you get angry?"

"We're here to be the shepherds of souls, not to burn with anger. Remember what Epictetus said."

"*I* don't want to lose my anger. If I lose that, I'll be accepting things exactly as they are."

"And tell me, why should this world need your acceptance?" Felipe slurped his tea, clattering the cup on the saucer. "We're here for other reasons, my son. Believe me, this isn't the priest in you that's speaking—it's the man. I know, my son, that you have your doubts, your troubles. I understand that. Truly, I understand and I sympathize. But that doesn't..."

John let it wash over him. They'd talked this way, oh, far too many times before in the six months he'd been here. It never got them anywhere. No matter how he tried, he couldn't engage anything in Felipe beyond this clever, weary, seen-it-all philosophizing. The old priest had spent too many years in the Endless City, lying back in the haze of the whisky and trisoma that he took to deaden the pain in his failing legs.

"John," Felipe said, crumbs trembling on his lips as he fished through his pockets for a flask to add to his tea, "this seedcake really is excellent. Lent or no Lent, you must try."

John reached to the old priest's plate and took a bite. It had the bitter, salt-sour taste of the reeking kelpbeds down at Chott from which the flour was processed. He forced himself to swallow.

After the evening service and the cleaning of the paten and the chalice, John locked the shutters over the windows of the church of Santa Cristina. Most of the glass and the original roof had been destroyed long ago by the weather and were now patched with panels and sheets. Still, even if the pillars were tidemarked with damp and the floor was crumbling to rubble, Santa Cristina had managed to survive the centuries. He'd read up on its history back in Millbrooke Seminary when he'd first heard that he was to be assigned here. Or had he read it on board the shuttle? Now he couldn't remember—any more than he could remember what the old analogue guidebook had said. Built by the Templars, sacked by the Merindes...Or was it the Berbers, the Saadians, the Alouites?

He paused beside the stone crusader in the east chancel. Time had eaten away the features, the cloak, the shield. Now, noseless and age-corroded, with hollow sockets for eyes, the figure resembled a skeleton more than anything else. He touched the stone with his gloved hands, crumbling away a little more. He didn't mind the decay of the church, this statue, the looted ornaments, the smell of damp that in another hour or two would override the lingering odor of incense and the characteristic sweat-smell of his departed Borderer congregation. The church was old anyway, dying.

8

The sound of scuffling and scratching came from the high arches as the large black indigenous birds squabbled for nesting space outside on the roof. The votive candles and chemlights of the side chapel of the Inmaculada gave a flickering, cheery glow. It was one of the few bright spots in the rambling church: Our Lady wearing a blue dress and a quizzical smile, surrounded by an oddly Christmassy pile of tributes. Her eyes were greenish brown, like the Bellinis and Titians he had seen in Paris museums. Christ and Our Lady had faces like those he saw here on the street, with a strange gaze of brown or green or blue. Drawn towards the statue as he always was, he noticed that a blackish rime had formed in the outstretched palm of her right hand.

It was probably dried blood, like the fresh red trail he'd found leading to the church's oak door one morning last winter when there'd been snow, and a purplish internal organ that had been left dripping on the altar rail. Looking closer at the candle-lit pile that surrounded Our Lady, he saw chewed baby teethers, wedding rings worn thin, cheap and treasured prosthetics. An unworkable hand. False teeth. The gleam of a glass eye. Cobwebby scraps of hair. These undying bits of the dead never accumulated the gritty dust that settled everywhere else in the Magulf: his parishioners were always picking them up, rubbing them with callused fingers and whispering *Madre.* He thought of Saint Paul in Athens, of the shrines and idols in that city full of unknown gods. Did they represent false images—or other pathways towards the light? Paul had been clear enough in his condemnation, but after all these centuries, after the death in the poisoned weather of half the world and with it the other great religions that had once vied with Christianity, there was still no real answer.

On a rusty stand beside the altar was a plate for offerings and prayers. As usual, it was well stocked. Each card crackled out its message as he picked it up. He could only make sense of a few on first hearing. The cards were thin and cheap—and even when his parishioners tried to speak clear European, the clotted Magulf vowels still came through.

A woman, with the sound of a baby crying in the background. "To Lady. Pray the soul of our son Josh."

Another woman. Something about the roof of her shack blowing in.

A man, in tears, too choked to say anything at all.

To get anywhere near understanding the rest, John had to take the translat from his belt and hold it close. Each time a card spoke, the translat's screen flickered and the power meter sagged before it barked out the words. The translat didn't get on well with the speech cards, but its flat, Eurospeak voice eventually echoed each message.

"Please mercy and forgiving. In the name of the gods."

"Pray now for rain, and for my friend Delo. As it was in time of the Dark King. Amen."

One card had pinned to the back of it a small plastic bag filled with titanium bolts. "For Jesus," it chirped, and the translat gave a clear but tinny echo a moment later. "Please remember."

Remember what? For whom? He gazed up at the face of Our Lady. She was smiling and sad, self-absorbed, and her carved lips always seemed to be holding back the same eternal secret. He wiped the rusty stand and then the main altar rail with a fresh dysol-impregnated cloth from the pack he always carried with him, an anointing that was part of the ritual of reassurance that took place between Borderer and European even when there were no witnesses. Then he changed gloves. Pulling at the thread and dropping the old pair to the floor, he watched them flare and dissolve, and brushed away the ash with the toe of his shoe.

He destroyed the unused wafers. Normally he would have gone through at least two of the sealed packs in an evening service, but today the congregation had been limited to a few old women, a few old men, and the babies that they'd agreed to look after while the rest of the people enjoyed the carnival. He'd had half a mind to acknowledge the fact during the service, even try—through the translat, or by testing his own stumbling command of the dialect—to crack a joke. But when he gazed down at those strange eyes, and at those warm and gnarled hands that he could never touch, the silence had closed in.

Freewheeling, his cassock flapping, he cycled down the cobbled hill from church.

These empty zigzag streets had once belonged to a town with its own name and history. The Endless City stretched along the north coast of old Africa, reaching through the dried-up regions of the Nile and the ancient battlefields of the Holy Land as far as the Black Sea before finally tapering out in the frozen wilderness of the Russian Plains. For the most part, the urban sprawl was narrow, hemmed in by mountains and the wildfire desert, pressed up against the gray waters of what had once been called the Mediterranean and was now named the Breathless Ocean. In this easterly part known as the Magulf, where John worked, the coastlines of Europe and old Africa almost touched. It had once been called Morocco—or possibly Algeria. The maps had blurred long ago.

Typically by this time on a warm, reddish dark spring Magulf evening, the candles and the cooking flames and the chemlights would be glowing, the streets would be spilling with beggars, vendors, fights, snake charmers, family arguments, scurrying children. Tonight it was much quieter. The alleyways were empty—even the dogs were single and furtive. Everyone who could manage to get there was farther down the hill in the old plazas, the bombsites, the open spaces. Enjoying the carnival.

He slowed and dismounted where the slick cobbles steepened and broke into a stairway of rubble between the houses, joined halfway down by the flow of what had probably started out as a stream somewhere up in the Northern Mountains. He picked his way with care, lifting the bicycle over a rock and banging his ankle in the process, conscious of the gaze of an old Borderer woman sitting at a window above him. She was watching the carnival's flickering lights, listening to the squawk of untuned trumpets and the thump of drums and firecrackers that filtered up along this damp maze.

"Hello," he called, looking up. "*Gunafana*. What can you see up there?"

He'd asked the question slowly, but the woman only blinked back at him. He was considering raising his voice or turning on the translat, when she spoke.

"Go home, *baraka*. We don't want you here," she said. "Get back to your own hell."

She pursed her thin lips and spat. The saliva plopped on a

mossy stone beside his feet, stained red from her chewing the koiyl leaf.

Then, with more accuracy, she spat again.

He had two calls to make that evening. He visited the homes of a few of his parishioners each day, even though those Borderers who were prepared to embrace the faith he represented were often unwilling to accept him personally. The only invariable exception came when someone was seriously ill. Then, the Borderers wanted him, and not simply because of the clinic he ran each morning from the old post office in the Plaza Princesa next to the bombed-out towerblock. Even when the doctor's medicines and scans had been exhausted, they wanted John to pray and touch his silver cross and mutter to Jesus, Mary, and the Lord.

His first call was down the hill on the Cruz de Marcenado, one of the main streets that bisected this part of the Endless City in line with the coast. Here, the music was louder—he was closer to the carnival's glittering fringe. Cooking smoke was rising over the patched rooftops, the light in it gleaming on the rancid lakes of winter mud that still filled the middle of the thoroughfare. A couple ran out towards him from an alleyway, laughing, hand in hand, the boy pulling the girl against a show of weak reluctance, her shirt flapping open to show her sweat-shining breasts. Riding his bicycle along the sticky pavement, John stopped; for a moment he thought that they hadn't noticed him. But the boy and girl had the same unerring sense for the presence of a European that all Borderers had. They halted and turned, their laughter momentarily stilled. Under a starless

Magulf sky, they studied him with grave and questioning eyes. Then, laughing again, they ran on.

John propped his bicycle against the wall in a nameless street, leaving it unlocked in the certain knowledge that its obvious cost and newness would warn any light-fingered Borderer kids to keep clear. He banged hard on an old doorframe. After a pause, the burlap nailed over it was jerked aside.

"Fatoo. You here. Please, he get worse."

He hesitated. Then, turning the translat to Transmit, he followed the woman inside.

She led him down a low corridor and into the one ground-floor room that was home for her and her family. He heard the familiar scurrying rustle of departing cockroaches as she turned up the lantern.

The air stank of sickness. There was a cheap, newish sofabed, a methane cooker in an alcove topped by a few cans of Quick-lunch, the drip of a water purifier in the corner. A screen hung at a slight angle on the wall, and in it hovering figures moved with a distorted impression of depth. She was picking up some faint transmission from Europe: through the jittery fuzz, he recognized the tanned, smiling faces. The silver eyes.

He asked, "How is he?"

A moment later, the translat's electronic voice declared *How ice uhe?* To John, it seemed a reasonable rendition of the Magulf dialect, but he didn't doubt that, booming out in this hot, dank place, it sounded as artificial to the woman as the translat's European sounded to him.

"He's worse, Father." She pulled back the blanket that screened off one corner of the room to show him her son. "Have you brought any medicine?"

"No. No medicine."

. . . meed-shun.

He studied the little figure that lay before him. The boy was about six or seven—the woman's only son. His name was Daudi. And her name, he now remembered, was Juanita. Unlike many of the Borderers who came to his morning clinics, Juanita had already been one of the regulars at Santa Cristina when her son fell ill. Usually it was the other way around. They'd turn up at the clinic, and if a treatment worked, they'd show an interest in Christianity. Even if things continued to get worse, the Borderers would often offer to take the sacrament in case John was holding something back from those patients who didn't embrace his faith.

"Will he live?"

She'd asked him that question several times before—even that first morning when she brought Daudi to the clinic. Then, Daudi had still been able to walk, although he was weak, dazed and bleeding from the gums and colon. After the buzzings and drillings of its consultation, the clinic's doctor, which for once had been almost fully operational, confirmed John's fears of acute myeloid leukemia.

"Will he live?"

"He's very ill. It's cancer, a disease that can't be cured. It's a cancer of the blood, leukemia."

. . . bludrut.

"In Europe? Even in Europe, he can't be cured?"

"In Europe, cancer is different."

"There is no cancer?"

He took a deep breath, feeling the sour wash of his own body heat. Juanita was standing at the usual safe distance the Borderers assumed, two or three steps from him—which in here meant that she was on the opposite side of the room.

"No," he said, "not in Europe—not until we grow old. There are these things, Juanita, special viruses in our blood, implants along our spines, inside our bodies. That's why I can't…"

Her brown eyes stared back at him as the translat repeated his words.

"I'm sorry, Juanita. Daudi's going to die."

"Will you pray for him?"

"Yes…of course."

"Then pray for him. Pray for him now."

John looked down at the child on the bed. He'd dealt with several leukemia cases and in his own laymanish way had become a kind of expert. The first case he'd had was a woman with lush, jet-black skin, still young enough to possess the bloom of beauty that Borderer women so rapidly lost. She'd come to him as they always did—too late. He still attempted treatment, but the ancient cytotoxic drugs that Tim Purdoe in the European Zone at Bab Mensor had synthesized for him were never intended for use outside a hospital, and the woman died anyway—pretty much as Tim had told him she would— but probably more horribly, from the green fungal growth of some secondary infection. He'd learned his lesson then; that the desire to help in useless cases was a selfish attempt to deal with his own guilt.

He unscrewed a flask of holy water and reached out towards the stained, sunken bed. The woman let out an instinctive gasp, but he knew she wouldn't stop him from touching her son. At least not as long as he kept his gloves on. His sheathed fingers brushed the boy's forehead, the skin as thin and pale as the bone it scarcely covered. Daudi was comatose, but for a moment the sunken eyelids seemed to quiver.

Speaking the too familiar words, pausing after each line for the translat to repeat them in a form that Juanita would recognize if not understand, John felt a sudden impulse to rip off the gloves. To heal, to touch. He shook his head and continued...

In the name of God the almighty Father who created you.
In the name of Jesus Christ, Son of the living God, who
  suffered for you.
In the name of the Holy Spirit, who was poured out upon
  you.
Go forth, faithful Christian.

As he spoke, the hot, silent room seemed to whiten.

The other call he'd planned to make was also on the edge of oldtown. Even he, a European, avoided going too far out in the Endless City at night, but he felt he was starting to acquire some feeling for navigation in the sprawling, unmapped, and ever-changing slum. It came from a mixture of many things: from the position of the sun when its glow could be discerned through the clouds, from the gritty feel of the almost constant southerly wind, from landmarks like the broken minaret of the Moulay Mosque and the rotted tower of his own Santa Cristina—or from the strength of the distinctive reek of the kelpbeds.

Down through the gateway in the old medina wall. A glimpse between the buildings of a tangled roof-fall all the way to the shores of the Breathless Ocean, where the kelpbeds gleamed in a break of moonlight like shattered green ice. And then right, and right again—into the blaze of the carnival in the Plaza El-Halili.

Too late, he realized the way he'd come. Inextricably entangled with the surrounding alleys, souks, and streets, the Plaza El-Halili was one of the bigger squares in the lower part of oldtown and usually crowded. But he'd never seen it like this. The buildings swam in a haze of light and smoke. People were everywhere. Bells and iron pots, drums and pipes were tooting and clanging. And there were the conflicting smells of incense, booze, the reek of stalls piled with fish, the fumes from fires, the sweet, teeth-aching aroma that came off graveyard piles of sugarballs in the shape of skulls, the smoke from tubes, the sweat-steam that sprayed off dancing bodies.

The instant that he stepped from the shade of an archway out into the light, the Borderers noticed him. They paused in their dancing, in their selling of wares and picking of pockets, in their arguments and their laughter. They fanned back and away. The sense of his presence passed through the square in a chilly, inaudible whisper.

Blue, green, and brown eyes studied him. Mothers reached down to grab the hands of children. Nearby music stopped, hanging on a discord. He nodded pointless thanks, wheeling his expensive bicycle through the space that parted for him, the battery coil slung beneath its crossbar and glowing, the big soft tires plowing through mud and litter.

Down the slope of the square, away from the frigid sphere of his influence, a stage had been erected against the castellated walls of the old Kasbah. The rusty scaffolding was draped with silks and flags, colored with smoky-pink chemlights, drifting fluorescent globes, endless shimmering ribbons. A play was in progress. A huge, leering mask loomed over a shrieking band of children. Their faces were blackened and their thin bodies smeared with ash. Their shrieks sounded alarmingly real.

"Hey, Fatoo," someone shouted out.

He saw a Borderer youth towering over the hunchback woman nearest him. The youth's hair was tangled with beads, and a cosmetic implant pulsed bluish red through the skin beneath his rib cage, like a second heart.

"Fatoo, you come anyway, huh? You here, and join in? Tonight..."

The lad was smiling—and John could see no trace of irony in the smile. Borderers weren't like Europeans anyway; they usually said exactly what they meant. The people around John began to nod and laugh. To beckon. The invitation spread. Koiyl-stained teeth grinned. Someone else laughed and pointed at the sky. Yes, come on, Fatoo. Join in. *Skay.* Come and share with us. *Cum.* Share...

John shook his head and pushed on towards the escape of the nearest archway. He passed quickly into the shadows, away from the carnival to where the blind walls and windows glistened in the faint red light of the Magulf sky and rats and caroni birds fought over something in the mud and the pulse of light and music faded.

He turned on his bicycle's front light, kicked in the standby motor, and rode slowly uphill. He could remember harvest carnivals back in Hemhill when he was a child, the great painted wagons, the good smell of the corn in the church beforehand, the Sunday perfume of the women, the beery breath of the men. And he remembered laughing and wrestling with Hal in the churchyard grass when the service ended, the two of them tumbling down the hill towards bright canopies, clangorous carnival engines, all the sweet discord of the fair. Thinking of vast European grainfields, the smell of dust, the hum of the compound in the valley that signified the end of summer, John dismounted from his bicycle in a dank Magulf square.

It was steeply enclosed on all sides, and in the center was the mouth of a communal sewer. His ears still rang from the carnival, but that only increased the sense of silence. Could *everyone* have possibly gone out tonight? Surely there had to be people other than the ill, the infirm, and the odd European priest who didn't want to participate.

He climbed the sagging steps and found the right door. It was open. Inside, he had to rely on touch. There was a passageway—a left turn?—definitely another set of stairs. He stumbled on through the darkness. The silence around him was no longer absolute. There were the creaks and stirrings that came from the flexing of the jelt floor and walls—also from the disturbance his passage was causing to the old building's many nonhuman inhabitants. He paused. Normally, there would be lights, kids in the corridors, music blaring…

But for the glow of his gloves—now pale red at the tips—and the faint light that came from the small personal monitoring screen of the watch set into the flesh just above his left wrist, the darkness was absolute. A few more steps, and he had to stop. Perhaps he should go back. He'd visit old Banori on the way to the clinic tomorrow morning. After all, the difference was only one night…But then he heard a sound, a low moaning that could have come from the livestock that the Borderers sometimes kept in their homes, but could just as easily have been human. He took another step forward. His right foot banged something, and he reached out to grab a wobbly stair rail. He began to climb.

The landing was illuminated in the glow of a chemlight from

the one open door, and he saw the dim shapes of waste barrels and of the water butts that in times of rain were fed from the roof by an elaborate system of pipes; otherwise they were filled laboriously by bucket from the pump in the yard. Such arrangements were always the subject of much local argument. It sometimes struck him that this was almost their primary purpose, especially as the things regularly broke through the weak floors to either comic or disastrous effect.

The open door was the one he wanted. He crossed the landing towards the light and entered.

He saw instantly that he'd come too late. Banori's corpse sat facing him from the old high-backed chair, its eyes already sunken and lifeless in the chemlight's dying radiance. The room was in an odd kind of mess, but John had picked his way around the furniture towards the body before the truth dawned. Even in the soupy atmosphere of a Borderer tenement, the place was filled with the bland, salty reek of blood. Black sprays of it garlanded the walls. They were still wet, scrawled by a strong, sweeping hand into hieroglyphs whose meaning he couldn't even guess at.

He looked around. He crossed himself. Whatever else it was that witchwomen did for the death rite, they generally left the place looking like an abattoir—although, as far as he could tell without undertaking a pointless analysis, the blood hadn't been the old man's. Not that it mattered now. In death, Banori smiled. He was wearing his best clothes, with his white hair slicked neatly down. He also had a set of teeth in, something John could never remember him wearing in life. Or perhaps the teeth were just another part of the ritual. They'd probably end up with all the other teeth in the chapel of the Inmaculada at Santa Cristina.

By Felipe's account, Banori had been a church regular even

before John's arrival in the Magulf, a true Christian, turning up every Sunday at Mass propped on his walking stick until a succession of strokes finally grounded him to his flat. The neighbors complained about his cantankerous and unsanitary ways, but as far as John could tell, they had always made sure that he had the necessities to live. And every week or so, John looked in. Usually, he offered to say prayers or Mass, and Banori would decline—in an accent that strained even the abilities of the translat—saying that he was close enough to God, to Scuro Rey, to be past that kind of thing.

Now, he'd gone the last mile. Maybe another stroke—but more likely he'd had enough of the indignities of age and got hold of something to end the pain. Peering at the clenched and smiling lips, John saw the glitter of tiny glass flakes that might have come from a crushed vial, and a sticky bubble that looked too black to be simply blood. Whatever it was, the presence of the witchwoman who'd scrawled these walls could hardly have been coincidental. It seemed as if this Church old faithful had finally chosen the witchwoman's comforts over those of a priest when he decided to bring his life to an end.

John pulled off his gloves. What difference could it make here? He took out the flask of holy water, flicking away the beetle that had crawled out from the sleeve onto the old man's hand. Once again, John began to recite the too familiar words: *May Christ be merciful in judging our brother...*

He heard the moaning sound again—obviously some pig or goat on the floor above. The clump of feet. The footsteps faded, then suddenly grew loud and close, bringing with them the moaning and a bizarre, Christmassy jingle of bells.

He ceased his blessing and spun around to look at the open doorway behind him, which was blocked by a shadow.

"There's a dead man in here." He buried his bare hands in the pockets of his cassock. "I'm from the Church of Santa Cristina. Do I—"

The figure spat out a chain of sound that lay far beyond his understanding of the Magulf dialect.

"Look—*danna-comma*—I don't understand—"

Still muttering, the witchwoman stepped into the room. John was torn between shock and curiosity—he'd never seen one at such close quarters before—and the first thing that struck him was the feverishly intense body heat she gave off. Even at two or three meters, it was like standing close to a fire. And then her eyes. She had some sort of fringed cape over her head, and the rest of her face was deep in shade, but the eyes were like wet slate and impossibly big. He tried to calm his breathing.

The witchwoman was breathing heavily, too. Her shoulders were shuddering, heaving, jingling the forest of silver and gold that hung on her. There were boxes dangling from the knotted ribbons, tiny cages that contained chittering insects, gilded skulls. The whole thing made a tinkling, whispering cacophony, like the crackle of frost...a flock of panicked sparrows...a thousand windchimes caught in a breeze. Then the pebble-bright eyes blinked back at him, and every sound stopped at the same instant.

In sudden, absolute silence—the chirping of every insect hushed, every bell magically still—the witchwoman stepped towards him.

"I suppose you and I..." His voice came out as a whisper. "We have something in common. We see to the needs of the dead."

The witchwoman studied him. More slowly this time, she spoke again. He still couldn't understand a word, but the voice was young, and he saw now that she wasn't as he'd imagined such creatures to be. All he could see of her face was her eyes, but through the silent curtain of bells and insect cages and the elaborately woven smock beneath, a sense of youth and physical power beat from her almost as strongly as the body heat.

Rocking gently, the witchwoman began to moan. And with her movement, the insects resumed chirping, the bells jingling. Tiny flashes of light sparkled through the swaying veils of her smock.

He stared. The noise seemed to pulse and sway with her movement, filling the room. The sound of it was as compelling as her heat and her scent. Glittering, unearthly, musical.

He saw her hands emerge from the frayed golden cloth around her waist and penetrate the chattering curtain of cages and bells. Transfixed, he watched her turn her palms towards him. They were bloodied red, and each bore a wide gash, a yawning mouth, a wound; like stigmata, a vulva.

He felt cold air break on his sweat-covered palms a moment before he realized that he had drawn his hands out of his pockets, and that he was reaching out towards the witchwoman.

Her eyes stared back at him.

Clearly, she said, "Touch me, Skiddle. Here—take my hands."

She was amused. Unafraid. He swayed and took an unthinking step backwards, bumping into the arm of the chair where Banori's corpse sat. That broke the spell. He ducked and ran out of the room, tumbling down the stairway, slamming from side to side along the main corridor. He slid down the steps into the mud of the square, falling to his knees. He could still feel the witchwoman's presence behind him, but the square was silent, and when he looked back, the tenement doorway was empty.

Somewhere, a dog began to bark. The air was spinning. Faintly, he could hear music. Wiping the mud off his bare hands onto his cassock, he mounted his bicycle and hurried away.

Pedaling along empty Gran Vía through the litter of tubes and chemlights left by the afternoon's procession, he saw that Felipe's top-floor light still shone from the Pandera presbytery. He parked his bicycle, kicked off his boots. He climbed through the freshly roped cobwebs of two empty stories that led to the building's inhabited quarter, and made his way along a corridor by the light of a bare electric bulb. Bella was obviously still up, too; it was always her final job to switch off the generator before turning in. Or perhaps she was out like everyone else tonight, enjoying the carnival.

He paused outside the door of Felipe's room. He could hear voices inside. Felipe's phlegmy rumble, then Bella's soft vowels. The pad of footsteps.

He stepped back in the moment that Bella opened the door.

"Ah..." She was in her nightgown, but still wearing the facemask. "Fatoo John." She glanced down at his bare, mud-smeared hands. With clumsy, cotton-gloved fingers she reached to button the collar that had loosened around her neck.

"Ah, John!"

Over Bella's shoulders, John saw Felipe sitting propped up in bed, surrounded by pillows, with the usual whisky tumbler and blisterpacks of trisoma on the table beside him.

"Fancy a word? Come in, come in."

John shrugged, then shook his head. "I'm tired. I'll go to bed."

"The Lord bless you tonight, my son..."

In his own room, he combed his hair rigorously, shaking out the dead husks of the lice killed by the phylum-specific poisons secreted from his skin, then washed himself with the greasy soap and bowl of tepid water that Bella had put out. He rubbed hard at the lump beneath his right armpit, where his powerpack projected slightly from the flesh, and at the watch's indentation in his wrist. Then he found himself leaning forward, peering into the mirror on the wall, studying his eyes. The whites were bloodshot tonight, the lids faintly trembling. Close up, the irises seemed translucent, like misted glass against a bright sky. Sometimes he imagined he could detect the blue that he guessed the silver pigment probably disguised in someone with his dark hair, his pale coloring.

The ceiling light blinked out as Bella switched off the generator on her way to bed. He turned from the mirror, pulled the shabby curtains back from the window, and completed his toilet in the red wash that came from the Magulf sky. There were voices along Gran Vía now. Singing, laughter, and the splash of footsteps as the revelers made their way home...

He dropped his cassock into the wicker box in the corner from which Bella took the washing. He picked up the translat. The red standby light was still glowing. He pressed rewind. How long had it been? An hour? The translat searched, stopped, searched again. Bella murmured *Fatoo John...*, and he heard the labored sound of his own breathing, the swish of tires as he cycled back through the empty streets to the presbytery.

Search. Stop. Search. His own voice, speaking a blessing for Banori. *May Christ be merciful in judging our brother...* Forward. The sound of moaning, footsteps from the floor above. He ran it on a few seconds. The jingling. Even through the translat's small speaker, it sounded like more than simply insects and bells.

Then the witchwoman's initial exclamation. He took the volume down, went back, pressed play. The red light flickered, the power meter sagged. For an extraordinary time, the screen flashed Wait. He waited for translat do its usual job of breaking any mystery by reducing all words to the dispassionate phonemes of Eurospeak. Finally, the screen announced: File not accessed. Try another language.

He stared at the bland message. So she hadn't been speaking the Magulf dialect—or any of its close variants. He supposed that that shouldn't come as too big a surprise. After all, even the Church still occasionally resorted to Latin. It was probably some garbled variant of an old African language, and maybe if he saved the data and accessed the net, he might get somewhere with it.

He ran the recording forward half a minute. He wanted to hear how she'd managed to speak so suddenly and clearly in European, in a voice that was so strong and that came—not that it was really possible—from his own past. He heard the jingling bells. The silence. The jingling again. The swaying. The moaning. The squawk of his own voice. The stutter of his agitated breath. Then the thump of feet and furniture as he stepped back into Banori and tumbled out of the room.

He ran it back again. And again. Whatever had happened, whatever words the witchwoman had said to him, the translat hadn't recorded. *Touch me.* Had he imagined it? It was easier to think so.

The screen flashed: File full. Store/Erase?

Crouched on his bed, with the Magulf sky flickering beyond the window, Father John selected Erase.

"Hey, skiddle, look at this."

It was a hot day, and the River Ocean was flat and clear, with blue fingers fanning through the rocks like the sky upturned. Crouching in cutoff jeans, Hal reached down and held something up. A stone. No, a jewel in the sun. A fragment of dripping fire.

"See..."

Skipping carelessly over the shingle, his shrimping net aloft, the soles of his feet hardened to grubby whorls by the long weeks of summer, John scampered over.

Hal lifted the stone to John's eye, a large red iris over his own of pale silver. John squinted through it, looking along the beach, scanning the horizon, then up at the clear and empty sky.

"What is it?"

"Just a piece of driftglass, Skiddle. Here. But you need to keep it wet..."

Hal dipped his hand in a shallow pool where anemones danced. He held the jewel out, and salt rivulets ran glinting down his arm.

"Look through it. See how everything changes. Even the sky..."

THE DOCTOR CREAKED in the stuttering light of the clinic's backroom, and the cards on the cartons of drugs along the shelves sagging behind it glowed in pinpricks of green, blue, and red. John's shoes went *stick* as he crossed the catalyzed dirt floor. The wind rattled the window. The sky boiled over the rooftops beyond. There were still a few voices in the frontroom of the clinic, chuckling laughter, *Ah, fornu,* as Nuru saw to the last of the callers who required the painkillers, antiseptics, and birth control devices that the clinic dispensed.

John sat down at the wobbly screen that was inset into the desk and ran his fingers through the cases he'd seen that morning. He felt the tug of the files as he copied and separated out each case, reordering it in a scatter of patterns according to illness, age, sex, treatment, severity. Here, at least, he could point to something that he'd accomplished in the Endless City.

Even though the doctor lacked the innate facilities, he'd used its memory to reorder and analyze not only all the cases he'd seen but also the records of the priests who'd been here before him. And, outside the clinic, counting, estimating, dictating into his translat, he'd trekked through the local maze of streets and souks, then along the coast, then by the kelpbeds, then the chemical plants, using the data to estimate total population, death rates, age ratios.

He stared at the morning's last case on the doctor's screen. Martínez. Hearing the man's wheezing breath, seeing his red cheeks and the way he waddled, John found that he was still almost as amazed by the fat people here in the Endless City as he was by the disabled and the very old. He had put Martínez down as a sufferer from the common Borderer complaint of circulatory disease, and had assumed that the red on his lips came from chewing the local leaf, until Martínez explained through Nuru that he was having trouble with bleeding gums.

A hard fan of AGTC lines indicated that the doctor's blood analyzer wasn't working, but the doctor recommended the taking of a hip-bone marrow sample. A pointless and agonizing procedure—without it, even without a blood test, John knew that a likely diagnosis for Martínez was acute myeloid leukemia.

He felt a sting from the alarm in his watch. Looking up, he saw that Nuru was already standing at the door, and that the frontroom behind him was empty. Nuru had his hands in the pockets of his smoothly creased black trousers, jingling the coins.

"Fatoo finished?"

"Yes, I've finished. I have to go to the Zone now. Can you get me a taxi?"

Nuru hesitated for a moment, the brown eyes under their dark fringe registering what could have been amusement, then he turned and went outside. John powered down the doctor, turned off the screen, changed and incinerated his gloves, pulled on his jacket, and began to lock up. Nuru had been a fixture at the clinic when John first arrived—that, anyway, was what he was told—and John had come to rely on him. The odd syringe, carton, and blisterpack went missing, and Nuru charged shamelessly for the supposedly free medicines that the clinic gave out, but he could persuade or manhandle those who panicked at the sight of the doctor's lobster arms, and he spoke reasonable European.

Nuru ran back into the Plaza Princesa just as John was keying in the clinic's alarms. Behind Nuru, hammering and rattling, scattering dogs, chickens, and children, came the taxi. It settled on its cushions, and the engine slowed to a dull thwack as John wrenched open the back door. The interior, filled with the smell of Borderer and the cinnamony smoke of a tube, was decked with a mixture of beads and ornaments. As the taxi turned and rose, John glanced through the rear window. Standing in the Plaza Princesa where the bombed-out towerblock clawed the sky like a malignant hand, Nuru smiled and waved.

Plunging between the high walls of a narrow offshoot of the Cruz de Marcenado, John was soon out of oldtown. Children crouched in the road ahead amid puddles reflecting the rusty Magulf sky, but the driver kept his foot firmly on the accelerator, and they scampered off between the piles of aged jelt, soggy cardboard, and corrugated metal. The driver swore, chuckled loudly, tilted back his head to shout *Hey, nach Fatoo...*

On higher ground, John could see the spires of the shuttleport of the European Zone at Bab Mensor, where four times a week the Paris shuttle skimmed down from its suborbital loop, turning west to follow the Magulf coast on a glide towards the corridor of lights that winked on beneath the waters of the Breathless Ocean.

The taxi neared the Zone through another part of oldtown, where the various Borderer service industries clustered around the perimeter fence. Some of the streets were paved, and suddenly there were many other vehicles for the driver to curse at. John spotted a number of wandering Europeans; easily identifiable even when he couldn't catch the color of their eyes, by their clothing, and by the glow—visible at noon under this sky—of their gloves and watches. The buildings along the main street were three- or four-storied for the most part, stuccoed pink, done out with seashell arches, keyhole windows, and bands of colored plastic mosaic in an attempt to recall things Moorish. In the souks that filled the narrow alleys between, leatherwork, embroidered silks, and silver trinkets predominated, with the prices aimed at the expats.

The taxi settled on its skirts outside the shockwire of gate C of the Zone, and a guard with the winged "H" Halcycon S.A. logo on his shoulderpads walked over. John wiped the coins for his fare with dysol, dropped them into the driver's tray, and climbed out of the taxi. Talking to the guard, he felt that odd click that came in his head nowadays when he spoke European.

The taxi rose in a cloud of dust, turning back into the narrow streets of the Endless City. He walked towards the bright net of shockwire.

The gate slid open.

———

The road inside led first though gray hectares of warehouses and the stalking shapes of robot cranes. A small passenger rail-truck was parked by a green sign and the door obligingly slid open as he passed, but he walked the kilometer or so to the medical center for his bimonthly check. He needed the time to readjust. The warehouse area was entirely automated, and the sidetracks, overbridges, and rail lines were festooned with warnings about the dangers of human trespass. There were signs of machine life all around him; two cars hissed by on the road with their windows blanked, but he didn't see another human until he'd gone into the suburbs beyond. Even then, there was an aura of silence as he wandered along the avenues beside the hill leading to the Governor's Residence. Just a few Borderer gardeners and roadsweepers carting barrows under a red sky, trimming hedges, pushing desultory brooms. The gray bunga-lows were all on short tenancies, owned and maintained by Halcycon.

The medical center lay by a lake amid rolling lawns. He wandered down corridors and through coffee-scented lobbies to the office where Tim Purdoe sat waiting with his feet on the desk, exuding his usual air of friendly boredom. Tim was an old Zone hand, used to people coming here for a quick tour of duty to help their careers, fuel their bank balance, or wipe out whatever problems they had at home. He was a familiar sight at gatherings, generally wearing the same crumpled tweed jacket, his graying blond hair cut with boyish fringe that would probably once have made him look younger.

"Let's get on with it then, shall we?" Tim swung his legs off the desk. "No point in wasting the Company's time when so many others are better than me at doing it..."

He dimmed the window, and John undressed, conscious of

every movement as he flattened and folded his clothes on the chair, feeling the goose bumps that always rose on these occasions, no matter how amicable the air. Tim, of course, would have left the room if John has asked him to for the period of the examination, but after his and Nuru's many attempts to reassure the Borderers at the clinic, that would have seemed like a failure of nerve.

The doctor, tall and yet folded over on itself like some wise mechanical heron, emerged from the alcove beside the window. John crossed the carpet barefoot as it opened itself to receive him. This is never an easy moment, he thought as the silver wings closed around him. Yet it was always a warm embrace, and surprisingly tender. He felt weightless as something passed into his mouth, then over his eyes. Ridges skipped down his spine as the output and integrity of his main recombinant was tested. He had really forgotten how pleasant much of this was. All he had to do was relax and forget about the tiny needles, the way something had apparently taken control of his breathing, and ignore the probe that was now entering his anus. To think of how his body was forming a perfect loop that spread though the nerve synapses of the doctor and out into the local net where the outputs and the calibrations and all the messy stuff of life were compared and contrasted with the thin stream of monitor levels that whispered through the Magulf skies up to the geosynchronous torus that punched the data back down through the atmosphere to be slowed and received and understood once again by the big medical roots and branches of the net back on earth. Yes, to think ... To truly ...

He opened his eyes and blinked as the ocular sheaths withdrew, feeling a fast extra beat already fading beneath his breastbone where his cpu had been downloaded, analyzed, reformatted. The doctor settled him back down on his feet, and, withdrawing, discreetly set about the process of cleaning itself of his fluids and secretions, stroking its mandibles in sweet puffs of machine oil and disinfectant. A strong chill passed over him as the conducting fluids evaporated into the air. He began to dress while Tim kept his head down, his fingers busy stirring and rearranging whatever story the figures on his screen were telling.

A printout whispered as John finished buttoning his shirt. Tim snatched it up, glanced at it, threw it at the bin. "You're sleeping all right?"

"Better than I was..." John glanced down at the screen of his watch, the gray blur of quaternary lines beneath the time display.

"You don't want another packet of sleepers?"

"I haven't finished the first lot you gave me."

"You haven't taken a single tablet."

John shrugged. Each night, as his mind finally began to relax, the figures and faces that paraded before him each day at the clinic began to emerge, gray and insubstantial now—Dickensian ghosts clanking chains of suffering—from the walls and ceiling of his room in the presbytery. "I'm not sure I ever needed the sleepers, Tim. The answer is to keep busy. More work—"

"Sure, and you'll end hopping around with your eyes bulging like some hyperactive frog. Believe me, I've seen it. There's only so much you can expect your body to do."

"You sound like there's some problem."

"There's no problem. You're under stress, but you're adjusting. Everyone adjusts."

"The doctor's blood analyzer's down again at the clinic," John said, staring across at the sleek silver heron in the corner.

"You're lucky that thing's still working at all. You know how old it is?"

"Don't give me that, Tim."

"I'll see if I can get one of the engineers to look in, but you know what it's like..." Tim shrugged. "They're on time-costing."

"Sure."

"Hey." Standing up, Tim came around the desk and clasped John's shoulder. "Don't look so glum—it isn't your fault. Everyone here gets upset by the hassles and restrictions. That, and the bloody-minded attitude of your average Gog."

John was surprised at the strength of his urge to shrink away when Tim touched him. He could never get used to people calling the Borderers Gogs.

"Look," Tim said, leaning back on his desk, "I'll show you what most people ask to see after their first couple of bimonthlies." He touched the screen, and the view from the window across the lake and lawns of the medical center dimmed once again. In its place, fuzzily at first, John saw a pinkish gray soup.

"That's your blood." Tim twirled the cursor, and the rimmed disk of a red cell jumped into view. He moved up a further magnification, then tapped out a series of commands. "Ah—right. Here's one of the little buggers."

John stared at the window where a single rod was floating, magnified to about a meter in length. A scrap of artificial genetic material, waiting to make contact with the living matter that would give it life. It was shaped like a walking stick. "That's from my recombinant?"

"Yeah."

"How can you tell it's not a natural virus?"

"*I* can't. But see those numbers in the corner? That means

that this particular fellow is combating a poliomyelitis variant. It's a thing called e-teneysis IV that's been around for a few years in this part of the Endless City. Methods of defense vary. This one doesn't attempt to attack the poliomyelitis virus direct, but instead enters your white myeloid cells and binds with the RNA, which in turn issues a new instruction, which *then* in turn..." Tim sighed and touched the screen. The virus vanished. "You get the idea, anyway."

"Yes. I'd be crippled or dead if I didn't have a few million of those things in my blood."

"It could be a false alarm—or you could even be naturally immune like most of the Gogs. You never know. But it does mean, I'm afraid, John, that you've probably been in contact with contaminated fecal matter. You're not drinking any of the pisswater the Gogs make do with, are you?"

"What difference does it make? You say I'm safe enough anyway."

"There are limits. Now—" Tim tapped the console again, and a new image appeared on the window. It looked like a small, and rather evil, spider. "See this fellow? Bet you didn't even know you had him in you, eh? Well, this isn't a product of your recombinant but a self-replicating virus that you were infected with when you were about three weeks old—has to be introduced, see, because it doesn't transfer through the placental barrier. After that it just spends its time floating around in your lymphatic system like a seed, waiting to settle down and multiply if it should ever make contact with any of its old friend, HIV. They like each other so much that they join and absorb into one unit, and then die soon after from terminal incompatibility. A bit like marriage, really..."

Smiling at his own drollery, Tim touched his console. The

window blurred back to the view of the lake and the lawns. The red sky was darkening again, possibly threatening rain. John stared out. No one had died from contact with a European for almost a century now, but—apart from that one incident with the witchwoman—he'd always been diligent with his gloves and about using dysol-impregnated cloths, surrounding himself in an antiseptic haze. Even so, there was a time early on in his stay here when Nuru wore an awkward-looking chin-high collar that John assumed was a fashionable affectation until he noticed the angry red rash beneath Nuru's ear that he was attempting to hide. But the rash disappeared, and the risk of anything more serious was minimal. The technology had improved, and the traditional Zone stories of expats who ran mad and naked through the Endless City, hugging people in the streets, had become simply humorous. It wouldn't be so very long, some now said, until the barriers came down altogether.

Tim ambled around from his desk and pulled on the famous aged sports jacket that was draped over the back of the chair. "Here," he said, opening a drawer. "Got this for you. Some cock-up when I ordered it." He tossed a white carton.

"Thanks." John caught it. It was heavier than he imagined. Brushing the card with his thumb, he saw that, powered up, it would produce over a thousand oral tablets of antibiotic. Crude stuff after what Tim had been showing him. But still. "You fancy a drink?" he said.

"You know me." Tim smiled, then extracted a comb from his top jacket pocket. "I even know where we can get one free."

Tim drove the two kilometers from the medical center to mid-Zone. His car was a huge vintage Corona with red fins and sidedoors that rose open like wings and a leather interior with wide backseats that John couldn't imagine him ever needing. Still, it was his pride and joy; as much a Tim Purdoe trademark as the tweed jacket. And, as usual, he insisted on keeping the car on manual, chattering as he drove, giving the current gossip. Who was on the way up, who was on the way out, and, as always, who was screwing whom. Several times as they passed through the suburbs, the proximity light flashed and the brakes kicked in to prevent them from climbing the verge. Tim was someone for whom the mere prospect of drink often seemed to act as an intoxicant.

He said, "I still wonder about you priests. I mean, you know what it's all about here. So what's the point in coming to the Zone if you're celibate?"

"I don't live in the Zone. I live outside."

"Ah—and how is the world outside?"

"Nothing much has changed. I had a close encounter with a witchwoman."

"They're all clinically insane, you know," Tim said, spinning the wheel to avoid a cleaner. "Something that used to be called schizophrenia, probably caused by a virus, although no one's ever bothered to locate it. What's amazing is the way that the Gogs fit them into their society. You know, all that moonrock crap—it provides a socially acceptable track along which their obsessions can go. Otherwise," he continued, belying as he did his general air of ignorance about anything beyond the Zone, "I suppose they'd all be locked up in some high room...

"But I like the simplicity of the Zone," he said as they finally pulled into the Trinity Gardens carpark next to the suddenly diminutive lines of Company Zephyrs, Furies, and Elysians. "Here, people work, they sleep, they eat, they screw. Then they go back home to Europe again. Everything's straightforward. You don't get all that baggage of hope and expectation..."

In the bandstand in the green bowl at the center of Trinity Gardens, a brass band was playing Elgar's *Nimrod*, with the musicians done out in uniforms to match the blue-striped marquees. The lake behind them was the color of rosé wine, stretching out to mirror every cornice and window of the Hyatt Hotel on the far shore.

Where the groupings of guests thinned at the top of the grass slope beside the tropical houses, there was a big floral display in the shape of a clock, with the words MEDERSA APPEAL picked out in houseleeks. Instead of hours, the clock was graduated in Eurodollars. Now the hands, decorated in red saxifrage, pointed up to the target.

"It's a fundraiser for some new kelpbeds at Medersa," Tim said, grabbing a glass of wine from a passing waiter. "You know, let's help the poor fucking Gogs..." Waving at some familiar face, he headed off into the crowd.

John stood alone, watching him depart. The clouds were low, but the afternoon air was pleasantly warm, incredibly still. For once, the wind had died down, and in the roseate light, with the Elgar, John felt that he could have been inside a sepia-tinted print. The women wore wide-brimmed hats, long dresses. The men were in pastel shirts, one-piece suits ornamented by jeweled brooches and cuffs. The screens said the nineteenth century was this year's theme, although he doubted that anyone in Europe would have taken it all quite so literally. But the look was appropriate: after all, these were colonial times.

He wandered, almost kicking a peacock that was pecking for

crumbs on the grass. The Borderer waiters were wearing the same blue uniforms as the band. They carried not only wine but also trays of red and green tubes, vol-au-vents, cactus fruit, steaming bowls of mint tea; all of it topped off with a discreet bow, a professional smile.

As John faltered over a choice of Chardonnay or Font de Michelle, the smiling waiter stood what would have been, outside in the Magulf, uncomfortably close to him. The Borderers who worked the Zones had a capsule implanted in their left upper arm that contained a synthetic protein to unzip any artificial European virus. It was called lydrin, and, in theory at least, it allowed Borderer and European to touch, talk, shake hands, share food, kiss, fight, exchange saliva, even semen and blood, without the risk of a fever, a rash, or some more serious and unlikely clash between recombinant and atavistic viruses.

Taking the Chardonnay, John walked on towards the lake and the walled gardens, passing through pockets of composed laughter, layers of pastel tubegas that carried the hint of chemical moods. Happy amber, relaxed pale blue. Red for lust—or was it joy? There were people here from main corporate admin, engineers and financiers. Even without his cassock, he was still known and recognized. It came with the job. As he passed each group, jokes and stories were briefly interrupted by the press of manicured hands. Silver eyes crinkled and smiled. Hello, Father. He nodded, tried to remember names. The young people here made him feel incredibly old—the old ones, incredibly young.

The Chardonnay was bitter; he left it on top of an urn and sat down at the edge of a pond. Goldfish and coy carp mouthed the surface in the hope of food. A fountain played over white lilies. From here, a honeysuckle arch opened out to the lawns, the marquees, the bandstand, the lake. He noticed the way the people leaned back as they laughed. The motion looked strange without the sound to go with it, like a dance. The stone rim of the pond where he sat was prettily weathered, covered in florets of lichen. He scraped at it with his fingernail. The color came away in flakes of paint.

The band stopped playing. A young, good-looking man came up to the front of the bandstand. John didn't recognize him, but even at this distance the man radiated the kind of assurance that made you feel that not recognizing him was your mistake.

"It's great to see so *many* of you here today," he said, the words coming out of the speakers hidden in the cypress trees, spinning in echoes towards the white hotel across the lake. "Our governor, Owen Price, really would have liked to come himself. He knows how important this project is for the whole of the Magulf." There was scattered applause. "Anyway..." Raising a deprecatory hand. "...there's one man present that I'm sure we'd all like to hear from. And here he is—our main contractor for the project, the man without whom none of this would ever get off the screen on my desk—Mister Mero!"

A rotund man in a flashy suit picked his way towards the mike. John knew he was a Borderer from the way the cheers grew louder as he stumbled over one of the music stands. Mister Mero would be some wealthy builder who would supervise the actual work on the new kelpbeds. He began to speak in clear and virtually unaccented European, expressing gratitude to the fundraisers. How the new kelpbeds at Medersa would provide much needed food, fuel, jobs... He seemed to be rounding off quickly, but then stopped glancing down at his screen and began to talk about A New Spirit of Cooperation. Attention wandered. Fresh drinks and smokes were found. Conversations started up again.

"Father John! So you made it."

A firm bony hand drew him by the elbow, through the honeysuckle arch and back into the crowd.

"Look, you haven't got a drink. *Have* you eaten? The food's not spectacular, but you may as well make the most of something that doesn't taste of kelp."

Father Orteau took a step back to study John. He didn't exactly tut.

"I'm fine," John said. "How are you?"

"Oh, *me*," Father Orteau laughed. "I'll be on top of the world when the bishop lets me out of here."

John nodded, trying not to smile. It had been Felipe who'd explained how the bishop in Paris, against the policy of regularly shifting priests around in the Magulf, had now reappointed Father Orteau to the Zone parish for a third consecutive year. The Church's usual fear was that, even in the Zones, priests would go odd, get an addiction, grow ill, mad—or go peculiarly native. But there was no chance of that happening to Father Orteau. Father Orteau was already peculiarly Father Orteau.

He dabbed at his forehead with a white handkerchief. His fingers strayed to check the precision of his center parting, the discreet diamond pinned to his right ear. He reinserted the handkerchief into his pocket, smoothed the crease of his suit.

"Well," he asked, "what do you think?"

"I'm sure," John said, surprised to discover just how easy it was to get into the ironic doublespeak of the Zone, "that more kelpbeds are just what the Borderers need."

"Really?" Father Orteau studied him for a moment, then

looked up. "You know, what I wouldn't give for some blue sky...a few mare's tails. And don't you think it looks particularly poisonous up there today? All that smoke and sand. Some more rainforest must have gone up, don't you think?"

John shrugged.

"One of the few things I have learned about Bab Mensor is that the wind always blows straight at my rooms in the Hyatt. I'm told the warm air has to go north to balance the Gulf Stream or something. That's the maître d's excuse for all the muck that gets blown onto my balcony, anyway." He peered up at the sky. "And I have a terrible feeling today that the net has bungled—or some satellite's gone down. I know it's not the time of year for it, but I really do think it's going to rain."

"Halcycon's probably got more important things to worry about than rainfall over Bab Mensor."

Father Orteau blinked at the suggestion, obviously taken aback.

John blinked back. "You must come and visit us at the Pandera presbytery," he said. "I'm sure Felipe would love to see you."

"I don't know what I'm thinking of—you still haven't got that drink. Hey, you..." A jeweled cuff fell back from an elegant wrist as Father Orteau raised his arm and snapped his fingers. "Over here. Quick! We have a man in thirst."

One of the Borderer waiters walked briskly over. John silently urged him to show some sign of reluctance or insolence, but the man kept up his unwavering smile, offering a choice of Chardonnay or Font de Michelle, neither of which John wanted.

———

45

Father Orteau was right: the low red sky really did signify rain.

It came chattering across the lake, obscuring the Hyatt, roiling the waters with reddish gray streamers of desert sand, drowning out the end of Mister Mero's speech, sailing hats over the trees and the bandstand, sending the guests scurrying to shelter.

John sat alone on a marble bench in the Temple of Winds. He could have made it into one of the big marquees or the tropical houses with everyone else. They'd be there now. Drinking, smoking, laughing, eating...

The path that wound through the pear trees to the sunken garden ahead of him was now a brown stream cascading down stone steps where roses and clematis raised drowning hands. Every now and then, the wind sucked in on itself, spraying water from the temple's sand-clogged gutters.

Still, it wasn't a mudstorm. Just ordinary rainfall by Magulf standards, turning the world rusty brown. And outside the Zone, the filters for the water butts would be clogging, overflowing, the sewers would be backing up, the streets running thick and fast. The Endless City would be sinking into mud. It was the same in the Zone. On the way from the carpark with Tim, John had seen the lines of yellow tractors that the Borderer gardeners used to cut and vacuum the lawns; the crabs and ladders for cleaning the tropical houses' acreage of glass; the pumping gear.

He shivered and shook his head, rubbing at the flesh around his watch, which still ached slightly from his examination, as it had when his recombinant was reformatted before he came here, to provide the viral barriers that lined his mouth and throat and lungs. The rain was thinning, but he was soaked by now anyway. The wind rocked the trees. A few more heavy droplets splattered down into his face. He could taste oxidized grit. Still, the gardens looked beautiful. The rain had almost stopped. And now, of all things, the sun was making a rare appearance. Bright rays, the lawns a sudden haze of steaming green, involving every sense. Tame birds started to squawk and sing. He saw a pair of the Trinity Gardens' famous blue macaws. Squabbling, perhaps mating, fluttering together from branch to branch down the pear tree avenue like tangled flags.

The air was heavy, wet, earthy, and alive. The sunken garden was already draining, rescued by hidden pumps. The paths gleamed. The sky was arched with a rainbow.

Standing up, feeling his wet trousers shift and cling, John saw a blue-striped umbrella approaching along the avenue of pear trees. He wondered if he should wander off to avoid the encounter, but decided that he'd already taken the easy option once too often this afternoon. And it would probably only be Tim, drunk by now on Armagnac.

But it wasn't Tim. It was a woman.

She climbed the steps, shook and folded her umbrella, and turned to sit on the bench.

"I wouldn't sit there," John said. "Everything here is soaked. Me included."

"All right." She straightened, twirling her umbrella. "Shall we walk? There's little else to do here."

He didn't recognize her. She was dressed in a blue business jacket, the cuffs hanging down to her knuckles, and a skirt that looked creased and a little less than new. Like him, she probably felt out of place this afternoon.

He got up. "I'm John Alston."

"The priest? I thought so."

"Is it that obvious?"

"Someone pointed you out."

His shoes squelched as he and she descended the steps towards the sunken garden. "The rain," he said. "It must have ruined the party."

"I thought it was rather picturesque, everyone running for shelter. Like an old movie."

"Or a sepia print."

"Hmmm."

"I'm afraid I don't know your name."

"Laurie Kalmar. I work the net."

He raised his eyes from the puddles, expecting her to offer a hand for him to shake. She didn't.

"I'm based at the presbytery beside Gran Vía," he said, "about ten kils from here..." He stopped there. Few people in the Zone knew or cared where he lived.

"Really? The Pandera presbytery? You live with old Father Felipe?"

"That's right." Surprised, he looked at her again. She was younger than he, no more than in her mid-twenties, which in itself was rare among expats, who generally came to the Zone after years of doing—or attempting to do—something else. Her dark hair was cut shoulder-length, and her thinnish face was dominated by wide, slightly protuberant silver eyes and a square jaw. "You seem to know your way around the Magulf a little better than most people," he said.

She laughed. Like her voice, her laughter was soft yet oddly precise. Both warm and constricted. "Just because I've heard of your presbytery? The truth is, I do sometimes get involved in charity things like this one. I would be a leading light if they'd let me."

"I guess it's got to be the way forward. More kelpbeds."

"That doesn't impress you."

"It doesn't matter whether I'm impressed. The Medersa project will feed more people than I'll ever be able to help. It's big money, high profile..."

"And all the Europeans sitting at home will be able to feel good for a little while longer about helping the poor bloody Gogs..." She shook her head. "This doesn't seem to be doing either of us any good, does it? Let's talk about something else."

They followed the path around the top of the lake. At first, they did talk about other things—about Father Orteau, the staff at Magulf Liaison; it seemed that he could mention any name and she would know who he meant—but mostly they still talked about the Endless City. Or he did: complaining about the antique doctor at the clinic, the erratic supplies, and the stupidity and ignorance that he encountered in the Zone—and outside, among the Borderers. What it was like to be forever alone in a crowded place: the sense of distant nearness.

"Your Church has always been obsessed with poverty," she said. "Like all those appeal leaflets—as though starvation had some kind of inherent dignity. You work in a clinic, you must realize that money and medicine could do so much more..."

She opened her umbrella as they passed beneath the dripping canopy of willows beside the boathouse. He was puzzled by her attitude. People were expected to argue with and question priests—it was one of priests' functions—but they rarely did. Workers on the net were notoriously eccentric—but *your* Church? As if there were some other.

"How long will you be staying here, Father John?"

"Just a year, unless the bishop extends my term."

"You think that's enough?"

"No, of course not. But the experience is that priests in the Endless City grow weary after a time."

"Is that how you feel?"

"Weary?" He raised his shoulders and shrugged. "Not yet. Confused, maybe. A year isn't anything like long enough. But how long would be enough—and for what?"

"And then, of course, you have your whole life in the Church."

He nodded. The grass and the lake were gleaming and steaming. He was walking with a young and apparently charming woman, but he felt weary and alone.

"You didn't happen to meet any of my predecessors?" he asked.

"I suppose I did. I meet a lot of people. You must know what it's like in the Zone. You really never get to know them."

"I passed the one before me, on the ferry," John said. "He was going out to the shuttle as I came in."

"That sounds quite typical."

"There's no continuity."

"Of course. No..."

"It's absurd, really, that so little attention is paid. Even the people you meet here seem in a dream—most of them, anyway."

"They probably wish they were somewhere else."

"Do you?"

She smiled and shook her head. Over the lake, blackish clouds were starting to ambush the sun. "And what would happen?"

"What?"

"If everyone woke up."

"I've noticed..." He paused. "Things about the people who come to the clinic. The kind of illnesses they have, disease rates. I'm sure that something could be done—simply—to help." Just then, the clouds met over the sun. As though someone had turned off a switch, the whole of Trinity Gardens darkened. The effect only lasted a moment. Stimulated by the change, all the lights around the gardens came on. The lake was suddenly glowing. Shadows flared out across the grass from the dripping trees.

In silence, they walked back up the slope to the noise and light of the tropical houses. The southerly wind had picked up too, almost as quickly as the change in the light, tumbling fallen branches, flailing the sodden beds of tulips and black daffodils, throwing scattershots of desert sand.

Suddenly Laurie Kalmar stooped, her hand to her face.

"What is it?" he asked. "Your eye?"

Leaning over the puddled path, she waved him away. "Just grit..."

Fumbling in the pocket of her dress, she produced a small vial. Tilting her head back, lifting the vial, she squeezed out a drop into her right eye.

"There." She blinked and looked at him. By the second blink, the green of her right iris had turned silver again. "You didn't realize," she said. "Did you?"

"No..."

"You thought we Gogs were all waiters, gardeners, cleaners, or peasants, right?"

"Of course I don't—"

"Come on. Let's go inside."

A uniformed waiter had seen them approach the tropical houses and was holding the door open. As it swung shut behind them, John was enclosed in a green wash of heat and the clink of glasses, the smell of European sweat, perfume, citrus fruit, wet clothes, buffet food, and tubes. He attempted to push through, but Laurie Kalmar was already squeezing away from him, between the hats and suits and dresses, between the birds and palm trees. The backs of her legs, John saw as she vanished, were striped with mud.

WEDNESDAY BREAKFAST AT the Pandera presbytery, and Father Felipe was spruced up in a much-mended brown suit, a silk tie and gold brooch, his best silver cross and chain, and polished black brogues that were cut along the soles to accommodate his feet. Felipe loved Wednesdays; they were his days at the Mirimar Bar.

He rumbled with pleasure and cracked his knuckles as Bella brought in trays of coffee and toast. The bread, the butter, and the coffee beans were all real, not a kelp synthesis but from one of the mysterious packages that often arrived on the presbytery doorstep. John had tried to refuse once or twice, but the smell of toast and fresh-ground coffee was persuasive.

Felipe lifted his slice of toast. Inspecting it, he pulled an elaborate face and replaced it on the plate. "Bella, my dear," he said, "I think you might find there's some of that rough-cut marmalade if you look top left in the kitchen."

"You finished it Monday, Fatoo."

"Damn."

The remainder of breakfast passed—apart from the noise of the old priest eating—in silence. John remembered his first days at the presbytery, when all this had seemed so gothic and strange. The empty rooms, the dark skies, Felipe with his bandaged and swollen feet, caused, so he said, by rheumatism brought on by his own body's defense against a minor fungus that had started between his toes. John, who had hardly ever seen a European with a chronic illness, believed that as much as he believed anything else Felipe told him. Sometimes at night, when John came back from the church or the clinic or from wandering the streets, there was music from an ancient piano and laughter in the presbytery's big upper room. Looking in through the smoke, he would find Felipe with a half dozen Borderers—generally old, male, and tattooed—seated in drink-drowsy poses on the armchairs around him. Of course, John would be beckoned in, encouraged—*amikay*—to find a seat and join and talk, but the music would already have been stilled and even the smoke seemed to hang frozen in the air. He knew enough about Borderer etiquette to understand when he wasn't welcome.

The old priest finished his breakfast, wiped his lips on the sleeve of the jacket that Bella had freshly cleaned for him, downed three trisoma capsules with his fourth cup of coffee, then levered himself up from his chair and into the leghelpers that waited beside him. He hissed and clicked his way to the window.

"Ah! I'm awaited! I must hurry, John."

The routine was the same every Wednesday. Felipe clanking down the stairs and across the street to the donkey cart that came to collect him for the bumpy ride along Gran Vía to the Mirimar Bar. There, watched by giggling Borderer kids, swigging from his flask and humming snatches of hymns and old popular songs, waving gleefully to passersby, he would climb out of the cart, and the barman Pérez would hold the door open for him, making genuflections of his own invention as he did so. Once or twice, John had gone along: Pérez was, after all, a convert to the Church; he kept an assortment of crosses and religious pictures hung on the Mirimar's smoke-blackened walls to prove it, even if he never did go to Santa Cristina. At the back table near the odorous toilets, Father Felipe, with his special seat by a screen decorated with cuttings from an illustrated Bible, a big glass and an even bigger bottle before him on the table, was set for the day.

When the front door had banged shut and Bella had returned to the kitchen, John checked his gloves and watch. Leaving his bicycle in the hallway, he started up the hill towards Santa Cristina. The streets were morning-crowded. The souks down the alleyways were busy and bright, roofed over with colored fabrics that sheened and fluttered in the wind. There were hawkers and beggars and people heading everywhere in and out of the alleys, including a koiyl vendor carrying a basket filled with the shriveled leaves said to give a sense of easy resignation, a release from pain. Everything parted in John's way.

John raised the chalice that contained the sealed packet and turned to face his congregation.

55

This is the Lamb of God
Who takes away the sins of the world.
Happy are those who are called to His table...

As those Borderers who knew the words repeated them after him, a loud thump came from the patched roof, followed by the sound of claws and wingbeats. Shadows floated over the windows as more birds came in to circle the hill. Primarily scavengers, messily communal, they were black with pink beaks and considerably bigger than rooks or crows. The Borderers called them caroni birds.

People were already drifting along the aisle towards the front of the church to receive the sacrament. John stood a few paces back from the altar rail, murmuring *The body of Christ* as each hand reached forward to take a tiny white circle from the freshly opened pack. Here was Juanita, her jaw working as she chewed on rice paper, mystery, and air, taking the blessing of God even now that her son Daudi was dead from leukemia. Here was Kassi Moss. And here were all the others, people John knew without knowing. Homes he had visited, babies he had blessed without the touch of his gloved and dysol-anointed hands.

The service ended with a ragged hymn. Afterwards, he stood waiting behind the altar rail as the congregation departed, muttering, blinking like sleepers, returning to the cares of their lives. Some came up and placed cards on the rail for him to pick up later, or paused to fumble the relics by the Inmaculada, or asked if Fatoo could come around and visit some member of their family who was *mal*—sick, old, or desperate. They were fat or thin, tall or short, dark or light-skinned, and had that air of vigorous health that Borderers, when they weren't actually ill, usually radiated, although one was scarred across the neck, another was missing a finger, another limped . . . John was still useless at remembering their names. A girl paused on her way out, scratching the flaky backs of her arms as she asked if in Europe they knew when it was going to rain, and did it always snow at Christmas? She nodded when he turned on the translat and explained that, *na*, no, it wasn't like that. But she still looked doubtful; it would have snowed at Christmas on every satellite broadcast from Europe she'd ever seen.

He was alone in the church, filled with the emptiness that now always came upon him after Communion. He remembered raising the chalice filled with the host for the first time, and how even then there had been no lightning bolts, no shivers; how it seemed to mean more to everyone else around him. Even his parents, so doubtful for so long, had been a little awed. Then his first solo duties had commenced, in a parish up in the high grazing lands of Yorkshire, where communities were scattered and the sheep were like boulders dotting the moors. The gray-green and purple landscape was fresh and new to him—in a way, it was almost like the Magulf, for there was deep cloud cover and often rain. He would stop on the way to his pastoral visits, get out of his car and watch as the wind silvered the hills. The sheep, slow and curious animals with heavy snouts and blunted horns, would amble over and gaze down at him. Close up, they were big as mammoths.

Soon he began to stop for the sheep, and talk to them, rehearsing the arguments and conversations that he might have at the big slate houses that waited beyond gates, walled gardens, windbreak pines. At least twice a week he was called to one of the local resthomes or some back bedroom and asked by sad and yet generally clear-eyed relatives to look down at the rags of flesh and bone on the bed. And was asked, Father, don't you think the time has come? He seemed so chipper in summer, but now. A shrug. He seems to have given up ... And, as if to emphasize its unhappiness, the figure might moan and turn in the shadows. A glimpse, perhaps, of an exposed powerpack or a silver thread protruding from the spine like a crude aerial, or a pool of blood thickening over the screen of a watch. Or, more alarming still, a quavery voice agreeing, saying, Yes, Father, it all seems to have gone from me now. My friends, my life. Even this room, the presence of my family and the scent of these flowers. I visit past times in old photographs, but nothing tastes. Someone once said that, didn't they? Nothing tastes. One of those phrases you remember even though you don't understand until later when something happens that makes it clear. Perhaps I've already lost my soul, Father, maybe that's what it is. Perhaps I'm already up there with my Lord, the part of me that matters. So you will say I should make an end to it, Father, won't you? Your prayers and a blessing would be a great help ...

Nothing tastes. John gazed up at Santa Cristina's stained and sagging roof, the rotting pillars, and he felt the cool and ancient air on his face and remembered the wild beauty of the moors, the streams in torrent as they hadn't been since the ice ages, scents and strange airy fruits on the breeze at the height of summer, the shining cars, the smiling silver-eyed people, and music in the old churches, the world perfected into some alien dream, and half wrecked in the process.

He destroyed his old gloves, changed from his cassock, wiped the surfaces with dysol, and went outside, looking up at the stained buttresses and weeping blocks of stone. His presence caused muted squawks and chattering, brief eruptions of wings. The caroni birds had made nests of Magulf litter and the torn remnants of the roof, choosing spots sheltered from the wind in the rotting stonework. The juveniles, this year's brood, still had scraps of down clinging to their new plumage.

He turned away from the church. Up here on the hill, in the flowing, powdery light, he could see the shimmering Breathless Ocean, the grainy tangles of oldtown, the levels, the smoking finger of the chimney of the incinerator plant at El Teuf, where he was sometimes asked to speak the funeral rite. As with everything else he did here, he was left drained afterwards with a mixture of humility, anger, and powerlessness. As if, like one of the cancers to which his body had been made and remade immune, a white and empty space was forever growing within him.

This slow loss of God, it seemed to John, must be like the loss of love in a marriage. It was something he'd never been able to trace back to a beginning; even in the early times of certainty, it seemed to him now, the seeds of emptiness must have already lain. His faith had been slipping away for many years now, but he'd thought at first that it was nothing more than a part of the normal adjustments of priestly life; a settling to a more solid and even plateau after the initial high peaks of his vocation. Then, as the emptiness deepened, he'd started to see it as a test. In a sense, it was almost to be welcomed. His belief had been so sure and easy until then. He discussed the problem avidly with friends and men of God, and he thought and read and shared with Saint Paul and Saint Augustine—great doubters all. And, like a dutiful spouse who fights to retain the affection that he feels is unaccountably slipping away, he threw himself more avidly into the external displays of devotion to the Church that he had once considered superficial, external, ultimately irrelevant.

He freely admitted to himself and, although he grew more circumspect as the gap became harder to bridge, to his seniors and tutors that he'd come to the Endless City hoping it would change his perspective on God: that he'd come to find a way back in. But the white emptiness only widened. All the books, all the knowledge, all the history—all the vows of the priesthood—counted for nothing without the fragile core of belief and certainty. And the world, as he'd always known, made at least as much sense without God as with Him. Probably more. In faith, as in marriage, you did no more than exchange one set of doubts and problems for another. And, like falling in love, faith was ultimately less an exercise in free will than an act of fearful and joyful surrender. Once the feeling had gone, it was irrecoverable.

Later that day, every face in the Plaza Princesa looked up when a veetol came out of the sky.

John had been between patients, studying the useless old cartons of drugs that he somehow couldn't face clearing, hoping without much hope to find the drug that the doctor had recommended—as though he might have missed it on the occasions when he looked before. Then the sound of fanjets grew unmistakably close, loud enough to set the vials jingling. He ran out of the clinic into the plaza just as a European veetol came into sight over the tangled concrete of the broken towerblock. The engines changed tone as the wings shifted angle. The Borderers who'd been queuing outside the clinic, bargaining, selling their wares, or absently chewing koiyl, were already dispersing, making the sign against the evil eye. Young children lingered in the storm of rising dust, torn between curiosity and the tugging hands of their elders.

Windows trembled. Pieces of jelt and stucco flew off into the red sky. Speaking in the flat tones of a translat amplified to the point of pain, a voice boomed in Magulf dialect, warning stragglers to clear the square.

The veetol, a fat orange beetle, settled on its legs. The fanjets slowed to a growl, and the door at the side swung open. Steps dropped. Standing beside John, Nuru crossed himself and muttered, "What the Jesus fuck."

A guard came out, her pistol raised. The man who followed her through the doorway saw John and waved to him through the dust. The two Europeans picked their way across the square to the clinic. John glanced to his side for Nuru, but he'd already vanished.

"What's happened?" John asked.

The guard was about thirty, and she had the pinched, watchful look that often came with her job. The man with her was wearing an engineer's insignia.

"I understand you've got a problem with a doctor, Father?"

"Yes, but I never—"

"We've been told to fix it as a priority. That's okay, isn't it, Father? We'll come back in a few hours. Just say."

"No, no, no—this is fine. Come in. I just wasn't expecting—"

"Neither were we . . ."

It took less than half an hour to repair the doctor. Shaking his head when he saw it squatting in the clinic's backroom, muttering about how the machine belonged in a museum, the engineer sent a nanocrab scurrying up into its main circuitry. Donning a helmet to steer through the dusty innards with movements of his hands, he was soon able to restructure the damaged nerves.

"Do you have a recent case to test?" he asked as he put his things away.

John nodded, and pulled up a file on the desk's screen.

Martínez
Blood monocytes 23.3 × 10^9/liter
Normal distribution 0.2 to 0.8

"Well there you are," the engineer said, leaning close over John's shoulder, his sweat smelling of meat and vinegar.

When the veetol had gone and the scream of the fanjets had finally faded, John slumped back on the stool in the surgery. He found that his hands were enormously tense. The guard and the engineer had left a faint sense of purpose and hope that still hovered in the gray air. He wanted to hold on to it, that promise that you could open a toolbox and produce a scrap of magic.

Nuru returned, then left. There were no more patients to see today; the veetol had scared them away. John tidied up, set the vermin traps, locked the clinic. Outside, the Plaza Princesa was busy again. People were still pointing towards the sky, making sweeping, expansive gestures. Many of them glanced at John as he mounted his bicycle, but he couldn't tell from their expressions whether the veetol's arrival had increased their fear of him, or their contempt.

He cycled up the street. It was late afternoon, and the sun was in decline behind the clouds, already breeding hints of darkness, deepening the browns and reds and blues around him, mingling the black shapes of the widow women with terra-cotta shadows, open doorways, glimpses of flesh, the bickering flocks of caroni birds. In Europe, evening came first out of the sky; in the Magulf, it always seemed to well up from the ground.

He went through the archway in the old medina wall, turned, and crossed the Plaza El-Halili. The wide square was barely recognizable from the last time he'd been here, on the night of the carnival. The scaffolding of the stage had been removed, and the few stalls that remained were selling recycled chemlights and rusty tins of Quicklunch: an old product that had been banned in Europe after an additives scare. People drifted here and there amid swirls of dust and queerly shaped bundles of litter that had caught and aggregated in the wind. They watched him go by.

He crossed the slope of ancient paving and turned right where the high, windowless, wire-strewn outer walls of the wealthy Borderer enclave of Mokifa turned its back on the Endless City. He cycled on beside the walls. Along Corpus Vali, parts of the ancient drybrick medina had been incorporated into gleaming stretches of modern shockwire. There were glimpses of stepped, neatly cobbled streets beyond the curving walls of the old Moorish fort, lit by unwavering light. Here, a modern gateway had been constructed from ornate, vine-encrusted pillars of jelt. A man toting a large-snouted subsound pistol stood guard. His expression was quite impossible to read.

John turned left down an alley he thought he recognized. Then right. But, as still often happened, he found that he'd gone a different way from the one he'd intended. He'd kept Mokifa to his right, but instead of reaching the square that led back into Corpus Vali he was driving down a series of stagnant alleys. Thick, moss-strewn cables reached overhead or, broken, lay coiled like nests of snakes. There was no sound other than the whirring of the bicycle motor, the hiss of tires over wet rubble, the rattle and sigh of the Magulf wind. He realized how unused he had become to emptiness and silence. It was almost like the vast squares and blind untenanted houses of his childhood dreams.

The sunken passage widened. The claws of a huge pylon hung over him, still crowned with white ceramics. Ahead in the fading light lay only ruined warehouses, stalking pylons, fallen cranes, shattered concrete. He realized that he was within the remains of the Kushiel geothermal project. By tapping the radioactive heat below the earth's crust, Kushiel had been intended to provide low-maintenance power—and, by implication, health, education, enlightenment—to a fifty-kilometer stretch of the Endless City. Before the funding ran out, only a single geothermal root had been sunk, and that had failed to generate sufficient power to supply even the needs of those who lived in the wealthy enclave of Mokifa. Now, nearly a century later, Kushiel was just a ruin.

He stopped and dismounted, looking up between the jagged buildings where the moon shone faintly through the clouds, roped by the veins of a ripple effect that was spreading rapidly across the sky. As he watched, the sky slowly boiled and unraveled. He walked on, wheeling the bicycle towards what he took to be the jeweled lights of Mokifa or Corpus Vali ahead.

A hole of large but uncertain dimensions lay off in the gloom to his left. He knew it wasn't possible for a geothermal pit to have been excavated and then left unplugged, but still the hole seemed to shift and extend towards him, and there was a prickling of his skin, a bluish density to the night air—a weird sense of outpouring. He turned back into a space between two warehouses. Above him, a loose cable clanged repeatedly in the wind against a corroded metal dome. He paused, rubbing at the pounding in his head.

A tingling electrical wash gave him goose bumps. Feeling a twinge of pain in his right armpit, he slid his hand beneath his cassock, then pulled it out sharply as he felt the jolt of a shock. Holding his hand up, he was sure he could detect a faint luminescence on it. Turning his bicycle, checking the power—it was low—he remounted. He followed the swaying powerlines through a short tunnel, past a hut and a barrier that still, impotently, guarded Kushiel's entrance, then went across a wide strip of wasteground to where the tumble of the Endless City resumed. Soon there were streets, houses, tenements, sounds of life. In a square filled with the smell of frying onion and fresh sweat, people twirled and swayed to the blare of music from a café.

He stood for a moment, watching from the shadows. There were grinning faces. Beautiful women. Spinning children. Men laughing and handsome, like pirates with their earrings and bandannas. Mothers, ignored, shouted and waved from windows for their children to come to bed while old ladies knitted and nodded their heads to the beat, and men at sidetables turned worry beads and smiled secret smiles, their eyes filmed with memories of other nights.

The people stopped dancing when John entered the light. Hands darted over chests in the sign of protection against the evil eye as he wheeled his bicycle beneath the colored lanterns strung across the square.

Several streets later, finally back along the way he'd intended, he dismounted outside the crumbling concrete facade of the old Cresta Motel and picked his way around the rubbish sacks and the clouds of flies that filled the open courtyard. He reached the beaded curtain beyond which Kassi Moss kept her office.

"Ah, Fatoo..." Even before he had fully parted the curtain, she was up and around her desk, throwing heaps of soiled linen off a chair, turning it and placing it just so for him. "*Gunafana*. So good you've come."

He sat down and waited for Kassi to return to her side of her desk. As always, the room was lit by a painfully bright portable halogen lamp. He realized that he was drenched with sweat.

Smiling, Kassi rocked back and forth in her chair. She was a round, gray-haired woman with brown, deeply lined skin. On the wall behind her, emphasized and enlarged by the white light, hung a large crucifix.

"I listened to you church Sunday, Fatoo," she said, perhaps noticing the direction of his gaze. "About Jesus knowing death when he entered the city gates. Was he such brave man?"

"Yes, he was a brave man."

Kassi nodded, wrinkling her eyes. Was she doubting Christ's bravery? Asking whether it was truly possible for God to be a man?

"Fatoo want coffee?"

"No. I just thought I'd look in, Kassi. And bring you this." Wiping down with dysol the antibiotic box that Tim Purdoe had given him in the Zone, John placed it within her reach on the desk. "I thought you'd probably make better use of this than I could. You have far more cases of septicemia..."

Kassi picked the box up, cocked her head to listen to the card on the side, and whistled. "This is..."—she looked at the box again, shaking her head as if she couldn't believe—"the best. *Bona*. Yes? The very?"

"That's right," he said. "The very."

His gaze drifted back to the wall behind Kassi, where the agony of Christ's delicately carved flesh was thrown into sharp relief by the halogen blaze.

"Would you like to see?" she asked.

"See?"

"My people."

"Yes. Of course."

Kassi led him back across the courtyard and up the creaking steps into the Cresta Motel. It was a hospital of sorts, although hospitals were uncommon in the Endless City, where illness wasn't anticipated by internal defenses but diagnosed only when symptoms showed and treated by the age-old remedies of tablet and injection, where even the practice of invasive surgery still sometimes occurred. The sick were generally looked after at home by their families. Money could still buy a reasonable degree of health with the drugs and treatments provided by healers, quacks, witchwomen, locally built doctors, and market stalls, but those Borderers who grew ill and had no one to see to them risked dying in the street. Kassi picked up a few of these, laid them on a mattress along one of the corridors of the Cresta Motel, pumped them up with what food and drugs a largely forgotten joint Magulf-Halcycon initiative still provided, and occasionally helped John with the cases he discovered. She had just four assistants.

There was an odd, whispering silence along the arched stone hallways that could never have belonged to any kind of motel. It came from the breathing of the patients; the exhalation of a sluggish sea, broken occasionally by coughs, grunts, cries of pain.

Kassi's lantern danced over the posters and screens that she had put up to disguise the wet gray walls; it arched shadows across the figures that lay curled on their pallets, it glistened on the faces that turned towards Kassi and John. Some were pale, sweat-sheened. Some were like skulls. In contrast, a young man sat smiling and nodding his head to the beat of whatever music he'd wired into his ear, the ulcer in his gut sealed by the miracle of a recombinant drug. He wanted, Kassi said, patting and squeezing his shoulder, to stay on and learn how to become a healer. But as they walked off, she added, in European, that her patients often said that when they were in the first rush of recovery. It was usually a different matter when the time actually came to leave. Not, of course, that she blamed them. She shrugged, waving her hands. Fatoo knew how it was—*fornu...*

As usual, deferring to a knowledge that she surely knew he didn't possess, Kassi stooped and pulled back the blankets of some of the more difficult or troubling cases to seek his advice. Here were the butchered legs of a young lad who had somehow managed to step on a landmine that must have lain buried beneath a wastepit for at least two centuries. And here was the pustulating flesh of a woman in the last phases of smallpox VII. She was still conscious enough to attempt to pull away when John leaned over her.

"Is right?" Kassi whispered, drawing him away, "that I give an ending? Is that the way of God?"

Every time he came, Kassi would take him to some hopeless case and ask if it was right to give an ending, if that was the way of God.

"You know what she has, Kassi," he said. "She'll be dead soon anyway."

"So I give an ending?"

Kassi gazed up at him.

"Yes," he said. "It's the way of God."

Her face relaxed a little. Later, she'd return to this bed with one of the tiny hand-blown glass vials he'd seen her secretly fingering. She'd break it and dribble the sticky poison onto the woman's lips or, if the woman was still conscious, Kassi would let her crush it with her own teeth and swallow. That, anyway, was what he supposed. Kassi led him farther along the stinking passageway where little rivers of blood, sweat-fever, and urine snaked across the floor. John spoke the last rites over an elderly woman, trying to ignore the bones, moonrocks, and bowls that lined the foot of her bed. Kassi had no choice but to allow the witchwomen to bring their own brand of madness into the Cresta Motel, but she grew flustered if he gave any indication of noticing.

Finally, he followed her back towards the courtyard, rubbing at the bands of pain in his head and the swimming blotches that were forming before his eyes. There were no obvious cases of leukemia here, and he'd asked about *bludrut* before. Yet the people Kassi Moss tended at the Cresta Motel were generally the poorest, the weakest, the most exposed to infection. He filed the fact away. It was meaningless as yet—but surely formed the part of some pattern.

EIGHT PEOPLE WERE seated around the table in conference room G in the main admin block of the European Zone at Bab Mensor. For various reasons, they were all paid to be here this morning. Otherwise, none of them would have attended—although, at the same time, these discussions, part of the complex fantail of Zone committees, had an addictive quality. There was always the sense that someday something might actually happen.

John propped his head in his hand to cover the muscle in his cheek that had started to judder. Surreptitiously he kneaded it with his fingers, looking along the conference table. Only the telepresences seemed attentive, leaning out from their screens— but he doubted if those postures were true of the people they represented. He glanced at his own screen and drew a squiggle with his finger. They were at item 3a. The agenda items went up to 10, and each was a signpost along a long road—like the times in Hemhill when he was young and every schoolday had a special quality dictated by its proximity to the weekend. Item 1 was like Monday morning, a gray shock. Item 3a was the depths of a dreary Tuesday. Item 10, of course, would be Friday afternoon. As the clock on his schoolscreen had blinked through the minutes of art and history, he could already feel the breeze of freedom blowing through the school gates. But the best of all Fridays were the Fridays at the ends of term, and the best of all ends of term was the end of summer term. In the clear eternal past of childhood, in the days when the world truly had been filled with giants, Hal was already finished at seniors and leaning against the railing under the oak tree as John ran out through the gates. The two brothers would walk home together, and the shops and cars and houses and rainbowed sprinklers circling the lawns had a brilliance that only holidays could bring. And at home the rooms would be in chaos, filled with the straining cases and endless piles of shoes that they would take with them next day to the summerhouse at Ley...

"I think we should move on to item 4," said Bevis Headley, the chairman, who represented Halcycon S.A.

The small globe-shaped secretary sitting in the middle of the table and feeding each member's display gave a discreet bleep and intoned: "Zone subcommittee on Magulf education. Meeting 28, item 4. Sat broadcasts."

Buttocks shifted in seats. Eyes scanned the ceiling. John drew another squiggle on his screen. He disliked item 4 more than any of the others. It was a long way from the start, a long way from the finish. A drab plateau.

Last night, he'd barely slept. Nowadays, even when he was fully awake, his head often filled with the same gray figures that had once only populated his dreams. Thin or bloated, half comatose or feverish, inflamed or limping, peeling back untaken patches of artificial skin with agonizing care to show him the head of a worm, a spine of metal, or the flesh of ribs and shoulders stripped away by a lurid secretion. European and Borderer, they floated entwined together, smoky fingers reaching out from the clinic, and from the Cresta Motel, and from Southlands, and the backrooms that he'd once visited in Yorkshire.

"Father, does the Church have a viewpoint on this?"

Faces along the committee table turned towards him. At such moments, he always felt torn between screaming out and falling asleep. "The Church," he said, "supports all positive measures to bring about enlightenment."

"Enlightenment. Good. Now, moving on..."

The air was stifling. Feeling faintly sick, the muscle in his cheek hammering faster than ever, John looked down again at his screen.

He had a late lunch with Tim Purdoe in the cozy fog of wood, brass, and firelight that was Thrials, the Zone's best restaurant, and thanked him, as the food arrived, for his help in getting the clinic's doctor fixed.

Tim impaled an asparagus tip with his fork. "I'm sorry," he said. "I forgot."

"Seriously."

"Look—" Tim dabbed butter from his chin. "I promise I'll get around to it."

"It's been fixed. The engineer actually came to the clinic in a veetol, oh, a week back."

"A *veetol?*" Tim speared another tip. "Much as I'd like to take the credit, John, it wasn't me."

"Well, it's fixed anyway."

"Good. That's great."

John was eating grilled steak; the cheapest item on the menu, although, as usual, Tim was paying for both of them. The food here was brought fresh on the shuttle in chilled containers. Meals cost a Borderer's monthly wage.

"Another beer, I think."

"Not for me."

"Take a soberup."

"It's not the same."

"Sometimes, John..." Tim put down his fork and reached over to touch John's bare ungloved hand. Without thinking, John pulled away.

Tim shook his head. "You really do need to lighten up."

"I have to go and visit someone later. He's a family man called Martínez, and he's dying."

"He doesn't know?"

"No."

"Will you tell him?"

"I'll try to play it by ear. I can't just decide, can I—sitting here? I'll have to wait and see. Isn't that what you'd do?"

Tim shrugged. "Working here, I really can't say I have that much..."

"Here, everything's different, isn't it? Here—and out there."

"Isn't that why you came?"

John pushed away his mostly untouched plate of food—the smell of freshly cooked meat was starting to disgust him, anyway—and saw, as he did so, that Tim was staring at the screen of his watch, the tiny flashing lines of AGTC, as if they contained some kind of message. He covered it with his sleeve.

"Tim—there's a link between cancer and radiation?"

"Well, yes."

"That would apply to cancers of the blood?"

"Which one?"

"Acute myeloid leukemia."

"Like that woman? The one that died?" The brown-eyed waitress placed a fresh beer beside Tim. He sipped, trying not to frown. He really didn't like giving specific advice on cases at the clinic. "Okay. Yes, leukemia could be caused by cell damage from radiation... Although there are viral, chemical, other factors."

"I've come across several cases like it, Tim. In the clinic, and in the doctor's records. I think there may be some specific and avoidable cause."

"And so you thought about radiation?"

"The Borderers are so naturally tough and resistant... I can't believe there isn't some external factor. Is it likely that they could somehow be exposed to radiation levels high enough to cause cancer? I mean, just this one specific kind. You must have access to figures on the net. We Europeans would be at risk from cell damage, too."

"We're not *at risk*, John." Tim raised his beer and drank, adding a line of foam to his lip. "Your viruses would easily recode a few precancerous cells."

"It's the Borderers I'm concerned about."

"Of course. The Gogs." Tim paused, gazing out the window, suppressing, John suspected, a professional's irritation with the dabblings of amateurs in his field. Outside, along the covered brownstone paving of Main Avenue, it was May and the cherry trees were losing their blossoms, scattering pink and white.

"Ordinarily," Tim continued, turning back towards John, "you're talking about lowish levels of radiation, here or anywhere else. There are solar rays out beyond the Last Hammada, and the products of old power station meltdowns, but you know that most of the nuclear arsenals were never used, and a lot of early climate control was directed towards scrubbing the skies clean above Europe anyway. The climate got almost the same benefit here. That was why the Gogs came."

"That's history."

The sweets arrived. Thrials specialized in architectural constructs of chocolate, toffee, and fudge to make up for the relative delicacy of their main courses. Tim had chosen a zero-calorie version, but to John that seemed a pointless final extravagance.

"So you're saying that radiation levels in the Magulf aren't exceptionally high?"

"There must be hot spots—I'm sure there were a few local conflicts and meltdowns—but many of the real nasties such as the iodine and thorium isotopes have a relatively short half-life. Others, like carbon 14, will be thinly distributed throughout the world. It's nearly all long gone, or left in tiny quantities."

"What do you mean? Nearly all?"

"I suppose a few could still be in the food chain around here. Something the Gogs are eating and we're not. Something odd that hasn't shown up."

"And no one ever tested for it?"

"For what? You said yourself you don't know."

"I'd just like to get to the truth."

"There's a difference between facts and the truth, you know." Tim lifted his spoon and excavated a syrupy lump from his dessert.

"About those radiation levels," John said, "my doctor's useless. If I provided you with tissue and food samples, could you do some tests?"

"For you," Tim said, his spoon still poised, "I'll do some tests. But I do have one question."

"What's that?"

"Just what do you expect to do with the truth if you find it?"

"The truth," John said, "will lead the way to an answer."

He parted with Tim after lunch and wandered along Main Avenue past the flashy clothiers and flowersellers to the nearest booth. He sat down inside and called up the Zone's directory from the net, finding the listing for Laurie Kalmar.

Her face appeared on the screen.

"Hello," she said. "I wasn't expecting your call..."

She was smiling. Her eyes were silver again.

"The doctor at my clinic's been fixed," he said. "A veetol came from the Zone. Which is about as likely as..." He took a breath. "Since I mentioned the problem when we talked in Trinity Gardens, I though it might be thanks to you."

"I really can't say, Father John," she said. "But of course I'll tell Laurie what you said as soon as she's available."

"You're not Laurie—you're just an answerer?"

The face on the screen nodded. She was smiling, as if amused. "I'm just the answerer. I'm sorry if you were confused."

He glanced at the cursor at the side of the screen, but it gave no indication. Another trick, like the silver eyes.

The answerer tilted her head, waiting for him to speak.

"Anyway," he said, "tell Laurie that if she ever goes into the Endless City, she should call in at the clinic sometime, and I'll show her."

"Of course, Father John. Goodb—"

He touched Exit, and sat for a moment. Then he called his parents, who still lived in the same house back in England.

"John...It *is* you..." His father sat down before him. He had a habit of leaning forward towards his own screen, which extended his neck and distorted the image slightly. Faintly, John could hear birdsong, and could smell something cooking. "I was just saying this morning to your mother that it was about time you called."

"Dad, how are you?"

"We're fine. How are you?"

John nodded. "I'm keeping well, thanks."

"Still curing the Gogs—Borderers?"

"I do my best." Ever since John could remember, his father had always called the Borderers Gogs, then corrected himself. John doubted whether his father even realized that he was doing it.

"That's good." His father was in his armchair in the lounge, where these days he spent most of his time, puffing his way though packs of mildly nostalgia-inducing tubes and listening to classical music, while John's mother, when she wasn't seeing to Hal, pottered in a garden that grew both neater and less attractive with the passing of every year. There, on the shelf just behind his father, stood the old willow-pattern vase with the chip still showing on the glaze. Kicking a football across the lounge one morning, preparatory to going to the park, John had sent it tumbling. "Is there anything," his father asked, "that you need?"

"Some powdered soup would be useful," John said. "You can get it in condensed blocks about so big..." He held up his fingers.

"You do your own *cooking* there?"

"No, but the maid..." John shrugged. In the rare event that the package actually made its way through the Magulf postage system to the Pandera presbytery, he'd give it to one of his patients at the clinic.

"Okay, Son, powdered soup it is. What flavor?"

"It doesn't matter."

"You're sure?"

"Yes."

His father looked doubtful.

"Asparagus would be fine, Dad. If you could get asparagus."

"I'll see what there is."

"Great."

The two men gazed at each other for a moment, holding on to their smiles. Then his father pulled back from the screen, and his face assumed its proper dimensions.

"I'll get your mother. Son, you take care."

"You too, Dad."

His father disappeared from view. John heard footsteps and shouts, the busy drone of a weeder cut short. He waited, looking at the chipped vase, the turning brass wheels of the clock on the wall that said a quarter past two (the same time as here, although that was hard to believe), the shifting shadows cast by the boughs of the cherry tree beyond the window, the pale dots of sunlight. He leaned forward and tilted his head a little to see if it was yet in full blossom.

"Ah, there you are." His mother sat down in the chair, plucking off her green gardening gloves. "You know, *he's* made me trudge all the way in here when there's a unit in the garage and he could have..." She stopped herself, put her gloves in her lap, and smiled. "How are you, love?"

"I'm fine." John read in her eyes that she thought he looked tired. "How's Hemhill?"

"Oh, I doubt if you'd notice much change. But you must come and see when you've finished there. No more promises."

He nodded. "Dad says he'll send me some soup."

"You don't *need* it, do you?"

"You know how he likes to send something. Tying stuff up."

They smiled, sharing their little conspiracy.

"And I want *you* to send me some pictures of that place you're staying at," his mother said. "Can you *do* that? I mean, I keep asking and you still haven't sent a thing. They do sell cameras there?"

"I can get one in the Zone, Mum. This isn't..."

"I want," his mother said, "to have something that I can show to Hal."

He nodded. "And how is he?"

"He's the same, John. Your father went up and sat with him for a while yesterday. He hasn't done *that* in years. Maybe he's finally starting to get used to it. He was always like this, you know, when we were younger, courting. A big kid. I don't think he's ever forgiven me for having these four extra years on him."

John smiled.

His mother glanced away from the screen, towards the clear

and sunlit window. "If it keeps like this, I may even try to get Hal downstairs and into the garden for a few hours. I'm sure he enjoys it."

"How are you coping?"

"The machines are a big help. They get a little better all the time. A good thing, really…"—she folded her hands in her lap—"…considering that the opposite is happening to me."

"You look very well, Mum."

"You know me. I'm only grouching. Would you like to send a message? I mean, to Hal?"

John said, "Sure."

"Then you may as well get on with it. These links are expensive. And you know I'll be thinking of you. Just break the connection when you've finished." Briskly as always, and with her usual aversion to farewells, his mother reached forward to reconfigure the screen. "Goodbye, John. Call again. And next time don't make it so long…"

The screen blanked over. With just the address cursor showing in the top right-hand corner, it felt as though contact with Hemhill had already been broken. And more than ever, sitting here in this booth nearly a thousand miles away, John was certain that nothing he could say to Hal would get through. Still, this wasn't the time to break his mother's hope—if, nowadays, hope was what it actually was.

He closed his eyes. He opened them again. He imagined Hal as he'd last seen him, almost a year ago, lying upstairs in his bedroom with its view, through the lime trees across the road, of the track and the playing fields. Nothing his mother had said in the year since indicated that there'd been any improvement. She used to call John at midnight on the net in a state of girlish excitement just to say how Hal had smiled at something or turned his head or had seemed to recognize a face. It had been years since John received that kind of call.

"It's me, Hal—John. I'm still at work in the Endless City, doing services at the old church, doling out treatment at the clinic." He paused. He licked his lips. "The clinic's the part of the work that I enjoy most here, Hal—although enjoy isn't the right word. I know it's not some great big ambitious project...But it's a way of saying, Here, look, we care, we want to help. If everyone did as much, there would be less of a problem..."

He gazed at the screen. Why, even now, was he still trying to justify himself to Hal? He let the cursor blink and let the silence extend. He could almost hear the humming of pumps, the pop, sigh, pop of the breather, smell the sour tang of antiseptic and bed-ridden flesh. He was wasting money on long-distance silence, but he didn't imagine that when the net finally edited and input this message into Hal's skull at some appropriate pause in his endless dream, the monitor would bother to relay any obvious gaps. And what did it matter, anyway, if the monitor did? John thought of the two thin silver wires that curled out from the terminal beside Hal's bed, snaking across the pillow that his mother changed every day, taped to the side of his cheek at the point where, in a tiny crust of blood, they entered his nose.

"One thing of interest, Hal, is that I'm getting further on the trail of a possible environmental factor in cancer rates in this section of the Endless City. But I don't know. It's early yet...

"People in Europe always seem to think that the Endless

City is some kind of ungovernable chaos, but in fact, with people living this close to one another, the rules of society are probably more complex than the kind of thing we get at home. It's just that no one's ever bothered to write them down. As for belief, religion..."

He gazed at the blank screen.

"As for that, I really don't know where to begin. I just wish you could answer back sometimes, Hal. I just wish that we could talk the way we used to. I know you'll have changed, whatever there is of you that's in there. But I don't know how. I just sometimes wonder who it is I'm supposed to be talking to. You, or the net..."

He took a breath. So much, anyway, for his priestly bedside manner. He wondered whether he shouldn't delete the last part of the message, but as it had already been stored at his parents' house, that would involve resummoning his mother or father to obtain the necessary authority, which in turn would give them the opportunity to listen for themselves to what he had just said.

"Anyway, Hal. Dad's sending me some powdered asparagus soup, and Mum insists she's been asking me for some pictures of where I'm staying so she can input them to you. She hasn't asked before, of course, but it's a good idea and I'll get some done as soon as I can. Meanwhile, I'll be thinking of you. I love you, Hal."

He touched Exit. His parents' address faded. He sat in the booth with his eyes on empty screen until the smell of carpets and cooking and new-mown lawns had faded. Then he called a car to take him to the edge of the Zone. A new Fury, Halcyon-logoed, as smoothly anonymous as a beach pebble, it bore him through the orderly wasteland of warehouses.

He climbed out by the shockwire. Here, the stale hot wind was always stronger, and night already seemed to be gathering in the hollow-eyed sockets of the buildings beyond. Pulling on his gloves, nodding to the guard as the gates swept open, John walked towards the weeping lights of the taxis that were always waiting at this time of day to pick up any stray European trade.

The house of Martínez glowed an ethereal cream and pastel in the dimming reddish light. In this heat, the smoke that swirled from the crooked chimney was a sign that someone was unwell: of the burning of soiled paper and linen. The doors and all but one of the shutters hung open, and the two younger children were squatting outside. They hesitated for a moment as John climbed out of the taxi, then they scuttled inside, shouting *Madre!*

Martínez was feverish today, and his wife Kailu was plainly angry when John offered the same drugs that she'd already bought herself at the souk. Still, she led John up the narrow stairs and pulled a chair away from the bed for him to sit on. The room had a pleasantly medicinal smell that came from the koiyl leaves that were heaped in a glass bowl on the table beneath the window. Left alone, John sat listening as Martínez muttered and tossed and turned, coughing mucus in a rust-red spray. His big arms were shrunken, and the skin of his fat cheeks was flaccid now. He seemed only half aware of John's presence, yet he still spoke more in European than Borderer as he talked ramblingly of blue skies, of the time he'd been to Europe on contract. The sun hot on his back. The green ruins of a city. How the tree-tappers flitted like silver birds. Gazing around at the yellow flower-patterned walls, hearing voices booming from a screen downstairs and the children shouting *danna-do,* smelling the kelp odor of cooking from the kitchen, John briefly wondered if it was possible that the work Martínez had done in Europe had been the cause of his disease. But he dismissed the idea. He'd learned long ago that Halcycon wouldn't permit dangerous processes in their complexes. The harvest work was simply hard and repetitive—and seasonal, migratory. That was why the Borderers did it.

When Martínez seemed to be sleeping, John wiped the chair with dysol and went back down the stairs.

"Comma mal?" Kailu asked, looking up at him, almost blocking his way in the hall, her gray eyes bloodshot with worry and lack of sleep.

"Fornu..." His hands a red-green blur, John made a Borderer shrug.

Perhaps he'd used the wrong word, but for a moment, as she let him by and pushed open the door into the street, Kailu's face seemed to lighten. There's always hope, he'd meant to imply—although with the translat on, or even in European, hope wasn't something he found easy to convey. There's always hope, until all hope has gone.

"Goodnight."

"Gonenanh."

The door closed. Running his fingers around the raised flesh where the white quaternary lines flickered, he checked the time on his watch. Then he walked back up the hill along the Cruz de Marcenado.

A BARELY TEENAGE BOY and girl were camped out-
side the clinic's doors. Their woolen djellabas, stiff with sweat
and dust, indicated that they came from the Northern Mountains. Whatever they had been wearing on their feet had given
out along the way. The girl held a small bundle close to her
chest. John realized it was a baby.

He turned on his translat.

"What can I do?"

Ee do hep?

They cringed away from him. They'd probably never seen a
European before.

The girl said something that the translat rendered as "Help
my baby."

"Come in."

Cum ha . . .

He unlocked the clinic, disabled the alarms, and gestured at the open doorway, trying to smile. There was likely to be little else he could do: anyone who came from beyond the Endless City would be seeking him as a last resort. The family remained huddled at the doorway. Deciding to wait for Nuru, he checked the rodent and insect traps for occupants, then packaged more samples to add to the box in the refrigerator he'd send by taxi to Tim in the Zone. It was grisly job, even with the neatly sealed tubes and cartons that the doctor, a couple of local healers, and workers at the incinerator plant at El Teuf had provided him with. Fishing a blank card from the desk, he activated it and said:

"Tim, I know I'm probably sending you far more than you need. Here's another card with copies of most of my case files on it. I took it as a backup a few weeks ago. And this card I got from Kassi Moss, the woman who runs the Cresta Motel. I tried playing it here but came up with nothing. So I suspect it's in binary..."

He fired up the small incinerator and placed the spare tissue samples inside, making the sign of the cross as the fats sizzled. A few minutes later, Nuru arrived and persuaded the family from the Northern Mountains to enter. Eventually, he also succeeded in prizing the baby from the girl's fear-rigid arms for the doctor to examine, but the tiny body was cold and stiff, with leathery skin and cavernous eyes: it had been dead for at least two days.

When John attempted to say a prayer, the girl bared her teeth in fear and made a sign against the evil eye. Snatching the corpse back from Nuru, she and the boy ran from the surgery. John blinked and rubbed his eyes, breathing the fecal stink of decay that they had left behind them. Surely they'd realized their baby was dead. So had they come all this way to the Plaza Princesa expecting a miracle?

"Peasants," Nuru said.

"Everyone is someone else's peasant," John said. "Have you ever been in the Northern Mountains? Do you know what it's like there?"

Nuru shook his head, amazed at the suggestion.

"But they're supposed to grow their own food, aren't they? They have some independence, they don't rely on the kelp-beds."

"They eat pig shit, grow koiyl."

"Is that where the koiyl leaf comes from? The Northern Mountains?"

"Yep. But don't Fatoo try the stuff. Nuru's *gramadre* say it rot your blood."

John stared at Nuru. *Bludrut.*

"Fatoo wanna see next?"

"Yes. But will you do me a favor?"

Nuru smiled and held out his hand.

John took out a coin, wiped it with dysol, and placed it on the surgery desk. Nuru picked it up.

John said, "I want you to buy me some koiyl."

Later, when Nuru and the last of the patients had gone, John was in the frontroom preparing to lock up when the main door creaked open again, letting in a roseate gust of Magulf wind and light.

Turning, he saw that it was Laurie Kalmar, and automatically took a step back before he remembered her lydrin implant.

"I got your message from my answerer," she said, picking

up from the desk the broken card of one of the old cartons that John had been trying to decipher. She turned it over in her hands. The leaking card trailed a few pinkish-gray nerves. Today, her eyes were green. "So I thought I'd have a look..."

"Did you really get the engineer to come here?"

"It was simple enough." She wiped her fingers and put the card down.

"No—I'm really curious. How did you do it? It usually takes so long to make anything happen."

"I had to access some maintenance systems." She fanned her hands in a shrug. "And I remembered what you'd said. It was easy to break through the right partition. Requests from your clinic will have a much higher priority from now on. I won't say what priority you were given before..." She smiled.

"I can imagine."

Dressed in a loose khaki suit and scuffed flat-heeled boots, she made an odd blend of the strange and the ordinary. And what happens, he wondered, when someone finds out that you've illegally tweaked the net? And how, anyway, does a young Borderer get trusted enough, and wanted enough, to work on it in the first place?

He showed her around the clinic, finding himself stupidly apologizing for the mess, the litter of books and cards, the empty boxes of drugs that he kept for fear of losing the dosage instructions. She looked at the doctor in the backroom for some time, standing closer than most people did. Sensing her presence, it clicked open its wide middle hip-grasping mandibles in a half-hopeful offer of embrace.

"How *old* is this?"

"Don't ask."

"Is it mobile? Do you take it out with you?"

He shook his head, smiling as he tried to imagine walking around the Endless City with this great red-armored knight clanking behind him.

"Do you have any plans this afternoon, Father John?" she asked.

He shrugged. "But I—"

"Then I'll show you where I used to live."

Here at last, he thought as he locked up the clinic and followed Laurie out into the Plaza Princesa in the shadow of the bombed-out towerblock, where she'd parked a rusty van, was a Borderer he could talk to—even if she did come from the Zone. Someone who was, but for the color of her eyes, really like him. She brushed away the litter of tube wrappers and tissues from the van's passenger seat for him, then inserted the card and started the engine. As the van rose and began to slide towards the nearest houses, gathering speed, zooming through a gap and down the narrow street, he decided that if Laurie stopped working on the net, she could always earn her living as a Magulf taxi driver.

She drove him fifteen kilometers west out through the Mella and along the coast to Chott. On the wide concrete ruin of the old highway they overtook vans, donkeys, wagons, big foline-powered twenty-wheelers, sheep, goats, and plodding Borderer families. This was farther out than he'd been before. Here where the road dipped close to the Breathless Ocean, the remains of ancient towerblocks stuck out from slate-colored slime. Laurie explained that they had once been part of a coastal resort, back in the time before the sea rose. Farther on were more kelpbeds, a much earlier project than the ones around Bab Mensor, divided by pipes and narrow concrete piers into a checkerboard that stretched halfway to the horizon across the sea, glossy in the afternoon light.

The old highway climbed where the coastline rose into cliffs. It veered, breaking perilously near the edge before giving out entirely where there had once been an ambitious suspension bridge. In the bridge's place, situated along a much used track a little more inland, a rickety span had been built out of wood, jelt, and scaffolding. On each side of the drop, children with guns and leaf tattoos on both cheeks were collecting the toll from the queuing vehicles, signaling across the gap to make sure that only one twenty-wheeler occupied the central span at a time.

"Take off your gloves," Laurie said as they waited in a fog of foline. "And keep your sleeve down over your watch. They'll charge ten times as much if they see you're a European."

He wound down the window, pulled at the threads, and quickly tossed his gloves out before the catalysts began to burn. "Okay now?"

She fumbled amid the old food wrappers beneath the dashboard and passed him a vial. "And drop this into your eyes."

She laughed when he hesitated. "What's the problem?"

"This isn't like you in Trinity Gardens. Out here, I can't play games with my identity."

She looked at him, no longer laughing, and he caught the faint seashore Borderer smell that, he realized, didn't come from the eating of kelp, as he'd always imagined. "Why come to the Endless City if you don't want to be involved? What is the point...?"

He opened the vial and tilted back his head. As the fluid spilled over his cheeks, Laurie turned up the fans and followed the sixteen-wheeler ahead of them to the lip of the bridge. He touched his eyelids.

"Do you have a mirror?"

She shook her head, winding down her window to pay the toll. The boy who took the money said *Ossar? skay*—hardly glancing at them.

A kilometer beyond the bridge, Laurie turned off the old highway towards Chott. Many of the sixteen-wheelers were also heading that way, and the buildings were scarred by their collisions. Chott was the site of some of the largest and most productive kelpbeds, and big effluent pipes ran downhill beside them. She turned again beneath a broken arch and killed the engine in a small square.

She opened the van's doors. "We can walk from here."

"What about my accent? What happens if someone tries to talk to me?"

"Act dumb—I'm sure you can manage that." She studied him. "It's good that you dress so poorly. You really don't look like a European."

"Well, thanks."

"Keep your hands in your pockets and keep your watch out of sight. Act sensibly."

"*This* is acting sensibly?"

He followed as she left the square. There was a small stall in the first street they came to. It sold chimes, dried gourds, and an assortment of ornamental mirrors. She held one up, tilting it towards his face, and laughed at his reaction.

"Brown," she said. "Is that right?"

"What do you mean, right?"

"Is that the color you were born with?"

"I don't know. Somehow, I always thought blue..."

As he walked on with Laurie, John could feel the faint breeze on his face from the passage of other bodies, the changes in the air as the street narrowed, widened, as they passed dank alleyways, noisy doorways, the swarming heat that issued from raked-up piles of dung, the drafts of koiyl and cinnamon from the spice souk, the white flutter of the tiers of washing hung overhead. The sounds seemed stronger too. Everything was more intense. Eyes that were green or brown or blue studied him—he was taller than most Borderers, and his fair skin was uncommon—but only in vague curiosity, and no one came close. He recalled something that he'd noticed many times before, but only as an observer: how the Borderers were able to move swiftly in a confined space without ever bumping into one another. It was a complex dance he was incapable of performing, but as long as he stuck close to Laurie, he felt safe.

Already it was late afternoon and the streets downhill were getting grimmer and darker, the reek of the kelpbeds was growing stronger. Laurie and John ended up picking their way across a slippery maze of piers and duckboards close to the shore. The mud here was topped by the sluggish tide of the Breathless Ocean, which seeped in past the protective pontoons and sluices. To the west, the thickening sky was netted with the lights and cranes of Chott's main depots and processing plants, where refined kelp was collected in anything from huge barge skips to wheelbarrows. From there the proteins, starches, and edible oils were taken to be boiled and flavored in the vats of cookshops, homes, and factories; the bulk fiber was pressed for a cheap kind of jelt; the flammable vapors and oils were refined into foline.

Laurie sat down on a smooth-topped rock, and John sat beside her. Oddly enough, there was something contemplative about this place.

"What are you thinking?" she asked eventually.

"How the old fathers in the seminary explained the kelpbeds. How anything can seem neat and elegant if you look at it from a wide enough distance..."

The nearest pontoons were gently rising, falling, slopping in and out of the mud. In the gloom beyond, he could just make out figures moving along the walkways. Kelp workers dragging nets, or poling canoes across the thick lagoons. As a rule, an individual worker owned and was responsible for his own kelp-bed, maintaining it, buying in quotas from the inflows, selling the product to the operators of the dryingpans, who in turn sold to the bigger bulk processors. A whole food chain based on market forces. It wasn't unknown for kelp workers, oper-ating alone and in competition with the owners of the pens around them, to fall from the walkways or out of their canoes into the thick unswimmable soup, and for their cries for help to go unheard. A drowned body could easily get tangled and hidden, lost into the process, and end up as food.

"I once tried to feed kelpbread to the ducks in Trinity Gar-dens," Laurie said. "But they wouldn't eat it."

"Before I came here, I imagined that I'd be eating nothing else," he said, "but Felipe has his friends and contacts. Still, Bella uses the stuff to bulk things up. I can always taste it..."

Behind them lay a scatter of huts and houses clinging to small islands of mud or raised on drunken stilts. There was an incredible stench, a smell so strong that it flowed into the other senses; it thickened the already dim light and muffled every sound.

"The place I was born is somewhere near," she said. "I can't be quite sure. There was a bad tide a few years back, and things collapse and change." She pointed out over the pontoons. "See the markerbuoy and the big pipe? I think my father's kelpbeds were in front and to the left. But it's easy to get lost."

"What was it like?"

"It was a long time ago. You invent things according to how other people tell you they were. I mean this *smell*—I don't remember that—but I do remember the way the kids whose parents weren't kelp workers used to fight us and say we stank. But the money wasn't bad, and kelp workers are used to doing things their own way. My father was very much like that—he was stubborn—and the tradition goes back in the family. The big upheaval was when my grandparents moved from the older beds at Tabia to the ones here. I remember how they used to talk about it..."

John gazed at her, wondering why she was telling him this.

"On my mother's side," she continued, staring out at the grainy horizon, "I know even less. I think her father used to repair old trucks, but she would never quite say. To be honest, she's what you Europeans call a snob, although there really isn't a Borderer word for it, and she never got over working with lydrin in her blood in Europe. And I never did understand why she married my father. It couldn't have been his looks. It couldn't have been his money. It certainly couldn't have been the way he smelled..."

Laurie shook her head in puzzlement. Perhaps, John thought, they'd been in love.

"My mother worked in Europe before they met," she continued, "but she buckled down to being a kelp worker even though she hated it. Helping my father, having kids—she probably hated that too. There were me and two brothers, and another brother who died. We all used to share this big cot up in the roof, and at night she would lie beside us and watch the lantern lights move across the ceiling as the workers walked up from the shore. The funny thing was, she never told us stories about Zazu or Peter Rabbit or Growling George. Night after night, she told us about her year in Europe.

"She was in personal service with a family in the Lowlands. The main house was huge—at least the way she told it. And outside there were mazes and lakes and pergolas. On one of the children's birthdays they put up this big carousel with bright wooden horses *inside* the house. Imagine..." Laurie smiled, far away. "...a carousel turning under the chandeliers in this big hall. And the woman, the lady of the house, for some reason, she singled my mother out. She made her a..." She paused, searching for the word. "Confidante. Is that right?"

John nodded.

"She used to have my mother sit beside her each afternoon in a white bedroom with a balcony and the sound of doves outside. And they would talk and drink iced coffee and tell each other stories of their different lives. And those stories would get tangled up with the ones our mother told us until it got so, when I was nearly asleep, I felt as though I had actually become that woman in that white bedroom with the doves and the balcony and the lakes and the lawns...

"Once in the winter, my mother took a flight with the rich family to London. And she had this wonderful night on her own with no responsibilities and everyone out at some show. It was foggy and dark outside, so she put on a coat and a scarf over her head so no one would see her eyes. And she just walked out. Just looking, staring. Seeing the big terraced houses and gardens and the lights of the cars and the trees and the shiny machines sweeping the leaves, and the glow of the roses, and the sweet green smell of the river. The people were out walking their dogs, and smiling hello because they thought she was a European. There was nothing but clear glass in the windows of the houses, and the curtains were open so she could see into all these happy, wealthy scenes. My mother kept telling us about that night in London as we lay in the big cot. About the time she went out pretending she was European...

"Then my father died, and my two brothers. The anchors to one of the outer pontoons gave way. Floated out. Sank. They tried to swim back through the Breathless Ocean, but of course they were poisoned and drowned. Anyway, that was the story. But it turned out that one of the big kelp processors had got hold of some European *cassan*—that's aid money—and needed some of our plots for bypass drainage, and that my father had been holding out without telling any of us. He was always groaning on about quotas and prices. His being stubborn over this drainage thing probably meant that he and Kerr and Tony were killed so that we'd sell out. But I don't know. Just my mother and I were left, and the joke was, we were paid a good price for the beds and pens. All those years of work—and we got more by simply giving up. Or maybe it was money for what had been done—guilt, compensation. It was enough for me and my mother to go Mokifa. You know Mokifa?"

"Yes."

"And she did her best to forget about life and get on with her dreams—which by now revolved entirely around me." Gazing out, elbows on knees, hands clasped, Laurie shrugged. "It gets boring after that, really. My mother put me on treatments of tetje. She didn't even say at first, but I remember the taste and how she tried to hide the taste in the food with curry and kelp sugar. I'd always been the bright one anyway, the clever prickly kid. I got through the entrance scans for Drezzar. It's intensive there. You spend five or six hours a day with a hood on your head, and the rest with screens. All day they make you speak European. By then I was taking the tetje myself, and the phenothate you need afterwards to keep you calm. My little secret. Huddled in the toilets with a syringe because the hit was quicker. I was always worried that if I didn't have the tetje, I'd fail the next scan. I'd be out..."

"Do you still take it?"

"No. And I probably would have done fine at Drezzar without it—most of the kids were there because of money instead of their brains. I quit the phenothate too. Anyway, the aptitude scans at Drezzar kept saying I was abstract/numerate, so they let me work on a screen that had an airwave link with the Zone. There was this routing problem with some of the processing drains at Chott that I sorted out. It was easy enough—I was just doing it as a student project—but it worked and I saved someone a whole lot of money. I was probably the first person looking at the program who'd ever actually got her hands filthy with the kelp...I was a whiz then, a minor celebrity. Word got out."

Laurie sat on the rock above the mud, hugging her knees.

"And from that," John prompted her, "you were selected to work with the net?"

"The net selected me. Or maybe it was politics—you know how they like to have the odd Gog in apparently trustworthy positions. So they can point and say *look*..."

"Laurie, how old are you?"

"Twenty-six. I don't know," she continued, answering an

internal question. "I'll maybe stay on at the Zone for another two years. The money is good. Then... *Then* I'll decide. I feel like I've been on this ride all my life. Pushed along on these rails. You don't like the way you're going, but at least it isn't your fault, you can blame others for what's been decided. But it's not always easy to step off..."

It was fully dark now, although people were still working on the kelpbeds. John could see the bobbing yellow lanterns, hear the ticking of a hand-pulled winch.

"Come on," Laurie said, "I'll take you back."

She stood up, rubbing at her legs. Her pale outline shimmered. Chill fingers of mist began to rise as the two of them walked towards the ramshackle nests of houses. They reached lights. Voices. The smoke of cooking. The streets up the hill were swarming, even more crowded than they had been that afternoon. But the people parted for Laurie, and John followed in her wake. A witchwoman sat at a narrow crossroads on an ornate rug, wreathed in smoking incense and surrounded by enamel bowls, tin rockets, chunks of moonrock, star charts, and the polished skulls of rats, goats, humans. John slowed, and saw a small green snake slide out from a candlelit eyesocket. The witchwoman scooped the snake up and held it out to him with a gap-toothed smile.

What had Tim said—that the witchwomen were infected by madness? This odd uniformity of behavior had to be based on something, and the tolerance, too, of the generally atheistic Borderers towards them. And why the obsession with the other planets? All that had been learned in the brief years of the exploration of Venus and Mars was that cycles of devastation were routinely at play. On the cinderblocks and the great gas giants as well. Planets routinely fostered and then shrugged off life.

But now that the world expended its resources exclusively on the great, orbital, winged solar deflectors and thermonuclear toruses that battled to sustain warmth and safe skies, he supposed it was better that the rocks and sand that men and women had journeyed across space for should end up being revered rather than stored and forgotten in some net-maintained warehouse.

Laurie drove back towards Gran Vía on the lower roads through the oldtowns and the gray-walled new housing projects, where even she was forced to stick to the sluggish pace dictated by the lumbering open buses, wandering cattle, scurrying flocks of children, aimless drunks.

"I never came this far," he said.

"When?"

"This way—when I was gathering data."

"Ah yes." She nodded. "I remember. There's a kind of disease, and you said you thought something could be done..."

"Tim Purdoe's checking some samples for me."

"For what?"

"A link between cancer and radiation. Leukemia—*bludrut.*"

Her mouth tightened. "I do know what leukemia is."

"Did you ever hear of any cases?"

"No—you're not disappointed, are you?"

He shook his head and looked out the window. The wind was weaving ribbons of dust and smoke through the lighted evening.

"I'm sorry." She handed him a tube. He broke the seal but couldn't tell the shade. "It's just the way you people always react when you come here. You all take one look and seem to think you have the answer. But if you're serious, if you really think there *is* something..."

"Yes. Of course."

"Then I'd like to see the cards sometime. I might be able to help with the net. I mean, it's not exactly my field..."

"Tim's doing tests on some tissue samples and food substances. If there is a cause, a pollutant, it has to be common, but it can't be something too obvious, like windblown dust or solar breakthrough or kelp—Halcycon wouldn't have let that through the system all these years. It has to be something else. Something with a slow buildup that's only present in tiny quantities. Something that has a strong affinity for living cells so that it's absorbed into the body rather than excreted." He stopped.

"Sounds like you're close," Laurie said after a while.

"I think I am..." He bit off the end of his tube and drew. It tasted of cinnamon, wood leaves, firesmoke, autumn. Briefly, he felt the way he was supposed to: filled with pointless nostalgia, both happy and sad. And the colors streaming from doorways and screens and signs were red, yellow, amber, orange. Sweat-covered faces and sliding limbs. "Where are we now?"

"You'll see."

She cranked down her window to let the smoke escape. Arms reached out, but she handled the van well, kept moving, spinning the wheel to avoid the bodies ahead. He heard shouts, laughter. And then there were mouths parting near him, glimpses of flesh. Here, there was no need for a translat. The meaning was universal: the offer of easy surprise. All eyes followed the van. Battered as it was, it still spelled *ossar*—money.

"Over there." Laurie pointed to a building that climbed out of the smog, where a faulty screen over the doorway stuttered with an image that John thought for a moment was a mouth, then an opening flower. "...you get the Europeans. It's a big treat, you know. To have a few drinks, smoke a few tubes, come out here from the Zone."

So this was Agouna. He drew again on the tube, wondering if it was that or the brown-iris pigment that was giving everything this blur of distance. And Laurie was still talking: See, Father John, over there, see those people across the street—they have their orifices electronically enhanced. And did you know, Father John, that they often die when the acid leaks from their implant batteries? Her words turned bitter, and he caught the dark breeze from the tube she was smoking, quite different from his own.

"I wanted you to see," she said.

She dropped him off outside the presbytery. His eyes were hurting him now, but in his groggy state he put it down to tiredness until, climbing to his room in the presbytery, he paused by the clouded mirror on the stairway to examine his face. What a joke it would be, he thought, if the catalyst were to hold permanently. But the iris of his left eye was already half-faded, barely a grayish brown. The silver, the iris-bleaching pigment that had started out as a whim of European fashion and then become an unshakable badge of identity, was returning. Vaguely disappointed, John walked the rest of the way up the stairs.

FELIPE IS SEATED in his chair in the Pandera presbytery's top room, smiling. Bella stands behind him, having removed her facemask at John's request. Uncovered, her mouth looks odd. The card's five available seconds go by as he silently urges them to speak, move—do at least something for the camera. But there is only the creak of the circling fan and sounds through the open window from the street below. A baby crying. A donkey braying. The hot Magulf wind.

Gran Vía, under a pouring sky where children dart like dragonflies and a koiyl vendor scowls, hauling his tall wheeled basket down the rutted street towards the Alcalá souk. In the background, a high tenement's rotting masonry.

Light falls through Santa Cristina's roof, pointing a finger in a drizzle of dust at the ravaged body of the stone crusader. John pans left for a glimpse through the open west doorway, where caroni birds are circling.

Tim Purdoe sits with his feet up in his surgery as the cleared window behind him shows the lawns and the lake beyond. The freezer box containing the tissue samples John sent over a week before lies unopened on the floor. Tim raises a hand and manages an affable but long-suffering smile. He is, as he's reminded John a few moments before, a very busy man.

Nuru is seated relaxed in the clinic, his feet also up in the front office desk in curious mimicry of Tim Purdoe at the medical center, although the two have never met and are unlikely to do so. He stretches out a hand and points.

"This your brother Hal? Fatoo John, do a fine job..."

The local healer Winah also stands in the clinic's frontroom, holding open the huge carpetbag she always carries with her. An Aladdin's cave of potions and vials, and the dried koiyl flowers, stronger and rarer than the leaves, which, so it is said, the women of the Endless City swallow to stifle the pains of labor. But John knows only what he's heard: women in pregnancy are more than usually wary of his presence, afraid he'll give their babies his silver eyes.

Beyond the rooftops of the Endless City and the rising spires of the Bab Mensor shuttleport, a river of light blinks across the Breathless Ocean. Then comes the roar of engines as the Tuesday evening Paris shuttle emerges through the darkening clouds from reentry, her fins glowing.

The wires and rails surrounding the smoking chimney-finger of the El Teuf incinerator flutter with thousands of offerings to the dead. A child's teddybear with the speech circuit hanging out, the skin of a cat, ribbons stippled with images of happier days, and endless messages, many on cards of the type given out at Santa Cristina. Some, damaged but still functioning, mutter and growl into the wind.

A Borderer family. Two teenage children, a baby, an old woman, a young man. They knew John was coming, and the glowing screen of a Borderer speak-and-talk Bible lies conspicuously open on the table in the corner. The deep gurgle of one of the main kelp-feed pipelines rumbles nearby like an endless train.

"What say, Fatoo?"

"Just anything, whatever."

The family frown as, uncertainly, they mouth the alien words *anything whatever.*

Back in his room at the Pandera presbytery in the hour before the generator goes down. The chair, the washstand, the bed. John is still dressed in his cassock and wishing that he'd also left his gloves on. That, after all, is the truth of how most people see him here.

"For now, Hal," he says, "I call this my home."

Laurie was already waiting for John in the Jubilee Bar of the Hyatt Hotel. The wine bottle on the table was half empty. There were the ends of four tubes in the ashtray.

"Father John . . ."

"Am I late? Are you early?"

She fanned her hands in a Borderer shrug, then tipped red wine into the other glass.

He sat down and unslung the camera from his shoulder.

"Your eyes are silver again," he said.

"It's easier in a place like this. Otherwise people ask you to bring them a drink or another tray of nuts."

"Really?"

"Do you want me to show you?"

He shook his head. Dimly, he could see his own outline reflected in her eyes. He still couldn't get used to the difference it made.

"So . . ." She nodded at the camera. "You've been taking pictures?"

"For my parents. And for my brother."

"Can I see?"

He handed her the camera and waited as she looked at the small flat screen on the back. Felipe. Bella. Santa Cristina. El

Teuf. Gran Vía. Nuru...Biting her lip, she paused, touching the pads to clear and focus on some part of an image, then moved on. The Jubilee Bar's wide windows looked out across the lake at the green of Trinity Gardens and the spire of All Saints where Father Orteau ministered to the needs of the Zone. The fountain in the middle of the room clattered. The empty glass-top tables caught the mid-afternoon light.

She placed the camera on the couch. "What is this brother of yours like? Is he much younger than you?"

"What makes you say that?"

"Just the way you spoke to him at the end."

"I only said about three words."

She nodded.

He put his hand around the glass on the table. He lifted it, took a sip of his wine, and swallowed. "Hal's older than me," he said, "but there was an accident in his late teens. We used to go to this house by the coast every summer. The last year, soon after we came home, Hal was supposed to go to study in London. But he didn't make it. It was obvious that he was depressed, although because it was Hal, no one really believed it. Then one night, late after the carnival, he got into the net from his bedroom terminal. He found this high-level port somewhere that they've never been able to locate, and used it to reprogram his implants. Since then he's been in a coma."

"Then there can't..." She paused. "There can't be much hope."

"Hope really isn't a thing you can weigh or quantify, is it? Hope's either there or it's not."

"I suppose so. A still small voice. And you wanted to show him the Endless City. You think that some of it might get through?"

"You know the story of Elijah?"

"Elijah?"

"A still small voice. You were quoting from the Bible..." He trailed off. Without even moving, Laurie seemed to be drifting away from him. "It doesn't matter."

She twisted around to rummage in her pockets for a tube. She offered him one. He shook his head. "Did you bring," she said, exhaling bluish smoke, "the cards?"

He placed them on the table. She took one, smoothed out a creased corner, and fed the card into the slot at the side of the table. Between the glasses and the bottles, the small screen brightened into life, throwing green and gold across her face. She paged up through the meal offers and lonely-heart adverts until she found the right port.

"How do you spell leukemia?"

Blinking though the tube haze, he reached over and pulled the letters up himself. Then they were looking down at the lattice of his main spreadsheet.

Laurie nodded. "Very impressive." The tips of her fingers dissolved as, shifting the cursor, she tiered back through the levels.

1A/924/K. (36) Male, adolescent. Bleeding from membranes. "Bone pain." N. Keno—place of origin and last name unknown. Doctor reports immature monocytes 6×10^9/liter. As usual recommends myelosuppression despite failed previous attempts to input.

3C/5626/K. (58) Female, mature. Skin lesions. Ulceration. Secondary gout. Worker at El Teuf. Doctor reports neutrophils 30×10^9/liter.

"What are all the numbers for?"

"I tried to think up a simple filing system based on the mission guidance. That way I was able to incorporate most of the data for the ten years since the last time the doctor was wholly reformatted. You know what it's like—you have to make a decision about groups and categories, then you're stuck with it."

Nodding in a way that suggested she didn't know what it was like at all, Laurie pushed deeper into the spreadsheet on the table. The entries became a blur. She hummed to herself and her eyes flickered, somehow seeming to take it all in even at this speed. John wondered if he wasn't making a mistake in showing her this. Like Tim, she was a professional. She'd see nothing but the faults and limitations in his work.

"This is just the top layer. Photographs—" He reached over and pulled something up from the screen. A brown-irised human eye appeared in close-up: swollen, streaked with blood.

"I saw that option on the menu," she said.

"But the point is a simple one. In the reports for the past ten years there have been a total of 78 separate cases of acute myeloid leukemia in the 63,000 entered into the doctor. With that number of people, there should have been only two or three." The blood-weeping eye on the screen blinked, and someone who'd just arrived at the bar glanced over and said something John didn't catch. Laurie picked up her glass and blanked the screen.

"Okay," she said. "At the clinic you are seeing whoever comes in the door—but they won't all be different people, will they? You'll get returns and repeats. And, how do you know how typical they are? You're bound to get people with unusual complaints, people who wouldn't ordinarily come to a clinic but are desperate for help."

John explained how he'd estimated the number of people in the surrounding Magulf who were likely to make some use of the surgery and how, even then, there were still far too many cases. And he'd gone back to the old analogue textbooks—not that they were perfect—but unless there had been some radical change, he knew that he shouldn't expect to see one case of leukemia a year, and that was all types, spleen and bone-marrow, acute and chronic...

"I have to deal with these people, Laurie," he said. "They'll let the doctor hold them because they think it'll stitch a wound or diagnose a problem. Then the readout comes up on the screen with this long list of pointless recommendations for drugs. Those that I can synthesize or get hold of through Tim only make the patients iller, quicker. And then I have to decide what to tell them. Whether they'll cope..."

He stopped. His voice had grown loud, and he realized that the people who were now filling the Jubilee Bar from the ending afternoon shift were glancing over at him and Laurie with undisguised irritation. Earlier that day he'd seen Martínez, who was still surviving, who was in fact looking better. The man had even managed to get back for a few hours to renovating and repairing his vans. Fatoo, it's just this fever, he'd said, sitting in the parlor as the silver-eyed people hung frozen on the screen he'd been watching and as his children peered in from the doorway. Martínez was a living advert for the incredible strength of the Borderers' natural defenses. He'd put on a little weight, and for the last few days he'd even stopped coughing up the pale-whitish blood. I'm making sure I still eat, he said, smiling as a fly crawled over the sweat on his face. So I don't need you to tell me it's *sumfo*—nothing, Fatoo. I know that already...

John finished off the glass of wine and stared at the empty

bottle, wondering whether he should blow half his weekly allowance and order another.

Laurie ground out her tube in the ashtray. "Anyway, Father John. You've convinced me. So. These are copies, yes...?" She rapped the cards together and placed them in her bag. "I'll see what I can do." She stood up.

"Hey—wait." He reached for the camera.

Laurie Kalmar in the Jubilee Bar of the Hyatt Hotel. She's smiling, and the cuffs of her jacket are down and her eyes are silver. There is music, and the murmur of voices. In the background, a uniformed Borderer waiter stands behind the bar polishing glasses. He's staring at her, and his face is blankly hostile.

"Wish you were here, Hal."

She turns away and walks out of the bar.

HERE WAS HAL at the carnival, here was Hal at the fair. Here was Hal on a bright late summer's afternoon where the great wheel was waiting, rising over the bustling tented city, its hub and vast circumference gaudily painted in man-thick streamers of red and yellow, trapped at the center of everything with struts and gantries straining against the sky.

"Come on Skiddle." Hal's hand surrounded John's own, drawing him on past the eye-shading onlookers, towards the fenced and looping archway that spelled out THE GREAT WHEEL and the first of the hugely anchored cables that were pulling hot and tight. "It'll be good."

And, yes, John knew that it truly would be good. To be up there, higher than the highest spire and coiled like the spring that kept the whole universe turning. He looked up. The great wheel creaked, and everything else seemed to lean. Already, could it be turning? Or could it be the earth? Or the sky? Could it be him?

"Skiddle, you *said* you would." Hal was smiling. "You said you would last year."

But last year, when John made his promise, he never really believed that this year would come. And he'd willingly give next year away with a promise too. By then he'd be different, more like Hal. He'd be strong.

They were drawing close to the back of the queue where there were faces he recognized: girls and lads mostly bigger and older than he was, rubbing at the sweat gathering on their eyebrows as they squinted up, and laughing about how it would be. All day they'd been waiting, holding back amid the sights and the stalls and the amusements, judging the moment. And people are asking, What's it really like—to be up there, turning? And surely that's a cloud right there at the top of the thing, caught like a piece of fleece in a spinning wheel, in the engine of the sky.

They were in the queue now, and Hal was finding the money he'd promised for John's ticket. A clown, a fire-eater, a juggler, a giant automated bear passed by, but the people here were looking up at the sky and their thoughts were already turning, feeling the scream of the wind and the flash of the sun and the drop in their bellies. Up ahead a barrier unhooked, and the first riders climbed up the steps. The open gondola swung as they settled; the thin golden bars of the cage; the creaking padded straps; the clunk of the catches. Then a drivebelt smoked and tensed, and the wheel growled on its bearings and turned flashing in a thunder that came up through the grass and from beyond the sun. The gondola bobbed up like a cork on a river. Already, it was halfway to the sky.

Another gondola. The queue shuffled forward. Again, the wheel flashed, growled, creaked, thundered, turned, and the sun was hot on John's neck and he could taste the fried onions he'd eaten earlier, could feel the pull of the ground through the soles of his shoes. Again the queue moved forward, and Hal was humming. John stared at the squashed grass. He knew that Hal was looking up. He knew that the great wheel was turning. A shadow passed over him. Silent and expectant as mourners now, filled with dread and excitement, the queue moved forward.

Another moment, and John was facing the steps leading up to the swaying gondola, which seemed high and huge and open and scary in itself. He waited. The great wheel was too close now to take in whole. He waited. Hal squeezed his shoulder and went up the steps first, climbing into the gondola and balancing just as he did at Ley when he was getting into *Omega*, their skittish little boat. Hal leaned back into the padded bench. The straps, the locks. John waited. A painted mermaid, many times life-size, smiled down at him.

Already far above, Hal beckoned from the swaying gondola, held out a hand. "Come on, Skiddle. Now it's your turn."

The whole carnival seemed to fall silent. The flags drooped. The engines stopped. The air whitened and froze over. John gazed at the first step leading to the gondola and saw how there was a nailed-down strip of metal at the edge, how the paint had been scuffed away by the passage of many feet.

"Come on, Skiddle! What is—"

Something broke inside him, and he turned and ran. Ran without thinking as the air washed the sweat from his face and roared laughter in his ears. Ran away, stumbling over guy ropes and cables, bumping into avuncular bellies and swinging disconnected arms. Away and through and over a hedge where litter and wild bramble clawed at his arms, across the dusty furrows of the freshly emptied fields where the machines slept like great black insects, and back towards the village. Finally, as the oaks beside the main road cast their shade over him and a spider brushed his face, John stumbled over a root, stopped, and turned.

He could still see the great wheel and hear the piping clangorous wash of the fair. And once again, the wheel glinted and turned. Even from across these fields it looked vast and the people on it were tiny as ants, almost too small to be seen. It turned and he knew that this time the turning would be different, faster. From under his tree, could he really hear the whoops and screams? The great wheel was truly spinning now, over and up and over, blurring, picking up wild momentum like a child's top, close to the moment of release. As he watched, he saw the puff of the stabilizers as the wheel started to lift from the gantry, saw as it began to rise. The motion was slow now, absurdly right, incredibly graceful. Turning as the earth turns, the great wheel rolled up the slope of an invisible mountain and bore its riders for their sweet and giddy hour tumbling in the skies of Hemhill.

Walking down the road, John felt guiltily grateful that he had run. No leap of the imagination would ever be big enough to put him up there, high in sunlight over the valley. He kicked at the dust. He passed the empty houses, walking on towards the center of the village.

High Street was Sunday-quiet. The trees hung still. The fountain was dead. The machines were resting. The shops were closed. From a window by the old theater came the tinny sound of music, but it only added to the sense of weird tranquillity. Here, deep in Hemhill's undersea heat, nothing would ever stir.

And there it was, up over the rooftops, far and distant, the great wheel with Hal in it, flashing through the deep rippling blue surface of the sky. It was unreal, and the stories the riders would tell when it returned to earth would never quite convey the meaning. The earth, the wind, the sun, the sky, the sky, the blue and lovely sky, and screaming at the top of your lungs. Next year, maybe next year, another year, he would go.

It seemed that Tilly's Café was still open; across the empty road, by the booth into the net, there was the green sunflash of its open door. But Tilly always was an old grouch. Farther along the wide street and vague in the heat, the shops and houses dissolved into fields and green haze. Hard to believe on a day like this that autumn would ever come. Yet it was waiting just around the corner and in the squat empty buildings beyond the shockwire at the edge of the village, ready to grab at him with its papery dry-leaf hands.

Inside Tilly's, the air smelled of dust and vanilla. The screens of the game machines at the far end of the row of empty chairs and tables glowed and beckoned. With the carnival here, no one needed them. Tilly himself was steering a broom across the checker-tiled floor. Seeing John, he stopped and scowled, resting his wrists. Would you believe, he said, that the cleaner's on the blink again. The rep says I've fed it the wrong kind of polish. I should get a Gog in here instead, a real human helper like those big places in the city. You know...

John sat down at one of the stools by the counter. Tilly sighed and gave the broom a few more pushes. But he was happy only when he was miserable. I thought you'd be at the... He nodded out the window at the hot blue undersea sky and the tiny wheel tumbling and gleaming, but he meant the carnival in general. Out there with the rest of them. And what'll it be? He poured John a chocolate shake, and waved the money away. Take it, son—business is bad anyway. Take it.

John sucked the cool sweet gritty stuff up through the straw, feeling it break and dissolve in his mouth, wondering why it was that things didn't taste the same when they were free. This is Hal's last year, isn't it? Tilly muttered. After that, he'll be off. Going to London around the time of the next carnival. And what is he talking of studying? Tilly asked, leaning his bare hairy arms on the counter. That brother of yours? Something to do with... Tilly shook his head. What is it to do with?

Structural communication, John said.

Tilly picked up the broom again, pushing at a smear on the floor. He'll be bound to be doing something smart, will that one. John nodded, stirring the foamy chocolate with his straw, thinking, earth, sky, earth... And what about you? Tilly nodded towards him, singling him out with his eyes as though there were someone else in the café. What is it that you're planning? Next year, John thought, Hal will be leaving for London, and I'll be up there with him before he goes. Up on that great wheel. And the year after, too.

I was thinking, he heard himself saying to Tilly for some reason, that I might study to become a priest.

STANDING ON THE granite steps of the Governor's Residence, John tugged at the white cuffs of his new suit. It was past six by his watch, and the Magulf sky was already starting to darken, draining the color of the stone between the shining yellow windows. He took a step forward when the doors of the residence swung in, expecting the figure who blocked his way to be some Borderer domestic. Then he recognized the governor's face.

"Father John—come in! I won't shake hands..." The governor was wearing an apron. His large hands were floured. "I'm in the middle of cooking dinner. One of my hobbies. Straight through to the patio. Help yourself to the drinks. You'll have to excuse me—I've got onions frying." Wagging a finger, he left.

John walked across the hallway and a wide, sparsely

furnished room. The far end, framed by curtains that lifted and fell in the wind, gave onto a patio, a circle of wicker seats, and a drinks trolley. As yet, no one else had arrived. He took the steps down into the garden, where a pathway led through clouds of rhododendron towards a fan of light and the *pock* of tennis balls. The man playing was bald, tall, and thin, clumsy yet quick in his movements. At the other side of the net a machine hissed and tumbled as it lobbed, returned.

"Thirty love, four games to three, final set," it intoned, trundling back to the line. The man briefly raised his racket to John in acknowledgment, then hunkered down to await the next serve, his bare skull gleaming under the court's floodlights, his cheeks forming deep hollows. His eyes were brown.

John sat on a bench outside the ball buffer and watched the game unfold. There had been evenings like this at the playing fields across the road from home in Hemhill, when he'd sat and watched Hal serve, run, volley, win... But there was something odd, he realized, about the Borderer's hands.

He waited for the match to finish; it was won by the machine against serve. Laughing, the man leaped over the net and, gravely ironic, shook the machine by the claw. John heard the clink of metal on metal.

"That's six-three. I must be losing my touch."

The man sat down at the other end of John's bench, still breathless. Inside the court, the machine proceeded to collect the balls from the troughs.

"You're here for the dinner tonight?" John asked, wondering why no one had ever thought to make the lydrin implant show itself the way the iris-bleaching pigment did for Europeans. "I'm John Alston—a priest. I work on Gran Vía."

"Call me Ryat." His fingers clicked. At the place where the

metal of his hands met his arms just above the wrists, the flesh had scarred and melted. "I was involved in supplying one of the main contracts for the kelpbeds at Medersa. I imagine that's why Owen Price has me here tonight. The token—is that the word?—the token Borderer. Although I gather that a girl who works on the net is coming too." The hands slid together with a sound like knives. He stood up. "I must change."

The garden was fully dark now. Away from the shelter of the windbreaks, the rhododendrons bowed and swayed. The two men passed the rim of a swimming pool rippling red as blood and entered the large changing hut beyond.

"Where do you live?" John asked as Ryat undressed.

"Mokifa. You know it?" Ryat balled up his clothes and tossed them into the disposer. His body was brown and well muscled but, like Nuru's, the healthy flesh was stretched over knobbed joints and a thin, angular frame. John studied Ryat's left arm for an implant scar, but there was no obvious sign.

"I've never been inside," John said. "I assumed that I wouldn't be welcome."

"And you have better things to do with your time than worry about *bereket*—a few rich Borderers?"

"If you put it like that." John shrugged. Ryat turned on a cubical shower. Even after six months in the clinic with the doctor examining Borderers, it was odd to see the clean, un-puckered line of a spine.

"And you know about Kushiel?" Ryat asked over the clatter of the water. The bar of soap, guided by metal fingers, slid, foaming, over his belly and thighs.

"I entered it once by accident."

Ryat turned off the shower and stepped out, shaking the water from his pointed fingers. Throwing damp towels into the disposer after drying himself, he reached into his locker, withdrew a small syringe, raised a pinch of flesh, and inserted the invisibly thin needle into his arm. Lydrin. So that was how. "On some nights before the rain," he said, "when the humidity is high, I stand at my window and watch Kushiel send great upward lights into the sky." He began to dress. "I'm sure one day it will have to be dismantled..."

"Even when it was built," John said, "it must have been too ambitious. A waste of money and land."

Ryat inspected himself in the mirror. Glancing over his shoulder, his face crinkled around a grin. "But there's a pattern, isn't there?" He straightened his tie. "The way things proceed here in the Endless City. It's not the ungoverned chaos that some people imagine..."

They walked back around the pool towards the lights of the house. From the patio, carried on the wind, came the tinkle of glasses, the hum of voices.

Laurie approached, wearing a long blue dress. She nodded at Ryat and drew John away.

"You know who that is?"

"Ryat. We met at the tennis courts."

Her eyes were their natural green tonight, but they still seemed closed off, covered by a layer. A gritty wind was picking up. The guests retired inside. They sat for dinner at a long table in a high room where the windows looked out across the Dustbowl towards the Northern Mountains, jagged and distant against a crimson sky. There was Jacques Montrel, a visitor from mainland Halcycon S.A. There was the deputy manager of the Bab Mensor shuttleport; John recalled the face. And Tim Purdoe, looking oddly lumpy in a suit instead of his usual tweed jacket, as if he had the thing on underneath. And Cal Edmead,

Price's deputy, who had introduced Mister Mero at Trinity Gardens what now seemed a long time ago.

"As soon as I saw the skies here, I thought—late Turner!" the governor said when the main course was finished and dessert came. He swooped around the table to pass out the dishes with his own big hands. "Swirling reds, oranges, golds. Laurie, would you see to the light over there?"

Laurie folded her napkin and stood up. She touched the room controls, and a big canvas loomed out from a paneled wall, showing a ship on a blood-red sea awash with bodies. The cream jug was passed.

Jacques Montrel, who sat opposite the governor, was obviously very senior in the Halcyon hierarchy—and made politely sure that everyone knew it—but he was also gray-haired, thin-faced, tired, and stooped as the bones hardened around his implants, a gaunt presence near the end of his time. "Tell me, Father John," he said in a near-whisper. "How do you manage with the Sacrament?"

"The packs are presealed, so I never actually touch the wafers."

"And there's no risk? Your parishioners don't object?"

"No."

A brief silence followed. Mozart played faintly in the background.

"The days," Tim Purdoe said, "when people had to go around wearing hoods and special suits are long gone."

"I suppose," Montrel said, "that that is progress. But don't you think we should aim to provide recombinant viral implants for all Borderers as well?" Slowly, he raised his trembling glass and sipped. His eyes were red-rimmed, and moisture had made trails down the furrows of his cheeks. He glanced up the table.

"Mister Ryat, you must have a different understanding of this. I mean, living in the Endless City..."

Ryat smiled. "What you are really asking me is whether I'd like to become a European."

"Would you? No"—Montrel smiled and corrected himself, the wattles of his neck sucking in—"of course not. That isn't what I mean, even if it really were possible. And you, Miss Kalmar?"

Laurie shook her head. "The reasons implant technology came about," she said, "had more to do with keeping out the great migrations than combating the spread of new disease."

Montrel gave a gray nod. His breath whistled. "And now?"

"Nothing's changed really, has it?" she said. "The only surprise is that we Borderers have survived and adapted, that the weather and the new diseases haven't killed us all."

The governor leaned forward briskly in his chair. "Of course Laurie's right," he said. He smiled, gazing upon his Turner. "There was a time when people feared that humanity would be taken over by machines. What they didn't expect was that machines would grow and expand inside us..."

The guests left the table. The music shifted to Chopin, rumbling from the keys of a piano, and doors opened, leading to a castellated terrace. White awnings flapped overhead. From here you could see north across most of the Zone, the lights of an orderly checkerboard. A few veetols were hovering at the shuttlebase: for a moment, they looked like twinkling stars. Beyond the Endless City was a well of darkness.

Montrel had been helped into a silver frame—a sleeker version of Felipe's leghelpers, but with support for the arms and back as well. He was talking to a few listeners about a trip across the globe to FarEast and Australasia where, as in Europe, the climate still held. Strange customs, strange people—his voice amplified now by the machine he was in—and, beyond in the dusty fringes, even stranger versions of the Endless City.

As John walked past Montrel to where Tim was leaning on the parapet, he caught the same stale papery smell of death that had filled the backrooms he'd once visited in Yorkshire.

"I know, John." Tim waved a hand. "You're going to ask me about all those tests."

John nodded, looking out, resting his elbows on the stone, breathing in the rich, living air of the Magulf.

"I've done the lot," Tim said.

John turned to him. "You *have?*"

"You could look a little less surprised."

"And?"

"You were right about the koiyl. Two of the five leaves you gave me contain significant levels of strontium 90, and traces of cesium 137 and plutonium 239. I found the isotopes in some of those tissue samples you sent me, too—although you didn't really give me the right kind, or tell me enough about the donors. But I imagine they're the ones who have the koiyl-chewing habit, or who absorbed the isotopes from their mothers. There was one case with a high concentration in the gut. Not a sample—I think it was on a pink card."

"That wasn't from the clinic," John said. "It was from the incinerator at El Teuf..." Looking out across the lights of the Zone, he was thinking of Daudi, comatose. And of the woman he'd tried to treat with cytotoxic drugs, her lush, jet-black skin paling under the bloom of a parasitic growth. And of Martínez, and the way Kailu had looked at him in that hallway off the Cruz de Marcenado.

The other guests were going back inside now to escape the rising wind.

"Of course," Tim added, squinting against a billow of dust, "this isn't proof. And there are bound to be other factors involved—a genetic predisposition to the disease, perhaps a chemical or viral trigger." He shrugged. "We could simply be witnessing some kind of random cluster..."

"There's nothing damaging about the leaf itself?"

"It does have a clever mix of neuropeptides, so I suppose you could make a nerve poison from it if you wanted. But that's not what's happening. The problem is definitely the strontium 90."

"What do we do? Put in more work to prove what we already know? Publish something on the net?"

Tim laughed and shook his head. "John, I remember asking you what you were going to do with the truth when you had it. Well, now you do. And you know what they'll say back in Europe: Why don't you just tell the Gogs to stop chewing that beastly koiyl?"

"It's not that easy. The whole point about the leaf is that it's simple and safe. The alternatives are alcohol, opiates, expensive tubes, even encephaline, and there have been cases of mass poisoning—"

"I *know*, John. I analyzed it. Your average Gog wouldn't believe there's a danger anyway. It's not like those two here..." Tim nodded over to where Laurie and Ryat still stood outside, talking. John could tell from the quick way they shrugged and gestured that they were speaking Borderer. "But what do the rest of them out there know about myeloid leukemia, John? The ones who work the phosphate plants and pour our drinks and hand-paint our Christmas baubles?"

"They have this generalized word. *Bludrut*—but that covers anemia, hepatitis D."

"It would be just another Zone-based campaign. More unwatched satellite time, the bloody *Outers* telling them what to do again. You try explaining how the remnants of some forgotten war could affect the Magulf now."

"Is that what you think the source is? A bomb? A weapon?"

"Here." Tim reached into the breastpocket of his lumpy suit. "I brought the main card you gave me from your doctor. I've updated it as best I can. You can read it yourself."

John stared at it. One little wedge of plastic.

Tim flicked the card with his thumb. Waiting.

John took it. "Okay," he sighed. "I'll speak to Price. And I'll play down how helpful you've been, Tim. That's what's worrying you, isn't it?"

"You never know what turn these things'll take. I'm not supposed to use my facilities for private research."

"Tim, you're the Chief Medical Officer."

"Yeah, and I'm CMO because I've learned how to keep my nose clean." He managed a smile. "And I'll still be here after you've gone. But fuck it, John. You go for it..." He gestured through the open doors at the room where the guests mingled, the lights glowed, a piano played. "I mean, what are we doing here otherwise? What's it about, eh?"

"That's right, Tim."

John turned and went inside. Conveniently, the governor was standing alone. John walked over to him.

"Mister Price."

"Call me Owen."

"I'd like to speak to you."

The governor steered John to a sofa in an alcove, and they

sat down. The man leaned forward, broad shoulders hunched, elbows on knees, nodding, listening, swirling a big balloon glass of brandy and asking brief clarifying questions as John explained about the leukemia, the koiyl, the tests that indicated radioactive isotopes. And, yes, Owen Price did know about the koiyl leaf, its popularity...

"It's not often," he said finally when John had finished, "that there's a simple answer to a problem in the Magulf."

John studied him. Every day, he supposed, he was presented with problems, solutions, conflicts of priority, disasters posing as triumphs. If you rose high enough in Halcycon S.A. to get to be governor of a zone, you probably learned to forget that there were simple answers to anything.

"I'll tell you what it's like, Father," the governor continued, with the air of confiding a great secret. "People come here, and they look around at what happens in the Zone and what goes on outside it, and they generally reach some conclusion. We all think that we're getting it wrong in one way or another. A lot say we should pull out of the Magulf entirely. Just trade with the Borderers for what we need and leave them to get on with it. It's mostly phosphates, ores—raw materials that we could find new ways to recycle or create if the pressure in Europe got tight enough..."

He downed the last of his brandy and leaned back. Around them, music played, voices rose and fell.

"That's supposed to be the whole basis of our society, isn't it?" he said. "Don't exploit, don't mine, don't hack, don't fell. Grow, nurture, reuse, make the best of what's left of the world...And then we trickle money and aid and investment into the Endless City. Just enough to unbalance things, never enough to really bring about a change. If we left. Left them to get on with their lives..." He shook his head. "But we're afraid to do that, too. That's the bottom line, isn't it? We're afraid of the Borderers. And we envy them. Like Jacques over there. Such a waste."

John nodded, and said nothing.

"How sure are you of this blood-cancer link, Father?" he asked. "Where's the koiyl grown? Do you know where the radiation is coming from?"

"I understand it's harvested in sheltered valleys up in the Northern Mountains. I would expect—"

The governor raised a hand. "Let's not speculate, Father. So you're saying we could save lives by stopping the trade of koiyl—or at least by stopping the supply from the contaminated area?"

"Exactly."

"Still, you've admitted that big gaps remain in what you know..." He gazed sadly at his empty brandy glass. "And I can tell you from bitter personal experience that common sense and reasonable evidence are never enough." He sighed and raised his handsome, wide-set silver eyes to John.

"You're telling me I should give this up?"

The governor shook his head. "I simply want you to be aware of what you're up against, Father. You really do need to find out more about the trade routes, the local supply— above all, what exactly the source of this contamination is. If you can point to that, I think we may be starting to get somewhere..." He levered himself up from the sofa. "You can of course continue to use my people to pursue your researches. But please be discreet. You must understand that a lot of Borderer goodwill can be lost if we meddle thoughtlessly in these areas. And do keep me informed. It would be counterproductive for any of this to get out in the wrong way. Have a quiet word with Cal Edmead over there when you feel the need..."

The governor turned, raised his hand, and headed off.

The voices were louder now. The air felt tired, talked-out. John stopped a drinks trolley as it tinkled by and grabbed a brandy. He had to admire the way that the governor had dealt with him. Even living in the Endless City, John realized that he still kept looking towards the Zone, hypnotized by its aura of power.

He got up and wandered around the room, looking to speak to Laurie Kalmar. But she'd already left.

It was too late to go back to the presbytery that night. Lying on the bed in the guestroom that he was given, he breathed the intrusively clean air and waited, even here, for the pleading white figures to emerge, the trailing hands and faces. But to-night, for the first time in many weeks, they didn't come.

He awoke just as the windows were letting in the first light of morning. He lay for a while watching the sky redden. The carpets were soundlessly thick as he went out along the empty corridors, and he startled a Borderer maid who was leading a linen-stacked trolley. Rubbing nervously at her implant, she directed him around a corner, through a doorway, and down a narrow flight of stairs.

He opened cupboards in the kitchen below, peered under the lids of tureens and jars, and wandered amid the hanging meats and cheeses in the coldroom until he found soft wheaten bread on the marble shelves, a knife, a plate, a pitcher of fresh-squeezed orange juice, salted and unsalted butter, numberless varieties of marmalade and jam. He ate breakfast at the scrubbed wooden table, then set about finding Laurie Kalmar's address on the kitchen screen.

One of the middle-rankers, she lived on a street half a kilometer from the governor's house. There was no birdsong as he walked down the sloping drive through the gardens of the Governor's Residence, which seemed odd amid the scent of damp earth and the flowers. He looked up at the sky, which was a bright early-morning Magulf pink, but circling caroni birds were absent, somehow discouraged from the Zone.

Blackberry Avenue. Hazel Oak Road. Whoever had christened these tight little grids of interchangeable bungalows, alien and gray-white under the seething Magulf sky, must have been exercising a dry humor. And All Saints Drive, with the spire of the similarly named Zone church showing at the end. Number 28—but for Laurie's battered van sticking out among the parked lines of clean and barely driven Elysians—was like all the rest, with a narrow facade fronted by the same square of tough low-maintenance grass.

The door clicked open when he spoke his name. He stepped into a hall that was the size of a cupboard. The air smelled of tubes and dust and breadcrumbs. Faintly, too, of Borderer.

"I'll be there in a minute..." A refrigerator door banged, and Laurie stood barefoot in a faded red dressing gown. "You stayed on? I saw you talking to the governor. You got what you wanted last night?"

"Not at all, really." He followed her into the kitchen. It was also tiny, and had obviously been designed by someone with a tidy mind. He unstuck a half-drunk mug from a stool to sit down. "But Tim's done all the tests for me on the leaves now. I'm a great deal wiser."

Laurie sneezed, rummaged in the pocket of her dressing gown, and blew her nose. She sneezed again. "I'm sorry." She sniffed and waved her handkerchief. "I get like this if I've been near someone who's just come over from Europe, like..." She thought about sneezing again, changed her mind. "Like Montrel. Didn't he seem pathetic?"

John shrugged. "Isn't lydrin supposed to stop any reaction?"

"I wish it did." She pocketed her handkerchief. "Do you want some coffee?" She turned on the grinder. Dirty plates jingled and rattled. She gave him a cup, and he touched the handle and watched as the brownish fluid began to heat and swirl.

"So..." She cleared a space and sat down across the cluttered counter from him. "Tell me what happened."

She watched and listened as he talked, and blew grayish tubesmoke through her slightly red-tipped nose.

"I don't think I'll get much more out of Tim for a while," John said finally. "And the governor seems to regard the leaf as just some extra problem—another way of rocking the boat. He said I should obtain more information about where the contaminated leaf is grown. And exactly what the source of radioactivity is. Which makes sense. I mean, how much do you know about this, Laurie?"

She waved her hands. "Koiyl wasn't commonly used where I came from. If you were old, in pain, you might...But my mother said it was a bad, disgusting habit."

"You've never tried it?"

"Is that why you came here? Because you thought—"

"Laurie." He shook his head. "I didn't think anything. I knew you were interested. I just wanted to talk."

She gazed at him for a moment over the empty mugs, her

chin cupped in her hand. "I suppose I could help you look in the net. Do you have the card Tim gave you?"

While she went to change, he cleared a space on the sofa in the lounge and sat down. Amid all the mess, the only thing in the room that seemed actively used was the screen by the window, which had several of what looked like gauzy stars drifting inside it. He could sometimes admire the chaos that other people created around them—all that life—but the scattered tube stubs and empty glasses and mugs gleaming dully in the reddish light here were too impersonal. It looked and smelled a little like the morning after someone else's party. He stood up and went over to the window. Across next door's wire fence, the stained sun-awning that some hopeful expat had erected over the patio flapped uselessly in the breeze.

Laurie reemerged. She seemed to have an infinite supply of unironed skirts of faded navy, with cream and white blouses to go with them. Outside, the Zone was at last showing signs of wakefulness. Vans and cars and cyclists swished past. Yawning, morning-robotic people ambled along the pavements. Laurie and John joined them. She walked quickly, chewing at her lip, not noticing anyone she passed. She worked at one of the big annexes bridge-linked to the main admin block where John attended his dreary subcommittees, a large white cube with sunken black windows like the pips on a die. Inside, through the tickling barrier that kept out the Magulf air, silver-eyed people yawned at desks, scratched, gazed absently, or chatted into screens. Laurie headed between the desks and down some steps, along a windowless corridor. No one said hello.

He asked, "Do many other Borderers work here?"

"A few," she said, opening a door into an office, "if you count the maintenance staff."

The office was as neat inside as her bungalow was messy, although just as tiny. Hardly an office at all, more a box with one wall occupied by the shimmering neutral standby gray of a very large screen. Otherwise, there was only a desk and two chairs; no notepads or calendars or cabinets or scraps of paper. Unlike the rest of the world, people who worked the net really had got used to doing everything on computer.

Laurie fed the card he'd given her, the one with Tim's analysis of the leaf, into the port in the desk. Humming to herself, she began to issue one-fingered instructions. The big screen blackened. Bars of glittering white light shot across the room, each bar filled with tiny specks that fizzed and danced like hyperactive dust motes.

"These strings are up at the main entry level," she said, still humming. "Look..." She said something else, and the bars across the room all froze. Each was entwined with an endless procession of the initials of the quaternary code of adenine, guanine, thymine, and cytosine nucleotides—A, G, T, C—the same code that, though in different ways, John and Laurie's bodies still shared.

She began to hum again. It was an odd sound, modulated into phrases, neither quite rhythmic nor musical. As the strings began to flow again, ATCGATGATGCCCTAGATC spreading and opening around them like a silver net, he understood that humming was her way of issuing commands.

"Can you actually read all of this?"

"You get used to it. Everything looks the same for a while, but..." She popped her lips and smiled, looking up at the lines that revolved through the ceiling above them, pulling down the lines, tunneling deeper. Spears of light threaded around Laurie and John. "You learn to find your way."

"And you sing to it?"

She chuckled. "Is that what it sounds like?"

More intersecting lines. Level after level. Slashing, blurring, dropping. Then a complex knot of intersections, a ball of jagged shining wool turning before them. The ball rolled at them, then Laurie clicked her tongue, and the lines snapped back. They were suddenly looking down over the Magulf from a stratospheric height. And falling. The view reminded John of the one he'd seen from the shuttle window as he approached Bab Mensor from Europe. First, the gray Breathless Ocean, with Spain reaching down towards the mottled land that had once been North Africa—mountain peaks and red gashes of desert dissolving into cloud. But everything was impossibly far, impossibly clear.

"See those lights over there?"

He nodded as the Northern Mountains, still vague with distance, tilted up. Specks of red flickered like cannonfire amid the lower slopes.

"The red indicates the main areas where the net thinks the koiyl leaf is grown." She muttered something. "But the data can get pretty thin. The net really isn't that interested in what happens in the Magulf, apart from the impact the Magulf has on sustaining the European climate." The horizon tilted back, and the Northern Mountains receded. Laurie nodded and began to hum again. The image shrunk, dissolved. They were back within the silver web.

As she sang a scatter of mid-pitch notes, the two of them veered up, down, left, and right through the matrix, hovering over gaps where the lines receded to a glimmering mesh, then diving in again, level through level, down towards a brittle rose, right into the tightly bound heart that widened back out into a space of darkness. She was obviously on the track of something and too involved to say what. John just sat beside her, wishing and waiting for the ride to stop.

Laurie glanced over at him. Light flaring across her face. Briefly, she stopped humming. "Are you all right? You look..."

"I'm fine."

They came to a massive cube, slowly revolving.

"This is the Zone's main scientific database."

"Why is it so isolated?"

She shrugged. "We've come at it a funny way." She made a soft whistling sound, and they lunged down to the cube where the silver bars loomed thicker and larger than those at any of the other levels. He looked at her. She was smiling as they hovered in the twirling pit, her green eyes twinkling with flecks of reflected silver. The detail of the network all around them here was incredible, like woven silk.

Laurie was clicking her tongue, humming in a tuneless, rambling way. Freezing, sometimes, the trembling strings, scrolling up and down silver lines dripping with ATGCGTATAGGAC like dew-laden wires. Then on and in, until she found the right sector, a tiny bundle of strings that grew and grew as she pulled.

"There is it. A couple of days old, but see that extra string up there, where it enters the subnetwork? It's been reentered. That must have been when Tim took the copy for your card. But..."

"What?"

"The code's wrong. It's been reentered since, and it wasn't Tim."

"Who, then?"

"I'm not sure. The code's odd. Old. From somewhere...
Maybe it's just me."

They gazed at the intricate silver tapestry of AGTC letters.
She popped her lips. "Here's the analysis of the leaves that Tim
made. See that bigger cluster off to the right? That will be the
tissue samples. Anyway, you gave him five leaves to analyze,
and it turned out that only two were contaminated. Now, it
also turns out that those two have the same blip in a no-read
area of their DNA."

He nodded.

"In other words," she said, "the two contaminated leaves are
from plants that are close relatives, probably from the same
valley. Makes sense, doesn't it? And, see..." She pointed at
another tangle of silver. "The balance of trace elements in those
two leaves is very similar, too. As is the growth pattern, if you
run it back. Again, a shared location. So we can ask the net to
try to filter out those factors until it finds the climate in a koiyl-
growing northern valley with the closest match. It'll still be
guesswork, of course..."

She smiled over at John as the lines swirled around her. She
looked pleased with herself.

"The net might get it wrong?"

"It wouldn't be truly intelligent," she said, "if it always got
everything right, now would it? Anyway." She whistled, and
the silver strings snapped away, the big screen grayed, and the
tiny office fell back into shape around them. "Let's eat."

They went to a bar on Main Avenue, where the tables on one
side had already been pushed together for a semidrunken

leaving party. Laurie took a corner booth and picked over their shared order of salad and paella.

"Seafood..." she said. "Why did we order seafood?" She pushed away her plate and took out a tube. "I'm not hungry anyway. Never am when I'm working. You look pale—would you like wine?"

He shook his head.

She drew at her tube and exhaled. She looked a little shaky, and exalted. "When I started my job," she said, "I just used to take food tabs and coffee in my office from the machine that went past. It was less trouble. But I kept getting these sore throats." She inhaled. The leaving party opposite erupted into laughter. "Then someone told me that people were spitting in the coffee before it got to me. Trying to make me ill..."

He shook his head. "You deserve better than this."

"I got the biggest break a Gog could imagine. No, really." She looked at him, then down at her uneaten plate. "I like a lot of it. The work. The net. The Zone. Last night..."

They fell into silence. At the row of tables, the people were trying to decide if there was anything about the Zone they would miss. *The money,* it was unanimously decided. They would miss the money. And each other, someone else said. Sure, they said, their voices more muted now as they shared glances and agreed. *Each other...*

"And what will you do, Father John?" she said. "What will you do if the net tells you where the bad koiyl is coming from? Will you try to ban the whole trade? Put up posters? Send in the veetols to destroy some village up in the hills?"

He shook his head. "The governor was right about one thing—I don't know enough yet. I'll have to go up to the Northern Mountains to confirm this."

"You, personally?"

"Why? Is that a problem?"

Coffee was brought to them. It was unusual for the Zone, but in this bar they were served by a long-armed chromium machine that hissed around the room on magnetized tracks. *Makes a change from all these fucking Gogs,* someone muttered on the other side. John glanced over, but he couldn't see who it was, couldn't tell for sure if they'd even noticed Laurie.

"How," she asked, blowing the steam from her cup, watching the machine depart, "are you planning to get there?"

"I'll manage. I see people at the clinic who've walked from the mountains barefoot."

"But you'll go?"

"I can't give up."

"Okay," she said, putting down her cup, grinding out her tube.

"Okay what?"

She looked at him. "I'll come with you."

He took a breath.

"Or perhaps you would rather be alone..."

"No," he said, finding that he was smiling. "I don't want to be alone."

T̲HIS WAY, HEADING south into the wind, they could already see the Northern Mountains. A fine red dust blew into the cabin, sticking to their skin, settling into their clothes, gathering somehow even beneath the fingers of John's gloved hands. On the van's backseat, along with their bags and clothing, were water purifiers, transmitters, security buffers, protective suits and masks, a radiation counter. Outside, amid the tarpools, the wreckage of prehistoric trucks, and the wind-picked bones of mules, there were other travelers along the broken concrete slabs of the twentieth-century Sadiir Highway. Foline-powered twenty-wheelers lumbering between the phosphate mines and the chemical plants on the coast. Vans like their own. Panniered mules ambling beside stooped figures with djellabas drawn tight across their faces. Individuals and families stumbling in from the mountains and the desert beyond, drawn by the promise of the coast.

What little open-sky agriculture there was in the Magulf was clustered over the first few inland kilometers, where the autumn rains still fell. At first, John and Laurie had passed farms and plantations, stunted orangegroves protected by ferocious pony-sized dogs. Then flocks of skinny sheep picking over slopes of withered grass. Farther on, there was nothing.

They stopped at noon by a roadside foline vendor, and John waited near the van as Laurie haggled for fuel. Reddish brown sandstone hills shimmered in the east. The air was filled with the droning hiss of the wind. The old woman who operated the handpump was half hidden in flapping rags, and her arms made incomprehensible circling gestures as she spoke to Laurie. Blinking in the wind, stretching his limbs, feeling his sweat-sodden clothing unstick and slide over his flesh like sandpaper, he waited for them to agree on a price. Was this how he'd imagined it—a world beyond the Endless City, a rim beyond the rim? Yet for all the heat, the wind, the discomfort, the bittersweet smell of foline, and the wary scowl on the old woman's face as she caught the silver of his eyes, it remained somehow distant.

They reached Sadiir as the light died. Climbing out of the van into purple night, feeling mosquitoes and nightflies bump seekingly into his face, hearing the clank of unoiled wind generators, breathing the ammoniac reek of humanity, John almost regretted leaving the dead plains.

Ahead through the rubble lay the lights of a hotel. Like the rest of Sadiir, it was ancient, half abandoned, tumbling in scraps of Moorish arch and colonial pillars. Dogs barked. Shutters creaked and turned. Music thrummed from doorways. Ulcerated children scurried out of the darkness as he and Laurie carried their bags up the broken steps of the hotel. Seeing the glowing arcs of his hands and the silver of his eyes, the children backed away.

Next morning, John was awakened by the crowing of cocks in the suddenly still air. He sat up, brushing off a layer of dead insects, and looked over to where Laurie lay asleep on her mattress beneath the shuttered window, stripes of morning light glittering in the quartz dust in her hair. He climbed out onto the gravelly floor and began to peel off his underclothes. He was in the process of picking dead bugs out of his pubic hair when he saw that Laurie's eyes were open.

"Good morning."

"*Gunahana,*" she said. "These private arrangements were something we didn't talk about."

He stopped, his shoulders hunched. "It hardly matters, does it?"

She gestured a shrug.

He turned away, using a rag and the bowl of disinfectant-clouded water to clean himself. Last night, tiredness and this filthy room had made him postpone any efforts at washing. He sat on the bed and grabbed fresh underpants and socks out of his bag. He found that he didn't feel particularly self-conscious.

"We'll have to pay off the local elder here," Laurie said, sitting up and pulling her teeshirt off over her head.

"How much?"

"I'll sort something out."

She began to gather up her clothes. He saw that she'd been bitten by bugs in the night, although she didn't seem to notice or care. Laurie had pale-brown skin, narrow shoulders, flattish breasts, a deep pit of a navel. Opening the seal on her bag and pulling on a fresh shirt, she pushed back the shutters from the window and took in a breath of the warm morning air.

John came over and rested his elbows beside hers, gazing out. Blue-gray near the peaks, with shreds of cloud and hints of green, the Northern Mountains seemed to lie just beyond the angular sprawl of Sadiir's corrugated roofs, almost close enough for him to touch.

They passed a sandy Christian graveyard filled with leaning crosses and angels as they drove out of Sadiir. Soon after, the jagged remains of a castle crowned the top of a hill to the east. As he looked west across the dead foothills, John wondered if he should ask Laurie how she got hold of the expensive cube of Halcycon nerve tissue that she'd used to pay off the village elder. But the moment never seemed quite right, and he guessed he knew what the answer was anyway: it was stolen. But why should Laurie's behavior be any different from that of the rest of the people who worked in the Zone?

He wound down his window and blinked in the scalding dust. It seemed that all history was buried and forgotten in sand drifts over abandoned villages, in the ruins of checkpoints marking forgotten frontiers, in the bleached carcasses of vehicles and animals.

At twilight, the highway gave out and became a pitted track. After hovering tantalizingly all day, the mountains had at last begun to draw closer. Bending forward to see more of their lavender peaks, John hooked the van around the next curve in the hillside, then braked hard as the fans kicked into mounds of ash. He punched on the headlights. The cabin filled with the carbony reek of dead bonfires. Everywhere there were blackened trunks and jagged charcoal branches. He pushed on, anxious to get out of this dead place, but they were still within the burnt-out forest when storms of ash and the gathering night made it impossible for them to continue. John pulled off the track into a clearing. The van's engines stilled. The flurries of ash settled. Clawing black trees encircled them.

They heated packs of stew inside the van. Laurie dropped a wine tablet into their water flask, then added two more. The cold deepened. Banging elbows, they climbed into their sleeping bags, reclining the seats and setting the keys for maximum heat. The scratchy darkness thickened, and the wind made the dead treetops click and rattle.

"I wonder how far you have to go," Laurie said, "until there's really nothing."

John shifted in the fragile warmth of his bag. He heard a pop as she opened a tube. In here, with the windows up, he guessed that he'd have to share whatever mood it created. "I mean, John, do you really believe there's something out there beyond what you can see and feel? Look at this place—you go so far and find it's just us. And after that, nothing... What else is there to believe in?"

"What about the witchwomen, the rituals, the moonrocks, the carnivals?"

"That's like a dance, John—something you let take over for a while. That's about the thrill of *this* world, not the hope of some other. It's a madness, too. The witchwomen take a burden from us. That's why we give them gifts and accept their strangeness. If you really think about the way things are, maybe madness is the only sane response."

"No."

"I'm sorry—you don't find this easy, do you, talking about what everything means?"

"It's my job."

"I mean your own faith. What you feel, what you are."

"Believing in God is like being in love, Laurie. You can't rationalize it. It has nothing to do with what's in your head."

"I don't see what's wrong with emptiness." Laurie ground out her tube and snuggled deeper into her seat, closing her eyes. "This world, and nothing else. Think about it. Is that really so bad?"

At one point, he awoke, hearing some other sound. Strange, half musical. He shifted and opened his eyes, gazing out at the witchy trees. Then he realized that it was Laurie. She was singing to the net, humming in her sleep.

They were back on the road before the light next morning and reached the walled town of Tiir at midday. The cold that had come in the night remained, and the wind still blew at them from the south. But it was different here. The air was scented with mountain sap and the tang of rain.

Tiir would have seemed a desolate place to anyone who hadn't crossed the plains. The houses were the same gray as the cliffs and outcrops they were built on. Flapping sheets covered the doorways of the stony houses; washed-out jelt alternated with mossy thatch as a roof covering. The smoke that wafted from stubby chimneys smelled of grass and donkey dung and charcoal from the burnt-out forest below. Faces peered at them from narrow unglazed windows, and small crowds hovered around corners. The people here wore brown capes woven with threads of indigo, crimson, chrome yellow. The women had beads in their hair, the colors vibrant in the gray light beneath the mountains.

Tiir was a place of transition, a buffer between the Endless City and the desert wastes beyond. The squat walls that surrounded the town were well maintained, and the guards who stopped and questioned John and Laurie at the gateway carried ancient rifles that obviously weren't for show. People from the coast, the koiyl merchants, the hawkers and dealers—John and Laurie, even—were admitted because they brought the trade on which the town depended. But the skulls in niches in the cliffs and outer walls declared that the others, the starving wanderers who still drifted in from beyond the Last Hammada, were as likely to be killed as sent away.

There was a market in the main square, overshadowed by the walls of an ancient castle keep. Wandering along the aisles, Laurie caused as much disruption as John: a Borderer walking close to a European! But the vendors shouted after them both and cheerily offered their wares. John was surprised not to find more hostility towards him from these people living on the fringe of Europe.

There were strung lines of cooking pans clanging in the wind, the wormy carcasses of lambs and hares, brilliant orange gourds, and scraps of European technology—screens, night-sights, transmitters, and sexual aids. They found a stall of the woven capes that they saw worn all around them. The cloth was stiff, warm, smelling richly of sheep oil. Watched by giggling, disbelieving children, they bought one each and pulled the capes over their dusty clothes. But they found no koiyl. The crop, Laurie was told by the stallkeeper, hadn't been harvested yet. But, yes, it would be gathered soon and sold here before it was taken down to the Endless City.

They already knew that Tiir would be the end of the line for the van, and had left it parked on a patch of ground outside the walls with a barrier field humming around it. From now on, they would have to go on foot—and would need a guide to show them the way.

It was hard to make sense of what was happening in the shadow of the keep where witchwomen had gathered. Bells were clanging, smoke was trailing. The air reeked of old sweat. The witchwomen, squatting under tented rugs, chattered, thumped goatskin drums, fanned the smoke from chalices. A few moaned and swayed, apparently in a trance. Others looked simply drunk. Laurie spat on a Magulf dollar and tossed it into a brass bowl. Then she began to pick her way between their nests of possessions.

"How do we know which one to choose?" John shouted after her.

She continued walking. "They'll choose us."

Glancing around him, John saw that a nearby witchwoman was tending a sore on a young man's thigh. He winced as he watched her prod at the open flesh with grubby fingernails and then, using a twig as a spool, begin to extract a long white length of worm. He hurried to catch up with Laurie.

She was asking questions in an unfamiliar dialect of Borderer. Whenever they paused by a ring of chemlights or a row of dried chickenheads, people pointed them on towards the far corner of the keep. There, a little apart at the end of the line, the last witchwoman sat. She was squatting alone, not under a tented rug but under a large black umbrella hung with rodent skulls.

Seeing John and Laurie, she beckoned for them to sit down on the paving. She leaned across the usual litter of figurines and glowing incense cones to peer closely at them. Although she must have registered the color of John's eyes, she looked at him in a way that was uncommon among Borderers; she actually seemed to study his features. Her own eyes were moist in the depths of a cracked face, and even the whites were brown. Then she nodded slowly to herself, muttering something.

John sat back as Laurie and the witchwoman began to talk, wishing he hadn't decided not to bring his translat on this journey. He couldn't make out a word of it: the accent here was strange, softer and quicker than the one he'd grown used to hearing in the Magulf, and he guessed from Laurie's expression that even she was occasionally struggling.

After a while, she said to him, "Her name's Hettie. She says you're a strange kind of *baraka*."

He smiled and nodded to the witchwoman, and her mouth broke into a one-toothed smile. From what he could make out in the gloom of the keep and the shade of her umbrella, he guessed that Hettie was no more than middle-aged, and that exposure to the elements probably explained the ancient leather of her skin. Whatever color her clothes had started out, they were now mostly black, and she gave off the dull, salty aroma that Borderers who never changed or washed eventually acquired.

"Well?" he asked when she and Laurie slapped hands in some sort of agreement. "Will she do it? Will she take us?"

"Yes."

"When?"

Laurie said something more to Hettie, then leaned back. "She says we must go right away."

"We've only got two or three hours of daylight left."

"She says, exactly."

"Does she want payment?"

"Not yet. I think she wants to get a better idea of how much we're worth."

Hettie licked her lips, turned slowly towards John.

She swallowed, wiped her mouth, licked her lips again.

"That right, Fatoo," she said.

Pausing on the steep track, John looked back one last time at the lights of Tiir in the bowl of the hills below. Where the path hooked around the ravine ahead, he could just make out Laurie as she clambered over a rock and, more faintly, the shape of Hettie still holding her umbrella aloft. Shifting the straps of his backpack until they bit into a different place on his shoulders, he forced his legs to continue on and up the dim path.

Hettie had managed to cram her entire belongings into an old carpetbag, but John and Laurie were more heavily burdened. After much agonizing at the van, they'd dumped the second barrier-field generator and a large portion of their spare clothing and replaced the food and water purifier with a tube of fizzy tablets they'd bought in the market. That still left a satellite transmitter for emergencies, a filter mask each, the radiation counter, and endless seemingly vital odds and ends. And after the cold of the dead forest the night before, neither of them wanted to leave their heated sleeping bags behind.

It was growing darker by the minute, and John's unease at

stumbling along the brink of shadowed drops was tempered only by the thought that they would soon have to stop. But he was wrong; skipping ahead, waving her umbrella through the dusk, Hettie obviously knew the way blindfold. He increased his pace to catch up with Laurie, then fought for his breath.

"What's the problem?" Laurie's eyes glittered at him. "Come on!"

She turned and headed quickly up the path. His legs aching, John trudged on behind her.

Hettie lit a fire when they finally camped. By then their breath was making clouds, and the sweat that had drenched John's clothing seemed about to freeze. They all crouched around the flames, their arms outstretched, shadows and smoke twining up over the rocks surrounding them.

Hettie wandered off, peering under stones. When she came back, she was swinging a bundle. As she stooped into the firelight and finally put down her umbrella, John saw that the bundle consisted of a bunch of lizards gripped by their tails, and that they were all still alive. One by one, Hettie tossed them onto the fire. He imagined that she was indulging in some kind of ritual until she found a stick to fish one out, lopped off its head and tail with a knife, ripped out the steaming guts, and began to eat. Her mouth full, blood and grease running down her wattled chin, she gestured for John and Laurie to do the same.

The thin sticks on the fire didn't last; cold darkness soon closed in. John climbed without much expectation into his sleeping bag, feeling queasiness in his belly and the rocky ground prodding his shoulders. He gazed up at a sky that, even in this darkness, churned with wind and movement, and felt himself falling up into it, as if, one by one, the strings of doubt, discomfort, and tiredness that bound him to the earth were snapping away. Sleep came easily.

He woke only once and saw Hettie sitting there, her umbrella swaying as she sang to herself, gently rocking to and fro. Closing his eyes, feeling the chill prickle of frost settling on his face, he tumbled back into a seamless dream.

Next morning, in exchange for the roast lizards of the night before, Laurie offered Hettie one of her foodpacks of sweet porridge. Hettie nodded eagerly. She obviously had no compunctions about sharing food. And once or twice she had even poked at John with a bare, bony finger. Remembering the witchwoman who'd confronted him in Banori's room, he wondered if this absence of fear, this willingness to come close, wasn't a part of their madness.

Puncturing the heat catalyst, Laurie handed the foodpack to Hettie and demonstrated how to slit it open. Hettie did so, sniffed the contents, and scooped out a blob on the tip of her finger. She studied the steaming oatmeal, put it into her mouth for a moment, spat it out into her palm, stirred the mash with her finger, and then began to eat in her usual lip-smacking way.

They packed their bags and began to climb. The ravine widened to a high valley floor where a small stream ran amid rocks, disappearing underground, reemerging, disappearing again. There were stunted conifers, meadows of tufted grass, and small bell-shaped flowers that shivered silver in the wind. The swift clouds were big-bellied with moisture. Far above, a hawk rode the thermals.

These living mountains seemed almost unchanged, but in truth they were a fluke, an unsought consequence of European climate control. The air that the satellites pulled across Africa contained little moisture, and much of that was used as a vast filter for the northeasterly flow of the Gulf Stream across the River Ocean. But the satellites and the millions of absorption panels couldn't rewrite the laws of nature entirely. Air cooled as it rose over these mountains, causing rain to fall, and the rain brought life, and the life held moisture, darkened the slopes, stabilized the temperature, and in turn encouraged more rain. Still, the cycle was as artificial as the wind from the south that brought it. Even to John's untrained eyes, there was a sameness about the vegetation here.

They were able to walk three abreast along the valley floor and talk, Laurie acting as intermediary between John and Hettie. Hettie explained that the village they were heading towards was called Lall. Her own dwelling lay a few kilometers beyond, and not far beyond that, where the pass began to dip down to the desert, the Last Hammada, was a site of special fear and significance. It was called Ifri Gotal, the place of fury.

John and Laurie exchanged glances. Had Hettie been to Ifri Gotal? Of course, but only once—nobody went there more than once. It was a terrible place. And would she show them the way? Hettie shrugged, and the skulls and bells of her umbrella jingled; from where she was going to take them, any fool could find Ifri Gotal. Even an *Outer*, a European.

They walked on, across an old stone bridge. A stream raced beneath. John began to see greenish purple clumps on the valley sides, which he guessed were koiyl.

By mid-morning, there were signs of habitation. Climbing a stairway of rock beside a waterfall, they reached a higher sweep of the valley. Here, where mountain peaks surrounded them through drifts of cloud, the lower, greener slopes were roughly walled into fields containing long-haired sheep. A figure stood watching them pass from the top of a high mesa, carrying a rifle. Hettie waved and shouted something. The figure waved back.

Patches of koiyl were common now, although John was careful not to show too obvious an interest. The koiyl bush grew semiwild, but it was still a crop; on the coast, one leaf would be worth a quarter of a day's wage. Undried, the leaves of this mutant succulent were plump, each a little larger than his thumb, bisected by a thick stem, covered with faint purple fuzz. The bushes were just coming into flower, and the blooms were tiny and off-white. They had a pleasant, musty odor.

The village of Lall lay over a final ridge. Cooking smoke rose, dogs barked, babies cried, and the tearing sound of a powersaw came from the open doors of a barn as they picked their way down the slope. Adults and young children emerged to watch. There was no sense of surprise in their stance; word of the approach of the three had obviously gone ahead.

"What do we do now?" John asked.

"Hettie says we should be *amikay*—accept their hospitality."

A large black dog ran up to him. Planting its paws on his thighs and nearly knocking him over, it tried to lick at his strange hands. An old woman in a shawl gave a whistle, and the dog ran back, its tail spiraling. As she leaned down and rubbed the creature behind its ears, John wondered whether the reports reaching Lall had omitted the fact that an *Outer* was coming. But when he drew nearer the muddy circle of low stone buildings, he saw that the villagers shuffled back from him, discreetly making the sign against the evil eye even before they could see the silver of his irises.

Laurie, Hettie, and John were seated out-of-doors around a large, flat-topped rock that served as a communal table. Soon, most of the village was sitting there too, and plates of food were being passed. In the circle there was a gap between John and Hettie. She ate voraciously, talking at the same time. He presumed that she was regaling the villagers with news from Tiir. There was certainly a fair amount of laughter. He glanced around. Whenever he met someone's eye, the person would nod politely, raise a beaker, try to smile.

The meal consisted of fatty lumps of lamb. The beer that came with it was better, but all of it weighed heavily in his stomach. What could these people possibly have to do with Daudi and Martínez, the river of death that flowed down into the Magulf? He thought of Tim, the blossoms falling from the cherry trees along the Zone's Main Avenue as Tim sat eating a mountainous dessert at Thrials, saying, John, just what do you expect to do with the truth if you find it?

Laurie was saying something to him. He turned.

"They say they've heard you're a *baraka*."

He raised his beaker and nodded.

"They want you to offer a prayer to your god."

"A prayer for what?"

"This year's harvest."

He gazed around at the expectant faces. Women nursing babies, men with faces scarred from disease, the old, the young, the frail.

"Go on, John. You must have something suitable."

Bringing his hands together, he recited:

The lord is my shepherd:
I shall not want...

When the food was finished and the goatskin of beer had been emptied, a large red-glazed bowl was produced, offered first to Hettie, then to Laurie. It contained fresh koiyl leaves. Nodding thanks, Laurie took two.

"Here's your big chance to try." She handed John a leaf.

The dried koiyl leaves sold in the Endless City were often small enough to be chewed entire, but a fresh one was too big. He watched Laurie bite off an end and drag it back over her teeth to remove the inedible stem, rather as if she were eating the leaf of an artichoke. He did the same. He knew that even for her there was no risk from one koiyl leaf—a harmful build-up of isotopes took years. But still he felt an odd frisson. The koiyl tasted...briefly strong, almost like nutmeg, and then a little like coal-tar soap. Then the flavor disappeared as the sap released some kind of anesthetic. His mouth went numb. He imagined that at least part of the skill of chewing koiyl involved learning not to bite your tongue. He swallowed and wiped his lips, certain that he was drooling. By now, he was beginning to experience the full effect of the leaf. The pain from his blistered feet and shoulders dissolved. The many aches in his limbs vanished. He felt both cool-headed and drunk. It was as when he had lain down the night before, looked up at the racing sky, and felt the ties of the earth snapping. Perhaps the influence was strong because the leaves were fresh, or because the drug was new to his system. Either way, if this was the effect that koiyl produced, it was easy to understand its popularity.

Laurie said, "They want to know what you think."

"Tell them *bona*—it works."

Laurie relayed the comment. There was general, red-toothed laughter. He looked around. In the flush of the koiyl, these villagers of Lall truly did seem to be a happy people. He saw a mother nursing a child, the dogs who were scolded as they hung around for scraps at the table, the old people, their faces lined with smiles. He looked up the hill at the unmistakable mounds where the dead were buried, at the well and the cooking houses, at the piled bricks and bloodied stones of a shrine, the tinkling foil and skulls, the ancient gauntlet of a spacesuit. The baby that the mother had been nursing was wailing now, opening the round red toothless O of its mouth, kicking and waving the smooth handless sausages of its arms.

The clouds that had obscured the mountains were now rolling down into the valley, bringing flurries of rain. John and Laurie were in no hurry to go on that day, but as usual Hettie was insistent. Didn't the Fatoo want to see her home? It was only a short way. She prodded her dripping umbrella in the direction of swirling mist, a steep hillside. Unsure that the villagers of Lall would welcome their continued presence, Laurie and John were in no position to argue.

Before they left, the village elder presented John with a bag of koiyl leaves. As they plodded up the valley behind Hettie, Lall and its waving villagers were soon lost in the mist. This time, even Laurie seemed to have little appetite for the climb.

———

The rain increased. Night came. They were still ascending. Once, skidding on the wet rubble that fringed some unguessable drop, John's feet went out from under him and he began a sickening slide until Laurie grabbed his flailing hand. He walked on, trying to still the shaking in his legs.

It hadn't occurred to him to ask Hettie what kind of home she kept in the mountains. It would probably have been impolite, anyway, but up here it was hard to imagine finding anything that resembled a roof and walls.

They entered a gorge. Even in the darkness, glistening rock was visible on either side. Finally, when it seemed as though night would soon turn into morning, Hettie began to climb a loose stairway in the cliffs. Every now and then there were handholds, but sometimes it was like scaling a sheet of wet ice. They passed a hole in the rock. Another hole. The mouth of a cave. John's questing hands touched odd outlines and depressions in the stone: carvings of some kind.

Hettie shouted something, then disappeared into the cliff face. Laurie followed, then John. Blissfully out of the rain.

Hettie poked along a fissure with the ferrule of her umbrella. Finding a pack of chemlights, she broke one open. The catalysts fizzed against the damp, then slowly brightened. The cave they stood in had been fashioned into walls, a floor, a stairway. There were friezes of men and animals, birds and lions and baboons, trees and flowers; scenes from a time when these mountains had been a vast forest of cedar and pine.

Hettie held the chemlight aloft. Gesturing to John and Laurie to follow, she went up stone steps intricately carved with ropes and whorls. The breath of the three smoked ahead of them, and the sound and the smell of the rain faded. They reached another chamber in the cliff. It was obvious from the smell alone that this was where Hettie lived. Crouching on a rug, she lit a foline lamp with the heat from her chemlight, pumping up the pressure until a sphere of light filled the chamber.

Most of the bare rock was covered with carpets and hangings. There were sagging tables and heaped cushions, corners filled with clean white deadfalls of bone, niches crammed with jars and oddments, dried and stuffed animals, broken mirrors, faded paper flowers, figurines, books, and bells. There were also bowls and spoons and neatly stacked tins of food, looking both reassuringly homely and oddly out of place amid all this witchwoman paraphernalia, and several small receivers, screens, and cameras in various states of disrepair. Peeling off the sodden top layers of her clothing, oily rivulets rolling down her surprisingly muscular arms, Hettie started a fire in a soot-blackened alcove. A natural chimney led up through the rock, drawing off the worst of the smoke.

John offered a blisterpack of tablets that swelled into biscuits when immersed in water, and Laurie produced a plump freeze-dried pack of processed steak. Soaking the steak and cooking it in an iron pan hooked over the fire, Hettie stirred various nuts and vegetables into the spitting juices. The firelight pulsed, briefly filling more corners of the chamber. John glimpsed a wooden crucifix about half a meter long hanging from the bare rock, nailed with the skeleton of a lizard.

After the food and the warmth of the fire had pushed out the cold, the three of them settled down in the smoky light, still steaming, smelling like wet dogs. Laurie dropped a handful of wine tablets into a jug of water. She offered it to Hettie to taste. Taking a sip, the witchwoman beamed.

"She says she has something similar that we should try."

"What does similar mean?"

"You'll see—it'll be fun."

Hettie produced a plastic jug. Filling it from a goatskin, she carefully dunked into it a fibrous lump on the end of a string, then tipped the contents into three crackle-glazed mugs, passing two to Laurie.

"Ghea!"

"Thanks—*bona.*" In the darkness, John couldn't even guess at the color of the liquid that Laurie had passed to him, and his sense of smell had departed in the aromatic smoke from the fire and in the steam that came off their bodies. *"Ghea..."*

He drank. The fire spat and rose, pouring out more smoke and light, revealing a shelf filled with poisonous jars of red Martian soil, lumps of moonrock, comet juice.

"Hettie wants to know what you're doing here."

John swayed forward, his eyes stinging, his vision blurred. Up here in the Northern Mountains, he'd sometimes actually felt that he was drifting closer to God. "The thing is, Hettie," he said, half convinced that the two of them would be able to understand each other if he spoke slowly enough, "it's a question of finding the truth. Do you think you're closer to it here? That place called"—he turned to Laurie—"what was it?"

"Ifri Gotal."

"Right. Ifri Gotal."

Hettie nodded vigorously and said something incomprehensible. Laurie shrugged. John smiled and shook his head, wondering whether it was some stray draft or a fluke in his own perception that made the tapestries around the walls belly in and out.

"I think she means her question more broadly."

"You mean, why are *any* of us here?"

"No, no." As Laurie tipped up her mug and drank, John gazed at the stray rivulets that ran down the soft geometries of her neck and shoulders. She banged the mug down. Hettie quickly refilled it. "What Hettie means is—why are you here in the Magulf?"

He placed his own mug on a tray, well out reach of Hettie's bottomless jug. "I'm here," he said, "because the bishop sent me here."

"No, it's a serious question."

Suddenly the only sound was the fire, the breathing of the two women, his own racing heartbeat.

"Why?"

Laurie's hair was a snake's nest—as wild as Hettie's—and somewhere in the last hours she'd thrown several necklaces of bells and skulls around her neck. The faces of the two women danced with soot and shadows, as if they were the same person caught at different ages.

"*Why?* Why did you come here?"

Hettie bent towards John, closer than she'd ever been, closer than any Borderer. He could feel her warmth. Her flesh. Her smell. They were breathing the same air. When she spoke, her spittle misted his face. "Tell truth," she said. "Fatoo is here for the truth."

Slowly, John nodded. "The truth. That's right. The *truth.*"

"Let Hettie show."

He felt fingers tugging at the glove that enclosed his right hand. Sliding the sheath of plastic away, snapping each of the spines. Warm flesh closed around his own. The motion was so smooth, so deep, that it was a long moment before he shuddered and tried to jerk his hand out of reach.

"It's all right, John." Laurie smiled, her lips and her voice close to his ear. Her fingers were twined with his, squeezing gently. "Coming this far, how can you be afraid of the truth?"

There was a curtained alcove. It gave off a stingingly strong aroma of earth and decay. When Hettie hooked back the cloth, he saw that it contained the blackened carcass of a goat. A few white growths sprouted from what had once been skin and fur—the fruiting bodies of some fungus.

Hettie plucked one, slicing off its tangle of roots with a knife. She pressed the white knob of fungus to her lips and inhaled. Her eyelids fluttered.

"What is it?"

"Trust."

"Memory."

"*Memory?*"

"The truth."

He discovered that he was sitting again before the fire and that Laurie was beside him. The fungus nesting in Hettie's outstretched palm was dimpled, innocuous. A puffball, little different from those that grew in the leafmold of Hemhill's woods.

But as she leaned forward, the cracked nails of her dirt-marbled hands pressing, breaking open the flesh to liberate the cloudy spores, the puffball swelled and changed. Grew larger and smoother, flattened at the top where it had been left to cool on greased paper, speared lopsidedly by a candy-spiraled stick. It was an apple dipped in toffee, gleaming with all the colors of carnival light.

He took it, and began to eat.

SKIDDLE? ARE YOU STILL AWAKE?"

John turned in his bed. The door was ajar. As he watched and waited, it seemed to breathe and widen. Everything about the house on this late summer's night—the scent and the feel of the air, the dry whispering that came from the trees that stirred outside his window, even the pressure of the old mattress against his spine—was strange and unreclaimed. They'd only got back from Ley that afternoon, and nothing yet really felt as it should. The long-dormant cleaner would be fussing over mountains of dirty washing in the kitchen. Fishing kit and Wellingtons were stacked in the hall. The smell of sand and salt and dried-on seaweed and fishscale competed with the odor of closed rooms. It was a time of year that he always wished would go quickly, impatient for this sense of strange unbelonging to dissolve in the closing of the days, the browning of the trees, the harvest, the carnival, the coming of the Borderers, the re-starting of school: impatient for the turning, as he always thought of it, of the year.

"Is it late?"

Hal came into the room, a darker shadow.

"Depends..."

"I couldn't sleep anyhow," John said.

"It's always like this." Hal sat down on the bed, a soft weight. The unsettled world shifted and formed a new center of gravity. "Coming back—home never feels like home."

"Are Mum and Dad still up?"

"Still sorting themselves out. Still looking for disasters. Dad, anyway..." The two brothers smiled at each other through the darkness, sharing the memory of their father's holiday-long obsession. All the time they'd been at Ley, he'd fretted that he'd somehow turned the house's systems up before they left. He tried calling through the net on the little booth along the quayside but was never quite able to make the final link and check the settings. Their mother kept saying that they'd be bound to have heard if the house exploded, froze, or burned down, that if it bothered him so much, all he had to do was call one of the neighbors. But their father being their father, he could never do anything as simple as that. He just carried on worrying. All things considered, their summer at Ley had been typical enough.

For a while John and Hal talked of the things they'd done and the things they'd do. They were reestablishing the old Hemhill ground rules. Coming home and waking the house from the hot long sleep of summer, preparing for autumn, having their separate lives and possessions again, friendships and pursuits that no longer depended on each other's presence, they always needed to rediscover their relationship. This autumn, an even greater transition loomed; in a few weeks' time, Hal would be leaving home, moving to London. Studying something called structural communication, an esoteric field that he'd never quite been able to explain to John or their parents. But it took good grades, and you could end up working on the satellites. No one was complaining.

"It seems funny to be coming back here..."

"I thought you'd go and see Annie tonight," John said.

"I called her. Told her I was too tired. I suppose I am," Hal said, almost admitting a rare lie. "Restless tonight anyway. You know."

"Yes."

"It's as if..."

John looked up at Hal, waiting for the sentence to finish. But Hal was staring away, his hand resting heavily like something forgotten on the blanket by John's chest. As if what? So unlike Hal to leave anything unresolved.

The silence hung, hissed, emptied, turned over. John could feel his bed and the whole dark house around him shifting like an animal relaxing into sleep. The quartzy sand was dissolving from his socks and shoes; his summer clothes were folding themselves back into the cupboards; the stale, slightly damp smell of unbreathed air was fading. Hal still sat unmoving at his bedside, but time—the nights, anyway—was shifting, draining, flickering by. The house was lived-in now and taken for granted, and the sheets no longer smelled soapy-fresh. Part of him understood. This could only mean he wasn't really here in bed, at night, at home, in Hemhill. This contraction of time meant that from somewhere, somehow, he was looking back.

As if...

Hal turned his head in the changing air, the sentence still unfinished as he looked at John. It was another night, and John could tell that Hal had returned from being out with Annie. He could see the near-fluorescent whiteness of the shirt his brother was wearing, slightly crumpled now, smelling of outdoors and the couple of beers he'd had. Smelling, too, of the lovely sea-lavender scent of Annie's hair.

Everyone agreed that they made a devastatingly good couple, but since Hal came back from Ley this year, a coldness had come between them. John suspected they were staying together now in this odd transitory time between Ley and London only because they didn't want to let down the people who so liked to see them together. Of course, when Hal did go to London, he'd call Annie and he'd still visit Hemhill with respectable regularity to see her and his parents and catch up with his old school friends. But the going out, the touching, the kissing, the whole boyfriend-girlfriend thing, that was over.

"What are you going to do Skiddle, eh?"

"When?"

"Next week. Tomorrow. Next year. The year after." Hal got up from the bed—and once more the gravity of the room shifted, the nights turned. John realized that the question hadn't really been meant for him anyway. It was some inward thing that Hal was chasing. Sighing, his brother went to the window and touched the control to let in more of the night. It was another night. Turning. Now Hal was in the faded denim shirt he always wore when he was dicking around with the wires and crystals and nerve fibers in his room. His passing wake no longer bore Annie's scent; it bore the soft, coaly odor of sweat and soldering crab oil. And outside the window, John saw that the nights were slipping by. The trees became a cloudy blur;

the cars and vans passing along the road were silent silver lines; the stars up in the deep darkness were streaks, smears, gray comets. Autumn was nearly here.

Leaning at the window, Hal gazed out for some time at the murmuring, spinning night. Faint shadows orbited the room.

"What do you do, Skiddle? How much is enough?" The air remained hot, close. John could see the wide sweatstains that stretched down and across Hal's shoulders and back like predatory wings.

"I was out with Annie this afternoon," he said. "I mean, you know how warm it's been here, to finish off the ripening. How hot. It'd be a shame not to go out on a day like this, and it was so quiet in the village anyway that Annie got the afternoon off. We went out for a drive in the old Elysian with the top down, and we stopped by Ludgate Hill and walked across the fields to take in the very last of the summer. The sky..." He gazed up through the window of John's bedroom. Amid the blur of the shifting stars hung a scowling, hooded moon. "...was blue, an incredible blue. And I was holding Annie's hand, and the corn they grow there was like a tall golden wood around us, and the skylarks were singing.

"We found this place to sit down. In the dell down by the pond where Gerry Barry almost drowned last summer. Or was it the summer before? The sky was so blue up there through the trees, shimmering like something underwater. We tried to think of a word for that blue. I mean, not a real word because there isn't one, but some new, better word for the blue of the summer sky that people would understand just from hearing the sound. And all the time, all the time, off in the grass beside the ruined millhouse we could hardly see because of all the hawthorn, there was this old agripede that someone had dumped.

The thing settled down on its rotting tires. And I couldn't help looking at it. My eyes just kept going back. Someone had broken open the controller, and the nerve tissue had seeped out in those thick green and purple strings with the flies buzzing around them. And there we were. There *I* was. With Annie lying back in the grass looking up at the sky though the trees on a late summer's afternoon, and all I could see in the dell were the flies buzzing around that broken nerve box. The one ugly thing. The rest of it—I don't know. I just can't break..."

Hal suddenly turned to John. The night turned. The stars beyond the window spun behind him, silvering the edge of his face.

"Skiddle, it's as though there's always something between it and me. As though I'm never quite there anymore. Not anywhere. I mean, I was just looking at the flies and the rot falling out of this tractor, even though I was with Annie and the sky was so blue and I should have been...ought to have been..."

Hal sighed, looked down for something he seemed to have lost on the floor, and pushed back his hair.

John knew that summer was passing. Winter was coming, bright and cold. London was waiting. Soon, it would be time for Hal to go. Every day, his mother produced more of the things she'd saved, the treasured odds and ends, and announced she'd throw them out if Hal didn't take them. Cups and cooking implements for this tiny flat he'd already found, where, if you stood on a chair in the shower and peered over the stately rooftops, you could just about see the green Thames. There was talk of a farewell party, a surprise party, although Hal would doubtless see it coming and then pretend with all his usual grace that he hadn't. There was talk of buying an engraved tankard, John chipping in what pocket money he could. But what really lay between Hal and London now—between Hal and the definite, incontrovertible end of summer—was the harvest carnival and the coming of the Borderers, the opening of the compound in the valley.

John wondered what the house would be like afterwards, half-emptied without Hal. He pictured it as a person he'd once seen with a limp: keeling over slightly, still trying hard to smile and adjust. He closed his eyes. And heard the rush of wheels approaching on the road outside. Yes. The sound gathering like a wind. Opening his eyes, he saw the play of headlights on the wall, catching in the mirror, redoubled, spraying golden wings across the ceiling, shifting through the black bars of the roadside trees. The sound of big wheels. Why did no other vehicle that passed through Hemhill ever sound like this? And why did they always have to come at night? But they did. They did. And now, as the headlights brightened and passed and faded and were gone like the flick of a switch, there was that other sound, a sound as autumnal as the crackle of leaves and the whoosh of fireworks and the wind-carried cry of crows. The hum of the compound in the valley.

"Come on, Skiddle," Hal said, standing over him, holding out a hand. "I have something to show you."

John took his brother's warm hand. Swinging on its leverage to lift himself up and out of bed, he felt the air of the house on his flesh, though his nightshirt, cooler now, though the controller was set to an even temperature. Another sign that autumn was nearly here, that winter was coming, that Hal would soon be gone.

"It's in my room..."

Barefoot in the darkness, John followed. The house was quiet. The lights were off. The doors were all closed. What time *was* it? Did time exist on a charmed and changing night such as this? And Hal, anyway, was breaking an unwritten rule by getting him out of bed. Not that their slumbering parents would really have minded if Hal occasionally let his younger brother wander the house late at night. But it had never been done; it wasn't part of the ritual.

John followed Hal along the landing, then turned and froze as something big and silvery nudged up the stairs. It bobbed and floated, squealing with big eyes, a leering face. Then he saw the trailing red string, and the face resolved into that of a storybook pirate, and he knew that it was only the balloon he'd bought that day at the carnival. *Today.* And that was why his teeth were sticky with toffee apple and candy floss. That was why his head ached from the beer he'd drunk for the first time in the gray-lit tent, and later from the beat of the carnival band. That was, underneath, why he felt so sick, so tired.

"Come on, Skiddle."

Hal turned on the light in his room. Now that he was this near to leaving, John half-expected to find it cleared and emptied, posters off the walls and rolled up, the bed piled with neat stacks of screens and clothes. But the room was the way it had always been: filled with all the stuff of Hal's life. If anything, messier. Being untidy, John sometimes thought, was Hal's single excuse for a vice, something he had to work hard at because he didn't have a real one. John could see his big brother forcing himself to take out and scatter stuff that he'd already put away. He could see him secretly sneaking back up the stairs to redistribute scraps of underbed dust he'd stolen from the bag inside the cleaner.

"I've been going through my things," Hal said. "Clearing out." He chuckled, waved his hands at the mess. "I started anyway. But you know how it is. You find things you haven't touched in years. And instead of clearing up, you spend hours remembering, messing around..."

John nodded. Squatting on the pillow of the bed beside the shining eyes of an old action doll, he saw a robot they'd once made together from scraps of other things that had fallen apart. Or, rather, Hal had allowed him to stand at his shoulder and ask questions and generally get in the way while he made it. They called it Lilith, and it was programmed to wander about the lawn collecting beetles for the insect project John was then working on at school. It soon disappeared, and after a thorough search of their and the neighboring gardens, they found it in the study, turning the pages of an antique wildlife book, busily snipping out all the insect pictures with its scissor hands.

Strewn around the floor were tennis shoes, laptop games, faceless piles of book palettes, a box filled with the twitching spidery angles of a self-construction kit, model cloudpickers, radio-controlled boats, shuttles, vans, and planes. Much of the stuff John was familiar with; Hal had never minded him playing with his old toys, although John knew his older brother well enough to make sure he gave them all back even if (*especially* if) they got broken. Hal never exactly minded lending things, but he could never let go of them either. He liked to know where everything was—even the presents he gave. John remembered how once Hal questioned their mother for what seemed like hours about how she'd managed to lose an umbrella he gave her.

"There's so much of it," Hal said, picking up a dodger ball that had fallen into a box by the bed. It rattled; the gyrostat was broken. John remembered years before: a November evening, looking out through the back window and seeing Hal still in the yard, Hal tossing the flashing ball against the garage wall. The fan of tiny spangled lights. The way he always seemed to catch it.

"And this." Hal picked something else up. Looked at it. Put it down. "And this..." As he wandered the room, he seemed to forget about John. Which, John reflected, was so unlike him. John glanced out the window, which had been cleared now like his own, and saw the lime trees standing sentry-still over the road and the unlit tennis courts beyond, and saw that the stars had ceased their odd spiraling and were hovering motionless in distant space. But perhaps, John thought, I'm not really in this room with Hal—otherwise he wouldn't be wandering around like this and muttering to himself. Otherwise he wouldn't be ignoring me. Perhaps, inside whatever dream this is, I'm actually asleep and dreaming...

But then Hal turned, and his eyes were clear and focused. "And see this." He pointed towards the tangle of wires, screens, links, and cannibalized nerve boxes that lay on the desk where he worked. "This was my big project of a year or two back. It had promise!" He let his hands drop, a little amazed. "I don't know why I gave it up. Really. Do you want to see?"

John nodded. He always wanted to see.

They sat down, Hal on a box, John on the swivel deskchair because he was smaller. Staring at the weird entanglements on the desk, he felt a tingle of the old anticipation. This was more like it—Hal about to wave his hands over junk and turn it into something magical. He'd rigged up connections to a three-sense screen that once belonged to a game of battle chess and run a wire to the low-level terminal in the wall, then spliced the connections and inserted a nerve cube. John had heard that this was a way of tricking the net into granting access to the next level up, although that was illegal. The scene was intensely familiar: Hal dicking around with nervestuff and electronics. Hal showing him something strange and wonderful and new. John smiled as he watched the soldering crab pick its way across a big old circuitboard, squatting and dropping its little globules of silver at regular intervals. This was going to be good...

He remembered how they'd once reprogrammed the cleaner to fall over and say *fuckit* at regular intervals as it trundled through the house. For a whole hilarious week, their parents had been too embarrassed to call out the repairman, or even say anything. Then, of course, Hal took pity on them and fixed it secretly and better than ever. In those days, Hal had an elaborate, wild streak in him. His eyes shone with a light that John saw less often now.

Hal powered up the screen. There was the usual electronic humming, a clean dark smell like seashores and armpits and whisky. He tapped at the keyboard that had its guts spilling out of it like a squashed beetle.

"If I just..."

The bedroom filled with ruddy light.

"This is a bit... Yes."

The light settled, began to pulse. The room was a deep shifting red, almost like a picture John had seen once of a foreign sky. But then he realized that the flowing all around them was blood, that the shuddering curtains that overlaid the walls were the insides of a body.

"And this here..."

The speaker membrane that used to be inside the big screen in the lounge began to give out a solid thu-thump underlaid by a gurgling, liquid hiss. A heartbeat.

"Right! We're in!"

It was obvious, but still John didn't understand. He gazed at Hal's bed, which was now red-lit, adrift like a boat on the pulsing tide.

Thu-thump. A heartbeat. But *in* where?

"Great!" Hal balled his fist, would have banged the desk in triumph if there had been space for him to do so.

The beat was quicker now. And beneath it, the sigh of breath and a rumble like thunder.

"You know where this is, don't you?"

't you?

Hal's voice, tumbling like rocks down a mountain. A deep, deep echo. Thu-thump. Sigh.

"Your heart?"

"Yeah, Skiddle. Incredible, isn't it? *My* heart."

John nodded, feeling a little disappointed. This was weird, but hardly in the same league as accessing a cloudpicker the way they'd done last spring. Or even simply climbing over the rocks at Ley and finding a lump of colored glass. Thu-thump, thu-thump. Hardly what you would call fun. Blood flowing red all around him as if driven by an invisible wind. The valve opening and closing like an undersea mouth. There it all was, too, represented on the monitor. Little blips like they showed you from the doctor when they gave you reformats at school. Hal's face was glistening crimson. He looked like he'd been cut. He touched John's hand and smiled. Now, listen...

It's not the walls of a real heart around us anyway, Skiddle; it isn't as though there's a tiny camera and microphone down there, but if you fiddle with the net in just the right way—if you tickle the electrons, if you trick the airwaves—you can access the implants that thread into your spine, input all the data from the tiny molecular messengers and viruses that go voyaging on the seas of your circulatory and lymphatic systems, and create an analogue of what it's like. Real enough, but ultimately unreal.

Hal touched the screen, and the shuddering red walls faded. The air in the room darkened again. There were darts and arrows now on the monitor—falling back, organized yet too quick to grasp, like a magnetized snowstorm. Another touch of the screen, and Hal and John were surrounded by a thousand white lines crisscrossing the room like dustmotes in winter sunlight.

This, Skiddle. This is data from my powerpack monitor. Hal moved the cursor, and the room seemed to tilt as the shimmering matrix turned. The strings ran close to John's face now, and looking down, he saw that he was pierced through his chest, his belly, his hand. Hal touched the screen again, and the strings all froze.

"See, Skiddle."

John looked, and saw

GGGGGCCATGTAAGTCCTATGCCTGTCATGTGCAA
GAATTGCAATTTCTACCGATGTGCAAGAACCGCAA

"That's the code for the supply monitor of my powerpack. If you break it down, it tells you that it's about two-thirds viable at the moment, which means I'll probably have to replace it next year, although there's no hurry..."

The letters dissolved into snow again. Then refroze. "And this, here—let me pull it in. That's the identifier from the cpu. That's not all of it, of course, but effectively an analogue of my own immune system's T-cell response."

Snow. Freeze. And this. And this. Incredible, isn't it? Touching the keys; Hal's voice and hands trembling a little. Snow. Freeze. This. This

TTGCATGCCGTAATATTATGCGTGCTAGGTAGCTCG
TCGTAGATCAATGTCGTAGTTCCTCTGCTCGTCGCT

Hal was going deeper now into the operating system that monitored his body, somehow accessing it on an unrestricted bandwidth, leaning over the terminal plug to fiddle with a stray wire, taking a pipette to squeeze fresh nutrients into the silver-crosshatched nervebox that he was keeping warm, from the heat generated by a small transmitter that John had last seen put to use when they were out on the high meadows chasing rabbits with the gyrfalcon. And where was the gyrfalcon now anyway? Those red eyes and silver clattering wings? He squinted around the blurred and fizzing room

ATAGTCGCTCGCTCGCTCGATAGCCGCTCGTAGAT
TATCAGGTCACCCCTTTTAAATGCTATGATCAATGA

and the litter of unstrung tennis rackets and worn-out clothing. Nowhere. Hal had probably cannibalized that, too.

TAGTACGCTAGATAGCTCGCTCAGATAGGATCAAT
GATCAATATATCGCAAACCTAGCTTAATTGCCGCC

"Now look, Skiddle. Bingo! Right into the main operating system!"

The letters were slower now, scrolling around them at an almost readable rate.

"Watch..."

Hal's quick fingers on the screen. The letters froze.

"Look..."

Close by their faces, as Hal typed, the letters began to tumble

173

over and change. A became T and T became G as he changed the codes in his own recombinant.

"We're in..."

AGCGCATCCGAATGCCTTGGGAAATAGTCGCTCGC
GCTAGGGATCGCGCTCGATAGCCGCTCGTAGATAT

"Will you look at this? Would you believe..."

The lattice turned and blurred. Bright points against the darkness. Where was he? The room tilted, dissolved, and John was falling up towards the whirling carousel of stars. And a voice somewhere was still saying, Will you look? Would you believe?

But John was losing his brother. He was falling through darkness towards the scent of cold sweat and old smoke and damp stone, and the gray of morning.

LIGHT FILTERED INTO the cave from a window set high in the rock. Streamers of smoke from the dead fire still hung in the air. John sat up, rubbing the cramp in his legs, his head and back aching. He'd been curled in a corner away from the chimney, and he felt cold and old and numb.

Laurie was busy repacking her backpack. She looked over at him.

"Hettie says she'll show us the way for another couple of kilometers. Then it's up to us."

He nodded, and winced as the pain in his head bit deeper.

"She says there's a climb. Are you up to it?"

"I'll be fine."

She smiled. "You don't look it."

"I'll take a paintab."

She shrugged, glanced at him once more, then continued packing.

Perched crosslegged on a rock across the dim cave, Hettie watched, singing to herself. He wondered how much of the previous night had been due to the puffball and how much had been simply him. He nodded *gunafana* to her and stood up. Before he had more time to think about it, he climbed down and out of the cave to the ledge below, where the wind blew back at him no matter which way he pissed.

Laurie and Hettie were eating the cold remains of last night's food when he returned. Burrowing through yeasty socks to find the paintabs, he checked the radiation counter that lay hidden beneath a flap at the very bottom of his bag. The counter had been sampling the whole journey, sniffing the air, its tiny green snout projecting through a rent he'd made. Every day, the line on the display had climbed a little higher towards the red.

Half an hour later, in time for the implants in his body to reach a rough accord, they set out. The wind had dried the rocks along the gorge, leaving them reddish gray, but with bright pools in the hollows, reflecting the hurrying sky.

As Hettie led John and Laurie up a screefall to higher ground, he saw that the cliff face was covered with arrowslit openings, ledges, and huge weathered carvings of the faces of forgotten kings. He pressed on through the continuing pain in his head. Foothold after foothold up the steepening rock, he could feel the kings' stern and implacable gaze on his back.

By mid-morning they had reached the rocky edge of an almost lifeless plateau. In the ashen valley below lay what looked to be a road—a path, at least—winding out of the mountains.

They stood, the wind pushing against them, to catch their breath and gaze down, and Hettie announced that she would leave them to go on by themselves from here. The route was straight enough. It had led nowhere for centuries—nowhere but Ifri Gotal. She agreed to meet with them again at this same place that evening.

"*Skay go?*"

"*Skay.*"

Levering herself up with her umbrella, Hettie was about to go, but frowned, turned, and said something else to Laurie.

"What's that?"

"She says Ifri Gotal's a dangerous place, that we shouldn't stay long."

"Tell her about the counter and the suits."

Laurie shook her head. "I'll just tell her that we understand."

There was more talk. Eventually, Hettie headed back the way they'd come, nodding dubiously, muttering to herself, prodding her umbrella at the sky. Slumped on a rock, watching as she became a black speck, John shivered. It was June, but he could feel the wind like ice on his face and through his clothing. In a gap in the mountains to the east, he could see the rippling orange plains of the Last Hammada, the edge of the desert that now covered most of Africa. Farther east still, where the hills fell away to purple, there was a glimpse of another landscape, a place where black clouds met the horizon and the land itself glimmered with a brightness that had nothing to do with the sun. He breathed the air again, realizing that the ugly tang nagging his senses all morning was actually burnt mineral oil. He saw now that there were smears on the rocks around him, sooty drifts of the oil in the crevices like black snow.

They descended from the plateau to the wide floor of valley.

The road was concrete, ancient, yet in better condition than most of the tracks they'd followed up to now. Here, there was hardly any vegetation left to destroy it. The radiation counter bleeped intermittently for the first hour or so, then settled into a prolonged, irritating whine. That was just a preliminary warning—the Zone engineer had calibrated it to go louder if the short-term exposure levels became truly dangerous.

After sitting on a old dry-stone wall and deciding against eating or drinking, they unfolded the protective suits and masks from their backpacks. The reflective material felt slick and cold as they pulled it over their clothing, and crackled slightly as they walked. The masks made their breathing congested and loud. They passed wrecked vehicles along the road, tires mingled with remains. And here, as John and Laurie walked through the canyon of this glimmering world, was a shrine, a washing line of tin cans, garish strips of plastic, and wind-picked bones clanging in the wind, and a rough table of rock on which crystals and stones from other planets were piled.

He tried to remember what the net's projections had shown of this desolate area on the far side of the Northern Mountains, but he'd never imagined they'd have to come this far. Anyway the data—or, as Laurie would have put it, the net's level of interest—were scant. But there *had* been a road, a road that was once a main route through these mountains and now blocked in a score of places by rockfalls, broken bridges, collapsed tunnels. Even before he had made any connection with Ifri Gotal, John remembered thinking that it must have been along roads such as this that the great migrations flowed north from the dying wastes. Now, the signs were all around them. Broken trucks and wagons and handcarts poking out of the dust. The debris of people on the move: migrating, dragging their lives behind them. Shoes. Spoons. The limbs of a plastic doll. Tatters of clothing. Broken bottles.

The valley narrowed to a cliff face on either side. With the piled wreckage, the road grew almost impassable. Clambering up over the top of a van, John caught a glimpse inside of hunched, mummified bodies, eyeless sockets staring out at him. Laurie's movements through the wreckage beside him were slow, and her face was barely discernible beneath the mask. Ifri Gotal: maybe this was it. Maybe they should turn back now. But Laurie was pushing on towards another dip and turn.

Here, where the road crested, the valley widened into a huge, ash-colored bowl. John stood swaying from exertion, looking down. As the haze of his mask began to clear, he saw that the expanse before him consisted mainly of human bones. Grayish white, a lapping shore reaching mountainside to mountainside.

So this was Ifri Gotal. The radiation counter was screaming in his backpack now, and he began to shiver. On impulse, he pulled off his mask. Laurie did the same. Now, real at last, the end of all speculation, Ifri Gotal lay all around them, the chattering wind and the powdery smell of death like an unremitting ache. His shivering was starting to get beyond control. Briefly, Laurie put an arm around him, and they stood together in the wind blowing from a sea of femurs, skulls, rags of clothing, broken possessions, teeth.

They stayed at Ifri Gotal for an hour, their breather masks back on as they struggled with the sampler scoops, hearing only the wind and the clink of disturbed rocks and the close hard sound of their own breathing. John lifted a stone to weigh down a small sampler that buzzed into the dust, but the stone turned out to be light and hollow, not a stone at all but a child's skull. He placed it back, trying to concentrate on the work he was doing, to see only what he needed to see. It was a trick he'd done his best to develop, focusing on the matter-of-fact details before him, shutting out everything else.

Later, he stood up and looked at the graveyard around him, knowing that he should pray. But all he saw were the fruits of an ancient conflict, the wind-picked bones of a people who had long ceased to be mourned. It seemed to him that all acts of violence, even ones as atrocious as this, eventually merged with the dust of history. What was truly terrible was the way that good and bad ultimately lost their distinction.

He stared at the child's skull. Meeting a bland empty gaze of sockets that had once contained flesh and life, he wondered why he had fought so hard to keep his faith. Laurie was right: if you ceased to expect purpose or meaning from the universe, then the knowledge of horrors such as this became a little easier to bear. You could forget, get on with your life.

He set to work again.

Squatting under her umbrella, Hettie was waiting at the rise in the rocky valley where she left them.

Driven on flakes of soot, a dry dusk was shining in the rain-bowed puddles. They had dumped their suits and masks on the way from Ifri Gotal, but their backpacks were heavier now with foil-shielded packages of samples. John had had to pull out the batteries of the radiation counter to stop its screaming.

"Ah fond?"

Yes, they'd found. Hettie studied them, her eyes gleaming in the shade of her umbrella, a fringe of glass and bone. Then, nodding to herself, she turned again to the north.

John and Laurie followed between the rocks and the high cliff walls. The sky overhead billowed and churned, but here in the valley it was almost windless, still.

Full darkness came. Hettie lit a chemlight and pushed it onto the tip of her umbrella, waving it over her head, jumping over puddles and from rock to rock as she led the way. The shadows slid back and forth, leaped over the cliffs—a witches' Sabbath—but John kept his eyes mostly at his feet, picking his way, occasionally stooping to collect another sample of stone or dry powder. When he looked up and saw the giant faces carved on the crags around Hettie's home, they too were demonic, with sightless stone eyes.

Watched by Hettie, John and Laurie removed and shook off their outer clothing beside the cut-stone steps leading to her cave. Then they climbed the stairway into the rock past the carvings of long-dead beasts, the whorled innards of stone, and they breathed the rank and yet now oddly refreshing human odors of smoke, sweat, urine.

John unslung his backpack and slumped down in a corner. Incinerating his gloves and wiping off with dysol the grit that had worked beneath them, he watched as Hettie prepared dinner. Laurie was holding a pan for her over the flames. Her arms, shoulders, and legs were bare, and he saw the play of light over and along them. Her hair was tangled, greasy, almost the same no-color now as Hettie's—and no doubt as his. She chewed at a strand of it as she swished melting fat in the pan, then asked Hettie a rising-falling question and reached into the pan, pushing at a barely warm scrap of meat with her finger. The stoop of her brown back raised notches. Hettie said something. Laurie smiled and shook her head. She scratched beneath her arm, pressed something dead with her fingernails, threw it into the flames. *Spat*, a little fusillade of sparks. Smoke drifted, and the smell of curried meat slowly rose.

Leaning more against the rock, he felt something dig into his shoulder but ignored it. It was good to be back amid life.

"Here." Laurie handed him a plate. She and Hettie sat closer to the fire, their faces shifting and changing like the stone giants outside.

"Ask her," he said, when the two of them finally fell to tooth-picking silence, "how she became *chicahta*—a witch-woman."

In response to Laurie's question, Hettie smiled and held her hands to the flames. She swayed as she spoke, and her voice was like a scatter of pebbles.

"She says it was when she was a girl," Laurie began. "On a night just before the rains, when the whole Endless City lies still and the sounds carry over miles, and people sweat in their beds and the air is like the breath of a dog panting close to your face . . ."

"She said *that?*"

"Shush, John. Listen—I know what it's like too. Hettie was up in her room at night, lying between her sisters, trying to lose the heat and get to sleep, when she heard this sound coming through the open window, singing like water. The tip-tapping of drums. It was faint, but so close too that it was almost inside her head. She crept from the room and down the stairs. She went out into the empty street dressed as she was.

"She walked barefoot through the dust. There was no one about. The world seemed different, but the sound that drew her was something she recognized even though she'd never heard it before. She followed it up the hill, and the sound grew louder in her head rather than in the air, and everything else was so quiet and empty that she thought she might be dreaming. But there were the clattering drums and cymbals and bells, so she walked on through the night, the cool sound drawing her...

"She found the witchwomen in a square, gathered around a fire, their shadows huge across the buildings behind them. As she drew closer, she realized that what the fire gave off wasn't heat, but it was like the music, refreshing and cool, and when the witchwomen drew her into their circle, she felt both rested and drowsy. She stayed with them for the rest of the night..."

Silent now as Laurie finished her tale, Hettie smiled, shivered, and drew her hands back from the flames.

"And they took her with them?" John asked. "She became a witchwoman?"

"No," Laurie said after Hettie spoke some more. "She went home in the morning, and her parents were furious. She didn't become a witchwoman until she'd had children of her own and they grew old enough to leave her. But it was *then* that she knew, that she decided."

Later into the night, Hettie grabbed up a seemingly random pile of electronics and shooed the red mites out of a large nervebox. Crouching over it, licking at the wires and pushing in the connectors, weaving it all together like a tapestry, she persuaded tiny green lights to glow. Music began to fill the cave. The looping strings of an orchestra...It started, stopped, played with a long and easy melody, drawing the listener on and in. John recognized it, although he couldn't quite place the name. Perhaps a Strauss waltz...

His eyes stinging with smoke and tiredness, he watched as Laurie and Hettie linked arms and danced, laughing, around the cave.

Hettie took them as far as Lall next morning. It grew warmer as they descended, and the high slopes around them were suddenly green and alive. Once or twice, watched by Hettie, John stopped to gather more samples. As far as he knew, Laurie had made no effort to explain the real purpose of their journey, yet the witchwoman, though curious, seemed to accept everything they did. He imagined that she thought the sample-taking was some priestly ritual; she'd naturally look upon their journey to Ifri Gotal as a pilgrimage.

The air grew brighter as they descended the widening valleys along the southern flanks of the mountains. A hawk circled. Rabbits darted under the gorse. And now, singly at first then in clumps amid the tall ragged grass, grew koiyl bushes. He could now smell the tarry, sweet pollen from the small white flowers that bowed and lifted here, sheltered from the wind that drove towards Europe.

When they reached the sharp rim of an overhanging valley that framed the toy village of Lall below, and the barking of dogs, the sawing of wood, the beat of generators, and the shouts of children filled the air, Hettie announced that she would leave them.

"We haven't talked about payment," John said.

"She says she doesn't want any."

"That's absurd—we have to give her something."

"I'll ask her again—if you really want me to offend her."

He shook his head. "But tell her . . . Tell her." He turned to

Hettie, who was standing a little apart and watching them with her head cocked expectantly. "Hettie, thanks. *Bona* I, *ah* can help, *hep*..."

Hettie muttered something to Laurie.

"She says she understands."

He nodded and looked at the witchwoman, her deep brown eyes, her wrinkled, mannish face. The koiyl-scented wind blew between them.

"Bye Fatoo."

She hugged Laurie, waved to John, then turned and began to climb the valley side—not back the way they'd come but up towards the grim wind-whistling peaks of the gray-blue mountains to the east. From a crag, she turned and waved to them once more, then continued her climb, umbrella balanced in one hand, black clothes flapping as she moved swiftly from perch to perch up the bare rock.

When she'd finally gone from sight, John and Laurie zigzagged down the slope to Lall. As they approached, the people came running out of their huts, shouting and waving to others who were working in the stony fields nearby and in the animal pens. Look! The girl! The *fatoo-baraka!* They've returned!

John and Laurie were clustered around, smiled at, offered water from the well, food from the smokinghouse, drink from the still. And would the *fatoo-baraka* like more koiyl? Perhaps some of the flowers. The flowers were special, the plant's greatest gift...

"You may as well take them," Laurie muttered, "in the interests of science."

She accepted them for him, and added them to the load on his back. Declining the offer of a meal, Laurie said they'd have to push on if they were to get to Tiir before nightfall. The villagers nodded. And would they need a guide—or a protector? No, they'd be fine. Waving, smiling, still nodding their thanks, John and Laurie walked through the village, past the low stone wall, across the footbridge over the stream, and along the path that led out of the Northern Mountains.

"What will happen to those people?" Laurie asked when they stopped to rest an hour later. "How can you stop the trade in their koiyl without destroying them?"

"Should we give up?"

"No..." She squinted back the way they'd come, where the path dissolved up the valley amid rich clusters of soft green and white. "But they're happy."

It was evening by the time they saw the lights of Tiir in the windy bowl of the hills. A donkey train had passed them hours before, going up into the mountains with jingling bells, swaying empty panniers, and the straw smell of the animals. The driver had scowled at them and hurried on, averting his eyes, saying nothing.

Down the final slope there were smoking lanterns, a gate, a guard, explanations to be offered, money to be paid. They went down the stone-paved streets to check that the van was where they had left it. It was untouched, but neither of them wanted to travel farther, or to have to sleep inside it. They went back up the steps and through the gates into the town, past the castle walls and the wide, empty space where Hettie and the other witchwomen had gathered three days before. The streets were almost empty. A few men and women crouched cross-legged around steaming hookahs and chemlights in the shelter of narrow alleys, engrossed in a complex game involving slow chanting and the tossing of colored stones. Few turned their heads, but John sensed from the shapes at windows and half-open doors that he was watched as he passed by.

A large graystone building leaned against the town's outer wall. A strip of lights proclaimed H EL, but the door seemed locked. Laurie banged and pushed until it gave way. They entered a bar of sorts, the tables and roof oddly bisected by the buttresses that presumably kept the front of the building from falling. They were shown up an irregular stairway to a room with a bare floor that heaved and sagged like a restless sea. One window was an unglazed arrowslit that looked out across the gray-lit valley through the thickness of Tiir's outer wall, while the other framed the dim street up which they had walked. Despite the insistent, wheezy rumbling of a nearby generator, there was no other source of light.

There were several pallets and a stone tub that the straining floor bellied down to accommodate. After considerable negotiation, Laurie agreed on a price for the provision of soap and the filling of the tub with water, and John and Laurie watched as the hotel's three children made a solemn procession up and down the stairs bearing a variety of buckets and bowls.

When the children were gone, Laurie flapped out the mottled blankets from one of the larger pallets, coughed and wiped her eyes in an invisible cloud of dust, smoothed out the blankets, and lay down. "You go first," she said, almost disappearing in the sag of mattress and floor.

John destroyed his gloves, then pulled off his clothes. Over the last few days, they'd stiffened and begun to mold themselves around him. He stepped into the bowl. The water was cloudy, knee-deep, and it stung. They hadn't been given the soap they'd asked for, but he supposed the pungent disinfectant would be strong enough to lift off the grime. Outside, through the larger window, he saw heaps of rubbish by a dead-end wall and heard the hum of insects that would probably turn to a roar when morning broke. When he crouched, a joist groaned. Splashing the oddly slimy water over his back and shoulders, he plucked away something that clung there and scrubbed at himself with his nails.

Stepping out, he reached for the nearest blanket, thought better of it, and tried to shake himself dry like a dog. Laurie chuckled. She was sitting up now, watching him.

"You're enjoying this?" he said, rummaging in his bag for a new shirt, finding that there were none left.

"Yes." She was cross-legged and smiling. "Aren't you?"

Sniffing experimentally at an old shirt, giving up, he picked his way naked over the boards. And yes, he was enjoying this, enjoying the sense of purpose that he'd sought throughout his life, even though, after seeing Lall and Ifri Gotal, he felt guilty about it.

He flattened out the bedclothes of a pallet that lay on a rise in the floor and lay down, expecting softness but feeling only boards beneath him. The blankets were greasy and gave off a sour vegetable smell. He could feel the billowing passage of air from the arrowslit window over his shoulders and face. He turned and saw Laurie washing, the gleam of her flesh in the light from the larger window. She was brisk, matter-of-fact. Her hair was wet, smoothed back over her ears and flat over her narrow shoulders, which jutted up and out as her arms moved. She turned slightly, balancing. Stripes of shining water trickled between her breasts and down the curve of her belly. As he watched, there was a soft, drunken kind of stirring within him.

Something that he'd grown used to forgetting over the years; that he'd isolated and studied and put aside.

Laurie stooped to wash her feet and shins, and between her buttocks and thighs he saw the downy line of her vulva. He looked away, at the wall, then up through the arrowslit at the dizzying movements of the clouds, and thought of the satellites somewhere beyond, the great wings shining against the moon ...But he could still feel his penis hardening, pressing painfully against the rough blankets, and his heart racing.

He heard the drip and sigh of water as Laurie stepped out from the tub, then the pat of her wet footsteps as she crossed the hilly floor. The seal hissed when she opened her bag, which lay on her pallet near the far wall. There followed many wing-beats of silence. The night seemed to turn and race. He almost expected to feel the air shifting, the room changing, to see the sky start to tumble and blur, the lights of the passing vehicles to fan across the walls. Hal to be there beside him. Then the silence broke. Again, Laurie's footsteps: the scuff of her bare feet, growing louder as she came towards him.

He turned and looked up. She stood over his pallet. Her shoulders were sloped, and in the darkness her face was blank, without expectation, staring through him. He sat up a little and pulled back the scratchy sheets. In silence, she stooped and rolled in beside him, still cold and a little wet, smelling of the disinfectant. And she was shivering—or perhaps it was him. Perhaps they were both shivering.

She put her arms around him. Across his shoulder and down to the small of his back, the tips of her fingers rested on the scar. He put his own right arm around her, and saw the spin-ning quaternary lights in his watch gleaming on the moisture that still beaded her shoulder. But his left arm didn't seem to belong quite anywhere, pinned awkwardly between them. He'd forgotten how strange it was, to hold someone else's body against your own.

He was observing himself, wondering where all this would lead, would end. Faint on her breath was the nutty odor of the biscuits they'd eaten back at the van. And she smelled warm and womanly too, clean and human, yet misty and so very different, of the sea, as Borderers always smelled, even when they lived in the Zone and didn't eat kelp. He was lying with his hips held a little away from her, conscious of the pressure of his erection. But then she drew in and pressed her hand harder against his back, pulling him closer, settling the wings of her hips against his, and in this strange and sudden contact he imagined his erection fading, could even feel the soft, apologetic space it would leave between them. He saw how she would roll back from him and away across the dark room. Morning would come, and the moment would be gone, easily forgotten.

But no. He closed his eyes and felt her breath and the sharing of their skin. She shifted a little, and there was the soft friction of her belly against him. Involuntarily, he pressed too, and she leaned her head to his from the unfocused dark and opened her lips against his mouth. He reached to touch her wet hair, the nape of her neck, traced the smoothly ridged line of her back and buttocks. As he did so, her breath grew in his throat and her mouth widened and she pressed harder against him. It seemed so natural now. He knew, too, as she raised and lifted her leg a little and his hand slid around and his fingers explored and parted the opening of her vulva that this moment would send cracks and ripples through his life. But it felt too sweet and plain and natural to be anything more than what it was: the joining of two people.

Their mouths popped apart. She rolled forward and eased herself higher up against him, offering her breasts. He took a nipple into his mouth, and her hand went around his penis and a finger traced a line and he wondered for a moment if he wasn't about to come.

But no. She settled back, drawing away more of the stiff blankets, lying with her legs raised and parted. He clambered around her knee and eased himself over her. She guided him in, and he pushed gently deeper, in no hurry now, looking down at her in the ribbon of arrowslit light as her throat arched and her eyelids quivered and the generator sounded somewhere even though there were no lights here and the south wind blew towards the Endless City. There was the sound, too, as he sunk and pressed deeper and their hips rolled, of soft slow moaning in her throat. A singing, almost. The sound Laurie Kalmar made in her dreams. The sound she made to the net.

She was far away now. Pushing deep with him. He could feel that his own moment was approaching too. The air shimmered. A series of shocks, jolts, close to pain. Yes. And even now. Far more than he'd expected. He looked down at Laurie. She'd ceased to push, was smiling. Had she come too? He hoped so. But he was no expert, he was Father John, a priest; there was no way of his telling. She squeezed his penis in farewell as he diminished inside her. He lay back, grabbing the edge of the sheet, pulling it over them.

Laurie turned over and pressed herself against him with her chin on his shoulder, her knee drawn over his thigh. He could feel her breathing, and knew from the pressure of her face against his neck that she was smiling. And how could this ever be wrong? The arguments and recriminations that he'd expected seemed reluctant to stir. No, you couldn't give yourself to everyone, equally. Not all the time...

"What made you decide?" he asked.

"When? Just now...?"

"I mean when you saw me in Trinity Gardens after the rain. What made you come over?"

"You looked lost," she said.

He closed his eyes. Somewhere in the hills outside the town, a bird or animal was screeching. Then the wind. He could feel it on his face, coming with the night through the arrowslit, cooling his sweat. Hot liquid was somehow filling his eyes. He felt a tear trickle down his cheek, meeting Laurie's mouth. He felt her tongue lick it away. And why was he crying? And what was that sound? Again, it was just the wind. The wind.

FEELING SLEEPLESS, HAPPY, puzzled, John collected his belongings in the morning gray of their many-bedded room. Laurie had already straightened the blankets of the pallet where they'd lain—as if it mattered, and the people wouldn't burn everything. Now her head was stooped while she reordered the contents of her bag, the fall of her hair parting to show the back of her neck and a pale line of scalp.

"Shouldn't we check about the koiyl market here?" she said, fishing for a tissue and then blowing her nose.

He shook his head. After last night he wanted to move on quickly. "The leaf hasn't been harvested yet. Who would there be to talk to?"

"As you say." Laurie walked over to him. She put her arms across his shoulders and looked up at him. Her scent was dark, real, sweet. He could feel the air from the arrowslit brushing

193

his hands as he placed them on her warm hips. He could feel the whole planet revolving.

"You didn't sleep much," she said, "did you? I mean, after we had..." She paused, careful. "After making love."

"I just liked watching you." He smiled at her, and she smiled back at him with her green eyes. Then she kissed him.

Just watching you. Was this, he wondered, the first lie?

It was not like any other morning as they carried their bags down through Tiir's tumbling, hay-scented streets to the van; it was brighter, the wind seemed sharper, with Laurie walking beside him. And as she hummed, and her eyes followed a kitten in a handcart, and she spoke to the guard at the walled gate and jumped the low stone wall of the field where the van was parked, he felt the tug of part of him moving with her.

After an hour of rattling and banging along the ill-made road, Laurie stopped the van for him to take over the driving. Later, he stopped for her. The rhythm of the journey began. Black dead trees surrounded them, and the reek of old fires. The burnt-out forest seemed endless, but they pushed on, neither of them wanting to spend the night in this place. Finally the trees faded to ashen scrub, and John and Laurie rejoined the bigger highway where the trucks and the grainy lights of the phosphate mines streamed in the distance. Reaching Sadiir after dark, they were stared at and followed by the same children, shown the same room in the same and only hotel by the same hotelkeeper.

A large and amazingly ugly insect scuttled into the wall when John and Laurie pushed the mattresses together. But there was an appealing domesticity about rearranging this filthy room. Here, far from anything, he almost wanted people to know. And the bed-making process was arousing, too. Laurie noticed and laughed. He hugged her, and the room seemed to brighten.

After they made love and all the lights went off, he lay tracing his tongue from the tip of her left breast to her shoulder, tasting her sweat and the charcoal of the forest. Finally she rolled away from him and padded out of the room and along the corridor to wash herself. He sat up and shook a few dead bugs off the sheets, hoping that this time his own phylum-specific secretions would be enough protection for both of them. This truly was a different life, a different way of seeing. Then she came back and lay beside him, propped on one elbow, smelling of soap.

"You're not entirely new to this," she said.

"There were times before I was a priest. A girl called Janis..." He frowned, unable to think of her last name. "She had a sense of the ridiculous, a sense of humor. It made up, I suppose, for what I didn't have myself. She was just someone I knew. We had the same friends and went to the same parties and dances. She'd look at me, and we'd share a joke at the stupidity of it all, which no one else saw. We'd be sniggering, and everyone would wonder why..."

He smiled, gazing up. Feeling, even now in this distant room, a ticklish, silvery bubble of mirth ready to rise and break inside him. "So we used to dance together, and of course people started thinking of us as a pair. And we began to kiss outside in the dusk the way the other kids did." He paused. This was at the same time—it had to be—that he was seeing Father

Gulvenny at the church, debating the meaning of existence, looking for the fire within. Also the time when he lost hope that Hal would ever recover. He wondered how it was that your life became arranged into these fragments. "I'd go around to her house in the evenings. We'd walk out down the drive holding hands, in our best clothes. I don't know..." he said, trying hard to remember those pastel evenings, Janis with her long chin and that gleam in her eye. But, along with her last name, so much had slipped from his memory.

"You made love with her?"

"Yes, but it was never serious. The joke was that we probably had more fun, physically, than the others who were so fumbling and intense, so ashamed to say what they wanted out of fear they might lose the person they wanted to do it with..." He smiled. "But I only realized that much later on, when I had to listen to people's problems as a priest. Janis and I drifted apart. We made love, but we were never really lovers. There wasn't much to keep us together."

"And Hal? Was he in a coma then, when you were seeing Janis?"

"Hal was pretty much then as he is now." John took a breath, feeling the tensions of his flesh where it touched Laurie's, the cramp that was coming into his muscles, the itch of some insect dying in the sweat that had pooled beneath his spine.

"Did he mean to kill himself?"

"I don't know."

"If not suicide, what would you call it?"

"An accident—that's what we always called it. Hal's still alive, and it was an accident. No one's ever thought of a better word. My mother's holding on, still hoping—and hope can become a kind of addiction. She's like me, I suppose. She still wants to know why..."

"Perhaps he just gave up."

"But if someone like Hal gives up," John said, "how are the rest of us supposed to keep going?"

THE FIRST MORNING back, he was up early. Bella gave him breakfast before Felipe came down, and he had time to cycle up to Santa Cristina before going to the clinic. There was no service until that evening, but he was grateful for the cool transparency, beneath a sky already glowing like hot iron, of the air inside the decrepit church. It smelled faintly of the incense that Felipe had used in the few services that he had given, clanking up here in his cart and on his leghelpers, while John was away. And the Inmaculada, John saw, had gained a few new ornaments in his absence. He played the cards that had been left in the tray, refraining, as he always did, from using the translat until he tried to decipher the words himself. But either way, they made little sense to him.

He arrived at the clinic to find a queue stretching around the block. Nuru, his feet up on the desk in the backroom, wore a new white coat and an air of importance.

"Fatoo find the mountains?" he asked.

John, already feeling tired and hot, disliked Nuru's newly proprietary attitude to his desk, and the reek of disinfectant had begun to sting his eyes. "Let's just see how you managed, shall we?"

Nuru raised his hands to shrug, then pointed at the doctor's screen, which was already on. He remained seated at the desk and watched as John scrolled through new records that detailed a treatment rate that was almost double anything he'd ever achieved.

He was out of the church quickly after Mass that evening and cycling down Corpus Vali in oddly mercurial light. Kassi Moss hadn't been in her usual spot midway back in the pews, and although he had no pickups or deliveries to make, he felt vaguely worried about her. Days in the Endless City were longer now. Places he was used to seeing only in darkness were exposed in flickering light. And the heat was everywhere, pushed and sucked by the wind, as if the air too was trying to settle somewhere in the coolness that never came. He saw a woman's face in the crowd that had gathered around an ice seller. She was jostled by those near her, and the drifting smoke revealed the brown flesh of a narrow cheekbone, strands of dark hair tucked behind one ear. She sensed his gaze, turned and looked at him, and quickly made the sign against the evil eye. She was older, thinner, not Laurie. A beggar called to him as he cycled past. But today he had no money. He'd forgotten his pouch—his translat too, he now realized, which lay with the pouch on the rail by the Inmaculada; a new and unplanned addition to the tributes to Our Lady. And the cassock he was wearing, in this heat, was absurd. He should have gone back to the presbytery after Mass and changed.

Mokifa now seemed just another part of the sprawl. The only difference he could see amid the buildings beyond the shock-wire was that the windows were closed. He imagined the people sheltering inside from the heat, clustered around coolers and purifiers. He dismounted in front of the Cresta Motel and walked under the archway into the shadow of the courtyard's walls, picking his way between bags of soiled laundry and rubbish, brushing away the flies that, too sluggish to rise into the air, crawled over his cassock.

As always, Kassi's office was open. But, pushing through the hot beads of the curtain, blinking in the windowless halogen-lit room, he saw that another woman was sitting at Kassi's desk. She was youngish, one of Kassi's helpers, her face scarred by the burrowings of the skin parasite for which she'd been treated here. John had seen her wandering in the background on his visits, emptying buckets and bundling up sheets as Kassi showed him from patient to patient along the dimming corridors and asked if it was all right to bring an end. But he and the woman had never spoken, and now she stared at him, her hands pressed to her narrow chest as if she'd never seen him or any other European before.

He reached to his belt and touched the space where the translat should have been.

"Where's Kassi?"

The woman shook her head.

He pointed. "Is she upstairs in the wards?"

The woman moved her lips. He waited while she swallowed. *"Kassi vendu,"* she said eventually.

Vendu? Gone—going? He wasn't sure. It was one of those context-dependent words.

"So she's not here?"

The woman shook her head.

John rubbed his gloved fingertips together, plastic on plastic with the sodden flesh trapped beneath, as he looked around at the tiny office. It seemed oddly empty without Kassi, and the halogen lamp threw everything out of proportion, made holes of the shadows. The cheap plastic Christ was on the wall above the desk, a clear presence in the darkness and the stink.

He said *gonenanh* and left. A family of rats watched him from a broken outflow in the courtyard, their paws delicately raised as they picked at something long and pale. Irritated, he walked towards them. After a moment of hesitation, they retreated.

Avoiding the temptation of shortcuts, he cycled back along Corpus Vali, then across the Plaza El-Halili to the Cruz de Marcenado. There was no discernible smoke rising from Martínez's gabled house, and light glowed from only one of the top windows. A wounded caroni bird disentangled itself from an alleyway and, mewing, dragged itself across the street as John knocked at the door. He waited.

When the door finally swung open, the sour gust of ill-smelling air and Kailu's face told him that Martínez was worse. John felt again for his forgotten translat, unable to remember whether Kailu spoke any European.

"How is he—*ice uhe?*"

With an odd, quick motion, Kailu shook her head.

"Look, if I..."

He made to step inside, but her face twisted. She spat at him. *"Inutel mal! Comma..."*

He stumbled back as she lunged forward, her hands clawing for his silver eyes. She was yelling in Borderer, her voice clamoring down the hot dark street where the wounded caroni bird was still mewing, trailing blood in the dust. Shutters swung open, figures stood in doorways. Kailu was saying, *Fatoobaraka*, you're killing him, you've made him ill! She lunged again. It was an awkward dance, and he sensed that she didn't quite have the final twist of whatever it took to actually touch him. Eventually a neighbor emerged, gripped her shoulders, muttered crooning words, and drew her away.

Breathless, weary, covered with sweat, John cycled back up to Gran Vía and left his bicycle in the presbytery hall. Peeling off his gloves, pulling the thread, and tossing them on the floor to curl and flare, he climbed the stairs and picked up and ignited a foline lamp. He worked open a damp-swollen door and stepped around the soggy piles of analogue books, paper printouts, unlabeled tapes, disks, and cards to get to the transmitter.

Sitting down on the old leather stool, he turned on the flat screen. Static buzzed as he scanned. There were faces and voices, rippling shapes from all the weird, cheap, faulty 2-D and half-encoded transmissions that flooded the Magulf, then the big winged silver H of the Halcyon logo demanding identification and his personal password. Entering the sudden order of the net, he called up Laurie. Her face smiled at him from the airwave's screen.

"Hello, Father John." Silver-eyed, she tilted her head. "How are you?" But even before she spoke, he knew it was the answerer.

"I want to speak to Laurie."

"I'm afraid she's busy at the moment. Can I help you?"

"Tell her I'd like to see her tomorrow. I'll be coming into the Zone."

The answerer nodded. "Of course." She waited, looking at him, amused.

"How well do you speak Borderer?" he asked.

"As well as you like." She blinked and pursed her lips. "Do you want me to talk—"

"No. I mean, I'm unsure about one particular word. *Vendu* —what does that mean. Gone? Away?"

"It all depends," the answerer said, still smiling, "on the context."

Next morning in the Zone, the tires of the cars and trucks ticked as they passed over the sticky roads. And the vans, sagging to wait at crossroads, their vents shimmering, seemed unlikely ever to rise again. Things worked at this time of year in the Magulf—but barely. The machines had all been designed for cooler, more generous skies, and the cost of fashioning anything specifically for so limited a market would have been prohibitive.

Beyond the admin blocks leading to the medical center, the people wandering through the haze that hung above the lawns were lightly dressed, in shortsleeves, cotton frocks, and shorts. A purplish scum had glazed the wind-rippled lake, and a Halcycon engineer crouched by the outfall and maneuvered a cleaning crab with helmet and joystick. He was watched from the water's edge by a line of ruffled and impatient ducks.

Entering the air-conditioned medical center, John felt his flesh tauten with the shock. Tim jumped up when he entered the office, seemingly surprised to see him despite the appointment John had made.

"So. The wanderer returns."

"Well," John said, sitting down, realizing as he did so that he was moving his hands as Borderers did when they shrugged. "Here I am."

With his usual eagerness to get things over and done with, Tim had already begun to tap commands into the screen on his desk. He'd had his hair cut while John was away; the fringe was a little shorter. When he leaned forward to peer at a corner of the display, John saw that the hair was combed and woven to hide its thinning. Funny, he thought, that we still can't do much about that. In the corner, the doctor hissed and clicked, reconfiguring its receivers and probes to Tim's commands, making minor adjustments. It looked sleek and predatory.

"Now. Let's get started, shall we?"

Tim blanked the windows. John discarded his clothes. The air raised bumps on his flesh as the doctor slid out on smooth runners. He submitted to its embrace.

"You've got the results there?" he asked afterward.

"Marvelous, isn't it?"

"You tell me."

Tim shrugged. "There's no problem, John. Of course there's no problem—you have God on your side."

John buttoned his shirt. "No isotopes?"

"There's a little in your intestines and lungs, but it's broadly distributed. No hot spots. The viruses haven't deprogrammed a single precancerous cell. Not that you should worry—you of all people. You're fit, John. To be honest, you were in a worse state before you left. There's a record of some blip in your cpu. But it self-corrected."

"And Laurie Kalmar. She'll be okay too?"

"She'll be fine," Tim said, "unless she was digging up the dust and eating it. Of course, I don't do the high-grade Borderer tests. It's a separate specialization. Not that I'd mind giving it a bash. With Laurie."

John concentrated on his socks.

"And what's it like out there?" Tim said. "Is it really as ghastly as everyone says it is?"

"The people up in the mountains are poor. But it's...more lifelike than here."

"Lifelike." Tim nodded. "That's not a word that often comes to mind, in or outside the Zone."

"I didn't know you went outside much."

"Oh..." Tim said. "Every now and then. And you got all the way there, I gather? To the site of the blast? You managed to take samples?"

"You've spoken to Laurie? To the engineer?"

"To neither, actually," Tim said. "But you know what it's like here, the way word gets around. We hardly need the net."

"I can imagine."

Tim gave John a glance that said he probably couldn't, then concentrated on the screen, tapping with his fingers. The window was still blanked, and the screen's lines of lights and letters scrolled over his face in the half darkness. John finished dressing. He had expected Tim to show more curiosity about the journey, though he knew now that the question of the contaminated koiyl in itself held little interest for him. But Tim didn't ask how John and Laurie had got on. What they'd got up to.

"It's a kind of holy place for the witchwomen," John said. "I collected some fresh leaves along the way. They were fresh five days ago, anyway. And the flowers of the plant, the people in the village just gave them to me. For free."

Tim kept his eyes on the screen. "You want me to look at them?" He seemed to be comparing sources of data, and John wondered momentarily if it was possible for Tim to tell from the readouts whether his patient had been sexually active with a Borderer woman.

"If you could. But tell me—and I know this is probably a stupid question—is there some way of filtering the isotopes out of the leaf? Some process? Or a way that people could chew the leaf without absorbing them?"

"You're right, John—it's a stupid question. The main contaminant at Ifri Gotal is strontium 90, which is a particularly nasty isotope because of the way it builds up inside living things. The reason it's in the leaf, and the reason it's finding its way into your patients' bones, is that it's so chemically similar to calcium that it gets absorbed along with it. It becomes part of what you are, John, and stays with you for up to thirty years. And all the while it's emitting beta waves that have more than enough energy to kill cells, or damage them—or make them cancerous."

"I just thought—I don't know. That there might be some way."

"There isn't. But I thought you just wanted to stop the contaminated leaves being sold." Now that John was fully dressed, Tim cleared the windows. The purplish scum had been cleared from the lake, and the ducks were back out, bobbing like little sailboats. "But yes, I'll take a look at the new leaves if you want."

"You're sure?"

"Of course I'm sure. Anyway, I have only one more appointment for this morning. What would you say to going out for a sip and a bite?"

"Sorry, Tim. It'll have to be some other day."

"Okay." Tim looked down and touched his screen again. "But let me know if your hear about any free drinks—remember, like we had at Trinity Gardens?" Glancing up from beneath his fringe, he seemed almost boyish again. "You will do that, John, won't you?"

John arrived at the little bar on Main Avenue ten minutes early. Laurie was already there.

It wasn't quite the place he remembered. The chromium machine was still busy serving, but there was no leaving party today; the tables were little islands occupied by solitary diners. She'd sat close to the window, in the motes of light that filtered through the glass from the cherry trees outside. She looked up at him and pushed back a chair.

He sat down. His throat was tight. She'd ordered wine while she waited but no food. The waiter whizzed between them to whisk away the butts of two tubes that lay in the steel saucer, and she watched with her chin propped on her hand. Her hair was tied back today. It was cool in here, but the strands that had escaped the ribboned knot curled damp against her neck and forehead.

They settled on cannelloni from the small nonseafood section of the menu. And more wine. The food came. They discussed the koiyl. Now, at least, John had the kind of evidence the governor had been talking about. Even if John feared for the fate of the village of Lall, he had a duty to make sure that something was done...

Despite the wine, his mouth was dry, and he found it difficult to talk and swallow. Yet Laurie was still Laurie and seemed
to be treating this as though it were all so ordinary, just the
meeting of two friends. He wondered if there was some subtle
Borderer sexual code that he, a European, had no knowledge
of. Or perhaps her expression was obscured by the wonderful,
continuing strangeness of her green eyes. He crossed his legs as
the waiter tinkled to another table.

"Did you hear," she asked, "what I just said?"

"I'm sorry Laurie, I was just..."

"I know. Elsewhere."

"What was it?"

She pushed back her plate and folded her arms. "Nothing. I
didn't say anything. That was how I could tell." She tilted her
head. "So what are you doing this afternoon?" There was gentle
mockery there, but at least she didn't call him Father John.

"Do you have anything planned?"

"Nothing. What about you?"

"Only things that can wait."

"Then let them wait."

He opened his eyes. He hadn't thought he'd been asleep, but
the glow of his watch told him that it was hours since they'd
come to the bungalow. They'd made love, and afterward Laurie
had gone to the bathroom, and he'd watched her shadow shift
across the tiles as she stooped to wash herself. Sex was, after
all, inherently messy. Now she was asleep. He raised himself
up on his arm and gazed down as she lay breathing, complete, composed, with that tiny puckered scar on her upper arm.
He turned over again, staring up into the dark, rubbing at the

crust around his eyes, wondering why the best moments always seemed to slip away.

He felt uncomfortable, it was true, under the silver-eyed gaze of people who, no matter how careful he and Laurie were, would soon be talking about yet another priest who'd gone a little strange here in the Endless City. And all his efforts with the koiyl, the meetings he would have to attend, the studies he would try to promote, would fit in so neatly as an excuse for these frequent visits to the Zone...

He turned and saw that Laurie was awake, staring at him.

"I should go to your church," she said, sitting up a little. "That might make it easier."

"Make what easier?"

"To understand what all this is doing..."

"I wouldn't worry," he said, laying his hand on her shoulder, breathing her scent, feeling the warmth of her skin.

"Did Hal ever want to be a priest?"

He smiled at the thought. "It was the last thing he'd be."

"Is that," Laurie said, pressing closer to him, "the reason you chose it?"

They walked out through the Zone. It was late, and quiet. The lights along the streets hummed, the occasional machine clattered by. They crossed the pale lawn past the gray spire of All Saints, where Father Orteau was just emerging. John raised a hand in acknowledgment, but the little man scuttled off through the hot wind towards his air-conditioned suite at the Hyatt, seeming not to notice them. They walked on, past the admin blocks towards the shuttleport, where lights shone out from the plain glass windows of the Borderer hostels and the sky seemed at its blackest and reddest, its most volcanic. Down by the shore, even after midnight—and in this heat—a shift was still working. Engines moaned, chains crackled, generators hummed, Borderer voices shouted. But a silence seemed to descend and the stares were hostile as John and Laurie walked by a great loading bay where a shuttle engine was being hauled up from a barge. From somewhere a frothy blob of spit patted the hot pavement in front of them.

"How long do you have left," Laurie asked, linking his arm as they turned the corner, "in the Endless City?"

"A few months. Four. No...three."

"You'll go back then?"

"No. I won't go back."

"Because of me?"

"Because of everything."

They walked on.

THIS WAS LIKE every other meeting he'd attended. There had been several about the koiyl over the last few weeks, and already they'd slipped into the general background roar of half-understood and half-acted-upon issues that pervaded the Zone. Most of the people here were deputies, or deputies of deputies, and there were several telepresences or simply empty screens. He knew that Laurie's attendance, as a potentially koiyl-chewing Borderer herself, would have been ill judged, so he was the only person around this table who had actually been to Ifri Gotal, or who even set foot regularly outside the Zone.

The engineer who'd initially prepared the radiation counter for him had done a fine job in analyzing the pollutants of Ifri Gotal. The weapon, it seemed, had essentially been a small fu-sion device of a type once known as an "enhanced radiation" or "neutron" bomb. Manufactured by several nation-states in the late twentieth and early twenty-first centuries, these bombs were intended to stop armored vehicles on the battlefield by killing their occupants. Essentially, they destroyed people rather than property—which, John supposed, explained why so many vehicles and possessions had survived at Ifri Gotal.

The explosion would have been like a tiny sun, pouring out deadly rain. Under what the engineer described as "ideal conditions," this type of bomb should have left behind relatively few long-term radioactive contaminants. This device, presumably, had been less than ideal; bought third-hand on the then-rampant nuclear weapons black market, or furtively constructed from stolen components. It was also likely, the engineer acknowledged in a chilling afterthought, that the area had then been deliberately seeded with additional contaminants to ensure that anyone else who tried to pass that way would die. John stared down at his screen, trying to imagine the state of mind of the person who had issued these orders to block the migrations from the weather-ravaged south.

The meeting was nearing an end, and Cal Edmead, the chairman, was now summing things up. He at least still came in person, and, as the governor's deputy, was in a position of some power—if he chose to use it.

"Obviously," Edmead was saying, "I can't sanction any attempt to ban the trade in the koiyl leaf, even if that were possible. Imagine what it would be like if we decided to ban tubes and alcohol in the Zone."

Laughter rippled down the table; the thought was genuinely comic.

"The success of the new kelpbeds at Medersa," he continued, keeping his hands apart in a composed gesture of honesty, challenging anyone, John thought, to doubt the intensity of his interest, "is still in the balance. In the long run it will save far more lives than a minor—although admittedly dangerous—pollutant will ever threaten. Of course, that doesn't mean that we should simply let the matter rest. Though it is still by no means clear that a link exists between the koiyl and this blood cancer. Some cases in the reports that Father John here has kindly provided—the, ah, boy, for example—"

"You mean Daudi?"

"Yes. There was no trace of abnormally high levels of strontium 90 in his body. You say that his father chews the leaf, but it's unlikely, isn't it, for an illness such as cancer to be communicated via a father's sperm?"

"That case may not fit into the pattern and may have occurred for other reasons," John acknowledged. He glanced over at the screen from which Tim Purdoe had made himself available by telepresence, at least for the first two meetings. It was now gray.

"As you say, Father. These things are possible, but they require further study. Now…"

John sat back. Eventually the meeting rambled to an end. Further study is required—is essential—but for now, of course, nothing must be said outside this room or on unsecured portions of the net. The matter is clearly sensitive, classified, to be kept within the Zone…

"These," John said, lifting his folder as the telepresences started to wink off, one by one, "are koiyl leaves from Lall, bought this morning on the streets of the Endless City." He shook out a dozen onto the table. "It's strange, really, that we've got this far without any of you actually seeing them."

He could feel a slight shifting away of bodies. The leaves looked black and shriveled in the clinical light of this room. Poor specimens, he had to admit.

"Here." He took one and held it out. "Have one each. There should be enough to go around..." The committee members seemed reluctant to touch the leaves; only Cal Edmead picked one up and kept it in his hand. The other leaves were stared and prodded at but remained scattered on the table—as though these people feared a link with the disease that they spent so many meetings trying to deny. John could smell the leaves, withered though they were. Clear and astringent over the odor of midmeeting coffee and tired sweat.

"I don't plan," he said, "to let this matter rest. It's probably unrealistic to expect the Zone to do much—you're right about that, Cal. But it's the Borderers who are at risk. I have to get the message through to them."

"I think," Edmead said, "that you need some kind of strategy first, Father. And more data to confirm the problem exists. Isn't that what we've established?"

The secretary bleeped. One or two heads nodded around the table.

"Nevertheless," John said, "I'm prepared to deal with this directly."

"With whom?"

"I have my contacts."

There was a pause. Someone coughed. *Contacts.* The word seemed to expand and float away from him on the scent of the leaves.

"That has to be your decision, Father," Edmead said. "And you act on your own authority. I still think that this phenomenon needs to be understood first. The minutes, of course, will show that that is the decision of this meeting."

Edmead pocketed a leaf and patted his cards and papers into place. It was the signal for other people to stand up and move away, for the few screens that were still active to darken.

John heard someone mutter *contacts*...He looked around. Smiles were exchanged and eyes were averted in an odd, frozen pantomime as his gaze swept the room. He sat there for some time after they had all gone, breathing the fresh tarry scent that came up from the leaves before him on the table.

When he reached the black-windowed block, Laurie was already walking towards him across the worn patch of lawn. They took a tram to the edge of the Zone, then stopped a taxi. She didn't even ask where he wanted to go; she sensed his mood. The place she'd found for them, beyond the shockwire, was accustomed to a mix of expats and business-chasing Borderers; it was virtually empty today. Their table was flicked for dust, and a chemlight was ignited to compensate for the dimness.

He looked up at the domed roof. Someone had once painted stars on it, and the glint of their gold caught as the chemlight brightened. The food came, but remained untouched. Laurie watched him.

"You haven't told me about the meeting."

"I got nowhere."

"You hate meetings—organizations, formal occasions, dressing up. You're perverse, do you know that?"

He lifted his glass. It was a small tumbler scoured to translucence by years of washing, but the fluid made it clear again.

He sipped. The drink was sweet and strong—not just alcohol. He'd be fuzzy-headed this afternoon if he didn't eat.

"I tried showing them the leaves. I put some on the table, and they pulled back as if the leaves were turds. There was only one vendor I could find this morning who claimed to have any leaves from Lall. They were lousy specimens. The bottom of the sack. How's that for luck? I doubt if even...if anyone would want to chew them. I left the leaves, anyway, in the meeting room, there on the table."

"Why do you expect quick results?" she said. "You've made a discovery—that's the easy part. What will happen now is the real test."

"I need to work out how the leaf is distributed. The vendors will talk to me—but they won't talk about that."

"You could follow them."

"At the end of the day they just go back home. You don't know, do you?"

"Know what?"

"Where the leaf is stored, who sells it to whom."

"This is a big city. Do *you* know what they do with the crops in Hemhill?"

"There's a compound at the end of the valley. I used to—"

"And then? Do you know what happens then?"

"No, of course I don't. Why can't we just..."

"Just what?"

The wind was moaning outside, rattling the door. It banged open on its hinges and brought in the roar of a passing taxi, the hiss of sand. The waiter came and pushed the door shut, wedging a chair against it.

Laurie took John's hand. The pressure was soft, insistent, but he knew that if he didn't reply to her question, she'd let go.

He continued. "At the end of the meeting, I said something about using Borderer contacts. And it was obvious from the way they reacted that they knew about..." He paused, still looking, after all these weeks, for another, less stupid, phrase. "About us."

She let go of his hand. "Didn't you expect that?"

"But it gives them an excuse to ignore what I'm saying—makes me just another priest who's gone odd."

The food sat untouched between them. He knew it hadn't been the right thing to say, but it was true.

"I'm sorry," she said.

"Yes." He nodded.

"What about tonight, John? Do you still plan to stay?"

"If they all know anyway," he said, "what difference does it make?"

After dark they left the Zone again, this time in Laurie's van. John felt a sense of release as the shockwire faded behind them. They swung out across the huge junction east of the Zone, where the headlights of massive trucks heading for the processing mills poured though the grit and mist, picking out cyclists, taxis, herds of goats, and thrusting them back swirling through the shadows. John marveled at the way everything seemed to move and slot in. Edmead had been right that the Endless City was a delicate mechanism. At least he knew enough to understand that.

Laurie smoked a tube. A fallen gantry went by. A bleeding, moaning, three-legged calf stumbled out of the gloom, almost too quick to be believed. John reached for another tube from her pack, curious. It was red tonight, as far as he could tell. He broke the seal and inhaled. His eyeballs seemed to shrivel. The columns of smoke that were balanced above the coolers and chimneys rippled against the shifting lights. He saw dragons over the Endless City, a horse's head, the giant healing arms of a doctor...

The streets turned downhill and narrowed. It was part of the game for him not to ask her where they were going—but wasn't that a minaret he saw above the houses? And, improbably, the long building to the right seemed to be coated with quivering leaves of vine.

The headlights skittered over the slats of a ramp, and Laurie stopped the van. There was nothing but darkness on all sides now.

"Is this it?"

She turned off the engine. The headlights disappeared. He guessed that they were out on the dry tidal flats beyond the kelpbeds. It smelled that way.

"Listen," she said. "What do you hear?"

"Nothing." Only the ticking of the cooling engine. Laurie breathing beside him. The wind.

She said, "That's okay then," moving across the duct in the middle of the van that separated them. *"Bona..."*

Her mouth had a flat taste that reminded him of European rain. Or perhaps he was just mixing his memories. And as she lifted her shirt over her head and peeled off his gloves, he wondered if she seriously planned to make love out here when they had the whole night and the cool sheets of her bungalow waiting for them back in the Zone. But she pressed against him, and his hand reached for the seat adjuster, trying to pull it back while at the same time helping her to roll his trousers back from his thighs. The hot wind blew through the window onto his skin. He heard her murmur *just concentrate.*

His erection bobbed up, and she slid down and took him in her mouth, holding him there in the van with her fingers clenched over his buttocks until he arched his back and came.

They were driving again, fully dressed, when Laurie suddenly said, "I have to stop."

"Again?"

But her voice was choked, and she opened the door and tumbled out even before the van's skirts had settled, and leaned with her head bowed and both hands pressed against a mossy wall beside them. He stared out through the windshield at the amber eyes of a slinking dog caught in the headlights, and heard the splatter of her vomit.

She climbed back into the van, wiping her mouth, pulling the door shut.

"Okay now?"

She nodded, looking ahead, her hands pressed on the wheel, the long tips of her fingers extended. "I'm all right."

"I wasn't—" he began.

"Forget it."

"But it was me, wasn't it? The viruses?"

"It's no big thing, John. I mean, really...But I still don't feel that great, to be honest. Perhaps we should just go back to the Zone."

She turned up the fans and drove on. The dog darted away. John sat in silence, remembering how she'd always climbed out of bed to wash herself after they made love. Even on their second night in that grubby room in Sadiir, she'd gone off somewhere looking for water. What did he know? He'd thought it was just some womanly habit. And hearing the splash of the taps in the bathroom on afternoons in her bungalow, seeing her nose and eyes red that morning after the governor's party...

She said, "You're not going to feel guilty about this, are you? It's only a minor reaction."

"I seems a pity that two people..."

"We'll get used to each other. It'll go away. Or I could ask for an increased dose of lydrin. That might work."

"But they'd know then, wouldn't they? If you had to ask."

He kept his eyes on the road, but he could feel her gaze.

"That bothers you?"

"No," he said. They were crossing the space of clean concrete towards the waiting guards and the Zone's heat-glimmering shockwire. "No."

Late that night in the bungalow, he slipped quietly out of bed and showered with the door shut. Laurie had dumped a towel on the toilet seat when she'd gone in earlier, and he saw that it was streaked with a dilution of her blood, his semen. He washed and used the fans in the shower, then tossed the towels into the chute, where they would be collected, cleaned, and redelivered by a Borderer maid. This whole place was like a vast hotel— no wonder people talked. They'd made love only once here in the bungalow, although Laurie had felt better by then and it had lasted long enough. He'd done the things she'd wanted him to do, pretending he was in the mood to be detached, interested only in her pleasure.

He pulled on his teeshirt. More lydrin. A new, bigger, implant. Or how about condoms? After all, he had a supply of those at the clinic. They were asked for only by hypochondriacs who feared diseases that had long since found less avoidable ways of jumping bodies; but the Church still insisted on providing the things, in vague atonement of some long-forgotten sin. He remembered now that there was a phrase for a boosted lydrin implant. Tim Purdoe had once used it in joking disparagement of something or other: a whore's muscle. Why had he forgotten that?

He stepped back into the bedroom, where Laurie lay. He loved her most this way, perfected in sleep, loved her with a deep Pentecostal fire that still awoke to reassure him that, between them, there was still everything to be gained. The sheet half-covered her shoulder, and one gracefully arched foot stuck out. She looked so old, so ageless, so young. He could see the dent that his body—almost impossibly, it now seemed to him—had made when he lay beside her, the way her arm now reached to try to close around it. Was she really still asleep? He bent over, but her eyelids were smooth and untroubled. No dreams, even. He tried to imagine her opening them, and the green of her eyes becoming true silver, and his not being a priest; nothing but love lying between them...

He picked up the rest of his clothes and went into the lounge to finish dressing. Bits of crumb and lint stuck to his feet. On the table beneath the screen, half obscured by drifts of Laurie-rubble, were some of the cards about the koiyl that he'd lent her before they went to Lall.

He picked one up, feeling nostalgia for the times of diligent search and the putting of pieces together. Since Martínez, he hadn't come across a new case of leukemia. Everything else: the torn flesh of dreadful accidents, burrowing parasites, fatal pneumonia. But people were still at risk from it—and dying—he had to remember that. He couldn't give up. The hazy stars on Laurie's screen glided or darted or didn't move, according to the whim of whatever program she was running.

He needed, he supposed, to start the process of unearthing the sale and distribution of the leaf. Easy enough in theory. If you weren't a European—and if it was really possible for anyone to know and understand the Endless City. He watched as the stars floated in their invisible matrix. One larger star hung center-screen, a pale sun around which the others orbited. It pulsed to some slow, cyclical pattern as he watched. A breathing star. The effect was soothing. It was a fuzzy mandala—drawing in, out. He breathed in, and saw it expand...

"Busy?"

He turned. Laurie stood in her dressing gown, yawning, pushing a hand back through her sleep-messed hair.

"I was trying to work out what to do about the leaf. The trouble is, the discussions in my head sound too much like what I hear in the Zone."

She muttered something, then put her hands into her pockets and leaned forward. From the corner of his eye, he saw the fuzzy stars dissolve from the screen. She flopped down on the sofa. Her dressing gown fell from her pale brown knees. She tugged it back over them.

He said, "I see you've kept those cards."

"I thought they were spares. Was that a problem? You can have them back."

"Have you copied them?"

She shrugged. "I can't remember." She pointed at the screen. "Put them in there if you want to find out what I've done."

"No. It's fine. It's fine..."

"Not that you don't trust me? Right?"

They stared at each other for a moment, then both looked away.

On the trip back from the Zone, he told the taxi driver to stop every time he saw a koiyl vendor. Some vendors, remembering John from the purchases he'd made the day before, called and waved. They were old men generally, with the big-mouthed wicker baskets they slung over their shoulders when they moved their wares. Close up, it was clear that most of them weren't users themselves; the dust that surrounded them wasn't sodden with red spittle, their teeth and gums weren't stained. John wiped his coins with dysol, handed them over, and took the first leaves that were offered. Not exactly a random sample, but it would have to do. It was late in the afternoon but still hot. As he climbed in and out of the taxi and trudged up alleys and across streets, the wind-driven grit seemed to stick more than usual under the sweat of his clothes. The last vendor he stopped for—younger than the rest, and with a fold-out tray set in the shelter of an arch—spoke comprehensible European.

"This is good," John said. The leaves were the best he'd been offered. Plumper, and without the hard leathery skin that signified age. He bit a corner off the one he'd been offered and smiled to indicate his pleasure as his mouth flooded with odd, slippery saliva. This, he realized, was the first dried leaf he'd actually chewed. It was tougher and sweeter than the fresh one at Lall. "Can you get me more?"

"More?" The vendor smiled. He had a crescent-shaped mark on his cheek that could have been either cosmetic or a birthmark. There had to be at least fifty more leaves in the trays.

"More this?" He gestured. Above them, shutters swung back from the houses in the street. A caroni bird settled on a gutter to preen itself.

"Yes, I want to take more with me, back across the water…" John was talking with a lisp. A scrap of koiyl seemed to have wedged in the roof of his mouth. It was about this time, he supposed, that you were supposed to spit out the remains.

"I get you more, Fatoo. How many? Hundred?"

"Could you show me where you get them from? Your supply?" he asked, thinking, *clumsy, clumsy*—this isn't the way.

"Supply?" The man gestured amazement. "This is my…" He looked up and around, searching for a word that was probably livelihood. John swallowed the lump of koiyl, waved *tak*, and, feeling suddenly cooler and light-headed, went back to the waiting taxi.

He told the driver to go to Rani Avenue, where Kassi Moss lived. She hadn't been to church for weeks, and he'd missed her twice now at the Cresta Motel; he was starting to worry. He'd never been to Kassi's home before, although he'd discovered that she lived only up the hill from the presbytery. She must have seen him cycle by, must have walked the same streets beyond the steps leading to the little covered market, yet she had never mentioned it to him or thought to invite him in.

He rang a prosaic-sounding doorbell on the ground floor, where mold hung from the ceiling and the discords of animal cries and argument and music came from the rooms around and the floors above. Outside, he'd seen patched and empty windows, cracked masonry, stains from broken outflows. A typical Borderer tenement, in fact, but it all seemed so chaotic and unlike Kassi, that he was convinced by the time the door opened that it wouldn't be she and he'd have to apologize to some shocked Borderer and say it was a mistake. He heard the shuffle of footsteps, coughing, a voice, the sound of something being knocked over. It was Kassi.

Unsmiling but unsurprised, she invited him in and bumbled around her home, trying to offer him something, not sure what he might want—what it was safe to offer a European. And yes, she'd missed a few days at the motel. She'd been *sumfo*. The translat was off, but he knew the word well enough from the clinic. It meant a mild chill—nothing. Then Kassi looked at him, her face half fearful, half challenging. He realized she thought he'd come here to remonstrate with her for missing Mass, and he found himself looking around at the plates and pictures she had hung on the walls; searching for a crucifix although there didn't seem to be one, or a bible or a rosary or any of the other religious impedimenta that filled the Cresta Motel. He thought it was unchristian of him to suddenly doubt her motives. And he wondered, for the first time, where the half of the funding that Halcycon didn't supply for the Cresta Motel came from.

Leaving Kassi, taking the taxi to the presbytery, he backed in through the door with his supply of koiyl in his arms and climbed the stairs past patches of mold and fallen plaster. At the turn where the mirror was, he dropped several of the leaves. As they tumbled over the hallway tiles, the fall activated the cheap cards he'd stuck on each, and a chorus of his own voices began describing vendors, impressions, locations. Bella emerged from one of the barely used ground-floor rooms. She stood watching with her arms folded for a moment, then nodded to herself and came over to help him pick them up.

She followed him up the stairs into the greater heat of the occupied floors with her share of the leaves cupped in her hands. In his room, John dumped his burden on the bed, and Bella followed suit before backing off, pinching her facemask higher with her gloved hands.

"Bella," he asked, "do you know where these leaves are stored? Who sells them to the vendors?"

She shook her head. "But my mother." She nodded at the leaves. "She have that smell. *Judia ee madre* . . . It make me think of her."

Bella was an orphan; her parents must have died—when? When she was young, left with memories of the koiyl smell her mother gave off. And her mother had died of what—*bludrut*, leukemia? Should he ask? Did he really need more proof? Was he starting to doubt the link? He sat down on the bed with the leaves scattered around him. Even though the windows were open, it was unbearably hot in here. A rich, soapy, sweet-sharp smell was rising from the leaves. He gazed at them, thinking of the cold gray of the Northern Mountains, the shimmer of the flowers, Hettie pressing ahead, Laurie beside him. He peeled off his gloves to touch them, and a chilly, ill-smelling wave rose off his skin. Bella stepped back into the doorway. He'd showered only a few hours ago at Laurie's bungalow, yet already he felt soiled.

"Fatoo want anything else?"

"Yes, can you run me a bath?"

She hesitated for a moment, then nodded and went away. A few minutes later, the pipes that threaded the house began to clang and rattle.

The hiss of the tank. The smell of dysol and damp wood.

John inhaled deeply and pushed his head back under the

water. His ears boomed. He could feel the rough, age-corroded enamel of the bath, but otherwise he could have been anywhere now, anyone...

He sat up, feeling the slide of water and the Magulf wind that came in through the window. The wind pushed away the steam, threw a film of silken dust over the tall mirror and the cracked marble washstand, which Bella had doubtless just wiped, and popped the bubbles on the water. He heard the cry of voices, pumps hammering, vanes creaking, and the tapping of the pipes. Louder than ever. Thump, pause, thump. Not the pipes at all, but Felipe's footsteps.

"There you are." The door swung open. "You're never where I expect you to be these days." Felipe hobbled to the middle of the room, glanced around, then reached to drag out the wicker chair that had been pushed beneath the washstand. "You're back, anyway. You had a good night in the Zone?"

"Yes." John sat up. "Let me—"

"No, no. You think I can't manage? After all the practice I've had?" With a cripple's way of making simple tasks appear alien, Felipe dragged the chair over to the window and slumped down. With the aid of his walking stick he pulled his feet up to rest on the ledge.

"There..." He sighed.

The tap dripped. Down Gran Vía in the west, shrouded by clouds yet shining crimson on Felipe's face, the Magulf sun was setting.

"This is always an odd time of year," the old priest said, gazing out. "And a little sad to me. I mean now, before the weather breaks...By autumn, it's always too late, isn't it?" He looked over at John, his face glowing. "But then, you and I, we're victims of the term-culture, aren't we? The academic and ecclesiastical year..."

John nodded. Felipe hadn't made the effort to come up these stairs to talk about the time of year. But he knew it was best to keep quiet and wait.

"Do you remember," Felipe was saying, chuckling, his stained teeth glinting between the red folds of his lips, "the orders and the rituals of spring?"

As the water cooled, the room darkened, and the hissing of the tank and the pipes finally stilled. Felipe spoke of the passing of the night vigil, the forty-hours' devotion, white smocks and candlelight, the sun coming up over the hills and the sharing of warm new bread, the greening land reborn...

"It all seems so distant now," he said, "and clearer with the distance."

"Do you think you'll ever leave the Endless City?" John asked.

"No, my son." By now, Felipe was just a shape against a window. "I imagine, anyway, that there would be problems with all these fancy wires inside me. I'm too old—and I've stayed too long. You can't just chop and change. Besides, I love to sit at these windows and look out. To listen. My eyes, I think, are failing me. But these ears... I wouldn't be without these ears. Listen, what do you hear?"

John shrugged. The chill water lapped. The wind, of course. The creak of a cart. The hiccuping generator that served the flats opposite and always sounded as if it was about to fail.

"Somewhere over there, across the street and down that way..." Felipe pointed his stick out at the dusk. "...towards Alcalá, a woman is cooing to her child. And closer, an old man sits talking, ignored by his family as they chatter and eat dinner.

And music is playing, of course. Music is always playing. And I can hear the bats now, wheeling and clicking. I can hear the crunch as their jaws meet their prey. I can hear the creak of bedsprings, John, and the sounds of love...The marvelous thing about these ears is that they filter, they analyze, they separate, yet for all that, they never judge. I love them for that, John. They take life as it is, they do not judge." He slowly shifted his legs off the window ledge. "You must be cold in there by now, my son. Bella tells me that you've been collecting leaves."

"The koiyl."

"Ah, yes. I remember now." Felipe lifted himself up from the chair. His breath became ragged for a moment. "The reason you went up to the mountains with that girl."

"Laurie."

"Laurie. You know," Felipe said, hobbling across the room, standing before him, "I almost forgot why I came up here." Leaning with one hand on his walking stick, he began to pat and feel his pockets with the other. Blisterpacks crackled. A flask clinked. "This arrived...Oh, when you were out this afternoon. Came through on the airwave, from Paris."

John took the card, his fingers dribbling. "From Paris," it whispered in confirmation. It was embossed with the bishop's gold seal, which already seemed to tell him all that he needed to know. But he touched the seal anyway and watched as it dissolved into the bishop's gray and kindly features.

"John," the bishop said, looking out at him from beneath a tree in a garden with the sigh of traffic in the distance, "I'd like you to come back here for a few days. Just for a word, you understand..."

LAURIE CAME TO the presbytery in her van to take John to catch the morning shuttle, and Felipe managed—as he always did when he actually wanted to—to get himself down the final flight of stairs unaided. He smiled and nodded, asking her what part of the city she was from, if she knew so-and-so, who used to work the net. He seemed genuinely pleased to see her. Standing in the hallway, dressed in boots and a smock, with a silver bracelet jingling at her wrist as she played with the vancard, Laurie smiled at Felipe and tilted her head and said yes, no, she might have heard...They would probably have stood around and talked for longer, but John already had his bag in his hand and was in too much of a hurry. He sat beside Laurie as she drove him towards the Zone through the morning-crowded streets, unsuccessfully willing himself and everything else to slow down.

They passed through the shockwire and on to the great gray buildings along the shore, where the van was taken over by the net and guided towards the concourse along with all the rest. He realized, when they were walking inside, that he'd be unable to kiss her good-bye in this public place.

She asked, "You *will* come back?"

"Yes—of course I'll come back. The bishop's not..." The air at the Bab Mensor shuttleport hummed with music and announcements. This was suddenly too much like a rehearsal for a more permanent parting. "I don't even know..."

"No."

A couple beside them were embracing, arms and bodies entwined, mouths crushed together. John looked away, down at the shining tiles of the concourse, then up again at Laurie. The wind had got to her hair when they crossed from the carpark, and a strand of it still clung to the corner of her mouth. He wanted to reach and brush it away.

"I'll call," he said.

"No, don't call. Just think."

"Anyway. I'll be back soon enough. A few days."

"Yes."

She stood watching him as he walked off amid the steel walkways and scurrying trolleys, holding up her hand to wave as he looked back a last time.

Just think. There was a party atmosphere on board the shuttle; most of the other passengers were expat workers leaving the Magulf for good. Cheers filled the long wide cabin as soon as the *Halcycon Phoenix* lifted from the Breathless Ocean. Hipflasks and tubes were passed along the aisles.

The shuttle climbed. Even the clouds faded. The sky deepened, and the moon and stars came out. For a timeless moment the cabin quieted as a marbled curve of sea and land and sky rolled far beneath them, then the *Halcycon Phoenix* began to dip. The thin air outside brightened. Glasses clinked, smoke drifted; you could get high just by breathing. The screen in front of John said the weather was good in Paris. By noon, the temperature was expected to rise to 27°, but with a refreshing easterly breeze. Just touch the middle cursor to get a fuller flavor...

"Going home, Father?"

John smiled at his neighbor and shook his head.

The Seine shuttleport was much like all European shuttleports. The foline tugs were automated, the moving walkways were covered over with views of the wide river, and the rolling countryside was dimmed behind layers of glass. It was only when he was outside, climbing into a taxi waiting under plane trees in the bright air, that the overwhelming strangeness of being back in Europe began to hit home. It was eleven o'clock, and his appointment with the bishop at St. Georges wasn't until two. He told the taxi to take him north along the river.

With the windows down, the breeze in his face was moist, smelling of clean wet soil, the river, vegetation. This close to the city, most of the countryside was semirecreational, with ornamentally small fields, brownstone farmhouses that had scattered hencoops and white geese, patches of woodland, gray-green rows of asparagus, market-garden strawberries, and dwarfish sheep and cattle.

The taxi crossed the Seine and passed into the ruined outer

suburbs. The vehicles on this new road scurried along between acres of fallen roofs and gables teetering under vine. The air smelled green. After the uncontrolled ravages of the weather, it had been easier to start anew rather than attempt to make the old roads and buildings fit the new demands of life. Many towns and cities were left to crumble back into the arms of nature; most Europeans now lived in the new villages such as Hemhill, servicing the various green industries that had replaced the gray ones. But London and Brussels and Paris—their centers, anyway—had been restored and saved.

A huge circle of parkland had been cleared around the inner-city area. There were gravel paths, bridges and streams, distant green hills. The lawns gave way to streets, tall elegant houses with dormer windows raised like questioning eyebrows. Rejoining the course of the Seine, passing fruitmarkets and hotels, John reached the Left Bank. In the absence of any further instructions, the taxi stopped on the wide avenue of the Boulevard St. Michel. He made to get out, but the door stayed shut and the taxi bleeped at him for the fare. He remembered to produce his personal card instead of cash, then searched his pockets for a dysol cloth to wipe it with.

As John sat and drank coffee at a pavement café, breathing the warm fresh air, time seemed to hang on one moment, then jump forward by an hour. He drummed his fingers on the tin table, still hardly able to believe he was here. Checking his watch again, he paid the European waitress the huge sum she'd asked for the coffee, quickly jerking back his hand as the tips of her fingers brushed his palm. Then he wandered amid the strutting pigeons, past the buildings, the striped awnings, the wrought-iron balconies adorned with potted plants and draped with washing. The silver-eyed people here were busy, happy, chatting, making the most of this predictably glorious summer day. Hurrying elbows brushed his own. It was strange, the way no one made way for him.

In the Luxembourg Gardens children played amid statues and fountains, and couples wandered hand in hand, flaunting their togetherness. Many nodded and smiled at John; showing the respect due to that familiar figure, the priest. From across the Rue de Vaugirard, church bells began to shiver the air. There were other spires and domes in the farther distance, rising over the trees at the soft edge of the sky.

Don't call—just think.

John sat down on a bench and covered his eyes.

St. Georges was a large seminary on the northern outskirts of Paris, built of brown brick in the heavy Gothic style that characterized the Second Empire. Climbing the tiled steps from the road at precisely ten to two, he was instantly struck by the smell of polish and incense, and by the same undertow of priestly aromas that even the Pandera presbytery harbored. Stone figures of saints and industrialists stared down from the echoing walls of the vestibule. He'd never been here before—his previous meetings with the bishop had always taken place in Rome or at the Millbrooke Seminary—but crossing the wide half-lit space towards the nun seated by the stairway, and despite everything, he found that he felt at home.

The nun smiled and slid across the counter a finger-smeared screen to show him the way to the bishop's office. He nodded thanks. Left down the gleaming corridor, past the refectory door, the clatter of cutlery, the rumble of voices, the floury smell of communal food. The bishop's door was half open, and she looked up from her desk before John had a chance to knock, was instantly up and taking his bag, urging him to sit down. She was dressed in a formal white gown, with a gold cross over her heart and a gold band in her graying hair.

"You look well, John. A little tired, if I may say so. But well."

"I'm fine."

"And Felipe?"

"He's bearing up."

She smiled. "Bearing up. I think that's how he likes it..." She was still standing beside her desk. Her hands clasped, unclasped. The white robe sighed and shifted. "Would you like something to drink? Tea, coffee?" She nodded towards the crystal decanter and glasses on the sidetable by the fireplace. "Anything weaker, stronger?"

"Thanks. I'm fine."

"Well..."

She drew in a breath. They looked at each other. John realized how little thought he'd given to this meeting.

"I read something this morning, John, and it set me thinking, knowing that you were coming. About the religious impulse being tied to the sky. The stars, the sun, the moon. Had we remained cavedwellers, we might never have found God."

John nodded, remembering the silence that had filled the shuttle as it rose into the troposphere. A breeze blew through the mullioned window into the bishop's office, lifting the edges of the cards and papers that were weighted by a sea-smoothed granite rock on her desk. He said, "I miss the stars."

"And I still miss the clouds," she said, alluding to her own missionary years in the Endless City, far east from the Magulf, in Mizraim, at the rim of the black mires where the Nile once flowed. "In my dreams, John, I'm always back in those tight, winding streets." The bishop clasped her hands again and shivered slightly. "But look outside, John. It's a lovely day. Even here, the sun is precious, something we should never take for granted." She held out a hand. He took hold of it. It felt light and hot, like a bird's. "Come. Let's walk in the gardens."

They went out and along the corridor, through a doorway into the rose-scented cloisters, where sunlight poured through the archways and the shadows between were deep and intense.

"And how are things at the clinic?"

"I manage well enough, Mother. I have the usual problems. An out-of-date doctor. Lack of supplies. Fortunately, I get some help from the Zone's CMO. He bends the rules a little, gives me advice and the few medicines he can slip through the system."

"I see." The bishop nodded, her hands now behind her, bony shoulders arched, fingers twining, untwining. She asked John about Bella; about the state, physical and spiritual, of the church. He walked beside her, answering each question, giving out nothing more. He admired this woman. He felt that she deserved his honesty. Still, he knew he was involved in some kind of negotiation—and as yet he wasn't sure of the terms. Was this summons really about Laurie? Perhaps he'd got it all wrong. Was it about the koiyl? She'd read, it seemed, his reports on the net...

"John, do you know how the leaf is dried once it reaches the Magulf?"

"There's talk of a place a few kilometers down Gran Vía, but the people are very secretive. The koiyl seems to disappear at the end of the growing season after it's taken from Tiir. Then it reappears on the streets. I suppose that's a way of controlling availability."

"A leaf probably won't keep unless it's properly cured, John. And that's not likely to be an easy process. More than just a question of hanging the things in the sun—if there were any sun. It will probably need moist conditions, or else it will powder and crack..."

"Was koiyl grown in Mizraim, so far east?"

"Not exactly, but there were parallels. The growing and smoking of the leaf of the tobacco plant—you've heard of tobacco? A venerable tradition. It was a habit, in fact, that I acquired while I was in Mizraim and then found hard to shake off. Like koiyl, it can be chewed as well as smoked. Do people smoke the koiyl leaf?"

"I've never seen it."

"Tobacco is also a dangerous substance, like koiyl. Cancer-causing, in fact, although for different reasons."

John nodded. He knew that tobacco was a kind of low-tech predecessor to the tubes that Laurie used. Though it was only mildly addictive, it had remained popular long after the harm it caused was established.

From the cloisters they passed into the gardens of stately trees and wide lawns. Walled in from the streets around it, St. Georges was much bigger than the map John had called up in the taxi suggested. There was a small lake with tame carp nosing the surface as they walked by. The bishop stooped to stroke a scaled golden head. The fish's wise, unblinking eyes gazed at them.

"I could walk around these gardens all day," she said. "I keep them as my direct responsibility. This green loveliness—

I admit it's become an obsession. New flowerbeds, new arrangements, little changes I've made. But, then, I suppose I need the escape. I have to spend hours, *days* pleading at meetings and on the net to raise money and awareness for projects in the Endless City. What to you, John, seems so sparse and grudging out there in the Magulf becomes a huge effort here. A rock that I must continually roll uphill if the work of places like your church and clinic are to continue."

They walked on across a circular lawn surrounded by trellises of nodding sweet pea.

"I look in eyes of the people I have to meet, John, and I often see the same conflict. They know that they should do, give, feel, more. But they try to shift, to look away, to find an excuse, an escape. Yes—I hear it said and I see it unsaid—we should help them, these godless Gogs. But shouldn't they also help themselves? Why must *we* always contribute and organize? Aren't we doing more harm than good? It's an ancient and inherently feeble argument, of course, and those of us who work to bring healing must try not to condemn, but we must also make sure that we do nothing that fosters that attitude. If we who bring aid seem compromised, if people can point at us and shake their heads, my task of generating money and interest becomes that much more difficult . . ."

They had stopped walking and now stood at the edge of a copse of trees. The bishop was right, of course. Any excuse: a design fault in a kelpbed, a priest who proclaimed one thing but did another. It offered people a way out.

"You've heard," John said, "that I'm sleeping with a Borderer woman?"

"Not quite that much," the bishop said, "but enough to feel

and pray of you. And to care and wonder." Like ripples trapped on green water, the sun danced through the branches overhead. She was tearing, John saw, at a leaf. "How is it, John? What is it?"

"I don't know," he said. "I don't know."

They walked on in the shade of the trees.

"Do you love her? Tell me about her. She must be special."

He told her about Chott, Drezzar, about Laurie's mother working in Europe. He told her about Laurie's bungalow and the net, about how she had to eat out at lunchtime because people where she worked spat in her coffee. The bishop was smiling at him now. For her, the moment of crisis was over, and her hands were calm again, clasped across her golden cross and white robe. The breeze caught a strand of silver hair, pushing it over her cheek.

She turned and began to walk. The trees shifted and played behind them. "God really does work in mysterious ways, John. Even now. Perhaps more now."

"I still have doubts about God, Mother, if that's what you mean."

"But perhaps the priesthood really isn't for you, John. I suppose you've thought of that...? Of course. Stupid of me. The breaking of a vow is sometimes just the way that leads out from the vocation to another role in life. At the end of the day, whether you continue within or outside the priesthood isn't important. You shouldn't turn your back on what's true to you."

"I just wish I knew what that was."

"You want to return to your work in the Magulf, yes? To see Laurie? Felipe? To do something about this leaf?"

"Yes."

She stopped again and turned to him. "Did you think I might refuse you that?"

"It had crossed my mind, Mother. Laurie and I will have to—"

"At the very least, be more discreet," she said. She took his arm and drew him on. Their feet sunk into the turf. "But you know my position. Hateful though it is, I do have to pay attention to appearances. You have—what?—less than three months left in the Magulf now, John. I'll give you that time. And trust you to use your own faith and judgment."

"Yes. I understand."

Her hand squeezed his arm. "*Don't* tell me you understand, John." The hand kept its grip on him. The bishop was bent over now, and her breathing was audible. The short walk had tired her. "Remember Bunyan's Pilgrim, called to return home by his wife and children but stuffing his fingers in his ears and running on and away, shouting about Salvation? I always thought how foolish that was, yet I imagined that one day I'd understand what Bunyan meant. I still don't, and I don't know if I'd live again this life I've chosen, John. God can wait for us—He has all eternity."

They turned back along a lavender-edged gravel border towards the sun-warmed brick expanse of St. Georges.

"You'll stay the night?"

"If that's possible."

"And then tomorrow I'd like you to do something else for me?" He looked at her. The hand clasped tighter. "John, it's not a demand or a favor, it's something you should do for the sake of yourself. Will you go and see your parents? Will you go to your brother?"

"Time is—"

"Just a day or two. I think you owe yourself that. Do you know how your brother is?"

"I spoke to my parents." When? Longer ago than he'd realized. "He's okay. He's still alive."

"How old is he now?"

A gardener was busy weeding a bed of pinks. It looked like a small cleaner, except that there was dirt on its pincers and it smelled of manure. Someone had painted roses on its dome.

"Hal's thirty-nine."

"Go and see him, John. Go and see your parents. Then return to Laurie, and tell me after the autumn rains who you are and where you want to be."

He had to smile. "I can't promise to answer all that, Mother."

She chuckled too. Her side was pressed against him, and he could feel the weak flutter of her breathing. He helped her as they walked thorough the sunshine back along the path to her office.

It was odd to take dinner at a communal table. The high-beamed ceiling of the refectory was held up by wooden angels. Bare hands served him vegetable soup and pork and potatoes, fresh bread and cheese. He was asked how long he was staying; if, for real or on the net, he played golf or bridge; if he could sing baritone. There were one or two faces that he knew. Silver eyes everywhere. Overpowered, he chose to sit alone for evening Mass as light flooded the stained-glass apostles and the air was filled with the rumble of the organ, the singing of the choir. It was all sweetly nostalgic, distant, unreal.

Next morning at St. Georges, John was woken by sparrows twittering on his window ledge. Looking out across prim lawns still dewy and hazed with mist, he decided to leave before breakfast. He shaved, opened drawers, packed away his cassock, pocketed the fresh card that, at the bishop's request, Brother Charles in Accounts had given him. He walked along the empty corridors, past the paintings of Christ and Our Lady, past the rails of coat hooks and the chapels and the dorms and the frosted windows of the classrooms. He let himself out through the main doors and headed down the street.

He was surprised to find that even an air-conditioned Elysian was within reach of the funds that the bishop had authorized for him, but he chose a smaller and less-equipped Zephyr and in it called up Hemhill on the screen. The bubble-shaped car took some time to reply; it had probably never traveled beyond Paris. Still, there it was: an estimated ten hours' journey along the main autoroutes.

By now, Paris was busy with the things of morning. The cobbled streets were filled with dog walkers, bike riders, buzzing cleaners, joggers. The cafés were opening, the markets and squares blossoming with purposeful life. His stomach ached for breakfast, but he instructed the car to hurry out of the city and through parkland dappled with the sailing shadows of clouds, past the ruins, into the wide green farmland beyond. Towards Hemhill.

IT WAS EVENING by the time he drew close to Hemhill. As the sights grew more familiar, the last part of the journey seemed to slow and expand. The lights of one of the great agripedes sparkled like moonlight through the tall hedges, and he braked the car and buzzed down the window to let in the summer smells of ripening jelt and corn.

After the long journey, it was odd to make this switch to the real and the particular. He remembered how he'd once had dreams of what it would be like to return home from somewhere far off. The dreams were unspecific, but in them he'd always done something marvelous while he was away, and everyone he knew would be waiting. Hal was there at the front, shaking his head and smiling down at his little brother. *I'd never have believed it. Skiddle...*

He passed the big oak at the railinged edge of Hemhill's

small central park where, swift and exulting—at least until he looked down—he'd once climbed. The streets and the houses were variations on neatness, with names that changed occasionally to suit the whims of death, divorce, company moves, and the house market. Sixpenny House. Arden. Leaves flashed overhead, and the white gate of his parents' house swung open at his approach. He stopped the car and stepped out, blinking as the lights came on.

"That is you...?"

His mother's shadow stretched out from the doorstep. His father waited in silhouette behind.

"I was saying, wasn't I? That you might be back. I had this feeling."

She planted a dry kiss on his cheek and pulled him swiftly inside.

"Come. It's..."

Their hands and words floated around him. He went into the lounge, where they had new chairs. He sat on one. And a new carpet; some kind of material that managed to be soft and smooth yet was dustless so as not to irritate their lungs. New wallpaper, too. And a new card in the picture in the wall, which displayed an almost white landscape clothed in either moonlight or snow. His mother had already shot off to the kitchen, and his father sat facing him, hands clasped, elbows on his knees, leaning forward in his chair. There were age mottles on his father's face now, and the thinning gray hair was swept from a shining sweep of skin-covered bone. His cheeks sagged. He was nearly sixty.

"You look well."

"Thanks. You too, Dad."

"It's...Hmmm."

John smiled at the house cleaner as it swiveled into the room to pick up the tray of tea china that lay on a sidetable. He raised a hand to delay the command and draw it over. He placed his palm on the warm brass dome, stroking to the rough edge of the cpu plate that he and Hal had so often removed.

"Exactly how long," his father was asking, "will you be staying, John?" He blinked. "What I mean is..."

"What he means," his mother called from the kitchen, "is that you're welcome to stay as long as you like."

"Just two days," John said. Squeaking slightly, the cleaner rattled out of the room. "I was in Paris," he added. "The bishop agreed I should take a short rest before going back to the Magulf."

His father regarded him. It had gone quiet in the kitchen. Rest. Bishop. By that quick statement, John had intended to forestall further questions, but he'd rehearsed it too often in the car, and it now implied all the things he'd meant not to say.

"Did you get the soup?"

"Soup?"

"The soup I sent you, Son. When you called us, you asked for powdered soup."

"No," John said. His father would have questioned him about the flavors and the brand if he'd lied and said yes. "These things take time, Dad. But I'm sure it'll come through."

"Time. Of course." But his father looked pained.

John shifted in the new chair. It was huge. His fingers strayed to the screen on the arm. He touched it, and the cushions softened and his feet rose into the air.

His father, still unsmiling, said, "If you'd have known you were coming, John, you could have picked it up and taken it with you. I mean, the soup."

"Yes. If I had known, that would have been simpler."

His mother came in with dinner steaming on a tray. He'd already stopped and eaten in the late afternoon. Shaking the salt out over sausages, French toast, chips, and bacon—and with every possibility of pudding to follow—he realized that that had been a stupid thing to do.

"We thought you could go up and see Hal afterward," his mother said. She perched on the edge of a chair, her hands pressed into her lap.

When he finished eating, he placed the tray on the floor and snapped his fingers, and the three of them watched as the cleaner came in and picked it up. When it left the room, his mother's face relaxed a little into a smile. "Would you like to go up now?" She half-stood from the chair. "I mean, if you're..."

"Yes," he said. "I'm ready."

"How *is* Hal?" he asked her in the glare of the hall.

"John, he's the same. I have this now." She raised her arm, tugged at her sleeve, and held her left wrist to him, as though inviting him to sample a new perfume. "It saves me having to worry and hang around him quite so much. Pricks at my nerves like a little needle." He saw a silver implant entwined around the veins above her watch. A pulsing light. She made a face. "And *I* had to have it done, of course. Your father wouldn't."

"No."

"Anyway, off you go."

She watched him from the foot of the stairs, one hand resting on the banister, the tiny ruby light in her wrist still showing through the wool of her cardigan. The air was noticeably dimmer on the landing. Past the door into John's own room, which was slightly ajar, Hal's door along the landing was shut. John started when, as he reached for it, it swung open. Then came the tingle of the molecular barrier that had kept the outside air at bay ever since Hal's minor fungal infection—something so odd that even his net-enhanced viruses hadn't reacted—of a couple of years before. The lighting grew slowly from darkness to a dull glow. That and the soundproofing were innovations made in the years when there were still things to be done to this room that hadn't yet been tried. Comatose patients, his mother once read in the ancient and esoteric medical books she buried herself in, could be precipitated into fatal crisis by sudden lights and noises.

John pushed through the wall of slightly warmer, moister air. Even the presence of his own body seemed to gather in slow increments inside this increasingly isolated box. He paused, took a breath. He crossed the soft and slightly sticky surface of the material that now covered the floor to the bed where Hal lay. So much about the room had changed, yet so much remained the same. The desk where Hal had worked, the books and cards and games on the shelves. Yet it was all so neat now, the way it would have been if he'd finished cleaning up the detritus of his childhood that night and gone to London to study—what was it called?—structural communication.

"Hello, Hal."

Click, sigh. The faint pepperminty scent of whatever it was that was used to repurify the air.

Click, sigh.

"It's me. John. I'm back. In the flesh this time."

It was so quiet, he could hear his own heartbeat—and the subterranean hum of the transformer in the unit beside the bed that pulled the monitoring data through a direct link with the big thermonuclear torus at Leominster. Enough power, his father had once said, to run a bloody factory. And to light, John now thought, a fair portion of the Endless City. Still, they could afford it on their Halcycon pensions and the extra medical grants they'd been given. If his parents hadn't had all this expense, they might not have put their summerhouse at Ley up for sale, but John doubted it. Even with Hal fully alive and working somewhere fabulous on things he couldn't explain, this room would still have remained a shrine.

"I'm just back for a couple of days. I've been to see the bishop in Paris. She suggested . . ." There was a chair by the bed that he recognized from the old diningroom set. The backrest dug into his spine when he sat down. It couldn't be comfortable to sit here for long hours, as his mother must do. "She suggested I come here. It's just a day or two, Hal. Then I go back."

Click, sigh. The peachy smell of the flowers on the other side of the bed washed over him in a sickly wave. Too-bright yellow chrysanthemums from the garden in a tall glass vase. He saw a spider climbing over the petals. Every movement seemed retarded, retracted, delayed.

"I haven't told Mum and Dad, but this visit is supposed to be a time of regrouping. Coming to terms. She's a decent woman, the bishop. The sort of thinking priest you always said you could just about come to terms with . . ."

Click, sigh. The warm starfield of bronzes, marbles, and cups on the far wall blazed and winked at him. Tennis, football, chess.

". . . but the fact is, Hal, I've been sleeping with this girl, a Borderer woman, Laurie, and word's got around the Zone. And the business about the contaminated leaf, that's also gone a little awry. I don't, anyway, seem to be getting very far."

He realized that he was speaking more to the screen on the

monitor box than to Hal. It was the instrument that sniffed at and sensed the room, monitored vital signs and brain activity for any traces of movement or pain, and fed data into the ravaged stump of Hal's consciousness. John could see the wires that ran from the box and tunneled into the pitted flesh of Hal's wrist where his watch had been—the final threads in the web—and the rainbow-thin but nevertheless slightly thicker cable that was taped to the side of his cheek and then entered his nose to mate with the internal implant that had been embedded through the bone amid the dead cells at the base of his skull.

"But apparently it doesn't jeopardize my immediate position—my term with Felipe in the presbytery. I'm going back, Hal. Day after tomorrow. It seems that no matter what you do, even if you step out of line, break your vows, discover a way of saving lives... nothing changes. Things remain the same."

Hal's flesh had a healthy gloss. Healthier than John's own. The bare arms and shoulders—lying above the special graygreen sheet that rippled constantly at some imperceptible molecular level to stimulate the skin and that could turn soft or rigid or liquid-smooth at the touch of a screen—had excellent tone and definition. They lay there, easy and relaxed as in an artist's drawing. A life study. But Hal's face, as always since the coma deepened, didn't quite connect with the real, remembered Hal. Like the muscles, it was too relaxed, too smooth. John gazed at the square jaw, the faint dimple in the chin, the broad, slightly compressed lips, the chiseled nose. The closed eyes set wide apart. John remembered the faces of the kings carved in the rocks above Hettie's cave, and how much, truly, Hal was like them—a king. That noble, unfurrowed brow. His mother kept his hair cut exactly as he used to have it cut. A little less fashionable now, and it still stuck up around the crown no matter what you did with it. That tuft would have always made him appear boyish as he grew older.

The cheeks were slightly hollower, the skin around the placid curve of his eyelids thinner and more stretched, but there was no real sign of age. Although...John leaned a little closer. Yes, his brother was graying at the temples. Quite a bit, once you noticed it. He wondered how his mother reacted when she saw that. Whether she had considered buying something to disguise it. At least Hal wasn't going bald like Tim Purdoe.

"So anyway, Hal. I'm here because I'm here. I wanted to look around. See you and Mum and Dad. See Annie..." he paused. *Annie.* "If she's still here. I haven't seen her in years. And I have fond memories." He stopped. "Fond memories, Hal, of the times when you both used to take me out to places with you. Remember Gloucester? Remember nights at the carnival?"

He reached out now, watching the slow, underwater movement of his arm as it stretched towards Hal, towards the hand that was resting, palm down and fingers loosely cupped, on the smooth sheet. Then his fingers touching, sliding beneath, closing on Hal's own. Hand clasping hand. Flesh on flesh. Hal's greater warmth, the slackness, and the slight dampness of sweat between them. John sniffed, and dabbed at his nose with the hand that wasn't holding Hal's. There was always this moment when, coming home and seeing Hal, he felt like crying. But the tears didn't quite come today. He took a breath. It would pass.

"Anyway, Hal..." The hand lay cupped in his own. A warm sleeper's hand, like the flesh of Laurie's body when she lay against him. "I'll look in again." He squeezed, felt bone and cartilage shifting. Was that a slight pressure in return? He dismissed the thought. He'd spent too many years listening as his mother pointed to screens and specially-brought-in monitors and timecharts that supposedly detailed Hal's responses to real-world events and input changes from the net. It was a blind alley, John decided long ago. If Hal ever recovered, there would be no doubting. The whole world would know.

Their flesh stuck slightly as John withdrew his hand. He stood up. Hal's right arm now lay a little crooked, the fingers and palm tipped over, no longer a mirror image of the left. He decided to leave it like that. His mother would rearrange it soon enough anyway, have Hal back the way she wanted. There was no real point in his interfering.

Click, sigh.

The door swung open. The barrier passed over him.

He left the room.

"We have a happy enough life," his mother said later as she prepared his room for him to sleep in. It was called the guest-room now, and few signs of his childhood remained beneath the freshly painted and papered surfaces. It seemed as if only the things that had never really been part of his room, like that vase, like that dreadful dampstained engraving of ancient Heidelberg, had been left as they were. "I wake up each morning," his mother said, "and I think of the whole day ahead. How lucky I am. My time's really my own. I embroider. And we play golf..."

He nodded. Her conversation seemed to be something that surfaced from an endless argument in her head. The blessings she had to count. Set against this, set against that...

"When I think of those poor people you must see every day in the Endless City."

"It's not as bad as people imagine."

The bed—a new bed he'd never slept on—was busy making itself. He watched the sheets billow and slide.

"But *do* people think, I wonder?" His mother glanced up at him, then returned to supervising the bed, smoothing out imagined rucks, crimping at the corners in a way that would once have infuriated him, fluffing and unstraightening the pillows, making little adjustments that the bed immediately attempted to rectify. He wondered why they'd bought the thing. He realized as he gazed down at her busy, trembling hands, at the pink of her scalp showing through the neatly trimmed helmet of silver hair, that he was intensely irritated by everything they'd done to his room.

"Next door, you know," she said, and for a moment he thought she meant Hal, "they have a pool. A pool now for swimming in, and this thing like a frog that swims around it every morning gobbling up all the insects and stuff and then sicking it out into the flowerbeds for mulch. That's the Youngsons. You remember the Youngsons?"

He nodded. He'd known the Youngsons all his life. "Do you ever use it? Their pool?"

"Not often. Stan and Helen say, come around anytime, but you know how it is." She fluffed the pillow again, then stood back, her head cocked. "Of course, your father complains about the kids always shouting and splashing. He likes to have his windows open when he listens to his music. He says that to get the proper transients you need fresh air."

"Don't *they* complain about the music?"

His mother shrugged, raising her shoulders. "Funnily enough, no. Did you enjoy your dinner?"

"It was fine, Mum."

"You look a bit thin. Do you really eat the sludge they grow out there? Seaweed?"

"It's just base protein and carbohydrates."

"Yes," she said. "And you know, that food I gave you—the sausage, the bacon—it's been staring at me in the larder for, I don't know. For years." She crossed her arms in front of her, her fingers linked. "You know how your father always loved his breakfast? What he called a proper breakfast? The first day of our retirement, I fried him two eggs myself instead of using the cleaner. And you know, he came and sat down and looked at them and he said, I think I should tell you that I've never really liked this kind of stuff. It sticks in my throat. And then he stood up and got himself some flakes." She smiled and clenched her fingers more tightly together. "Can you imagine? All those years? And then he says he's never even liked the stuff."

"Dad's Dad."

"Yes." She looked at him, blinking. "He really is, isn't he? Still..."

"And you're managing?"

"Oh yes." His mother smiled. "I'm managing." She untangled her hands, opened them. "Come here, John."

He walked around the bed and into her embrace. Her face was close against his chest. She smelled of dust and lavender water, like her wardrobe, where he used to hide.

"There." She stepped back. "You must be tired. You know where everything is? Of course."

He nodded, looking around the room.

"I'll leave you, then."

His mother turned and walked out, palming the screen by the door to turn off the light as she left. He stood in the darkness, then heard her tut to herself and stop on the stairs as she realized what she'd done. She came back in, flustered and laughing—girlish, even, for a moment—in the wash of light.

He slept for little of the night, lying in ridiculous discomfort on the shifting, ever accommodating sheets of this huge, hideously comfortable bed. The room around him kept shimmering, trying to regain shape and familiarity. Here of all places, the pleading white figures that he'd shaken off in the Endless City were trying to get through again. He left the window cleared, but the room remained darker than he was used to. The shadows leaped and re-formed as the headlights of occasional vans and cars swept across the ceiling. Every time, they settled into greater darkness. He could hear the humming of the house, a sound that seemed so distant to him now, when once it had been close and warm.

He slept through the dawn. When he awoke, the room was a penumbral gray. He got up, and spent some time fiddling with the controls for the window before he realized that the world outside was bathed in mist. Everything had a luminous sheen: the trees, the houses, the tennis courts, the dissolving fields and hills beyond. A car went by, its headlights a cloud of amber. He buzzed down the window, resting his hands on the wet edge of the frame. He licked the dew from his lips, and tasted Laurie. Laurie who didn't taste of sea and rain, as he'd imagined, but European mist.

"We generally go to church in the mornings now," his mother said later in the kitchen, peeling the cards off the packs of food and feeding them into the cooker. The sound of Mozart and the smell of his father's tubes already came from the lounge. "Of course, people are always asking how you are. I thought you, oh, might have wanted to let Father Leon know you were coming. You're a real celebrity."

"Father Leon? Yes..."

His mother gave him a significant look as she ripped open the milk carton and it spilled over her fingers. He knew that one of the things his parents still disliked about his being a priest was the sense of obligation it placed on them.

After breakfast she took him out into the garden. The evilly spiked shrub that had punctured many a football was gone. So was much of the privet border—replaced by white paling, or fluffed up and trimmed into squared-off runs that bore little resemblance to the scrappy bushes of his youth. His mother showed him a bright purple-pink bush: a mass of dewy, up-turned sunset- and sky-colored flowers. *Hydrangea quercifolia aspera,* she told him, pronouncing the words with pride, an active member of Hemhill's garden club now that she had the time. He cupped one of the heavy blooms and sniffed, lifting it to his face.

"There's no scent."

"No."

He held it, breathing deeply. Sap and earth and mist and Laurie. His mother hooked her arm around his, and they walked slowly along the razor-straight flowerbeds, their feet leaving a trail on the wet grass. And this. A cactus, its genes rearranged to accommodate this loamy soil and temperate climate, yet still looking grumpy and out of place. *Cerus echino-cereus saloni.* And this. *Wilsoni millefolium,* which produces flowers in the autumn. If you catch them before they separate and drift on the air, the flowers dry into little golden-yellow pouches or envelopes that can be placed in drawers. He remembered how they felt when he used to crush them, the oil and the unlikely scent of fruitcake that clung to your fingers. And this. Of course, an old favorite, *Malus corinia,* a small tree that will soon be bearing tiny inedible apples. But the scent: mellow sweetness, the distillation of autumn. And the new hedge, *Fusci magellanica.* He trailed his hands amid the hanging pink and white flowers, seeing the tiny stamens that quivered beneath the furled petals, thinking, *dancing ladies.* Why can't you just call them dancing ladies, Mother, the way we used to when we collected them wild along the hedgerows above the sea at Ley? Or perhaps you don't even remember. And here, the roses. *Rosa* in the Latin, of course. *Deo gratias. Amen.* The elderflower tree at the far end of the garden was caught in the time between flower and berry. He counted the crooks and angles he'd once climbed, counted until they dissolved into the mist. *A cruce salus.* Bringing the salvation that comes only through the way of the cross. And the roses, yes, he knew about the roses. Even now, when they competed with the new sharp odor that wafted from the Youngsons' pool across the fence next door, unseen but for the blue glow it refracted into the air. *Domino optimo maximo . . .*

Back in the house, he followed the smell of tubes and the chords of the slow movement of Schubert's *Unfinished Symphony* into the lounge. As if in prayer, his father was crouched on his knees in the corner. His back had an almost painful curve to it, and his tanned and wrinkled neck looked exposed. John made a noise, picking up the big polished shell on the table. His father remained bowed. John rapped the shell harder.

"Ah, John." His father turned, but stayed on his knees. "I was wondering when you'd..."

"This is new, isn't it?" John gestured at the speakers that loomed like obelisks spaced between the chairs—faceless Easter Islanders.

"Yes." His father made a hunched gesture that John interpreted as an invitation to crouch beside him on the floor. Racks of machines, dials, displays. And, reaching out of sight behind the sofa, there were shelves lined with various types of recorded media, like an organized version of the room in the Pandera presbytery where they kept the airwave transmitter. In the background, the music had changed. Now there was a single phrase from the main melody, repeated at the start of the second movement. Dee dah... dee dah... And again, unresolved. Little more than half a dozen notes.

His father raised a finger. "That's Bernstein. Now Barbirolli and the LSO... Early Toscanini. A wax roll, of course, so it's not..." And so on. An endless parade of the string sections of different orchestras playing the same phrase. His father ran a knotted finger along the dustless shelves. "This," he said, drawing out a black disk from a card square, "is probably what I would choose. Ancient, of course..." John saw the whorled grooves. "...but much closer to the music. True analogue. Everything since, every format, has been sampled. They take slices of the music, John, but no matter how many samples you take, there's always the gap between them, isn't there?"

He put the disk on a wheel and rested a pivoting arm on it as the wheel turned. Over the hiss, bangs, and crackles, John heard the same opening notes of the second movement.

"Real, isn't it?" But then the recording began to play a sequence of notes over and over again, giving an especially loud click each time. John thought the effect was intentional, but his father frowned and lifted the arm from the disk, which gave an even louder screech.

"Of course," his father said after the sound of a modern recording again filled the room, "I normally go for something baroque at this time in the morning. That seems about right, doesn't it? The correct choice. Don't you think?"

"Well, yes. I—"

"Then Mozart at noon. In the afternoon, piano music, but not, of course, Liszt. And then we have a big symphony in the evening. Elgar. Mahler. Or Puccini—an opera. The full gamut of emotion, the wider range. Not something you'd want all day. Too much of—do you agree?"

Confused, John nodded.

"Of course, your mother says I play too much to him anyway."

He understood then that his father was talking about the music he was inputting through the net into whatever remained of Hal's consciousness.

"Do you listen to the same stuff yourself, Dad?"

"It's a good thing to share, isn't it? Music's a great healer. There are cases, recorded cases."

"Yes."

"And you were always very fond of this piece, too. The Schubert, weren't you?"

"Well, yes."

The *Unfinished Symphony* was nearing its end. John had never been a great one for music, but his father, so keen to share, interpreted a vaguely expressed liking as undying love.

"It's a shame, isn't it," John said, making an effort to get on something approximating his father's wavelength, "that Schubert died before he wrote the last two movements."

"Oh no. It wasn't like that, John. Schubert may have died young, but he wrote a great deal of other music after this. It was just that the challenge of this particular symphony was too great. He was overconscious of Beethoven, and perhaps also the greatness of what he had written..."

"You mean he gave up?"

"Yes," his father said, as the long last chord faded and the room became briefly and blessedly silent. "If that's how you want to put it. He gave up."

The mist was rising as they walked to church; it filled the valley with white. His parents seemed a little stiff and self-conscious —parading, unannounced, their distant, living son—but otherwise there was a true morning air of celebration. The world once again freshly remade. The people came out of the fog, the children running ahead, the older folks behind, and as they drew closer, their shapes gained identity and substance. The damp air smelled incredibly ripe, green, roaring life into the lungs. And John. *Father* John. You're back, you're here. This, he thought, is what it will be like on the Last Day, when people are supposed to rise in raiments of white, holding palm leaves in their hands. Seeing those laughing, dew-shining faces, and as the little cars buzzed by and the invisible church bells began to clang, he truly wished that he believed.

It was a steeper climb to the Church of Saint Vigor than he remembered. Sleepy headstones, solitary yews. A low stone wall with a ha-ha on the other side that had once been used to keep out the glebe's flock of sheep; lines of roof and spire washed out and vague on this beautiful morning—an engraving etched into the dim, distant present from the real, solid past. Yet the people still came here, came in greater numbers and with greater joy than in the stern medieval Old Testament days of back-breaking labor under the threat of hellfire. They came as John's parents came, and as he and Hal had generally come in their youth. Thoughtful and grateful, almost puzzled—like all of humanity—to find themselves still here and somehow thriving on this wrecked planet.

The Holy Apostolic Church of Rome had indeed survived well, learning the lessons of history. There were few rules now; after all, God understood all, God forgave. That was the thing, John remembered, that he had found most contemptible when he was in his young and most questioning phase. This lack of fire. At the porch, the new priest was nodding, arms behind his back, counting in his flock. Seeing John, he beckoned him over and placed a pastoral hand on his shoulder.

"I've heard of you, of course," he said. He was younger than John, with blond hair and sharp silver eyes that almost seemed to bear a shade of blue. "Leon Hardimann," he said. John felt a warm hand being placed within his own, and smelled the sweet musk of the man's aftershave. His mouth felt rubbery from smiling. "You *will* say something in church, won't you? I'll call on you..."

John nodded. The churchyard was almost empty now. Rooks cawed and circled. The stained-glass windows were brightly lit, filled with organ notes and the deeds of saints and color and song.

"Your mother," Father Leon said, "she does a fine—a splendid—job with Hal. Ahhummm..." He looked wistful. "She keeps the hope alive. I do so admire her. And your father. That strength. You must be proud."

"I am," John said, disturbed by this man's familiarity with his family, and more so by the thought of him standing in Hal's bedroom with that smug smile on his face.

They walked into the church.

"John, but you will speak, won't you? A few words. Sorry to drop it on you, but I'd only learned you were here this morning. Of course, if I'd heard earlier, I'd have said..."

John sat in a front pew, his hands pushed between his thighs and his fingers tightly laced, conscious of flesh on flesh, cold sweat on sweat, a nervousness he'd thought he'd long shaken off for such occasions. As he climbed to the pulpit, he could feel the outstretched arms of Christ floating on the screen behind him like an eagle at his shoulders. Votive candles glittered. A baby was crying, and the mother was saying shush, shush. An old woman in a hat mopped her eyes. Everything was neater than in Santa Cristina, the rows of faces, the neatly spaced way the people sat. Yet the differences were marginal. Seen from up here, he thought, with the pages of the parish bible open before him and smelling of mildew, nothing is ever very different.

"We read in the Bible," he began, slipping into that old phrase because his mind would come up with no other, pausing only fractionally to wait for the echo of the translat that didn't come, "of God's anger, of God's wrath, even of God's jealousy. These are all emotions that we understand and recognize within ourselves, yet they seem strange when we try to apply them to an all-powerful being. So, how is it that God feels these often destructive and impotent emotions... ?"

After the congregation had gone, John sat in the vestry with Father Leon. Father Leon reminded him a little of the priest he'd seen across the water when he first took the ferry from the shuttle to Bab Mensor; his immediate predecessor. The man had the same blond hair.

"I was unsure," Leon said, pouring John coffee, "when they offered me this posting. It's my first, and it seemed like something suited for a more elderly priest. I didn't know..."

John took the cup, touched the handle with his bare fingers, and felt it begin to warm.

"I thought it wouldn't be a sufficient challenge." Leon smiled, smoothed out his cassock, and sat. Crossing his legs, he made small circles in the air with the polished tip of a shoe.

"You met Father Gulvenny?" John asked.

Leon nodded. "But he was ill by then, up at Southlands. He was your priest here, I suppose, when you were younger?" His eyes narrowed. He sipped his coffee. "John, I tell you I came here determined to make everything change. Not at once, of course. I decided I'd give myself a year to settle in and reach a decision about the appropriate action. But by then..." Leon gestured around, smiling. This room was clear testimony to how little he'd changed things.

John was grateful that some of Father Gulvenny's presence remained. Soon after what his parents were already starting to call Hal's accident, Father Gulvenny had been a big influence on John's life. He had been Hemhill's parish priest for some years by then, but John—and, it seemed, the rest of Hemhill— had taken little notice of him. Father Virat, who'd come before Father Gulvenny, had been a rich fund of stories of drunken tomfoolery, gaffes in the pulpit, and odd sightings of him wandering the fields. In comparison, Father Gulvenny was functional and gray. He had a cracked voice, an awkward smile, long cheekbones, and a long body. After Hal's accident, as the initial exclamations and concerns gave way to the dull realization that Hal would never recover, when his parents turned inward and the people who used to come by began to avoid them, Father Gulvenny was the one person who actually sought John out, and made the effort to talk to him like an adult.

This old church, Father Gulvenny had said—sitting in the same overstuffed chair where Father Leon now sat, and where even the surplices seemed to cover the stone in the same folds —this village, this sky, this earth, you have to learn to see through them all and feel the fire that's beneath. Most people are dreamers, John. They dream their way through life. They know of nothing but the tiles of this fireplace, that cobweb (could it be the same cobweb now? or at least an ancestor of the same spider?), that triangle of light at the window. And the Church, the whole Holy Apostolic Church, is mostly the same.

Father Gulvenny would talk for hours in that notched and crackly voice, his eyes wandering the room, rarely meeting John's. To others, it might have seemed that this priest was simply conducting an awkward inner dialogue with his faith, but John was fascinated, not least by Father Gulvenny's willingness—obsession—to criticize the Church that he supposedly represented. All of it nothing, a sham. And yet, and yet...

Through all those evenings and afternoons, in the summers and winters of John's teenage years, as the logs sighed in the fire or the windows lay open to the sound of birdsong drifting with the haze of pollen up the valley, Father Gulvenny, charged and yet soothing, personal and impersonal, deeply attentive and far away, had tried to express the things that lay beyond the everyday. The things that he could never reach. John now understood that Father Gulvenny's short, awkward sermons, which had passed over most of his congregation, were also an attempt to express this same unlikely spiritual fire. And all from a gray man in a small, insignificant village. A sense of meaning beyond the ordinary. A sense, if not quite of purpose, at least of a direction in which purpose might lie...

"I suppose it must come as a relief," Father Leon was saying, "to speak directly to a congregation as you did this morning. I mean, after the Endless City."

"I hadn't thought. But, yes. It is."

"To express more...ah, complex feelings." Father Leon gazed into his empty mug. John realized that he'd expected a talk rather than a sermon from him. Bringing the Good News to the Magulf. This new priest certainly hadn't expected an off-center exploration of God's anger. To John, the connection between what he'd said and his work in the Endless City had seemed obvious. And he had—or hadn't he?—mentioned the cases of suffering he saw in the streets and at the clinic. But, looking at the still warm, blue-flowered mug he was holding, seeing it was the same one that he used to drink from years ago, sitting with Father Gulvenny, he understood that things had come full circle. This morning, he'd done little more than ape one of Father Gulvenny's old sermons.

With the coffee finished, the two priests crossed the empty church and stepped out into the brightening noonday light.

The sky was still hazy, but the valley below them was clear of fog, a brilliant undersea world held beneath a dazzling white that frothed and lapped around the hilltops. The heraldic gold of the cornfields. The soft greens of the meadows and the jelt reaching up to the forest. So many greens. John could scarcely believe there were this many shades of green in the world. And the spirit, he thought, the fire beneath. Of the three personages of God, Father Gulvenny would say, the most important is the Holy Spirit; it must come first. Without it, the Father and the Son could not exist. Yet people hardly talk...Hardly ever. The fire. The spirit.

He looked up at the sky, where something seemed to be moving. A shadow, shifting. A wave-tip glint of light. And a whoosh, a crackle in the air. He felt the hairs on his neck and arms prickle.

With a great swooping sigh, the cloudpicker fell out of the mist towards them. Ionized cloud churned, shivered, and dissolved. There were tracks of white spirals, and a brisk, sea-scented wind tugged at his clothes, pushing the hair back from his face. The sun flickered through. The trees bowed, the rooks took flight. Ghost-ship spiderwebs of spars glistened. Close to, the thing was so large and yet so fragile that it seemed to be sustained more by aspiration than the rules of flight.

The cloudpicker's delicate shadow was over them now. John could just see the tiny silver bubble where the pilot sat, and both he and Leon raised a hand. This whole display was obviously intended for them. There was no need to come this low; a drone would have cleared the fog easily—if it had actually needed clearing. But that was one of the reasons they put people instead of telepresences inside the cloudpickers. Forget about fractional lightspeed delays and the need for conscious, random, and intuitive levels of response that the net found hard to imitate in realtime: surely humans piloted the big cloudpickers for the joy of doing so.

The shadow passed. The air was clear now, and the sun shone as a dazzling disk through the haze, glinting on the river. John glanced at Leon, but nothing was left to be said between them now. They shook hands, and he walked out through the graveyard and back down the hill towards his parents' house, taking a diversionary route along a green-tunneled hawthorn lane. Harebells lay amid the grass, their heads still drowsy with the dew. And the sky through the branches above was now the same color. Harebell blue? he thought, looking up. But no, the shades weren't the same. He walked on into the village.

There were few children along his parents' road by the park now, and the paintwork was pristine, the gardens all neat, done out in complex ways that no one would ever bother to program a machine for. The days of mossy lawns and pollarded trees and goalposts by the garage were gone. Now, it was all genuine human effort; a sign to the world that the people who lived in these houses were still able-bodied and alive.

His father was playing *The Ride of the Valkyries*. He went upstairs and saw that the door to Hal's room was open.

"There you are," his mother said, looking up. "What you said was *interesting*, dear. There in church."

"Do you need help?"

"No," she said flatly.

He nodded and remained in the doorway, feeling the tingle

of the molecular barrier as it brushed and retreated from his face. His mother had lifted the top sheet back from Hal, and it hovered stiff and frozen at the foot of the bed. Underneath, Hal was naked. The base of the mattress twitched, lifting him a little to one side. His mother raised his arm by hand, and wiped his flank with a disposable towel. Of all things, the air smelled of dysol.

"You don't really seem to be back, John," she said, "if you don't mind me saying so."

"Back?"

"You're still thinking about the Endless City."

She walked around to Hal's other side. Her back was to him. She wouldn't press her questions.

"I suppose I am," he said.

They still used, he saw, a crude-looking catheter to extract urine—the kind of thing you might see Kassi Moss using at the Cresta Motel, although a large and serious pipe extracted the solid waste directly from Hal's gut, and probably went deep inside him to aid digestion. A more advanced method of dealing with Hal's urine would probably involve some form of emasculation. The technology was well proven, but it had been perfected for the elderly for whom such indignities no longer mattered, and his mother wouldn't have that done to Hal, not anything that would damage his life when he eventually rose from that bed. John remembered once, what was already years ago, watching his brother's penis flip over and stiffen as his mother tried to perform the delicate task of removing the condom-shaped thing that they then used, and hearing her recite, under her breath from one of her textbooks, "The penis may sometimes become engorged during manipulation..." At the time, he'd been faintly horrified, but now he thought that she'd probably been pleased to think that Hal could still get an erection. It was a sign of life.

"There," his mother said, dropping a sealed bag into the disposer. She touched a screen, and bed settled down again, the sheets slid back.

She turned and stood there with her arms folded, looking at John. Perhaps, he thought, I'm supposed to say something now. Outside, across the road, white-suited figures were out on the tennis courts. And machines were parrying with a thrust and a glide. A blur, the last fragments of the mist.

"Hal was always such a bad patient before, you know," she said.

For a moment John was confused. "Oh, you mean..."

"When he had that bug that his recombinants made a mess of. Remember that? He would wander around coughing and with his nose blocked and mutter about lousy programming, how any idiot could do better than this. And that time he fell and broke his foot. Being ill was always such an effort for Hal. It was as though he had put so much of himself into it." She glanced back at the bed, touching the now soft sheets. "You know, he ricked his shoulder recently. When he did his exercises. I had to get him on his tummy and rub in this warm foul-smelling stuff. Eliot Farrar says it's best done by hand. For the contact."

"So it's still Farrar? I remember him saying he was going to move on."

"Everyone says that here, dear. You'll probably find him down at Southlands today."

Southlands. John nodded.

"He made a terrible sound when it happened. When he pulled his shoulder."

"It must have hurt."

"But he didn't show it."

John, who was squeamish about the treatment of Hal's apparently healthy body in a way that the sicknesses of the Borderers at the clinic never affected him, had always found the spectacle of Hal's exercises unbearable. He remembered the first time he came into the room, and that brief bubble of hope that rose inside him as he saw his brother sitting up with his head turned, one arm outstretched. Then he noticed the jaggedly angular movement and realized that Hal was under the control of the net. But they'd probably improved things by now. He had this brief vision of Hal up and walking, of Hal dressed and coming down the stairs, of Hal sitting at his old place for breakfast, a fleshy mannequin with the eyes dead and closed. John lowered his gaze to the old bedside rug, so out of place on the new, smooth flooring.

From the hallway, louder this time, came the sound of Wagner.

"Come on," his mother said. "Dinner's probably ready. I leave a lot of it to the kitchen and the cleaner now. I keep out of the way, although I sometimes feel like a guest in my own house." Hal's door closed behind them. Explosions of string and brass crashed up the stairwell, and she smiled and rolled her eyes. "And it all happens so *quickly* if I leave it to the house. I end up racing to keep up. But time really seems to be running faster now, don't you think? Just these last couple of years, and the summers more than the winters. Everyone else I've asked says so. The clocks are all running faster too, even the particles around the atoms..." Her grip tightened on John as they descended the stairs. "Everything's speeding up. But there's some part of us that runs to a different time, that still knows."

The music grew even louder at the foot of the stairs, but to John it sounded oddly sterile and fractured. Perhaps his father was right and something did slip out between the samples.

He asked, "Does Dad really feed this racket into Hal's console all day?"

"He thinks he does, dear." His mother patted his hand. They shared one of their old conspiratorial smiles. "He thinks he does. And it keeps him happy."

After dinner, heavy with the weight of more food than he'd wanted, John announced that he was going out. His father stood outside on the drive watching him as he climbed into his rented Zephyr. The sun was bright now. John took a left down the road, away from the compound and towards the center of Hemhill. He studied the screens. Annie, he thought. He'd been at her wedding—already a novitiate and a target for smirks and the confidences of elderly relatives, but content with his lot because he was still looking into the fire beneath. He found her address easily enough; and he remembered it now anyway. Annie lived at Radway Farm. Near the ruins.

The farmhouse was centuries old, even if it was now surrounded by cleverly landscaped areas of warehousing, storage, silaging, and stocks. Looking down into the sunny bowl at the squared-off jumbles of flowering meadowgrass that covered the acres of flat roofs with their colors, angles, and heights all at slight variance, he was reminded of expressionist paintings where everything was rendered as a series of overlapping blocks, created in a time when artists were trying to take apart the world rather than keep it whole.

He had to announce his name into the gate, and there was a pause as it paged for human advice. Getting out of the car as he waited, taking deep breaths of this deep country air, he looked up at the sky, which was an incredible blue. He hadn't been here since—when?

The gate swung open, and there was Annie in dungarees and Wellingtons, walking towards him through the bright afternoon.

"John," she said, offhand and smiling. "You're back?"

"Just today."

They left the car to park itself and walked down the springy track and into the brown of the yards. Chickens scattered around them. His shoes quickly became heavy with mud. He felt clumsy and earthbound here, but Annie took his hand to steer him onto a sterile blue walkway and found him boots in an old barn.

"I don't get rid of anything," she said. "I did once, but I lived to regret it."

"I should have come to see you before, Annie," he said. "You haven't changed."

She turned her head away from him. Of course, she had changed. The skin around her eyes had lines. There were lank strands of gray in her hair. But that wasn't what he meant. In his own way, he'd always loved Annie. Adored her when she and Hal were courting and they used to take him with them when they visited places. Even now, he couldn't really understand why they'd wanted to bring this gooseberry kid along with them. But they had, and by doing so left him with eternal memories of a boat amid swans on a river in some town whose shining cobbled streets he saw as vividly as daylight. And the giant golden walls of Gloucester Cathedral. Annie, with her boyish hands, bare freckled arms, thin shoulders, strong lips, and short dark-brown hair, had always been the kind of girl he liked. But not wanted for himself, not in any real sense.

Annie was proud of her farm. A tenant, but she said by now she felt it was as much hers as it was Halcycon's. She seemed immersed in the present, in the particular warm minute of this particular warm afternoon. The smell of bovine feed and excrement was leaking from the pipes that led to the stocks. That smell, too, he associated with Annie. With coming here with Hal to see her after her parents had moved from Brimfield to run the place.

She showed him a tiled room, once a dairy, where the new calves were checked and encoded. ATGCTA unraveling on the screens. As they walked on towards the open fields, a black-and-white dog ran up and sniffed at John's crotch. He reached to stroke its silver-collared head, but it growled. Annie aimed a kick at it, sending it away. She said that farm dogs were never any good with people, even when they were linked into the net.

Pipes and lines stretched overhead. It was as if an industrial plant had been dumped lopsidedly into this fecund country mud. They passed under the sentinel figures of the pickers and diggers and harvesters, most as high as a house and with years of mud encrusted on their tracks and claws. There wasn't much going on today, Annie said. Nowadays the workers were all on contract, and moved from farm to farm. You had to wait. Things changed, but it remained one of the essentials of farming that you always had to wait.

"Do you ever go and see Hal?" John asked as they walked between the barns.

"I used to," she said, "when I thought it would do any good." She grabbed a blade of grass and began to shred it. "And of course I tried to keep going after you left. But I'd already mourned for him. I lost him, John. Long ago...Before that stunt of his, to be honest."

John nodded, glad at least that someone else was still angry.

"Come on." She tossed the grass away. "I'll show you the milkers."

They took an open lift up the side of the largest of the stocks. This is new, she said, pointing to something in the jumble of slurry tanks, silage processors, and silos. But it was still the same farm, the same organized mess. And her cheeks were flushed, and the same sweet air that rose from the woodlands still ruffled her hair.

The lift stopped. The upper door irised open. There were pipes everywhere inside, even in the control room, where a young man sat with his feet up on the console eating a sandwich. Beyond, in the main pens, there was a stinging intensification of the smell that pervaded the whole of Radway Farm. John remembered getting lost in the stocks once when he wandered off on his own. He remembered the moist sound of so many creatures breathing, the sourceless lighting, the animal warmth.

Each milker was encased in a rack. Wires, pipes, and monitors drooped above and below it, crossing in great knitted sheaves over the walkways along which Annie led John. He traced the line of a red tube, quivering and warm to the touch, to where it passed through bars and entered a grayish wall of flesh. A tight ring of muscle pulsed and relaxed to receive it, and a pink bovine eye that was pushed against the racking of the pen blinked and seemed to regard him, although he doubted that the nerves reached the brain. It was a great brick of an animal. Tiny stumps for legs, mottled and almost hairless. In the rack above, he could see the pendulous udder of her neighbor. No teats as such, just two long fleshy tubes that faded at some indeterminate point into the plumbing of the machinery.

"What do they think about?"

"They don't think," she said. "Not these ones, anyway. But I've heard that people are getting an extra twenty-percent yield down in Montgomery from reconstructing their sense receptors and inputting VR."

"You mean they think they're grazing out on a meadow?"

She chuckled. "Imagine, having this place filled with cow dreams! Come on. I'll take you to the house. You should meet the kids and Bill."

The old redbrick farmhouse. Stone-capped windows, and the gate into the garden that still needed a good hard push. The cats sleeping on the sunny porch, and the smell of damp tiling.

"Wear these," she said, kicking some slippers across to him. He put them on, wiggling his right toe from the hole in the front as Annie peeled off her socks and rolled her dungarees up above her knees. She picked up a rag from where a cat had been sitting, frowned at the rag, then used it to wipe the stripes of mud that had adhered to her calves. Her legs were still shapely and pale, and a fine down covered the shins. She'd shared a cabin room with him during the one summer that she came to Ley, and he remembered her bending over in the bluish seathrown moonlight to fold her clothes, dressed only in panties and a bra. He was used to seeing her in a considerably skimpier swimsuit on the beach, but the intimacy of that moment gave the sight of her a new charge. It was easily the most erotic thing he'd ever seen, and became his secret masturbatory icon in many teenage nights to come.

She looked up, and caught his gaze.

In the kitchen, straggles of laundry hung from beams on the ceiling. John sat on a stool, and a little girl with long blond hair falling from a crimson ribbon immediately started to use him as a climbing frame. As she slid down his legs, all sweaty absorption, another blond child came to stand beside him. She placed a frank hand on his shoulder and said, "Would you like to play?" It was only when he looked into her impossibly silver eyes and saw the emptiness in her mouth that he realized she was a doll.

"That's my friend Samantha," the climbing girl said, "and she wets the bed."

Annie was doing something on the counter that involved oddly shaped implements of a kind that John had never seen before. The room filled with the smell of raw meat and garlic.

Annie's husband, Bill, came in, dressed only in y-fronts and a crumpled blue shirt.

"This is John Alston. Remember? Hal's brother? He's a priest now."

Bill shook John's hand and shooed the doll and the girl away. Then he yawned, scratched his head, and looked around.

"You haven't seen my trousers?"

"They're wherever you put them."

Bill turned to John. His face was mostly hidden beneath a whitening beard, eyebrows, and bushy hair. "It's a permanent rubbish tip around here."

"And whose fault is that?"

"Anyway, John. You must be...where?"

"The Endless City."

"Ahh. You people."

Bill waved a hand, then lifted it to his mouth as he yawned again.

"He does the nights," Annie said, still attending to the meat.

From a previously quiet and undisturbed corner of the kitchen, from what John had thought was a box containing more laundry, noises began to emanate and sheets to stir. A pink arm emerged and waved as if drowning. There was a moment of stillness, then the baby began to squall.

"He'll be wanting milk," Bill said.

"Yeah, but—can't you see?—in a moment. Let John have him."

The baby was lifted up and placed, struggling amid a caul-like trail of blankets, into John's arms. Surprised at this big new human, it stopped crying, and John instantly felt more relaxed. It smelled so sweet. And no one ever really expected you to say or do much when you were holding a baby. It nuzzled towards his thumb. He let it suck.

"You must be a big hit at Borderer christenings," Bill said, taking a bowl of uneaten breakfast cereal from a stool across the kitchen and sitting down.

"They don't have them," John said.

Bill nodded, crossed his legs, took the spoon from the breakfast bowl, and began to eat.

The baby still sucked John's thumb. The sensation was warm and strong; it actually felt as though something nourishing were being drawn out of him. Then the baby pulled away and looked up. In the growing lattice of silver in its irises, there was still a hint of brown.

"He came a bit late," Annie said. "A surprise gift. Isn't that right?"

Bill grinned, milky oatflakes on his beard.

Annie gestured with bloody fingers around the kitchen. "We thought we'd finished with all this."

Accidental pregnancies didn't happen, but here John could almost believe in them. Annie coming down one morning with her breasts already swollen to give Bill the news with a sour-breathed kiss, a big hug. He envied the chaos of their happy, busy life.

"Here." She took the baby from John. Her hands made red smears as she unbuttoned her blouse and offered a nipple.

"I'll have to stop this soon," she said as the baby began to suck. Her chin bulged as she looked down. "He's five months already. They planted the crystals, oh, early summer, wasn't it, Bill?"

Gazing absently at his wife's breast, Bill nodded.

"There's inflammation there still," she said, "and they expect him to be ready in the autumn for his first format." The baby's mouth went *tick, tick*. "You read preliminary medicine, didn't you, John? Don't you work in some kind of clinic?"

"Well. Yes."

"I've been using Calcymix in bottles, too. But the screen says I have to stop breastfeeding soon. It's so bloody stupid. I'm sure I did it later with Jennie. It's the only way in the middle of the night when he won't stop crying."

"He looks very healthy," John said, wondering what he could possibly tell these people about babies. "It's just there's a danger of your natural antibodies conflicting with the recombinants his implant will be producing. They start that even before formatting, and those antibodies are far more powerful than the intravenous ones you'll have been giving him. But there would be a rash first if there was a problem..."

"Oh, right."

There was silence in the room now. The baby had stopped sucking.

Before he left, Annie insisted on showing John the baby's back. She peeled off his vest and rompersuit, performed whatever trick was necessary to unseal and remove the diaper, and wiped the baby down. He lay there, legs and arms slightly curled in this warm room on a toweling sheet flecked with cat hairs. John turned him over, wishing he'd asked the name. But the baby didn't cry. And of course there was some inflammation around the scabbed indentation in the baby's spine. John glanced at Annie as she leaned intently over. He inhaled the soft milky smell of her and the baby. Didn't she remember her other children? Didn't she at least remember the last main implant she'd had herself when she was a teenager?

"Do you think I should try applying more cream?"

"Best to just let the air get to it for a while each day. Find him a warm place to lie and dry off after his bath. The inflammation's not coming from outside, Annie, its coming from him. His own immune system is starting to work for the first time, and he's reacting against this alien presence."

"*Alien?*"

"Well, it is when you think about it, isn't it?" he said, thinking, You must see this, Annie, every day outside in the stocks. "I'm sure they'd give him a suppressant if they thought there was any real problem, but it's generally best to let these things work themselves out on their own."

The baby was clothed, powdered, put away. John shook hands with Bill and walked with Annie back across the yard.

He said, "I'll be going back tomorrow."

"Oh? Right."

"That baby boy..."

"He's sweet, isn't he? I'm so glad we had him." Annie was looking away. One of her contractors had arrived and was doing something with an odd dome-shaped machine that squatted in the mud, giving off puffs of steam from a curved funnel that projected like the spout of a kettle. "*He* shouldn't be here today," she muttered. "Look, I'll save you the walk and call your car."

John stood on the worn brick lip of a doorway as Annie went to the nearest screen. By the time his car arrived, she was on the other side of the yard arguing with the kettle contractor. Waving her arms. They were too far away for their words to reach John, but he could catch the sharp European accents of their voices, and the sun, low and golden now, brimmed over the grassy rooftops like a fluid into his eyes. A cock crowed. The Zephyr waited humming beside him. He was tempted just to climb in and drive off.

Then Annie saw him and hurried back over. "You must come again," she said, pecking his cheek. "When I have more—"

"I still think about you, Annie. The good times. With Hal."

This time, Hal's name seemed to pass through her without touching. "I have to dash now. This idiot's come a day early. He needs someone in the screehopper and that's muggins here. Bye."

"Bye."

John watched her go, then got into his car and drove up the hill. Stopping by the gate, looking back, he saw the kettle rattling across the livid brown-and-green expanse of the early fields of superkale, trailing a scarf of steam. Behind it strode a larger two-legged machine. The machine paused for a moment, turned at an angle, and raised a claw in John's direction, then strode on.

He drove up the valley, through the woods, and past one of the golf courses where his parents now played. Shadowed by the hills, the figures moved in pairs across a landscape of undulating grass. He saw the lighted balls twirling through the air into the deepening blue sky, then settling into the grass. He didn't want to go home yet. He turned left, right, waited as a giant machine lumbered past him up the road, walking in a corn-dust haze towards farm buildings and the sunset beyond. He remembered Annie, the flow of moonlight on her body as she undressed when they shared the cabin room at Ley. She and Hal hadn't been prepared to admit then that they were sleeping together. Thinking back, John really wasn't sure if they'd ever made love.

The gates at Southlands opened for him. The trees at the far reach of the gardens stretched their shadows across the lawns. Water clattered softly over ornamental rocks. A piano somewhere played a nursery tune. The main doors up the steps of the pale building also opened immediately on John's approach. The security was good here, this deep into the net. Simplicity of access was just a sign that you had already been monitored and recognized.

The great hall was scattered with chairs, lined with huge paintings of extinct animals, filled with the smells of stone and lavender. A door swung open quicker than John had expected, and he held out his hand, trying not to look surprised. Eliot Farrar had dark hair, a square face, slightly strained and studious eyes.

"This way, Father."

Here, no one would be surprised to see a priest. John was led along corridors and through open wards. There were voices in the dim air, although they shifted and changed, so that it was hard to locate their source among the shrouded, silver-wired, and screen-surrounded shapes. An eye gleamed. From several beds, the fall of hair; a frozen waterfall. A knobbled foot, the ball of its big toe like polished wood, poked incongruously. This was much the same technology that kept Hal alive, although here it fought a losing battle. What was it now? John wondered. How many years were likely? Fifty-eight? Fifty-nine? Sixty? Now that his parents were close to it, he didn't want to know. Halcyon would reconfigure the implants, of course, and an extra year or two of life might be gained. But the huge invasion of recombinant technology started an unstoppable clock in the human body; the strain was killing. Your days were numbered. Here were the late-mobile wards. Nowadays, the wheelchairs had no wheels and didn't possess chairs. They looked more like miniature versions of the great farm implements that many of the ward patients had operated all their lives.

"Virtual reality's a great bonus when you get to this stage," Farrar said. An old lady, her eyes fed by wires, hissed and clicked by them. "Sometimes I think you could extend it all indefinitely. Like, ah..." He wiped a hand across his face. "We call in the priest, of course, before we make that final decision. Father Hardimann. You've met?"

John pictured the two of them shaking their heads over some helpless case. Then Kassi Moss at the Cresta Motel. "Don't you find it depressing?"

"Of course." Farrar shot him a look. "But it's a necessity, it's a job. And we consult the family. It's really up to them. I'm sure you understand that, Father."

The better cases, still able-bodied, were gathered in a big anteroom with a domed glass ceiling filled with the intense blue of the evening sky and pricked by the first stars. Many came here after a fall at home or some other crisis, only to recover and check out again. Or perhaps they would move for a while into one of the sheltered machine-served chalets that dotted the grounds. For others, for most, this was the beginning of the progression along the wards through which John had already passed. One group, drawn in a corral of high-backed chairs, were laughing and nudging one another at the antics of the actors in a comedy show who argued at cross-purposes and paced, semireal, in the lighted space before them. There was, on the surface, a holiday atmosphere in this big room.

Through illusory gardens scented with pollen, a quavering voice shouted after him. "Look. Isn't it...?"

John turned. Even without the cassock, he was recognized. But then he heard the hiss and mutter of disappointment, the careful rearranging of limbs, the turning away of eyes. Shaken heads. Not Hal. Hal's brother. And don't you remember? Sad. How sad. People, John imagined, who'd taught them both at school. Or served them in the shops. And wasn't the face over there a strange age-distorted version of Tilly? He didn't want to ask.

John sat down in Farrar's office, and the door slid shut behind them, clicking some kind of lock. There was a sudden formality about the occasion as the two men faced each other across the wooden table.

"How often," John asked, "do you see Hal?"

"Once or twice a week." Farrar gazed just over the top of John's head. A tiny nerve in the corner of his right eye was twitching. "But really I go to see your parents, John. I mean, to check their state of mind. I can monitor how they and Hal are doing physically just as easily from here."

A big screen filled a corner, of a grade even higher than the one Laurie had in the Zone. Spinning stars drifted deep within it.

"What's that?" John asked.

"That's how I keep track of the people here. See those two over there?" Farrar clicked his fingers, and the screen scrolled up towards two circling nebulae. The nebulae sailed across the room. "That's us, sitting here."

Hovering over the desk, like tiny glowing balls of wire or wool. Each strand, John saw, was alive with swarming lines of AGTC.

"And you can tell where we are?"

"It's a simple matter of triangulation." Farrar frowned at the stars. Obediently, they disappeared. "You did say you saw Father Leon?"

"This morning."

"Did he tell you anything about Hal? I mean, specifically?"

"He said he admired my parents. Most people say that."

"This, ah... This can't go on forever."

"No. Of course. Hal will probably decline and die. We've known that for years. My mother still—"

"What I mean, Father John, is that that time may have come already. Is, in fact, overdue."

John stared back, wondering if Farrar was going to have the nerve to talk about resources to someone who worked at a clinic in the Endless City.

"Hal is hopeless, John. There's nothing left there to save. You're an educated man—you know about medicine—you don't need me to tell you that no matter how close we get to understanding the mind and body, we still can't isolate consciousness. But there's no mystery to that. Consciousness is everywhere, it's a function of life. Look for it in a specific place, and it disappears. But I'd say with certainty that Hal has no consciousness left. Or that, if he somehow does, he's suffering."

"Those are two separate possibilities."

"What?"

But John was grateful to this man for defining the issue, for pushing him into a corner. "I don't," he said, "want Hal to stop being alive."

"Look, I walked you through the wards. You must know by now what it's like. Your own mother and father—I know, I've spoken to them—have been faced with similar decisions about their own parents and relatives."

"That's different. People who are aging know that they've lived their lives. Hal hasn't. Not yet. It's unfinished business. I know *that*"—John heard himself saying—"with a greater certainty than I can probably convey to you. I know it with more certainty than I know anything else in my life."

"Okay." Farrar sat back from his desk. "Have it your way, Father John." From his expression, from the Laurie-like emphasis on the word Father, John didn't doubt that all the usual battles between medics and priests took place across this table. "But the decision still remains to be taken, I'm afraid. Your parents—and I hate to have to put it this way," he said, un-blinking, "are what? Now?"

"Whatever," John said. "It's a responsibility I'm prepared to shoulder."

The two men regarded each other. The window at Farrar's back was open. Faintly, John could hear the chatter of water, the sound of a piano playing, could feel the pull of the night. The silence in the room seemed to lapse, and the tension was lost. It became apparent to both of them that, for now, there was no more to be said.

He drove out into the summer dark. All the gates opened for him. He kept the windows down to blow away the heat that had risen to his face. He felt tired, confused, hungry.

The little car hurried along the main road to Hemhill. The occasional lights of other cars flashed by him, but the houses he passed were mostly dark, seemingly deserted. He stopped when he saw the lights of a roadside café. His parents would probably have something waiting for him, cooked hours before and now congealing on the plate. It seemed easier not to bother them.

He took a seat in the café, and the table asked him what he wanted. He shrugged, which would normally have been taken as a signal to recite Today's Specials, but his body language was too compromised by the ways of the Magulf. The table repeated the question. He chose a green salad and pepper steak.

He looked around. There were a few other people here in the yellow-lit gloom. Solitary diners like himself. People in transit from one place to another. He jumped when the plate arrived, rising through an opening in the table. This kind of arrangement had been a fad of his youth, but now people preferred more traditional ways of ordering and serving. Unless in his absence all this trickery had come back in fashion.

He pecked at the food, which was rich and ornate on his tongue.

"Mind if I sit with you?" It was a woman with close-cropped blond hair, stripes of sunburn across her cheeks.

"Sure."

She straddled the chair. She wore a sleeveless shirt, and the muscles in her arms and shoulders were sharply defined. Nobody needed to be that fit and strong these days. No European, anyway. He guessed that she used one of the reconfiguring recombinants that Halcycon, amid a maze of warnings, permitted.

"I'm passing through now," he said. "But this place used to be my home. I mean, Hemhill."

She nodded, a gold crucifix dangling between her breasts, called up a dry wine from the table, and asked, "Where do you work now?"

"The Endless City."

"Yes."

"You can tell? Most people seem surprised."

"It's your coloring, and the way you look around. I nearly took a contract there myself."

They talked. Her breasts, outlined beneath the shirt, were more like a man's pectorals. A few months ago, he probably wouldn't have consciously registered the fact. He realized she'd seen that he was staring. He looked up into her eyes, then away.

"I have a bunk in my truck outside," she said. "Sometimes I find that having company's a more natural way to end the day."

"I've got to go home soon," he said.

"I thought you said you didn't live here now."

"My parents do. They're still alive. They used to talk about moving to this place they had by the sea. But it never quite came off. They ended up selling it."

"I know what you mean. It's all talk, isn't it?"

She told him about her own parents, who were dead, and he sat and listened. Then she told him about her work. Like most people of this age of quick and easy travel, she was from the same part of the country. She'd been born in Ross on Wye, had trained for one of the low fliers that captured the purple blooms that lay through the summer like a knobbly carpet over the flatlands from Cambridge to Norwich. With the first cool days, they snapped their stalks and rose into the air. "It used to be a real skill to capture them," she said, "a trick you never thought you'd master. And then you did..." She had another drink. "But Halcycon thought of a way of polarizing the plants as they grow. Some new twist in the genes, positive to negative charge. Now it's like shooting fish in a barrel. They come hissing and cracking after you even if you try to turn your scoop away."

He nodded. He still hadn't told her what he did for a living. If she asked now, he'd lie.

"I aimed too low, I guess. I had the right marks to be a pilot, all the synapses. I should have studied harder. Spent less time...less time..." Her gaze faded as he wondered what it was she'd spent her time doing. "Should have studied structural communication, like my father used to say."

"That's for controlling the satellites, isn't it?"

"That's changed too. A lot of the people are switching over to cloudpickers now. It's all so automated and implanted that you hardly need the old special aptitudes to fly. It's all part of the net."

"Studying structural communication would get you a job flying a cloudpicker?"

"I should have seen it coming. Me, up in the sky with the angels instead of down here. You want another drink?"

"I'd better be going."

"Me too." She took his hand and squeezed it. There was a surprising softness in the touch of her broad palm and fingers. "You know, it's the story of my life..."

His parents had a comedy show on in the lounge when he got back. It looked, in fact, like part of the same broadcast that the better Southlands patients had been running. The characters paced, and the audience's ragged laughter sighed and broke like the sea. But his parents seemed uninvolved. He guessed that they'd been waiting for him.

"Ah, it's you. Where have you been?"

He sat down, feeling the years of his youth tumbling back over him again as he fumbled for an excuse. But when he looked at their faces, he saw that they were showing a polite interest, nothing more.

"If this is what you're telling me," the fading man in the comedy said, "then I..." And he was gone. The room seemed very large and quiet without him.

"I went to see Annie."

"Yes. How is she?"

"She's fine. She has a new baby. A boy."

"How lovely. What's he called?"

John did his best to spin out a story of the way the farm was now. His parents leaned forward, smiling. From there, the conversation wandered back to the Magulf, the Endless City.

2 8 8

"Where do you think they'll send you next?" his father asked.

"I don't know. I may choose to stay on. Try something—something a bit different... with my life." He looked for a reaction. There was none.

Soon it was bedtime. John went to his room. His mother followed him and stood there as he undressed. He saw how selfish he'd been this visit, how little time he'd spent with them, trying to get beneath the surface of this life they were living.

She touched his shoulder and smiled. "Are you happy, Son? Something's changed about you this time."

He smiled back and kissed her cheek.

"Here." She gave him his old pajamas. The tang of fresh linen.

"Thanks." He pulled them on and climbed into bed, conscious now that they were both reenacting a childhood ritual. She looked down at him, then her hand went to her wrist. The red standby light that linked her with Hal. He wondered if she was turning something off, or checking.

She sat down on the edge of the bed. It was still early; the windows were clear, and the passing cars beat waves of light across her face and hands. The effect made her seem old, then young again.

"You know if there's anything—*anything*, Mum. When you need me, you know I'll come back."

She leaned down and kissed him. "Now it's time for sleep." When she stood up, the center of gravity didn't shift the way it had with his old mattress.

"Goodnight, John."

She left the room.

He lay there, watching the lights, counting the cars. Soon he was asleep, dreaming about something he couldn't remember. Even as he dreamed, he knew that he was losing it.

THE BROWNSTONE BUILDINGS along Gran Vía seemed translucent where the big-bellied clouds hung above them like swathes of soiled velvet. As John backed through the screeching door and the wind-stirred dust and clotted cobwebs of the presbytery hallway, he decided that the Magulf light really had thickened and changed. He climbed the stairs. The presbytery was quiet, and there was no sign of Bella—it was, he remembered, her afternoon off—but his bed was freshly made, the sheets taut. He dropped his bag with a clink of the bottles he'd bought for Felipe and sat down, peeling off and destroying his gloves, kicking off his shoes. The koiyl leaves he'd collected still lay in the corner, in a Quicklunch box he'd found. Part of the welcoming aura of the room, he realized, came from the smoky undertow that emanated from them.

He sorted out his bag, then climbed the stairs and found

Felipe in the top room overlooking Gran Vía. The old priest sat with his feet up on a stool, the fan circling, whisky and trisoma on the low table.

"There you are," Felipe said. "A good trip?"

"Good enough." John handed him the bottles. "I brought you these."

Felipe studied the labels. "Herefordshire. So you've been home?"

"The bishop suggested it. She wanted to give me time to think. To readjust."

"She would..." Felipe sighed and put the bottles down. "Although I'd have thought that home would be a poor place for contemplation."

"She gave me an ultimatum," John said. "About my seeing Laurie Kalmar."

Felipe nodded.

"But I've decided now what I'm going to do."

"That's good, my son." With a wince, Felipe shifted in his chair. "Of course, you'll still be staying your term here?"

"Yes, I plan to remain a priest until then."

"And after that?"

"I don't think so. No."

"Do you have any plans?"

"Not really, Felipe. It's a big step. I can still hardly see as far as my taking it, let alone beyond."

"These things are sometimes for the best."

"That's pretty much what the bishop said."

Felipe nodded, and crinkled his eyes. The fan on the roof creaked and circled. "And Laurie?"

"I don't know. But I don't want to lose her." Outside, a truck went by. John looked down at the green spines of his gloves; the tiny Halcyon logo, which he noticed for the first time, was incorporated into the thread of the cuff, with the blur of his flesh beneath.

"Up to the west," Felipe said, "where the coast of Africa meets the River Ocean, the climate is better. Things grow unaided. Life is said to be easier there. I mean"—Felipe made a face and waved his hand at a fly—"that society between Europeans and Borderers is more relaxed. They work jointly, and there's no fence around the Zone. The freighters that head from there for Australasia have mixed crews. After all, if people live closely enough together, they forget their prejudices, they develop a physical and a mental tolerance..."

John nodded. He'd heard this before—from Borderers here in the Endless City, from priests at Millbrooke Seminary—but it was always about another place, some part of the Endless City they'd heard about but never actually seen.

"You managed," John asked, "when I was away?"

"Oh, you know."

"I'm sorry if I've been...a little preoccupied."

He heard the bang of a door and the tramp of footsteps on the stairs. That would be Bella returning. Although this was her afternoon off, she'd have managed to come back laden with shopping.

"I've been thinking about that leaf while you were away," Felipe said. "The koiyl. Not really the kind of thing that a European priest—even I—would be expected to show any curiosity about. Still, I made my inquiries." He smiled. "I think we should go out later tonight, my son, after you've done Mass. See what we can see..."

Nuru was waiting at the church for him, his hands clamped under his armpits, his dapper black clothes flapping in the wind. They were both early, and the door was unlocked, but Nuru hadn't bothered to go in: here, unlike at the clinic, he had no plans to take over.

"Fatoo John." Nuru spread his hands and followed John into the church as a cawing black squall clattered up from the roof. The emphasis was on the *John*. Who had he expected to see? Some new priest? He knew, after all, that John had been called back unexpectedly by the Fatoo Bishop. He probably knew about Laurie, too.

Dim light and cool air. John went alone into the vestry and dressed for Mass. The damp surplice was torn at the hem and smelled of incense and Felipe; even after Paris and Hemhill, the smell of a European was instantly recognizable to him. He tried to remember who had said to him that he hadn't really come back at all, and where it had been. He drew a breath and attempted to compose himself as the sound of footsteps and laughter came through the open doorway with the first of the arriving congregation. He changed his gloves and unlocked the sealed box that contained the Sacrament, wishing that Laurie would come at least once to the church during a service.

When he returned to the presbytery, he went into the backroom and called her on the airwave. All he got was her answerer. He stared at the answerer's face and said, "You've changed the color of your eyes."

"We thought it was time."

"We?"

"It was causing confusion. I always told Laurie that it would."

"Blue eyes make you look very different."

"I know."

"Almost the same as Laurie."

The answerer smiled.

"I'd like to meet her tomorrow," he said.

"I'm sure she'll be free. Would it be lunchtime, as usual?"

"I was thinking of that bar just outside the Zone."

"Which one? Is it one that you've been to before?"

"It has stars on the roof. A big place—"

"It's called Red Heat."

"Red Heat? Are you sure?"

"I'm sure."

Back in his room, waiting for whatever it was that Felipe had arranged to happen that night, John settled on the bed with the Quicklunch box of koiyl leaves beside him. The window was open. Across the street, the lights of most of the tenements were on and people were moving. Bella had certainly got their generator started by now, but he decided to work in darkness. The black shapes of the leaves in the box reminded him of figs at Christmas. Even the smell. And of old-fashioned Christmas soap, the kind shaped to look like something else. Touching one of the cards he'd attached to the leaves, he heard the sound of his own voice and the rumble of the taxi's engine in the background. A street name, and a description—deeply unflattering—of the vendor.

As he worked through the box, he found that the leaves were surprisingly varied. Of course, Laurie had pointed that out long ago. There were other high valleys that grew a product that was harmless and pure. This fat leaf, for example, was almost wider than his palm. And the stem was cut farther down—another local variation. He licked the rough and slightly oily skin. Sweet and tarry. He took a bite, and his mouth flooded with juice—or was it his own saliva? He pulled the wastebin over to the bed and spat out the reddish lump.

The next leaf was thinner, cut higher up the stem. Less sweet, more astringent. He spat that out too, aiming and hitting the bin from a slight distance, beginning to see that this would be part of the pleasure of the chewing: expectorating as a sport. His mouth, initially numb, seemed to swell and regain sensation.

It was fully dark now. Little stars rose and expired inside his eyes. Another leaf. Another. He heard his voice from the cards describing the taste and sensation, heard the wet smacking of his lips. Here, now, was a leaf from Lall. Not a particularly good specimen. Smaller than the rest. Almost shriveled. His voice on the card told him that he'd even managed to buy it at a slightly lower price. It was nothing like the fat green specimen that he'd been offered in the village, and after the others it seemed to have little effect on him. Perhaps he'd reached the maximum active dose, or was developing a tolerance. He got up and went to the window.

The lights were off in many of the tenements across the street, and the sky was a deep impenetrable crimson. He looked at his watch. Time was barely moving, and even the tiny flickering quaternary lines seemed half frozen, but it was too late now to try Laurie again—the real Laurie—without waking her. Off to the east, towards the coast, his eyes caught a flicker of blue-white. Probably lightning, but no rumble came on the wind, and it seemed too low even for these skies. His fingers picked at the paint of the windowledge as he tried to remember something that someone had once said...

A low rumble, long delayed, broke over the rooftops. It came, with typical Borderer lack of logic, from the direction opposite to the lightning flicker. The sound continued, then grew and resolved, sending the cats and rats and the few people who were still out scurrying to the edges of Gran Vía. He watched as a big forty-wheeler came churning between the houses, spewing a fog of dust and exhaust. The baroque cabin and the rusty fuselage slid by, then stopped, still thrumming, beneath his window, blocking the frontage of the presbytery and its neighbors.

In the corridor, John could hear Felipe shouting. He pulled on fresh gloves, grabbed his translat, and ran to help the old priest down the stairs and outside into the street, where the local children had reawakened and were already climbing over the truck as yawning adults looked on. A forty-wheeler had no place here on Gran Vía, especially this late, but it was hard for the people not to smile, especially as Felipe was winched, waving and turning, to the cabin. John clambered up the ladder alongside him, almost losing his footing as he helped lift Felipe in.

The horn moaned, the door swung shut. The engine roared, and the truck began to roll forward, tumbling John across a screeslope of cushions and rags at the back of the cabin. He climbed over the long front seat at the far end while the driver sat at some distance from him in the middle, with Felipe on the other side. The driver was a small man, grinning and elfin, with sharp bones and pointed ears. John vaguely recognized him as one of Felipe's drinking cronies, but the man wasn't a church-goer. They rarely were.

Windows and walls slid by close enough to touch. Watching Felipe through the swaying forest of cables and screens that filled the cabin, John saw him gulp from his flask, swallow one tablet, and start sucking at the next. As he did so, his eyelids quivered, his hands trembled. He was also humming snatches of a psalm, and belching between verses. John had noticed before that the haze of alcohol and trisoma was always stronger on the occasions that Felipe went out, and he wondered why it had never occurred to him before that the old priest was prob-ably agoraphobic.

Up onto the main highway, where the vehicles were larger although still mostly dwarfed by this one. The little driver was talking now—saying something about *fatoo muu;* John's mouth. Then cackling again. John wiped his lips on the back of his hand and saw the wet red stain from the koiyl.

They trundled on. Over, he guessed by the sag in his stom-ach and the splintering creaks, the loose bridge that he and Laurie had crossed on their way to Chott. The tiny driver leaped up in his seat to peer over the rusty plain of the truck's hood, pulling down screens on knotted ribbons. He hardly seemed in control. John could see where an access panel had flipped open on the seat between them, and could smell the semeny smell of hot nerve tissue.

The long fuselage creaked and snapped as they veered west, where mudflats and the Breathless Ocean shone, mirroring the clouds, and they headed downhill, picking up speed. The tiny man stroked the nerve tissue, grinning at John, and gave it a sexual squeeze. The sound of the engines, John was almost sure, grew more agonized, louder. Glittering ribbons and screens scythed pendulum arcs, and on the far side of the cab Felipe began to recede like a tunnel in a dream. The whole long body of the truck seemed to rise and buck as the little man's thin hands dug deeper and harder into a nerve's mucus-thick sheaf...

Finally they slowed and stopped in a wide parking area by the shore. John climbed shakily down the ladder and walked around the truck's long hot maw to help Felipe out of his cradle, slotting his right arm under his back and easing him to the ground. By now it was past midnight, and the parking area gleamed with flanks of cooling metal. The tiny driver watched from a few paces off, twitching his head and shoulders.

"You should have put on your leghelpers," John said.

"Why, my son? I've got you." But already Felipe was panting, and the breath in John's face consisted more of whisky than air. "But don't worry. It's not far. Not unless..."

They were at Seagates, which lay east of Mokifa and Kushiel. Ahead were the great cranes and gantries John had seen in the distance when he sat by the kelpbeds at Chott and Laurie told him about her father and mother. Close up, rearing towards the clouds, the cranes were truly impressive, far bigger than anything that served the automated warehouses in the Zone. Felipe leaned against a brick wall, gasping. He mopped his face with his red-tinged gloves, then began to fumble in his pockets. John found the flask for him within the folds. He looked around for the driver, but the driver was gone.

He linked an arm once more under Felipe's shoulder, and they started to walk. They passed through iron gates where water glinted up ahead and an engine chattered into life as a boat's white beam nodded across rotted moorings and break-waters. Looking down while he hauled Felipe's weight, he saw a tangle of keels bobbing in the water. A questioning lantern was held up towards them. There was a hiss of surprise as it caught the gleam of John's eyes. Then things took a predictable path: confusion at the presence of Outers was followed by a shrug, and glee at the thought of *cassan*—their money.

Felipe pulled himself away from John and stood swaying at the edge of the dock, waving his arms, barking at the boat hold-ers in his own version of their dialect. Somehow, an agreement was reached without the help of a translat, and a small boat was hauled close to the steps.

"How much did you pay to use it tonight?" John asked.

"I bought it, my son. But perhaps we should also try to hire a guide."

"Do you know where we're going?"

"Roughly, but—"

"Then come on."

The steps were slippery, and the boat rocked wildly, but somehow John managed to get Felipe down and seated at the prow. Scrambling to the stern, he sparked up the lantern and traced the outboard's flywheel, smoothing out the kinks in the rope and looping the end twice around his palm, pulling it out and through. A puff of exhaust stung his eyes once, twice, and the motor started. He turned the throttle and threw off the mooring rope.

"Where did you learn to do that?" asked Felipe.

John simply shrugged.

Many other craft were emerging from the wharves. Some with lights strung along their spars like Christmas trees, others frothing by on skirts or bobbing with only the creak of an oar. Rounding the last thrust of the pier, John saw the lights of the Seagates market stretching far along the coast.

He shouted to Felipe, "Which way do we go?"

The old priest waved his hands in a vague sweep. Farther east, John saw the funnels of the bulk carriers that plied the shores of the Breathless Ocean, but the smaller craft seemed to be heading straight inshore towards lights and rooftops. He tillered the boat that way, twisting up the throttle. The boat creaked and bucked on the soupy water where irregular lines of wharves, warehouses, and narrowing channels loomed. The gathering flotilla bobbed closer. Faces and prow lights flickered their way. Sitting on the loose plank that served as a seat, John steered under a low footbridge into a canal.

Afloat on either side were platforms seething with lobsters. He watched as one big creature flopped into the canal, its pincers flailed, drowning in water after a lifetime of wading in nutrient sludge. Some of the boats were already pulling in at the low piers. Deals were being haggled. The clamor grew louder. Lights dangled from a long, beamed roof. On other wharves there were heaps of brightly colored bowls, boxes of tubes, the inevitable tins of Quicklunch. Garish and incredible clothes hung on pulleys over the water, and cooking boats nudged around with their stoves blazing, streaming the smell of caramelized kelp and onion. The priests were passing now through stripes of lavender light that caught in the steam billowing from the water. Brass pots swayed and clanged. Here, every new turn and angle was a surprise. John slowed the engines, looking around him.

He smiled and watched as a child swung rope to chain from one section of roof to another, taking long, elaborate detours, whooping, agile as a monkey. They passed, it seemed, the same stall selling miniglaciers of pink-tainted sugar crystals that they'd seen earlier. There was no sign of the koiyl, but this whole night seemed to have developed an arcane logic of its own. He could see it as a kind of board game played through the long afternoons of a European winter. The latest craze—find the secret of the leaf. He could even see the screen, swirling and gilded as you entered it. The outboard stalled, and the boat touched a low bank of sand. He wound the motor, started it up again, and pushed off, steering towards the mouth of another tunnel.

"John!" Felipe pointed. "Over there..."

A soft scent broke over the water. There, piled on matting, heaped in baskets and buckets, lined out on patterned silks, were the koiyl leaves. Extracts and pickles too, and dried bunches of the flowers.

About a dozen merchants. John caught the flatter accents of the mountains in their voices. The leaves, he saw, were fresh, as yet undried: this season's crop. He nudged the boat closer in. The market was open to the sky here but darker than many of the various lit tunnels, and it was some time before the few bobbing lanterns caught the glow of their gloves and watches, the silver of their eyes. The disturbance then was predictable, but the merchants did their best to answer the questions that John shouted across to them. Yes, they knew Lall. Good leaves. *Bona.* Leaves were tentatively held across the water, more for him to see than to touch and thus cheapen. But this year, not many. Not this year, and not last year either, although they knew of no problem with the crop. Maybe someone else... But with each merchant it was the same, and John realized then just how good he'd become at identifying the Lall leaves. He didn't even need to ask. There were far fewer than he'd expected, and they were all of poor quality. The ratio he'd found recently on the streets was something like one in ten, but here the leaf from Lall seemed to be even scarcer. Which was odd, considering that Lall was on the main route through the mountains to this part of the Magulf. Perhaps, he asked, there was some other market that sold leaves, or some other section of this one? No; not within fifty kilometers, anyway. And up at Al-Fhican, they slept with beasts and had tails like animals—those people wouldn't deal with Lall. Or another day? But no, also. No. And so it went.

John eventually poled the boat back from the crowd towards a small and empty island, and sat watching as the koiyl merchants got on with the business of the night. An absurd thought, but it almost seemed as if, now that he knew they were dangerous, the Lall leaves were disappearing of their own accord.

At the prow, Felipe popped out more tablets from his blisterpack. They were the last, and he seemed drowsy. For some time now he'd given up trying to keep his split shoes and bandaged feet out of the bilgewater.

"Can you think," John asked, "of anywhere else?"

"For what?" Felipe folded his arms over his chest. His eyelids trembled.

"Other than here, for the leaf."

"Ah..." Felipe chuckled. "You were hoping for a single dealer, weren't you? Someone who could have simply waved his hands and... What you're trying to do here is very difficult."

"I understand, Felipe."

"I know what you think of me, my son, and of the little gifts that arrive at the presbytery. Old Felipe with a finger in

302

every imaginable pie..." He paused a moment, his fingers tracing the empty depressions of his blisterpack. "You think I have—all these deals and arrangements. It's not like that. The reason people bring me things, the reason I'm tolerated and possibly occasionally even liked and respected here, is that I keep my distance. I leave the Borderers to live their own lives. I leave them. As they wish. You see... And because I don't..." The old priest's eyes were closed now. After this brief animation, his voice had become a mumble. "Because I don't..."

He grunted, nodded, was asleep. John restarted the outboard and steered the boat back past the koiyl vendors into the first of the chambered tunnels. The night had gone quickly, and the crowds and the boats around the stalls were already thinning. Scaffolding was being dismantled, barges were being towed away. The piles of unsold wares had a disappointed look.

In the open air again, where the sky was lightening, John shifted and looked around. His bladder was starting to ache, and pissing was always a tricky operation in the Endless City; because of the viruses, you needed somewhere away from habitation. The boat puttered on. Rusting iron bars blocked the wide mouth of a tunnel, so he reversed the throttle and turned back. Felipe began to snore. John took a side canal, which threatened a dead end but then opened to a long, newish concrete wharf. There was no one about as he leaned over to grab a mooring post, threw the rope over, and killed the engine. Keeping his balance, remastering an old trick, he stood urinating into the water. Sparks erupted before his eyes. The air was clear and almost cold here. There was little wind. They were surrounded by the silence of large, dark buildings. He closed himself up and looked around again.

"Felipe?"

The old priest remained slumped in the prow. Now that John had stood up, his back ached terribly. It was probably just from sitting half the night with his hand on the tiller of the boat, but he couldn't ever remember a pain quite like this one, and he wondered briefly if the crystal rigidity of his recombinant wasn't starting, even this early in his life, to damage his spine. He clambered onto the wharf and secured the rope. He stretched and rubbed himself, thinking of the faces at Southlands and the metal jutting from flesh in those Yorkshire backrooms. But already the ache was starting to ease...

He walked beside the wall away from the water's edge. Beyond were the empty frames of stalls, a few caroni birds, a great deal of litter. He glanced back at the boat, then wandered on up through the empty shore market, where his feet slipped and skidded on a mush of discarded food, loose wet packaging, the perennial soggy balls of chewed koiyl. A green light twinkling in the mud caught his eye, and he bent cautiously—waiting for the pain to come back into his spine, using his knees to stoop as he'd seen his mother do on that misty Hemhill morning in her garden not long ago—and peeled the flattened carton from the stones. The emerald pinprick was one of the signal shades Halcycon used to indicate when medicines had passed their use-by date. In another place he saw a misty starfield glinting in the mud. Not just *reinventory* greens, but *potency retarded* blues, *immediate discard* reds. In fact, more than he'd ever seen, even on the shelves at the clinic. Some, now that the moisture had corrupted their circuitry, were giving out muffled versions of the final beep-barp danger signal that he'd often had to ignore. The safety parameters were excessive anyway, and there was the trick Tim Purdoe had shown him—how to bring the lights on or shut them off with the simple passing of a magnet.

He looked again at the sodden carton in his hand—it had contained a mild immune-suppressant, something he'd asked for many times at the clinic—then, hearing voices approaching, he threw it back into the mud. A small cluster of Borderers came into view. The one with the most audible voice was much taller than the rest. As John stood and waited, he caught the flash of metallic hands. When the tall man saw him, he dismissed the others and walked up to him alone.

"Father John." Ryat smiled. "You should have told me that you were coming here."

John pointed back at the wharf. "I arrived in a boat with my partner-priest, Felipe."

Ryat waved an arm. John felt the breeze from his fingers. "Most everything comes through here...But you already know that? From what you have seen?"

"Actually, I was looking for something specific."

"And could not find it?"

John opened his mouth.

"Come." Ryat was turning, walking away. "My office is near. We can talk there."

As the sky brightened and the wind picked up, they left the empty aisles and crossed the iron ridge of an old railtrack towards an ancient building that stood alone. It had tall windows and a portico, and beneath the crusted dirt seemed to have been made from blocks of real stone. John gazed up at the entrance. The inspiring scenes and scrolled cod-Latin inscriptions had weathered away, but a tarnished plate riveted to a pillar still read CONTROLE DE PASSPORTS. A beggar sat in a hollow of the worn steps, her face a black mass of flies. Ryat paused to give her some money, and John noticed the little ritual they went through with their hands to avoid the touch of flesh to metal.

Apart from the checkered tiles, the stumps of gaslights, and the broken mosaic of a frieze, most of the interior had given way to scaffolding and rubble. Bats clattered high in the roof, and the few unbroken panes of the domed skylight filtered the already reddish light of the sky with the green of their scum, turning everything gray. Yet, perched at the top of a new set of stairs, Ryat's office was as rich as the whole building must once have been when harbormasters and customs officers sweated in their uniforms in this colonial rim of Empire.

John sat down. Everything in the office seemed to be made of brass, leather, or wood, and the air smelled of old varnish. There were sash-framed windows looking out on three sides, although the room lay in the middle of the building. John traced the stitching on the arm of his high-backed chair. The spines of his gloves were two-thirds red now.

"From here," Ryat said, stretching out his booted legs on the desk. "I can watch things." Outside, it was mostly quiet on the canals and walkways, although a dredger was working off-shore and a large tanker was nosing in to port. The scene switched to a view from a high crane, and the tanker became a toy, spreading a white V across the water.

"The reason I came here," John said, "was to find out about the distribution of the koiyl leaf. Felipe suggested to me that it might come here first from the mountains."

"Of course. The koiyl comes here. East dock, sector three."

John nodded—although he didn't think that east dock, sector three, would be what the Borderers called it. The leather chair squealed as he shifted position. Should he simply say that the koiyl from Lall was contaminated? The silence began to weigh, yet there was no real sense of tension: Ryat was a

Borderer, used to not filling in every pause with empty babbling. John asked, "Have you heard of Lall?"

"Lall?" Ryat thought, nodded. "A place in the mountains where the leaf is grown. Yes?"

"I've been trying to trace the crop from there. This year's should be in the Endless City by now if it's going to be cured and marketed."

"I presume it is."

"There seems to be surprisingly little."

"Perhaps you came here on the wrong night?"

"Is there a way you could find out?"

"Ah..." Ryat kicked back his chair and walked over to the neat rows of tiny brass-plated drawers that reached floor to ceiling on the unwindowed wall to his right. His fingers clicked down the wood and brass. One and then another drawer slid open. The cards buzzed, and the scenes of the empty market in the windows flickered and changed. Once, John thought he glimpsed Felipe lying in the boat, then a flock of caroni birds. Another drawer flew open. Ryat's hands were quick and graceful here—working in a way that no human hands could—but something was wrong. Why hadn't he asked John what he was after?

"Yes..." A drawer flashed. "I think we have something. But I see what you mean. There was much leaf from Lall five years ago..." Another drawer. "But now, each year, less."

"Do you have any idea why?"

Ryat turned to him. "I provide only facilities here." He still had one card in his hand. The tip of a finger traced the magnetic strip along the back. He seemed to be reading it. "And, of course, Seagates is just a staging post, a channel. The main sales are always at Tiir."

"I've been to Tiir."

"You did not get an answer?"

"I wasn't there long. And perhaps I didn't ask the right questions."

"These things are difficult, Father John. You ask a simple question in the Endless City and get no answer—or get many. Too many. But never just the one."

Ryat returned the final card to its drawer. Linking his metal hands behind his back, he crossed to the far window and stood looking out. Despite its depth and clarity, the view through the glass was pixel-based. From the distance he was standing, it had to have been little more than a blur.

"But I will ask for you," he said. "Of course, I will make inquiries."

Folding his own hands, John felt the adhesion of his gloves. "Do you know," he asked, "why I'm doing this? Why I'm asking?"

Ryat raised his shoulders. His fingers slid. "The curiosity of a European fatoo is explanation enough."

John told him about Ifri Gotal, the strontium 90, the tests, and the cases of *bludrut* at the clinic. Ryat nodded and listened, but he didn't seem surprised.

When John finished, Ryat spread his hands. "There have been rumors," he said. "Even allowing for the poor standard of the leaf from Lall that is available, I understand that the price is down."

"But you didn't know?"

The corners of Ryat's mouth twitched. In profile against the changing window, his face flickered slightly. "These things always do come out, Father John. Why do you think I go to the Zone? I do not expect I will ever get very far with the tennis..." He grinned. "And these ancient weapons are terrible, yes? To be feared even now. The laws of nature have not changed. Why, think what would happen if the weapons were to be developed again—here, for example, in the Endless City. Of course, it would require a different culture, the kind of organization and government that I sometimes suspect that your people in the Zone are here to discourage. To keep us dependent, moderately happy, but not too wise . . ."

"But at least there are no wars."

"No," Ryat said. "There are no wars."

"And now that you know there is a poison in the Lall leaves, will you help?"

Ryat pointed to the racks of drawers. "As you see, I cannot stop something that is already—"

"The leaves will still eventually come through Seagates—at least some of them."

"What do you expect me to do? Destroy them? Or should I speak out, intentionally devalue them, as you or someone else seems to have done already? You tell me that a few people die here in the Endless City, but how many people live in Lall? And do you imagine you can warn about the leaf from one area and not harm the trade as a whole? And the traders, what will you do for them?"

"It isn't—"

"Father John, let me tell you I once spoke with another European. Someone who came from the Zone here to this room and explained that we Borderers must not sell Quicklunch, that it causes the stomachs of our children to ulcer. Do you not see that too, at your clinic?"

John nodded, but the symmetry of someone else sitting here and arguing about food contamination was too neat. It was true that Quicklunch had been dumped on the Magulf after a scare in Europe, but that had been a recombinant-precipitated reaction, and the figures at the clinic for stomach problems had never stood out.

"I am sorry." Ryat sighed. "I only wish to tell you that the answer is not easy."

"I understand there are problems. I agree with at least some of what you say about the hypocrisy of the Zone. But you haven't seen these people dying. They're young people, Ryat—children, sometimes—and many haven't even chewed the leaf themselves. I know there are other injustices, but will you at least help me to do something about this one? Will you look out for the Lall leaf in Seagates, and keep me informed?"

Ryat pursed his lips. "Yes," he said. "If I can."

"I'm grateful." John stood up from his chair. The ache in his back had returned. He felt weary, dazed. The light at the end of the tunnel, he remembered Hal once saying, can be an oncoming train.

"Come on, Father John." Ryat strode around the table and placed a hand on his shoulder. The metal clenched, and John forced himself not to pull back. "This crop from Lall will turn up. And from here...There will be ways to change things. Have you thought perhaps that you are trying too hard? A material thing can sometimes be as elusive as a feeling. If you seek too strongly, it may disappear..."

John looked at Ryat as the hand released and withdrew. He felt a sudden twist of anger. At close quarters, as with everyone else here in the Endless City, Ryat's breath reeked of kelp.

Finding his own way out from Ryat's office, John wiped a Magulf dollar and tossed it at the beggar on the steps. Now that there was no point in keeping it secret, he had half a mind to ask her too what she knew about the leaf, but she shrank from the coin as it spun on the eroded marble between them. He walked back to the boat through the market where the glowing cartons flapped and soggy balls of litter scuttled towards him. The world was dimmer than ever this morning. Even the wind and heat seemed frail.

He turned the corner. A thick scum of lobster husks, sodden kelp, koiyl leaves, and the twisting body of an animated doll broke and slapped at the concrete wharf. Beyond the wharf, a path of flames trailed across the water. He stared at it for a moment, rubbing his back, his feet slowing. Then he broke into a run. Farther up, past where the boat should have been, gray figures clustered at the water's edge. Filaments of their clothing unfurled, and he could hear them shouting and whooping. *Chicahta... Scuro... Rojo...*

Tumbling, nearly falling, he yelled Felipe's name.

He found Felipe propped against the boat's mooring post. His shoes were off, and his sodden bandages had been un-raveled. Oily bolts and screws had been removed from the boat's torn-off outboard and pushed between his toes. John shook Felipe's shoulders, but the old priest only muttered and smacked his lips, still deep in trisoma dreams. John slumped down beside him. Smoke was rising across the water, stinging his eyes as the wind drew at the flames. For a while, the boat shone as brightly as the sun that was so rare in these Magulf skies. Then the blaze died, as the boat, raising its blackened prow like a drowning hand, slid beneath the water.

Down the wharf, the witchwoman cackled and waved.

THE BAR REALLY was called Red Heat. He saw the letters—no longer straight, and colored a chill powdery blue—framed above the doorway. And, as always with the places he and Laurie visited at lunchtime, there were few diners. A wealthy-looking Borderer sat eating alone, and two European males who'd bothered to make the journey out past the shock-wire were hunched over a table; from what John caught of their conversation, he guessed that they were engineers at the phosphate plant. They probably hadn't been in the Magulf long, either, from the sullen way they kept looking around. As well as being cold, the Red Heat was big, dim, and empty, and smelled of damp and burnt fat.

John glanced up at the high ceiling, which glinted with the gilded light of stars. Not stars as you might see them, but pointed, filament-waving, storybook stars. Those stars, and the way that all the tumblers had frosted to a driftglass translucence from frequent washing, had been his main memories of their last visit here. Certainly not the name.

He glanced at his watch. Laurie was ten minutes late. Worried about going to the wrong place and missing her, he'd arrived early. She was usually early too, but now she was ten minutes late. With anyone else, that would be...

The door swung open, and there was Laurie, peering around for a moment as her eyes adjusted from the gloom outside to the Red Heat's greater gloom. He watched as she stood with her face and body still unfocused, still not conscious of him— he had, after all, chosen the farthest, darkest corner. She looked strange and lovely, gawky and yet strong. For a moment, he thought, she was like a new and different person; like an actress in that unguarded moment when her face relaxes as she walks offstage.

"Laurie..." He raised an arm. The two phosphate engineers looked over.

She truly seemed different today. As she moved between the empty tables and chairs, he saw that she was wearing a newer, shorter dress. Something that he'd never seen her in before. Pale red stockings. Shoes with raised heels. She came and stood by him.

"Sorry I'm late. I..." She gestured at the outfit. Now that he'd finished noticing her legs, he also saw that she was wearing a short navy jacket brocaded at the edges. Her eyes seemed wider, too, her lips redder, and she smelled of the primitive dab-on perfume that he once saw on the shelf in her bathroom but had never actually caught her wearing. And her hair—even though the wind had got to it—was held back by two gold bands. All this for me? he thought, quite overwhelmed as she sat down. He felt clumsy and unworthy. The ache had come back into his throat.

"You look great, incredible."

"Thanks. So do you." She looked at him and tilted her head, changing her mind. "Are you hungry? Have you ordered?"

He shook his head. The tiredness of the long night at Sea-gates and this more-than-alcohol drink were starting to have an effect.

"Well?" she asked, feeling in her bag. "What was it like?"

"After Paris, I went back to England—to Herefordshire. Home."

"I had wondered why you returned on the London shuttle."

"You knew that?"

"I asked the net to check the flight lists for me. Why?"

His eyes stung a little as the tubegas reached him.

"You know I missed you."

"I missed you too."

She reached her hand across the table, and he took it. The two phosphate engineers watched in silence. John was dressed in secular civvies, but perhaps they knew he was a priest. Or it could have been just the sight of a European male and a Borderer female touching—although if every story he'd heard was to be believed, most expats paid at least one visit to do more than just touch the flesh at Agouna, if only so that they could say that they'd been. But that was different. Just another transaction.

They ordered food. Mainly bread and fungi. Laurie said she wasn't hungry, and John could still taste the koiyl he'd chewed before he went to Seagates. It wasn't actually unpleasant, but it dulled his appetite.

"You got the afternoon off?" she asked.

"Yes," he said. "I don't have Mass till six this evening."

"Anyway"—her cheeks hollowed as she drew on her tube—"some things don't change."

"In Paris," he said, "when I saw the bishop, it was pretty obvious that everyone in the Zone had been talking."

"Everyone?"

"Well, you know."

"I suppose we could have been more careful. But I'm used to being..." She thought for a moment. "Ignored and noticed at the same time."

"We both stand out, Laurie. I don't know what I was bothering to hide from anyway. I'm not ashamed."

"You've said that before."

"It's true."

"From the bishop, did you get a telling off?"

"It's not like that. When all is said and done, my vows are between me and God. She—"

"She?"

"It does happen. She was sympathetic, really, Laurie. She asked about you. She knows about the problems I've had with my faith. She wanted to know how I felt. She wanted to know if I was in love."

"Are you?"

"I don't know. I'm still not sure..." He blinked. This was all coming out too quickly. Laurie was watching him, and part of him wanted to shout yes, to hug her and hold her. "Anyway," he said, "the ache's in my throat again, and even my back is now aching—"

"That's lust," Laurie said, "not love."

Seeing the change in his expression, she sat back a little.

"You don't know either, do you?" he said. "Where this is taking us?"

He picked at his food. He asked Laurie what she'd been doing. She shifted her second or third tube between her fingers.

"Nothing much," she said. "Just working."

The two phosphate engineers left. Someone else came in, but this place was so dark, it was impossible to tell the person's sex or even whether the person was Borderer or European. The door swung forward, back. Outside, some kind of procession was going on—a funeral, to judge by the witchwoman wails and the jangling music. It was headed straight for the incinerator at El Teuf. Nothing that he would be involved in.

"How are your parents?" Laurie asked. "How's Hal?"

"Hemhill's the same. Nothing seems to have changed."

"What are you going to do?"

"I'll give the three or so months I have left here to the priesthood," he said, feeling suddenly breathless, his heart racing. "Then I'll quit. Laurie, I'm going to leave."

She made to say something, then stopped, gazing over his shoulder as her hands fiddled with the tube. "This is for me? You can't throw away..."

"No, Laurie, it isn't for you, it's for me. Nothing else is clear to me at the moment, but I do know that it's for me. I don't feel free. I don't understand myself. I can't even come to terms with God..."

Laurie ground out her tube in the saucer between them. As she leaned forward, a soft hollow formed at the base of her throat.

He asked, "Why do they call this place Red Heat?"

"Isn't it obvious? It's because it's so big and cold."

They paid the bill and left. Outside, she walked away from him, moving quickly. He shouted after her. The street was overfull. There were women carrying great swaying bundles of kelp-sausage on their heads. A screaming child was snatched into a doorway. Someone muttered *something-outer*—and from somewhere there was a deep, growling rumble. It was early afternoon, but the lights were on in the rooms above the shops, and it could almost have been twilight. He looked at a passing koiyl vendor, trying to see if he remembered the face. The displays on a stall that sold Magulf lace were flapping madly. The chemical smoke from the hot pans of a dye maker whipped around them. A Halcycon-logoed Elysian whispered by, its windows blanked.

"Come on." She pulled him around the corner, where her van sat in the dust between the windowless sides of two tenements. The rumbling came again, and the wind was suddenly stronger. Up ahead, supported by a post between the two buildings, a child's swing rocked wildly.

They tumbled into the van, and the wind banged the doors shut behind them as Laurie leaned over and began to kiss him. He placed his arms gently around her shoulders, feeling the intricate stitching of the collar, the press of her tongue into his mouth. He could smell the perfume she wore, the way the chemicals had reacted with and almost drowned out the Laurie scent of sea and mist and rain and her skin. He opened his eyes and saw her closed lids and the delicate whorl of her ear, the lobe pierced by a gold stud. The wind boomed. Her stockings sighed as she shifted her legs. The van creaked and rocked slightly. He felt the nub of an old tube pressing into his right thigh. When Laurie kissed, there was always a faint grunt in the back of her throat. She was making it now. Then suddenly she pulled back.

"I'm sorry," he said. "I'm really not here."

"Where are you, then?" She fished in her bag.

"No." He took her hand. "Wait a minute. Look..." He squeezed her hand. "I'm sorry. This whole thing needs explaining."

"You mean kissing? I thought it was a straightforward process for two people."

"It's..." He shook his head. Laurie looked crumpled now, with her makeup smudged and her skirt no longer straight. "I don't think it's something that I'm ready for yet. I mean, sex," he said. "I'd like to call a truce."

"Truce?"

"I know it's the wrong word—a stupid word." He laughed. The wind rattled over the van. "I want to see you, Laurie. I *long* to see you—you know that. But can't we just keep it the way it is for now, Laurie? Just being together until I've finished here, as a priest?"

"People will still talk if we are seen with each other."

"That's not what this is about."

"I suppose you gave your word to your bishop not to fuck me?"

"Yes. *No.* This is all happening so quickly, Laurie. Can't we just give ourselves time to breathe?"

"All right." She pushed the card into the slot, and the engine started, the van began to rise. "It's a kind of relief for me also. I hate hiding. I'm sick of eating lunches I don't want at places no one goes to."

"I won't go back to Europe at the end of my term," he said.

"I'll stay on and find work in the Endless City. That isn't long. And you, Laurie—you always said you wanted to leave the Zone."

She took the wheel of the van and gave him a kind of smile.

"...and when you asked if I loved you, Laurie, I wish I hadn't said I wasn't sure. That's not true, I..."

Her hand came down on his knee to silence him. Then she touched the grubby dashboard screen. Dust swirled.

"We couldn't have made it more difficult," she said, "could we? Not if we'd worked at it. Not just Borderer and European—but you a priest."

He laughed and stretched his hand along the back of the seat, touching her padded, embroidered shoulder, his sleeve riding up, the pale light from his watch glinting on the colored beads.

"But, then, you could have been a homosexual too, John. Isn't that what most priests are?"

She pulled into the darkening, crowded street. There's not much point after this, he thought, in our going back to the bungalow the way we used to most afternoons. But Laurie had turned the other way in any case—west and away from the Zone.

"It's not far to Mokifa," she said, peering up through the windshield at the low sky.

"Mokifa?"

"It's where my mother lives."

As she drove on, he glimpsed a hitherto unseen variant of Santa Cristina's blackened silhouette over the shanty roofs.

"I went to Seagates last night," he said, "with Felipe."

"Oh?" She nodded. "The market."

"I was looking for the Lall koiyl."

"Did you find it?" She slowed for a flock of children. One

of them waved and banged the hood of the van. John watched her eyes crinkle with a smile.

"And I met Ryat. Remember Ryat? He was at the Governor's Residence that night."

"Yes. I remember."

"Do you think I should trust him?"

"Trust him for what?"

"He seemed... Well, not unhelpful, but evasive. And he already knew about the leaf being contaminated. Somehow, the news of that must have got out to him."

"I'm not surprised," Laurie said.

"Then he went on about Quicklunch, about how there were so many other kinds of wrongs..."

"And he's right, really," Laurie said. "The Endless City is bound to have things like the Lall leaf, by its nature."

"What do you mean, by its nature?"

"No one is in control to say—this is, that will be, you must. You're from a structured society, you expect simple answers."

"You're starting to sound like Ryat now."

"Is that surprising?"

They slowed at a scalloped archway leading into Mokifa. Even before she cranked down the window to show her face to the tattooed child-guard, Laurie was waved on.

"People know you here?"

"This was my home."

"What about Chott?"

"Chott was when I was young."

He said nothing, irritated that anyone should cordon off a part of the Endless City. The roads were paved here, and there were more taxis and vans than he was used to—their headlights, today, blazing through the gloom—but otherwise Mokifa wasn't that different. There were even beggars (perhaps they were the beggar gentry). He did notice fewer animals—and fewer children. Many of the houses and tenements were more modern—uglier, disfigured by external pipes and wires.

Laurie stopped the van. "We are here."

He climbed out and looked around. Even with the wind howling, the air was filled with the discordant throb and rattle of generators. A building opposite had been configured to look something like a Roman palazzo, but the ornate golden arches fizzed and brightened unevenly. Through them he could see ghost outlines of corrugated jelt. The people walking by seemed the same here as everywhere else—although there were perhaps fewer obvious oddities and deformities among them, and they stared a little less obviously at him. Were they better dressed? It was hard to tell, wrapped up and hunched as they were against this stormy afternoon.

"I didn't think you'd approve," Laurie muttered.

The tenement where her mother lived consisted of various boxlike levels of individual dwellings linked and cocooned by a loose network of cables and scaffolding. The steel gate of a lift slid open when Laurie spoke to it. Creaking, it drew them slowly up through the lattice of girders. There was a green scent in the air that could have been polish or a mood change in Laurie's perfume. She gave him a look, standing by him, then gazed back at the door. The steel caught the reflection of two figures; faceless outlines and colors. Laurie's pale red legs. Her squared shoulders. Her frilled skirt. He thought *dancing ladies,* then the lift turned right, juddered, and stopped. The door slid open, and the scented air escaped into the wind.

"Your mother knows about me?" he shouted, following her on the open walkway.

"Oh yes," she said, pulling at her cuffs in the shelter of a doorway, straightening the bands in her hair. "She knows."

The apartment was windowless, strung high amid the girders. There was a screen on the sealed door. It greeted them as the door hissed open, and they stepped into a sudden hush and warmly lit gloom. Laurie's mother had the bustle of someone who was expecting guests—but not quite yet.

The décor was all very complicated and neat. Furred red wallpaper, the brassy glow of many small electric lanterns, chairs with lacy edges, mobile and unsubtle pictures of scenery; waterfalls and seascapes. A half-meter-tall clown stood atop an implausibly ugly chest of drawers, hopping from foot to foot and juggling tiny balls. The carpet was lumpy from all the cabling.

Laurie seemed relaxed, and her mother sat facing John in the kind of advanced interactive chair that no elderly European would have sat in—it proclaimed too conspicuously the need for help. Yet she'd moved around easily enough when she saw them in, and she didn't even look that old. He guessed she was in her late fifties, like his own parents, yet her dark hair was thick and full, her jaw was strong, and the flesh on her hands and face, if slightly crimped, was still plump.

"I used to go to Santa Cristina," she told him. "Once. But I did not really go for Christ, for the religion. The priest..."

"Father Felipe?"

She thought, then shook her head. "It was many years ago."

Did you take Laurie there with you, too? he wondered. Did she sit at the back swinging her legs—and why has she never told me about it?

"It would be good," he said, "if you could come to the church again. I see so few people from here, from Mokifa."

She smiled and said, "Yes, I will see if I can." But she looked and sounded so much like Laurie that he knew that that meant no.

"You worked in Europe, didn't you?"

"Yes," she said. "Laurie told you about that." It was a statement rather than a question. They gazed at each other for a moment, then looked over as the trolley came rattling in through the wall.

"Didn't you say you were going to get the wheel fixed on that thing?" Laurie asked.

"You know how it is..." Her mother spread her arms. *"Fornu."*

Fornu... That one Borderer word hung in this rich, dark room. John wondered whether it was his imagination, or whether this whole tenement really was rocking in the wind.

The cups were filled and passed around. The biscuits on the plate that had been reserved for him were warm and tasted of sugar, butter, and flour in the fractional moment before they dissolved into nothing. John couldn't remember when he'd sat in a Borderer room and eaten food before—yet it all felt eerily normal, almost boring. Tea with the priest; as though Laurie and her mother were acting out some kind of play.

"You are good friends, I hear."

"Yes," he nodded. "We've got to know each other very well. Even these days, I suppose, that's uncommon. Ah..." He realized he didn't know what to call her. *Mrs. Kalmar, I'd like to marry your lovely daughter.* How did that sound? Like one of those stupid tunes Felipe was always humming.

"You have not many months here?"

"A couple—two—in this posting. But then I think I'll try to find work that will keep me in the Endless City."

"You miss Europe?"

"No, I don't miss Europe. I was just there."

"Yes. Laurie told me."

Behind her, on a shelf above the juggling clown, was propped a smaller picture, less elaborate than the heaving landscapes on the walls. A younger version of this primly dressed woman looked down on him. The man standing with her, grinning and with his long hair tied back, also managed to look like Laurie, although he could not have been more different from his wife. A stubborn man, Laurie had told John, and her father looked it, although he was relaxed with his two sons beside him, one already fuller and broader than he was, unmistakably self-possessed and handsome, the other thinner, like a poorer and wrongly sexed shadow of Laurie. A girl in a print dress stood in front of them, holding herself still with a tension that suggested she wanted to squirm away from the proprietary hand that her father was trying to place on her shoulder. She had a mischievous face. The background had been blanked to gray—no pens and ramshackle houses and black pillars, none of the stench and gleam of the old kelpbeds. But for the color of their eyes, he thought, the photograph could have been taken at any time, anywhere.

"And you have both been," Laurie's mother said, "to the mountains? So I hear?"

He tried to tell Laurie's mother about the koiyl and Ifri Gotal. He hoped that his newly decided policy about the koiyl—the idea of being open, telling everyone—might suggest new leads and possibilities. But he sensed that her attention was as poorly focused as his own. No doubt she was more concerned about the company her daughter was keeping with this alien holy man.

The conversation faltered. Laurie stood up and said to John that she'd like to show him her old room. Moving carefully around ornaments and the low table, he followed her through the wall. The illusion was thin; as they passed through, it gave no sensation at all.

"My money keeps this place going now," Laurie said as they stood in a bare jelt-walled room with a narrow mattress. "My mother's ran out some time ago."

The room was blank, like a cell. "Were you really *here*?"

"Try it like this."

She touched a screen on the wall. Now there were pictures, a glittering starfield for a ceiling. "This is mostly how I used to have it. It seems smaller to me now."

"None of it is real."

"Everything is real, John—or as unreal as you make it."

He looked around. Compared to the sort of thing Laurie could achieve on the net, the projections here lacked definition. The shelf of analogue books that had appeared by the bed would probably require some kind of physical amplification. It was like a hotel room; offhand, impersonal. And so neat.

"What do you do, Laurie," he said, "turn it off at night to save power?" Then he realized, from the look on her face, that that was exactly what you did here in Mokifa.

"I need to check the kitchen appliances," she said, turning to go. Then she stopped. "Think of your own life, John, before you criticize and judge others. At least I'm not forcing someone to have pretentious ancient European music churning around in their head all day."

She went out through the door without bothering to open

it. He caught the leap of static as the frilled edge of her skirt brushed against him. Dulled, confused, expecting no response from the room, he leaned over to the bookcase and tried to take out one of the volumes. To his surprise, it moved—if jerkily— and his fingers received a vague impression of size and weight. The book split open in his hands, and there were words inside it—the shimmering print of a language even stranger than Borderer. It was English-American.

The door, he read, *irised open.* Looking up and around Laurie's room, he saw that the night-sky ceiling now encompassed the floor and walls. Unlike the stars at the Red Heat bar, these looked real enough, but there were also golden arrow-shaped spacerockets whooshing by between pretty, many-ringed planets. The book was telling, he guessed, some long-forgotten tale of the never-to-be future.

Laurie came back into the room. She clicked her fingers, and the book, with the rocket-threaded stars and planets, faded and vanished. She said, "We'll have to go soon. Arra comes at four, and anyone else being here gets in her way."

"Arra?"

"She cleans for my mother. I don't suppose," Laurie said, "that you feel that you know me any better now."

"I keep thinking how much I take for granted."

They left the room, and said goodbye to Laurie's mother. The chair lifted her up, and she studied John gravely. Her face was broader than Laurie's, reminding him of the distortion that came into his parents' features when they leaned too close to the console. Touch another screen, he thought, and Laurie and her mother, or this whole place, might disappear. Laurie was good, after all—a quaternary wizard. And now she hung close to the exit, fiddling with the brocade of her sleeve, suddenly anxious to go.

"Goodbye."

"Gonenanh."

A deep crackling sound came from the sky as they stood waiting for the lift.

"Laurie," he said, holding the railing, which quivered in his hand. "What you said about the music...It was about Hal, wasn't it?"

"Music?"

Something wheezed and snapped somewhere, and he felt the railing shudder. "How did you know about the music my father plays to Hal?"

"How do you think?"

He said nothing. Laurie looked around at the webbing and the racked clusters of houses, the wind furrowing her hair, then frowned and waved her hands.

"I used the net."

"You used the net?"

"Of course I used the net."

They stared at each other. The lift arrived. The door squeaked open.

"If you want to know about my life, Laurie, why don't you just ask?"

"I do ask—I just don't get a great many answers."

He was breathing hard. The sky tore at the rooftops. The wind roared. Grit pattered his face. He wished that he could shut it all off for a moment, that the two of them could stand together in some empty place where there was no Europe, no Magulf, no sex, no God, no viruses, no preconceptions.

The lift peeped to remind them of its presence. Laurie stepped in, and he stood beside her as the door closed, shutting them off.

"So you already knew," he said, "that I'd been to Hemhill? Back at that bar, there was no need for you even to ask."

"No. Actually, I didn't know."

"You didn't—"

"I accessed Hal some time ago, John. I'm sorry if you think I was curious."

Sorry. Curious. Some time ago. These words, he supposed, should be helping. That was what they were for. But Laurie— he knew so much about her, her flesh at every soft and rainy shade and flavor and angle—he could even sense the precise moment when she would reach into her bag for a tube. There—she was doing it now, and the lift was creaking, turning, taking them down.

"Curious?" he said.

"Yes." The space grayed with smoke. "I was curious."

"And the koiyl? You were curious about that too?"

"What?"

"Is that why you copied the cards? Because you thought Ryat should know? Was it to satisfy his or your curiosity?"

She raised her head and nodded quickly, as though getting the final twist of an elaborate joke. Then the door slid open, and she walked to the van.

"You did tell him, didn't you?"

"I didn't tell anyone."

The palazzo opposite glowed and fluttered. Something was screaming in the wind. Looking up, he saw lines, electric cables. One was snapping and swaying; another had broken loose, twisting like a snake. There was no sense of power in them.

She fumbled for the card, nearly losing it to the wind. He was standing on the van's passenger side, as though he might actually get back in with her.

"What..." she muttered, her head down, words lost. Then she faced him with her green eyes across the dented and dusty roof. "You think I went all the way to Ifri Gotal with you...? Fucked you...? For the sake of some stupid..." She gestured, searching for the word. "Conspiracy."

He pointed at Mokifa, at the tenements. "Then where do you get all the money?"

Her face went a little blank. Ah! he thought, weirdly triumphant.

"Yes." She nodded. "I do sometimes copy cards and let things out. Sometimes, for money that I need for here and for myself. But not you, John." Her eyes narrowed. "What do you think I am?" Everything seemed to be slowing down, growing more gray and solid. "It's just stuff about the kelpbed contracts...I..." She thumped the roof of the van. "Why should I tell you this?"

"Because we're supposed to trust each other. And Hal!" he shouted in a sudden red burst, disbelieving. "Why did you have to pry?"

"Pry." She nodded again, as if that explained something, and he wondered for a moment if she'd misheard and thought he'd said *pray*.

"...if you could just see how you are now," she was shouting, "the way you're standing there. The way you never really seem to move. The way you never really left Europe. Just what are you, John? A priest, and you don't even believe in God— do you? You don't believe in love either..." She shook her head. Her hair obscured her face. She pushed it back from her mouth and eyes. "I'm sick of these discussions with you."

The street was empty. The air was truly foul with grit now, and even the spectacle of a Borderer and a European having an argument wouldn't have been enough to draw people out. He squeezed his eyes shut, then opened them again. They were dry and ached in the wind. He was sick of life, sick of memories.

"And please will you tell me some time," Laurie said, "what it is that you're planning to do when you stay in the Endless City? What skill do you have? What is it that makes you think any of us would ever want you here?"

The doors clunked as she pushed the card into the van. He stepped back as the fans roared. There was a brief warm rush around his feet as the van pulled up and away, rattling down the street, taking the corner so fast that the skirts screeched, and disappearing.

There was no trace of red left now in the sky above the pipe-threaded buildings. Just black, gray, and the flicker of colorless light. He let the wind push him as it chose; it had the weight and presence of the whole angry earth. It couldn't just have been satellite-made. A metal shutter flapped off its hinges and twirled not that far from his head, on through the fractured images of the houses until it buried itself into something solid. The child-guard had gone from Mokifa's scalloped archway. Even the beggars had taken shelter.

Outside, in the real Endless City, the cables swayed uselessly down the lanes towards Kushiel. There was even a junction box on the wall above a boarded-up shop, still intact and bearing an ancient version of the Halcyon logo. John wandered for hours, unthinking and at random, through alleys and wide, empty squares, across dry bridges, past buildings of gaunt brick and concrete, or between shuddering clusters of shanty dwellings that threatened to detonate in the wind. The few people who were out made the sign against the evil eye when they saw him, pausing as they hurried home or hammered back loosened flaps of sheeting.

The sky had a dimensionless texture. The air seemed to be growing darker. He walked on. Cars and vans occasionally sped by, their bodies tilted half-sideways to counteract the force of the wind. He had to turn away from them as the dirt swirled in his face. When he finally looked around to see where he was, he saw that there were lights and signs along the street here, a grainy fog of reds and yellows. He sensed movement and heard voices—figures were sheltering in doorways and crowded at the windows nearby. A woman stepped out, smiling against the billowing grit, opening her robe to display the roped scars that crisscrossed her breasts. A boy, sitting on a ledge, grinned and made a lewd motion. Shaking his head, walking on, John saw that many of what he'd taken for brightly lit windows were in fact screens designed to entice customers. As he watched—it was quite impossible not to—and the twisting naked figures threw out funnels of flickering pink light into the dust, it was hard to imagine that the flesh ever ended, that the spirit ever truly began. But this evening he seemed to be the only pedestrian in Agouna, and most of the cars were going by too fast to consider stopping. Cries, suggestions, and shouts followed him as he pushed against the wind, but no one bothered to come close. This odd change in the climate was like a cold bath—a good sexual anesthetic.

Another car came down the street now, its wide lights blazing through the haze. It stopped before reaching him, and the doors of the nearest buildings flew open. Discords of light and music blew by as several adolescent boys, all elbows and yells, clustered around it. It was a long car, too clean and ornate to be from anywhere other than the Zone, but it was only when John saw the doors rise like beetle wings that he could be sure that it really was Tim Purdoe's red Corona.

After the brakelights had vanished and the boys who'd been left standing had gone back inside, John walked on. Out of Agouna. The day's incipient darkness had finally given way to near-night. He pressed into it, pushing through the stabbing pain in his back, filled with a sense of urgency that, by its very suddenness, made him stop, turn into the lee of an abandoned truck, and look at his watch.

Hovering above the shimmering quaternary lines, the numerical time display read 6:30. He leaned against the truck's rusted metal surface, clanging his head. He'd missed Mass. It was hard to imagine more than a handful of his usual two or three dozen worshipers turning out for church on a night like this, but that wasn't the point. He walked on, the wind tearing at his clothing, bowing his back, furrowing his hair. He looked again at his watch, deciding that he should try to work out where exactly he was, find and climb the right hill, go to Santa Cristina. See, at the very least, how the roof was faring...

The night was deceptive; he was nearer Santa Cristina than he'd imagined. He soon saw it rising over the rooftops, black, wintry, and solid, backlit by an opalescence that was either the moon or an electromagnetic effect from the racing clouds. The roof was holding, although even the caroni birds had left it tonight to find better shelter, and he could tell from the screech of the swinging door that his congregation had gone. Whirl-

pools of leaves and discarded cards hovered over the graffiti-
corroded pews. Glittering with lights, little bells, and the call of
many tiny misactivated voices, the Inmaculada stretched out her
arms towards him. Tonight, shamed by missing Mass and by
the pettiness and finality of his argument with Laurie, John
found it harder than ever to meet her brown eyes.

He heard something flapping. Unmistakably separate from a
sudden booming increase in the wind outside, it seemed to be
coming from the sleeping stone crusader. John began to walk
around the pews towards it, imagining at first that a piece of
jelt had fallen, then that it was perhaps a rat or trapped sparrow
or pigeon; even, as the sound began to heave and scrape like
the claws of something bigger, a caroni bird.

He rounded the last pew and saw the thing squatting by the
ancient pediment that supported the dead knight. Not a bird,
but a human, clothed in ragged black and flashing stripes of
gold and silver. It began to hiss and chatter, waving long hands,
shrinking away from him. John surprised himself by taking a
step forward. The dimly golden light from the Inmaculada and
the altar fell on the witchwoman's face, showing her bulging
eyes, the shifting slit of her mouth. Her hands danced again, a
white blur as she drew herself up and away from him. Something black dripped on the floor between them. Then she turned
and ran.

He ran after her, but she was quick, slamming open the
doors, leaping, half-flying over the rough grass and fallen gravestones, blown and disappearing through rags of darkness into
the streets below, swallowed up by the cackling wind. He went
back inside the church and saw the crisscrossed outline of her
palm where she'd pushed back the wooden door, the dribbles
on the floor, the circles and stripes that she had smeared over

the stone crusader. He could smell salt and wet stone. The knight's hollowed face now had the shocked animation of a child's painting: round eyes, a grinning slit for a mouth. The stumps of his hands had fingers of a kind again—two on one, three on the other, a bird's hooked claw for a thumb, still beaded and gleaming as the blood formed tiny bubbles and sank into the spongy stone. She'd drawn a phallus too, although, like the knight, that was also slumbering. Staring down, he decided that taking a bucket and washing it all off would be more of a desecration than leaving the figure as it was. He removed a glove and touched the blood, already sticky and fibrous, and sniffed and studied the spot it left on his fingertip. Then he pulled the glove back on and crossed himself.

He closed the church and walked the rest of the way back to the presbytery, his head bowed in the wind. Just before he reached Gran Vía, the clouds broke, and, beating in heavy droplets like fists, it began to rain.

THERE WERE NIGHTS when the River Ocean was at one
with the sky. Entering one element, you broke the surface of
the other.

Omega's prow scattered constellations and billowing nebulae
of jellyfish drifting on the tide. Here, sometimes, it was just
possible to catch a clear glint and a flash of something so high,
that it could only be the solar wings of a satellite. The cloudpickers were far away, anyway, and the night was warm enough
to touch. There were no clouds.

John sat at the stern of the boat with the throttle of the
outboard alive in his hands as they skimmed the outer harbor,
away from the hills that cupped the lights of Ley. The engine
went *chuck, chuck* as they steered out between the last of the
shining yachts and the undersea bubbles, and he imagined the

people in their beds, in hotels and in holiday homes, in cabin rooms or tangled together in love, sinking half asleep as this sound rocked by them, soothing them, it and the tinkle of spars and the beat of the sea. He was proud of this engine, of the way it puffed and clucked, the way it broke the deep black water, shattering the stars. Yesterday, it wouldn't even start, and this very morning he took tools from the house's small cellar and walked along the cool early streets past the cottage with the yellow windows to the stretch of sand in the inner harbor. There he unbolted *Omega*'s engine, wiped it, drained it, and stripped it down, laying it out on a canvas sheet amid the wormcasts in the seagull-wheeling sunlight as the sky blued and brightened. When it was readjusted, made fresh and new, he pieced it all together again. He did it just as he'd watched Hal do it every summer before—always believing, until now, that the task was difficult, complex, arcane, and probably permanently beyond him. But from the time he opened his eyes and gazed up at the pine beams of the cabin this morning, everything had clicked. There was only *here*, only *now*, only pure and intense certainty as the bolts unslid and the two polished pistons began to gleam.

John looked now at his brother's silhouette as Hal sat gazing out from the prow across a moonlight-skimmed patch of water and, although he knew the night at Seagates would not happen for many years, he was reminded of Felipe. He blinked and frowned, looking back at the dark of the harbor. Even here, his memories were compromised by other memories. Time had become disordered, but he knew that if he tried to explain this, it would only distract and confuse Hal. *Omega* began to buck and rise when they hit open water. He sensed that Hal was annoyed because of his servicing and fixing *Omega*'s outboard this morning, or at least a little distant—and puzzled, and strained. But then he'd been waiting for Hal to do something about it for weeks. He couldn't wait forever. The holiday would end. What else was he supposed to do?

"You know, Hal," he said, trying a slightly different tack, "I don't don't feel as though I've ever really left here. I don't mean this particular night. I mean here—I mean Ley. I mean those—*these* summers that we spent together."

Hal grunts and keeps looking forward, out across the water. Perhaps John has said the wrong thing. It has to be admitted that this summer at Ley isn't Hal's finest hour. Even the mackerel in the outer harbor haven't been biting as they usually do. Last year, when Annie came along, was better. Far better. John now even entertains the heretical thought that Annie's company—or at least Annie-with-Hal's company—is better than Hal on his own. They've walked their usual walks over the clifftops this year mostly in silence, and found their secret coves and wrecks and drowned houses, but they have all been frozen, spectacularly unchanged. Now, he misses Annie's laughter and her scent. And he misses, although the moment will always be with him, the nights when she stooped to undress close beside him in the cabin. Although this summer separation was apparently agreed on without rancor between the two of them, he senses that Hal misses Annie too.

They were beyond the headland now, and the water dropped and rose around them, throwing waves against the side of the boat in easy sucking blows. Hal and Annie, he supposed, were less of an item than they used to be. After all, he could understand that himself now. Better, at least, than he did. People come apart. They drift together. And briefly, not that you'd ever understand it, there's the possibility of love. You must never look

337

for it, but you know that somewhere, over your shoulder and fleeing even as the thought occurs, it's there.

"It's like that moment," he said to Hal, "when you reach out to take something—say, a cup, just a cup from a table. And you know, even as your arm extends and your hand opens, that your grip isn't right, there's something about the whole movement that you've misjudged. You're already certain that the thing will drop from your fingers, yet you can't stop reaching and pull back. You can't simply pause and give up, or try again. You take the cup in your hand, and it falls even as you take it. Do you understand what I'm saying by that, Hal? To you, does that make any kind of sense?"

Hal grunted. At least this time John got a grunt out of him. The whole coastline stretched in darkness behind them now, and there was a gantry up in the hills that linked with the satellites, and the pale lights of a car. He ran his hand along the boat's thick, paint-slick gunwale and shifted his feet to keep them out of the oily slop of water that gleamed on the floor. An old lobsterpot lay there too. Most summers, they'd have charged it up long ago and tossed it over the side. And the receiver, lost as usual in one of house's back drawers, would have started to bleep at some wildly inappropriate time, and they'd pile into the boat anyway to trace it and set the flotation ring to draw the thing up. And later in the kitchen, feelers still waving, the lobster would crawl drunkenly around the counter until Hal, laughing at everyone's squeamishness, tossed it into the boiling water and the shell began to scream.

The days have all been different this year, although no matter how hard John tries, he cannot trace the reason back to any root. The sun is as hot, the sky is as blue. This afternoon, for example, on Chapel Beach: lying with Hal on a wide white space of sand, petals of sunlight and sails flecking the water and the drowning heat pressing down. And kids laughing from somewhere by the waves...

Leaning on his elbows, he'd seen their heat-quivering shapes move as they redirected the stream that ran from the apparently undrinkable well (although they'd all gulped it down with salt-hungry lips) at the promenade above the beach. Just figures stooping, carrying, digging, searching for stuff along the strand. Hal had his eyes closed, and his breathing was slow as he lay beside John on the towel, but John knew that he wouldn't be asleep. He knew that if he gazed too long at the strong chest and arms, at the little coppery line of hair that ran from his navel into his trunks, that Hal's eyes would open and he'd say, What is it, Skiddle? What would you like us to do? But that question would have been too much responsibility today, and John hoped, anyway, that they would take *Omega* out late this evening now that he'd fixed the engine. Just go where the water hung cool over the jellyfish and the stars, where you hovered between two worlds, where the sky was blackly bright. He closed his eyes on the beach, listened to the shouts of the kids and the pulling sigh of the tide, and let the afternoon slip by.

When he looked again, the sky had changed color, the wind had picked up, and he was almost within the extending shadow of the promenade wall. He sat up and saw Hal standing a little way off, hands on hips, elbows at right angles, the pink scar like a tightly closed mouth along his spine. The beach was empty now. The kids had gone. The ice-cream machine had gone. The surfers and pedalos had all been moored.

"What is it?"

John stood up. His feet scuttled across sand that was still warm on the surface, cooler beneath.

"Skiddle, look..."

He walked with Hal to the edge of the waves, where the children had been playing and an elaborate mandalalike complex of sandcastles and canals had been embroidered by the tide. Even now, with the stream left to its own whims and the walls picked at by waves, the canals functioned perfectly. Moats filled. Little pebble-banked falls frothed and cascaded. Elaborate windows and shell-scalloped arches still held. The walls of the bigger structures were embellished with seaweed and shells and other catchings from the strand. Polished glass, driftwood, and bones. A string of foil turned and flashed in the sun's rays, and at the top of one mound higher than John's waist there was an old beaker filled with something that could have been oil or blood but certainly wasn't water from the spring or the sea. They stepped to the center of the complex, and found it enclosed by a high wall in such a way that, as the sea rose around and destroyed the city, the center would remain dry and be the last to fall. The wide, scooped-out, and flattened hollow inside was ornamented with a mosaic of beads, scraps of sea-corroded circuitry, bottle caps, and pebbles. In the middle was a gull's head. As John stared, he saw the eye twitch, and the black-tipped beak parted slightly.

He and Hal looked at the buried gull. The waves, warm and curdled with sand, broke around their feet. Up on the promenade, music was playing; a brass band. But they seemed to be alone here, separated in a frozen counterworld.

When Hal stepped over the bank, the sand slid and the beads and the pebbles were scattered. The spell was broken. Working together, the brothers dug the seagull out with their hands. It had been buried so that its wings were outstretched as if in flight, but both were broken, and the pecks it tried to aim at them were feeble. One of its eyes, John saw, had run out, and the sharp edge of a shell had been used to pierce its breast. Why, he thought, would anyone do this? But the question somehow seemed irrelevant. He hadn't recognized the kids who were playing here, but, even if he had, it was the kind of act for which you could never know the real truth about. And the seagull had probably been injured in the first place. Otherwise, how could they have caught and buried it in the sand? He looked over at Hal, the bleached stubble and eyelashes and the falling blond shock of hair, and felt, as he always felt when he was troubled, an unworthy sense of release; of knowing that it was really his brother who bore the burden of all these questions, and that Hal would pass the answers on to John someday when he'd worked them out.

Hal lifted the bird. Its sand-clotted wings stirred and flapped. It mewed, turned, twisted its head. He stepped across the falling walls of sand to a nearby flat rock, and John looked away as his brother raised a stick of driftwood to smash its skull. But even so he heard the repeated sound that was made—hard at first, then soft—and when he looked again, he saw Hal standing with the stick raised and the bloody feathers clinging to it, his brow furrowed. And he knew then that he and Hal, as much as the kids who'd buried the gull, were a part of this thing that had happened.

He was glad that the gull was dead. Hal carried it along the beach, swinging its dead weight by the legs, up the steps to the causeway above the rocks where the water always pulled. And when they broke the beam of the sign that warned of the danger to swimmers, John knew it was right that he should take the seagull from his brother and toss it into the quickening water himself. There, he thought, there goes something, feeling the weight and the swing, then watching as it bobbed and turned like a crushed flower, feeling the smile that cracked his face. There goes something. But I don't know what.

Now, he scanned the water near *Omega*'s hull, briefly wondering if the seagull would float by, still caught on the gleaming surface between the water and the stars. But the sea was clean and sweet here, dark with the fragrance of brine, and the cliffs were now rising and falling behind them, where the caves went deep. Sometimes, on quiet afternoons on the clifftops, you could put your ear to the flat hot earth and hear, hidden and far below, the boom and roar and rage of a subterranean sea. But the land looked tiny now, and although tonight John was holding the tiller and was in control, he felt that without his willing or deciding it they'd somehow gone farther out than they should have. If they continued, they'd hit the colder water that rose off the continental shelf. Too strong, really, for this little boat to cope with—certainly without a navigator, at night. He was afraid that this outboard would fail them, that some vital piece of the ancient engine still lay gleaming where he'd left it on the sand of the inner harbor. He thought of his parents, probably contentedly asleep. He thought of his own bed, empty, and the creaking of the house around it.

"We should go back now."

But the motor kept puttering, and the water broke in a curve of glass at the prow, and Hal looked ahead and said nothing. They were heading, John realized, straight for the horizon.

"That gull..." he began. "It's a kind of madness, Hal. A release. I think I understand that now..."

His voice trailed off. Far ahead, where there should have been nothing but water and the planetary curve, there were glinting mountains. White and sharp, clear yet distant.

Once or twice in his life, he'd seen them: on a pale and windy day, when people were standing on Ley's promenade, holding up binoculars and cameras, and then on the net, in a news story of how, by some trick of the tide, an iceberg had actually come ashore. In the screen, the white mountain had been gray and dirty, pocked, smelling of old fish. But this, John thought as he looked over his brother's shoulder, was how icebergs should be. Clear and pure and distant as the mountains of the moon.

"I think," he said, "we should go back now."

This time, he exercised some control. He wasn't quite able to counter his brother's will and turn the boat back yet, but at least he killed the motor. Sudden silence. The waves slapped. He felt the cooling water, pushing, rising. They were adrift.

"I think we should go back now."

A booming detonation came from far off, from the ice. Unless he did something, the boat would drift rapidly. He could feel it moving, turning already. Quickly he rewound the starter rope, smoothing out the kinks. He tensed it, pulled sharply the way Hal had shown him, and the outboard barked back into life. But as he reached for the tiller to turn back to the shore, Hal half-stood in the prow and—barely rocking the boat as he did so—tipped himself over the gunwale, into the water. The River Ocean sighed its surprise. For a moment, Hal floated beside the boat, his body slick and smooth now, neither clothed nor naked but coated in creamy gray. Then he kicked out easily, arms glistening, lifting and falling, towards the icebergs, and for a while he seemed to grow larger as well as smaller. He paused, raised a hand for the last time, then flopped back to eject a gleaming arc of water from his mouth before swimming on towards the whiteness at the horizon.

THE TAXI HISSED along Gran Vía, trailing plumes of water. Encased in steam and chattering beads, his feet wet and his gloved palms clammy, John swallowed down the tarry residue that had formed in the back of his throat, and his fingers squealed a space in the window. In the fractional moment before the glass misted over, he saw black figures on bobbing duckboards, sheet water cascading from gutters, an alley that had become a fast-running slide of mud. The wipers thwacked. The fans growled. The driver, his bony shoulders hunched almost to the level of the cockerel-like crest of his hair, peered ahead.

John realized he was shivering. He'd never felt cold before in the Endless City—this weather front came from the rain-sodden air that was diverted from Europe when the corn there was ripe, brittle, and erect and the big machines moved in. But the people here, despite the chill and the discomfort, actually seemed to welcome it. It was a different discomfort, in any case, to the heat: like shifting your buttocks on a bed of nails. Prized duckboards, sandbags, pumps, and rickety walkways were dragged out from storehouses and lofts; discussed, tutted over, compared, and arrayed. Bridges, ladders, and ropes stretched at improbable heights between the buildings while Bella, humming snatches of Felipe's ditties, splashed around the presbytery in boots to distribute and empty the pots that caught the many drips, and she wiped down the bizarre flowerings of mold that draped the ceilings and walls like Christmas decorations. The clinic and the church, at least, were both on higher ground, above the brown and frankly turd-infested waters. The markets had been selling stomach remedies and T-cell injections for at least a month in anticipation of what John had thought would be a rapid increase in cholera and nematodes, but the rains were a yearly occurrence here and the Borderers knew how to deal with them. The sky itself provided a plentiful supply of distilled, if gritty, water. Still, he wondered what else was blown in by the storms.

"Here, Fatoo."

He paid the driver and climbed out. Water instantly began to leak through his supposedly rainproof cape. Black acres of umbrella jumbled around him; a steaming, hidden city of feet and heads and sodden shopping. He looked over them at the gleaming buildings and a fallen stretch of the medina wall, then took shelter beneath an archway. When he shifted his arms, the water from the cuffs ran down inside. A reddish river coiled and uncoiled across the cobbles at his feet like a lazy whip.

He hadn't thought that Ryat had meant much by his offer of help at Seagates. Ryat was, after all, a major local figure. The message that had come through on the presbytery's airwave suggesting that they meet here still had the feeling of a fluke, a chance twist of the ether. John really didn't believe that it was in Ryat's interest to upset the delicate balance of Magulf trade —but, then, he was finding it hard to accept anyone's good faith at the moment.

"Father John."

Ryat stood in the archway, his skull beaded wet, droplets hanging from his nose and the metal tips of every finger.

"I'm truly grateful—" John began, but Ryat waved it away. They stepped out into the rain. Ryat made no effort, John saw, to keep himself dry; whatever clothes he had on were plastered colorless against his body. The air, John knew, wasn't really that cold, despite the chill that had worked its way into him. He followed Ryat to the end of the narrowing street and then across a puddled and treacherous stretch of wasteland. Ahead of them in the rain, jaggedly shaped buildings rose and fell like the undulations of an angry sea.

"This is new to you?" Ryat asked as they climbed over the remains of a broken barrier. Looking up at the black pylons that vanished into mist, John shook his head. This was Kushiel. The ground here, consisting of curving concrete, was slimy and treacherous, punctuated occasionally by small crooked chimneys that spouted clouds of steam into the rain. The ragged mouth of a tunnel reared up, and they splashed down steps and through a low doorway, where a dense, warm wave broke over them. The rain here was a dull rumble. Chains of lights and pipes stretched before them.

"This," Ryat said in an almost reverent whisper, "is where the koiyl is dried."

He rattled the tines of his fingers along the pipe that ran beside them, and they waited. John could feel hot air rising, billowing against the low ceiling, and smelled a deep, intrusive smell that was a mixture of growth and decay.

Ahh. Fatoo. Outer...

Faces peered at them. Glinting teeth and eyes and tongues, skin the texture of well-tanned leather. John waited as Ryat conversed. He heard the word *koiyl,* but they were speaking too quickly for him to catch much else.

Div, far...

He and Ryat followed a woman who waddled along the passageway on dropsy-laden legs. Here and there he saw pots seething with beetles, heard the chuckle of water, and smelled, overpowering even in this air, the reek of drains. At first, the walls and ceiling were one curved, fused surface. Then the passage widened, and they pushed their way through dangling fronds of fungi. In many places there were no pipes; the warmth came simply from the walls, which seemed to be giving off a deep red light close to the borders of vision. Lightless plants reared up. Beetles scuttled, chomped, and burrowed in the mulch. Ryat and John crossed a junction of tunnels where the currents stirred and embraced. Here, although the light was almost too dim to focus, dream colors formed. There were neon chrysanthemums, albino ferns like comet tails. Drowsy red buddleia hissed and swayed their lips of moisture-swollen petals.

"This is for the carnival," Ryat said, cupping and inhaling a pink rose that shone in his hands. "After the rains."

"It seems a waste."

"What?"

"A waste, when staple food could be grown down here."

"But you do not live on just food? Is there some saying like that—in your Bible?"

Ryat turned and walked on.

"So when does it happen?" John asked, following. "This carnival?"

"A week or so. It will come when the rain stops."

Blue hyacinths studded the walls and covered even the ceiling, their upwards-growth gene suppressed either by happy accident or design. Beyond were steps, doors, and curtains leading to softer odors. There, shimmering in the faintest imaginable light, shadow waves of koiyl leaves lay heaped.

"In these tunnels," Ryat explained, "the leaf must lose moisture or it will rot. There must be heat and no light for perhaps two, three months..."

John kept his head lowered as they moved slowly along the tunnels, expecting at any moment to crack his skull on some invisible obstruction. He felt a growling pain in his back.

Ryat paused, muttered, and extended his arm to John.

"Here. Try. These ones are ready."

John reached out. His gloved fingers, as the spines left a radiance hanging in the darkness behind them, touched metal, then the outline of the leaf. He could tell simply from the shape that it wasn't from Lall, but he took a bite anyway, another, and crammed the whole thing into his mouth. He'd been salivating from their scent, and the red wetness slid easily between his teeth and tongue. His cheeks bulged. The pain in his back and the pricking flashes of heat and cold began to recede. Even his sight improved a little. Aroused by his and Ryat's presence, the Borderers who cured the koiyl began to shuffle from the darkness. They were stooped, muttering in softer accents than those heard on the surface, and wide-eyed. Faces from a painting by Rembrandt—*The Night Watch*. Ryat was asking about Lall. A pump was humming somewhere, and John had to put out a hand to steady himself against the wall. A red blur, the wall seemed to pass through a layer of mist without finding substance.

"Are you feeling well?" Ryat asked.

"Yes..." He swallowed, in the absence of a spittoon, most of the leaf and felt it rise and sink in his throat, then, with a warm blush like a falling firework, go all the way down. "It's just the heat."

Another tunnel, another pattern of leaves. Speaking slowly enough for John to catch most of his meaning, one of the curers was explaining that the Lall leaf was *ca bona*—one of the best—but hard to get. They were grown in a holy place, had special healing properties. The man reached, still talking, to take a leaf. He bit and chewed at the tip with a quick, rabbitlike motion, and spat it out in a black stream. Much, John thought, as would any European winetaster. And why, Ryat asked, why was the place holy? The man frowned and shook his head. The whole thing sounded, John thought, forcing his mind back into concentration, like little more than a salespitch. If prompted, these leaf curers could probably suggest special properties for all the leaf-growing areas. But the aroma seemed stronger here, reminiscent of an apothecary's shop where amid the jars there was a promise not just of healing but of a little wisdom. A trick, perhaps, that would turn base metal into gold—or at the very least summon the face of a loved one from the heart of a fire...

Ryat was chewing a Lall leaf. He offered another to John, who bit just a quarter off this time and pocketed the rest. This was a small tunnel, no more than an offshoot of what appeared to be the main drying rooms, and John now had to bend his knees as well as his head and back. Pushing the damp wad of koiyl towards his molars, he felt it thicken and enlarge as the walls shrank around him. His head was swelling. As they climbed, the tunnel seemed steeper. He had to lean forward to keep from falling.

They ducked through a curtain, and the tunnel cooled and widened in a pale glow. Faintly again, he could hear the hiss of the rain. A man stepped aside to let John and Ryat pass, his hands sheltering his puckered eyes as if from a blazing sun. Squinting himself, his head pulsing, John saw that the man's upper lip was scarred where a piece had been lasered off. There had been some kind of growth, probably.

And how much of the leaf from Lall, Ryat was asking, still keeping his words slow and distinct so that John could follow, do you have down here? How much of this year's crop? The man made a vertical gesture with his tannin-browned hands, which suggested that they had less than a quarter. And what about the rest? Was it here—or elsewhere in the Kushiel tunnels? Did one of the other curers perhaps have it? No. Definitely no. They trusted each other, they worked together.

Ryat thanked him, and he and John climbed back up to the surface. Outside, rainswept Kushiel seemed almost white, and Ryat stood watching as John blinked and spat his wad of koiyl into a gutter. Then he began to cough, and had to swallow the vomit that tried to follow it.

"It seems," Ryat said, "that we have but a portion of the crop here, Father John."

John blinked again, his head swimming. *Potion?* Portion. His ears boomed. Whiteness poured around him as the rain, with cold impartial fingers, explored his back.

"Perhaps they were suspicious. Of course..." Ryat shrugged elaborately, in a spray of steel, his clothes still steaming from the heat. "But they are speaking the truth."

"When the leaves from Lall are taken to Seagates, will you let them be sold?" John sniffed as a cloud of richly scented steam from one of the low crooked chimneys passed over his face, and a shiver, bigger than the ones that had preceded it, ran through him. The rain rattled in the puddles. But at least the whiteness was fading. Kushiel had sunk back to gray. He looked around and saw twisted powerlines and fallen fences, the illegible signs and the faint blackened ruins. He felt a dull and distant humming, a sense of power.

"I have other obligations, Father John. I have partners. And this year's leaf—you saw yourself—most of it is not here." Ryat clicked his fingers. He seemed amused. "I will see. It is a time of goodwill, with the carnival. *Gonenanh...*"

John stood watching as Ryat walked away. Steam and smoke, gusting through the rain from the chimneys of the half-buried drying sheds, formed the shapes of imaginary continents. Farther off, just where the gleaming backs of the houses began, was an odd and rusty dome-shaped building, and a blue light that rippled from the haze. He walked towards it.

Inside, in a space of concrete and streaming glass, bodies were splashing and diving. The pool itself was almost lost in steam; it was impossible to tell, if you peered down from the slippery rim, just how deep it was. A boy surfaced. Puffing his cheeks, he saw John, blew out a plume of water, then kicked off again. Shouts and cries echoed. Younger children paddled where the floor sloped into the water, busy with buckets, absently peeing or plucking at the fronds of mold on the walls. Deeper in, John saw a teenage lad helping his younger brother keep his head above water. *It's like this.* The older boy let go to gesture with his arms, and his brother bubbled under. John smiled, remembering similar scenes at the big outdoor pool in Hemhill. There, you could actually breathe underwater if you inhaled the stinging gas from the poolside vendor first. But it took courage to draw the water into your lungs. He remembered Hal, hair flattened and chest gleaming, holding him. *You're out of your depth now, Skiddle. All I have to do now is push you under.* Knowing what was to come, he'd kicked and struggled. Would have screamed, too, if the water hadn't flooded his mouth. And then down, his ears blocked, his eyes burning. Endlessly down.

The tips of his gloves dripped red beads as he walked along Cruz de Marcenado, and the indentation of his watch formed a milky pool when he raised his arm to bang the door beneath the gables of Martínez's house. He waited. A face peered at a streaming window. The damp door wheezed open, and Kailu stood with her head lowered. *Fatoo,* she murmured, and stepped back, letting him in and past her, watching without following as he ascended the creaking stairs. There were no screens murmuring today, and no smell of cooking. Through the doorway in the frontroom John glimpsed the children sitting silently with their hands clasped around their knees. He pushed open the door into the bedroom, expecting, if not blood-strewn walls, at least the gold-threaded simples that draped the bedposts of even his most regular parishioners when they were this near the end, the heaped powdery soil of some planet even deader than this one.

Martínez's eyes were open, although John couldn't tell until he leaned over that the man was conscious. Martínez blinked and mumbled something. Blood bubbled at his lips. John stooped closer and felt the dry inhuman heat.

"I didn't..."

Surely he wasn't speaking European? But he was, and the thin screens tacked around the room to the yellow-papered walls were filled with silent green and golden landscapes, skies that were glorious—even beneath the dusty and corrupted surfaces that browned at the corners where rust had set in—glorious with clouds or the sun or the moon or the stars or empty of everything, a deep and endless blue that was really no color at all, only a sensation of letting go, of falling...

"...want it to end."

"Yes."

John nodded, conscious of how close to Martínez he was, of the droplets of rain that had fallen from his hair and clothes onto the blankets, of one that even gleamed like a tear on the taut drumskin of Martínez's cheeks. He sat down on the chair beside the bed. There's always hope, he remembered once thinking, where there's hope. Even here.

The mattress creaked as Martínez coughed and then turned his head on the red-speckled pillow. His lips split apart.

"I don't want..."

One arm lay outside the blankets, the flesh pooled and sagging where the muscle inside had dissolved.

"I still need to..."

The hand moved. Once it had been a strong wide hand and had worked foline engines and held his children and touched his wife in love. The fingers slowly hooked across the rucked blanket. John glanced over at the leaves that lay in the chipped glass bowl on the far table, wondering if Martínez was trying to reach them. They'd probably help at a time like this, although John doubted whether Martínez could chew anything now. But the hand was moving not towards the leaves but towards something that lay closer. John looked down but saw merely the rug on the floor, a shoe sticking out from under the bed, and his own gloved hands resting on his thighs.

"...to..."

John gazed at Martínez and thought of Christ, of the Inmaculada, and of the other Mary, the Magdalene, her hands reaching out to her resurrected Lord in the sepulchre. *Woman, why weepest thou? Touch me not, for I am not yet ascended to my Father, but go to your brethren and tell them...*

Touch me not.

John unpeeled his gloves. He broke the spines and pushed the gloves into his pocket. He reached out and gripped Martínez's hand. The flesh was loose and hot. He waited for a sign, for a return of pressure, but when he looked up at Martínez's face, he saw that the eyes were closed and that the breathing had grown easier. Martínez was asleep.

John got up, unsealed a pair of fresh green-spined gloves, and wiped with dysol the chair he'd been sitting on. Kailu watched him from the hallway as he descended the stairs. She stepped back, pushing open the door, saying nothing. Outside, it was still raining.

Coughing and whispers in the stone air. The sleeping knight. The smiling Christ. Brown-eyed Mary's arms reaching out through the tumble and glitter of a fresh snowfield of cards and mementos. The failing roof creaking and pattering with the claws of caroni birds. Silver threads plinking into buckets. So few people here. No Nuru. No Kassi. No Juanita. Just the indeterminably aged who came up to take the wafer and then shrank back, watching him over the pews from the unimaginable distance of their alien eyes.

John turned on the translat and studied the little screen. He pressed Close, then touched down into the main files, with the gloved tip of his finger drawing the pattern that was his own codeword, down into the phrase banks and sound types, the fuzzy circuitry that supposedly dealt with humor and twists of meaning, again and again pressing Close. He turned it off when it was fully blank, and, gripping the pulpit, breathing in the scent of dysol and the salt odor of Borderer flesh, he began to speak.

"It is good, Paul says in First, Corinthians, for a man not to touch a woman. He is talking of sexual touching, there is no doubt about that, for he goes on to say that a man should take a wife to avoid fornication. Yet simple touch and contact—especially between a man and a woman—is regarded as a less than ideal thing in most of the Bible. It is true that Jesus heals and teaches by the laying on of hands, by the washing of feet, yet at the same time this is ultimately seen as a sign not of God's spirit in Christ but of His earthbound humanity."

He paused and licked his lips. It was a strange nakedness to hear his voice unechoed by the translat.

"Mary Magdalene, who was the symbol, if ever there was one, of God's forgiveness of the weaknesses and the strivings of humanity, is the first to come to the sepulchre and see that the stone has been rolled away, that Christ has arisen..."

There was a disturbance as the first of the congregation, muttering at the strange babble of this European *baraka,* began to leave. The door banged open. Streamers of rainy light filled the church, throwing long shadows from the pews, transforming the shapes of the people that remained into globular disconnected heads and bodies.

"Imagine her feelings as she stood weeping and alone before that empty tomb, then turning, seeing this man, so full and vigorous that for a moment she does not know him, cannot comprehend..."

The door banged shut.

"...that it is truly her Lord. She thinks he's a gardener! Can you imagine, a human gardener—not a machine that clicks and buzzes and trims the roses for you. But a human gardener."

The church door swung open again, grinding over the unswept porch.

"But then," John continued, swallowing back the bitterness in his throat, staring out across the empty pews and deep into the pouring light, "he speaks her name. And he says, Touch me not, for I am not yet ascended." He coughed. "Touch me not. Now, what are we supposed to make of that? Later, Jesus greets his disciples and shares food with them. According to Luke, he even lets them handle him. But Mary Magdalene, being a woman, wasn't allowed to. And in the book of John, Thomas, who doubts that Christ actually is who he claims to be, does not, as you might imagine—for surely he must recognize Christ's face—touch him. Instead, he passes his finger through the holes in Christ's hands. His hand reaches to touch his Lord, whom he longs to recognize and love, and it passes through. And there, in the emptiness—in the space beneath Christ's flesh, in the evidence of agony, inhumanity, and suffering—he somehow finds faith."

It was late at the Zone's medical center. Even the Borderer cleaners had finished work. John walked along the corridors alone, his footsteps dirtying the fresh floors. The door to Tim's office was ajar. Tim sat at the desk, surrounded by cards and papers, his head lowered; he seemed to be busy.

"Ah." He looked up. "I wasn't expecting..."

John sat down. Rainwater from his clothes pattered on the carpet.

After a moment, Tim smiled and pushed the cards away. "Things have changed a bit," he said, "haven't they?"

"About as much as they ever do here."

Tim nodded slowly, watching him. "You're still seeing Laurie?"

"That seems to have ended."

"I'm sorry, John. I just wish we could have talked honestly about it."

"I suppose you and most other people knew anyway?"

"Well. You know."

Tim stood and walked over to the doctor in the corner, placing his hand on it. The curved panels reflected back an older, wearier version of his face. "You should have said, John. I mean, about Laurie. The physical stuff, anyway—I could have helped you with that."

"It wouldn't have made any difference."

The rain gelled silently across the window. Father Orteau's Church of All Saints across the black lake was a misty lantern.

"Why have you stayed on here so long, Tim?" he asked. "Is it because of Agouna?"

"Agouna's one of the reasons." Tim turned to him. "Why?"

"I saw your car there. That big Corona."

"I go at odd times."

"You pay them?"

"Of *course* I pay them." Tim came back to the desk and began to pick at the furballs on the shoulders of his jacket, which lay draped over the chair. "And—to save you asking— I sometimes give them medicines too, and money. I help their uncles get jobs at the shuttleport or across the water. I do all that, John. It's part of the exchange."

"Exchange—is that what you call it?"

"Being in the Magulf for me isn't just some odd exercise to find out where my life is going, John. I'm not like you—and all the rest of them." Tim shook his head. "This is it, my life. All there is."

"So you copied my data on the koiyl?"

"Copied?"

"Gave it out. About Ifri Gotal and Lall and the leaf. People in the Endless City seem to know. I spoke to Ryat—"

"Is that what he says?"

"He said there had been rumors. I thought at first that it was Laurie."

"And now you think it's me? *Jesus*, John. This place is alive with rumor. Amid all that, don't you think some of the truth gets out?"

The silence stretched between them.

Tim sat back down. "So," he said, "where do we go from here?"

"I don't suppose it matters. I don't have long left here anyway."

"It's a shame. And you don't look well, John. Do you know that?" Tim glanced at the screen on his desk. "The signal I'm picking up from your implants is very weak. You haven't been..."

"What?"

"Deliberately damaging yourself in some way? People sometimes do odd things when they come out here." Tim touched the screen. Tiny flutters of AGTC lined his face and caught in the silver of his eyes. The doctor stirred in the corner. "John, I'd like to take a closer look." Mandibles unfurled, and the doctor's eyes began to glow.

Beneath his wet clothes, John felt his flesh turn colder than ever. He shook his head.

He said, "I'm not going into that thing."

The gutters ran in shooting rapids past the sleek trees and buildings of the Zone. The lights in Laurie's bungalow were off when he
walked past, and her van wasn't there. At the end of Main Avenue,
a group of drunken expats swayed arm in arm through the rain. He
walked along the dry brownstone, looking in the shops, scarcely
able to believe the profusion of the goods, the incredible displays,
the ridiculous prices. Most of the bars were closed now or closing,
but the place with the chromium waiter stayed open all night.
He sat there alone in the warmth, shivering, drinking whisky,
gazing at the empty space opposite him, where Laurie once sat.

When he finally felt drunk enough, he went back out, found
a booth, and called her number.

"Father John." The answerer smiled. "It's good to see you
again."

"You mean that?"

"I'm always pleased to do my job."

"You're really not like Laurie—you just talk with her voice,
and have her mannerisms."

"If I talk as Laurie talks, if I behave as she behaves, doesn't
that make me like her?"

"Will you put me through?"

"I'm sorry—you know she's asked me not to do that. But
of course, I will advise her that—"

"Laurie would never do what you're doing. Just slavishly
following orders."

"Under certain circumstances I have free will."

"Such as?"

"Now. Talking to you, Father John. I could show you her
bungalow if you want."

"She's not there."

"But *I* can be. Look." The blank space behind the answerer became Laurie's bedroom, with the same mess as always. And the air, too, smelled the same, taking over the booth, blocking out the empty street outside. The screen widened, pulling him in. "Is this what you want to see?"

As usual, Laurie had left her wardrobe open, and he saw the row of her clothes, so few of which she actually wore. But there was the skirt from that last afternoon at Mokifa: he remembered the spark of static that had jumped from the hem as she turned, the growling wind, the loss of every right word.

"You know," he said to the answerer, "that we were lovers."

"Yes." The answerer was dim now but beside him.

"I suppose Tim's right," he said. "And you're the net, aren't you? If you don't know these things, who does?"

"I'm just a small portion, John. Something Laurie's taken and partially controlled. But Tim Purdoe was also right, earlier, when he said that you needed a doctor to examine you. I, too, find that your signal is weak."

"We can't be the only Borderer and European," he said, "ever to be..."

"No. Of course."

"Does it ever work?"

"There's sometimes talk," the answerer said, "of a way of making the recombinants entirely safe so there will be no fear of touching, no need for dysol or lydrin or the gloves. But then something else comes in from the deserts, one of the new viral predators that attack your recombinants directly. It never seems to end, Father John, and I doubt if it ever will. Every time you get close to touching the Borderers, the world will push you back."

"You accept that only because your priorities are the same as ours," he said, turning in the booth to look for Laurie's answerer. She seemed real beside him now, with blue eyes and standing in a blouse and skirt that needed pressing. "Do you think anyone in Europe really wants the barriers to come down?"

Spreading her hands, the answerer shrugged. "I suppose not. The shockwire, the cheap labor, the hand-painted trinkets..."

He looked at her eyes, her face, her hair. She held out her hand. "Would you like to touch me, Father John? There's enough processing space available to go up to five-sense on this partition. We could even make love."

"I can't."

She smiled and nodded, and his fingers reached and found the quaternary lines and dug in, pulling down the cursor and fading the screen, bringing back Main Avenue, the warmly lit booth.

He walked all the way back to the presbytery, out of the Zone and through the flooded streets of the Endless City. Gran Vía was shining and empty, but he stopped at the twisted crossroads on Cruz de Marcenado when he saw the headlights of one of the low-backed funeral vans that plied to and from the incinerator at El Teuf, beating white tracks through the rain. It stopped at a place where people stood outside in black oilskins, holding chemlights, their shoulders sloping like the wet roofs of the houses from which they had emerged. As John, hidden by the night and the rain, watched, the long box bearing Martínez's body was carried out of the house, and the women began to wail.

H E   W A S   W O R K I N G   most evenings at the clinic now, updating and reordering the doctor's data. He doubted whether his successor would continue the task, but he persisted in drawing links and lines, surprising himself repeatedly by his own absorption and persistence, his speed and decisiveness. The leaf helped. Chewing it regularly, he was coming to understand its true function: although it worked superficially as an anesthetic, in the longer term it gave an ability to shut off areas of thought.

It was more than just forgetting. With the leaf, it sometimes seemed that he could reorder the whole rambling house of his mind, redecorate and close off wings, demolish stairways, brick up unwanted doors, throw out old furniture, repaint the walls in clean whites and then wander the pale and empty rooms at will, always turning exactly where he wanted to turn, seeing only the views that he wished to see through the gleaming windows, hearing only the clean clear music of silence. There were blissful periods working late and alone in the clinic's backroom when he was filled with nothing but the pure and intense energy of this orderly task. No Laurie or Hal at his shoulder. No worries about quitting the priesthood. Just the sound of his breath, the beating of the rain, the creak of the doctor's mandibles, and the tumbling figures on the screen. He paged back through the years of anonymous entries, calling up the varied graphs of disease and fatality rates. Overlaid, they formed a pattern even more jagged and complex than the rooflines of the Endless City, or of Paris or London at dawn. There were soaring towers and yawning canyons. Here were the Monuments of Smallpox II, the Steeples of Leukemia. The vast spire, too, of stomach complaints, if you combined ulcers and lesions in a single category. Could there be some external cause for this as well? But the question had come too late. It was an edifice he could not begin to scale. This city was truly terrible and grand, with its jeweled streets and blazing foundations. A place beyond this earth entirely.

One night, there came a persistent tap that seemed to signify more than the endless drip-knocking of the rain. He paused the screen and went through the outer office to check the door, where two children were standing. Between them, backlit by the fires that burned in the towerblock opposite, was a horned goat.

The girl and boy came inside when he beckoned. He recognized them as Sarai and Mo, and knew that their parents lived in a tenement not far from the church. The parents were intermittent regulars, and worked at one of the big food processors—their hands and arms stained a permanent blue from the catalysts they stirred in to solidify the blocks. When the doctor raised a creaking sensor to sniff the air as the children dragged the goat into the backroom, the girl Sarai turned and stuck her tongue out at it.

The goat was a male, a well-hung breeder of the kind that supposedly gave good milkers for offspring, with long unbudded horns curving from a dense white coat. It reeked, of course. Competition for servicing was fierce, and in the absence of any ability to pick and choose genetic traits, the creatures had to be an advertisement in themselves. Over the years, attempts to breed placidity into goats had given way to the expedient of routinely sprinkling suppressant powders on their feed. In the summers goats were mostly tethered outside in courtyards or in patches of wasteground, and often could be seen grazing with their backs to the wind. Now, John supposed, ways had to be found of keeping them indoors out of the rain.

He crouched and looked at the legs, which were puffy and scabbed to the hooves. In Borderer, interrupting each other, Sarai and Mo told him that it wasn't like the usual foot rot. John turned on the translat to keep track as their explanation became more and more complicated. For several weeks now, they said, since the rains had started, they'd tried giving the normal injections and creams. He took a sample from one of the flaking red scabs and kidded the doctor into doing an analysis. After several outraged pronouncements about nonhuman tissue, he got what he wanted from the screen.

"It's caused by a fungus," he said, "like the stuff that grows on the walls." He selected a syringe. The goat, either too ill or too drugged to notice, barely moved as he jabbed its rump.

Uncomfortable, the boy was shredding the end of the tether with his fingers. He and Sarai were avoiding John's eyes. Weren't penicillin and antifungal systemics sold in the souks?

They'd have heard, anyway, that he normally refused to treat animals. Nuru, he knew, would see it as a lowering of standards and be quietly outraged. Then Sarai said something the translat didn't catch, and they led the goat out through the surgery.

He called, "You'll bring it back, won't you?"

The translat echoed *unt oo?* as the children vanished into the rain.

He was at the clinic again next evening, still working on correlating the doctor's data. Time was short now, but he didn't know how short, having blanked out the screen's calendar a while ago. He was surprised at how easy it had been to forget the actual date his term in the Magulf ended. He knew that he'd come here after the rains, and he knew that the streets had been dry and windy and cold, that there had been an almost Ley-like tang of salt on the waters of the Breathless Ocean, but he'd given up counting the days.

He began to search his pockets for a new leaf of koiyl, patting and squeezing each pocket in turn, wondering as he did so why it felt odd, until he realized that he was mimicking Felipe's regular search for blisterpacks. There. His gloved fingers closed on the familiar rounded shape and traced the notched and indented spine, the little stub of the cut-off stalk. He took the leaf out and looked at it, feeling his mouth stretch into a smile. Not a Lall leaf. He put it whole between his lips, his cheeks bulging, his tongue tracing the sharp underridge, and felt his saliva sweeten and thicken as the surface oils were released. The leaf swelled and grew more pliant, inviting his teeth to sink in. His heart began to skip. Dee-dah, dee-dah, like one of Felipe's stupid half-remembered tunes, drowning out the sound of the rain on the roof. There. He bit, and felt the leaf open up, break, separate. The rush of his senses, the ease of his pain, the stars that always floated momentarily before his eyes.

When a tap at the door came, he swallowed the fibers, paused the screen, and went out to where Sarai, Mo, and the goat were standing, again backlit by the bonfire lights in the towerblock. The echo from the day before was so complete that he had to stop for a moment, his back stiffly arched and his hand on the doorframe.

We keep him in our room now, they told him as they shuffled in. We don't mind the smell—but he tries to eat our beds. The goat looked no worse, perhaps even a little better, but Sarai and Mo seemed disappointed: they must have expected more than this gradual remission. The creature butted John when he crouched down to examine the legs. Sarai and Mo cheered up a little at that.

John asked, "Doesn't he have a name?"

No name. They shook their heads.

"Who does he belong to?"

They waved their hands, and said the Borderer word that meant both no one and everyone.

He jabbed in more penicillin. "He's for the carnival, isn't he? The sacrifice?"

They nodded, and the goat blinked drugged brown eyes. John took a tin of zinc oxide off the shelf.

"So when is it? The carnival?"

They shrugged, and waved their fingers. Two, three days— or even tomorrow.

"Why did you come to me?"

They said nothing and shuffled closer together. Their brown eyes were as impenetrable as the goat's. Then Sarai nudged Mo, and John guessed that they had noticed his red koiyl-stained teeth.

"Okay." He disengaged the doctor. "The goat should be fine soon anyway."

"Fatoo pray no rain?"

"Yes. But I want you to show me something."

He closed the clinic and followed Sarai and Mo up the hill. The climb was steep this way, and he had to stop as a hot chill ran over him. He spat out a series of stringy lumps. Then a gout of reddish fluid followed. He coughed and blinked back stars as the mess washed into the gutter, then hurried up the street and stood waiting, leaning on the bottom rail as Sarai and Mo took the goat up the steps of their tenement. When they returned, he followed them across the square to a lighted doorway that gleamed over the cobbles. The inside was filled with a drumming and tapping that came only partly from the rain. Faces turned towards him as people paused in their work on the carnival floats, but no one seemed that surprised to see him here.

He wandered the aisles, where arc lights sparkled, hammers hammered, drills and saws howled. A huge glittering dragon that clawed the air of the warehouse ceiling was almost lost in misty, methane-lit space, its jaws roaring out the smell of glue. Children were scolded when they climbed scaffolding or tried to use one of the great skeins of new material for a slide. He found Sarai and Mo with their parents, painting an ornate sash around the flatbed that would carry the goat. *Fatoo,* they said, and blinked slowly at him as their brushes dripped red pools onto the floor.

Where the darkness was deeper, a giant screen-demon reared

up towards the roof. Its head was a vague triangular lump, with slotted irises that reminded John of the sheep he'd used to talk to on his way across the Yorkshire moors to some deathbed; the eyes had the same bland and unquestioning gaze. Beyond that was an antique float, nothing more than a half-collapsed frame, a squashed spider. John ran a gloved hand along one of the rusty poles and saw a flicker of light that came from an old man who sat working almost hidden in a corner. The man pulled whispering transparent material through a machine. Without using his translat, John tried asking what the float was going to be. He got nowhere. The man only gestured at the sky, saying something about the *Scuro Rey*—the gods, the Dark King.

There was no Mass this evening, and John felt more than usually empty as he wandered out into the rain. He checked his watch, running his finger over the slight inflammation that had appeared in the ridged flesh around it. Walking back up Gran Vía to the presbytery, stopping to spit into the running gutter, watching as the red froth was swept away, he saw snatches of life through windows that the weeks of rain had washed almost invisibly clean. Pans steamed on stoves. Cats preened by fires. A man stood buttoning his shirt. John stopped outside a window set almost level with the street. It was dry and warm inside, and children crouched in the light, painting each other's faces. Powdery white first, then black for the eyes and nose, hair drawn back and lips clenched for them to draw skull-grinning teeth. One of the children caught sight of the figure outside the window, and their fluttering hands streaked their faces as, silently through the glass and the rain, they began to scream.

He walked quickly on. Dripping power cables stretched uselessly overhead, segmenting the disordered sky. On Gran Vía, he saw that the presbytery lights were still shining, and that a van had parked outside. Laurie's van.

He pushed the door aside and climbed the stairs and halted halfway, breathless, to inspect his face in the mirror. Corpse-white skin, straggling rivulets of hair, bloody mouth, and silver eyes—but it was too late to do anything about the way he looked, and he could hear voices, female Borderer voices conversing, warm and engaged, along the corridor at the top of the stairs.

"Ah!" he said, standing at the edge of the light that opened into the smoky fragrance of Bella's kitchen, thinking he might as well dramatize his newly awful appearance.

Bella sat on a stool, the light from the stove gleaming on her bare knees. She had a cup in her hand. The other woman seemed so different that for a moment, as she turned, John thought she wasn't Laurie.

He said, "You've grown your hair."

"Yes." Laurie held out her hands, palms down, to show him her fingernails. "The stuff you have to take plays havoc with these. Where have you been?"

"At the clinic." He shrugged, fanning his hands. "I had a special case. Were you—"

Laurie said something quick and unfathomable to Bella, then picked up her pack of tubes and bag, pushing back her newly lengthened hair with a half-formed gesture. It shone, combed and washed, but John noticed, with a hot, weary tug, that, Laurie being Laurie, the ends were already split.

"John, we need to talk . . . Your room's down there, isn't it?"

Bella watched as he and Laurie went out into the corridor

and down, their paths separate but interlocked. He opened the door, and Laurie lifted the crumpled cards off the chair by the dresser and sat down with her legs crossed, her back to the streaming window.

"Bella says she's turning off the generator now," she said.

He nodded and took out a chemlight. On cue, the bulb in the ceiling dimmed. The darkness pulsed in, then rearranged itself to the corners of the room as the chemlight's catalysts hissed. He took a seat on the bed, conscious of the snap of the springs, the rug's faded pattern, the crucifix on the wall. No wonder, he thought, that I never wanted to bring her here.

"John, you look dreadful."

He smiled.

"This place smells of..." She looked around and saw the old Quicklunch box full of koiyl leaves. Her hair swayed. The fall of it made her face look thinner. Too thin, perhaps—but he thought he could get used to it. "Bella says you're chewing those now."

"They're harmless. Everyone says they're harmless." He chuckled. "Apart from me, that is. And it would have been presumptuous, don't you think, to try to do something about the koiyl trade without understanding what it was really about. I have a good supply now. There's a room half full of them down the corridor. I was given them by Ryat—you remember Ryat?"

She reached into her bag and broke open a maroon-colored tube. "You must be wet. Cold..."

"You've spent too long in the Zone, Laurie," he said. "Out here we have to get used to the rains. And why, when you grew your hair, didn't you change the look of your answerer?"

"I thought about it, knowing that you were always calling. But I decided you might try to...To make some interpretation."

"Then why did you let the answerer talk to me at all?"

She waved the question away with her hand, the smoke from the tube drawing a jagged symbol that suggested in the moment before it dissipated that the whole matter was complex, beyond the scope of anything that they might have to say to each other.

"But I'm sorry," she said, "that it's ended like this."

He nodded. The room swayed. "So am I."

"It had so much...promise. I suppose that having sex was a mistake."

"I've made worse ones."

She smiled. "It was really Tim Purdoe," she said, "who talked me into coming here." She gestured at the room. "Although I didn't want you to go back without..." She searched for the right word. "A farewell."

"I saw Tim—a while back. He said that he wanted to examine me. But I suppose you know that, looking through the net. I seem to remember that your answerer knew."

"I'm not my answerer, John. It's just a trick of the net. Something I once did, overdid really, just playing around, looking for someone to talk to. Anyway, this is all ridiculous."

"What is?"

"The way you think you're being betrayed, let down." She squeezed out the tip of her tube and stooped to pull out the tin wastecan that lay between her and the bed, noticing as she did so, he was sure, the chewed red lumps in it. "It isn't true."

"I suppose you've spoken to Felipe. And of course to Bella."

"I just wanted to see if you were taking care of yourself."

"Here I am. You can see that I'm taking care."

"When are you going back to Europe? Has the bishop said?"

"No, she hasn't."

"What do you expect to achieve this late?"

"The leaf—"

"You're not the only person in the world, John. And I'm not saying that you should give up everything, forever. Just..."

"You think I should leave here?"

"Now that I've seen you, yes. I think you should go back. There are other healers and helpers. And you've said often enough that Nuru can cope with the clinic. I don't want you to break up here, John, I don't want you to get hurt. I have no idea how you've managed to get like this, but I'm sure it's not that difficult to damage your recombinant if you really try. Even a child could."

"You don't know what you're talking about, Laurie," he said. The chemlight was starting to fade now, and a space of darkness was flowing in the room between them. But how could she dismiss the silver tangle beneath his flesh so easily? As though it was something you could step out of, discard...

"I see now," she said, "why you're like this. It's simple with you, really, John. Everything you do and say keeps coming back to..." She broke open another tube and blew out a stream of smoke. "You're not like him. I know you well enough at least to know that. *He* thought that life would be easy just because he had talent and advantage. By the time he learned it wasn't, it was too late."

"I wish I could have taken you back to Europe, Laurie," he said. "Not Hemhill, I don't think Hemhill. But Ley. It's part of my life, and I needed...Someone else to go back there with."

She smiled, keeping her distance.

373

"So you'll go back?" she asked. "Can I tell Tim that? Or at least you'll speak to the bishop? As for the rest, John. The leaf. Us. Everything. Sometimes you have to break things off, separate from them, leave them truly behind, before you can find out what the truth was about them."

Laurie picked up her bag, her tubes, shook out and reparted her long hair with her fingers. He followed her from the room and into the corridor, past the closed door where Felipe was snoring. He stood in the hallway with the rain seeping in through the front door, hearing the slip of her footsteps as she moved away from him.

"The carnival should be soon now," she said. "You can feel the change in the air. It's like..." Her hands moved in the mottled light. "Do you remember some time when you wanted to throw your head back and laugh for no reason? You once asked what the carnival was like, John. Do you remember a time like that?"

He stood on the last stair, his hand burning on the damp rail, searching for a face and time in his mind, finding only a clear white space of emptiness.

The door screeched open. He heard the swish and patter of the street.

"So," she said. "Goodbye."

"*Gonenanh.*"

She closed the door. Her van was barely audible through the rain as it started down Gran Vía.

SOMETHING IN THE air, clear and metallic, turned and flashed, then cracked into separate notes. He opened his eyes as the room snapped back around him, and the tang of tube-smoke still hovered above the soggy earthbound scent of koiyl leaves, his own sweat, the dust and damp of the presbytery. He sat up, and pain ran through his spine.

He crossed the room, gripping the waxy corners of the ancient furniture. No leaf today, he thought, seeing the chair by the window set at an angle, and the scatter of Laurie's tubes in the wastebin beside it. He dressed in the dysol-reeking clothes that Bella had put out, and light poured with him into the corridor as he descended towards the smell of cooking.

Felipe was already seated at the table, the steam rising from his coffee.

"A good day for it," he said. "Don't you think so, my son?"

John went over to the window and looked out. The air was still. Every brick, lintel, and patch of flaking plaster on the tenement opposite was sharply etched. The windows and rooftops were held in glassy suspension as the sky glowed white—no, the sky was gray, like the pressure he felt at the back of his eyes. Still somehow gray despite all the brightness.

He turned when Bella emerged through the doorway with the breakfast tray tinkling in her hands. He sat down, and Felipe grunted and flapped out his napkin as she leaned over the table, the bare stretch of her forearm touching John's shoulder as she placed the plates before them. There were fungi leaking grayish juice, fried kelpbread, several crustacea, two rashers each of bacon, the pale watery eye of a fresh egg.

He said, "Laurie was here last night."

"Yes." Felipe watched the sway of Bella's departing rump. "So I gather."

"There seems to be some concern about me," John said. "Tim Purdoe thinks I'm unwell." He looked down at his plate, the blue pattern that he'd stared at many times before without really noticing. "Not, I think, that I'm exactly..." The beaded black eye of the shrimp stared back at him. He knew that if he put the thing into his mouth, he'd only spit it out again. "Not that I'm entirely fit. I've been taking the leaf..." He swallowed, conscious of the brightness flooding from the window at his back; of how the noises in the street sounded so different now that there was no rain and even the wind had stilled; of the dry, odd-sounding croak of his own voice. "I've been chewing it in a spirit of scientific experiment. But now I seem to be coughing up a little blood."

"I've seen people looking worse, my son," Felipe said. "But

also better. If you really want to stay here, then you should stay." He waved the eggy tines of his fork at his feet. "That is, if you want to become like me. But otherwise, I think you should go back to Europe right away. You only have—what is it?—two weeks left of your term."

"Is that all? I'd thought..." He felt as though he should be getting up. Running somewhere. Doing something.

Felipe chuckled, mopping kelpbread around his plate. "After all, you've left me often enough already. And I see the bishop's flag is flashing on the airwave again. Has been for the last couple of days... But this time I decided not to take a message for you."

"I'd like to see today through at least. This carnival after the rains..."

"Of course." Felipe pushed back his plate and folded his arms over his stomach. "Bella," he called, "excellent as always!" He turned to John. "And after that? Your plans for the priesthood?"

"I'm still going to leave."

Felipe nodded. Then he leaned forward across the table, his face suddenly grave.

"Now, my son." His gaze shifted down to the untouched breakfast. "If you're not wanting that, perhaps I might...?"

He checked his bicycle in the hall; he'd used it little lately, but the powerlight still gleamed and the tires were firm as he wheeled it out into the street. The clear flat puddles reflected fractured images of the roof-segmented sky as he cycled down to the clinic. Outside, a queue was forming, although Nuru had already arrived and unlocked the doors. He was sitting inside at his desk in the outer office, little columns of coins on the desk before him, busy with his preparations.

"Fatoo..."

"*Gunahana.*"

John changed gloves and took out a fresh wad of dysol cloths. The doctor's lens followed him as he entered the backroom. He heard the usual chatter of voices when Nuru began to sort out the queue. Those who were keeping a place for someone else, those who'd let a friend in, those who weren't really sure why they'd come. John listened, smiling, watching the play of shadows through the half-open door.

The first patient came in. A tall man, he mistakenly held his wounded hand out to John rather than to the doctor, his eyes downcast.

"Not many this morning," Nuru said cheerfully from behind him. "People got other..."

"Yes. The carnival."

The man mumbled, and Nuru explained that he should step towards the doctor's suite of mandibles. Sitting on the edge of the desk, John watched. This patient was, for all the difference in his clothes, the spiky hair, the stubble on his jowls, the unmatched shoes, and the bloodshot green eyes, almost the exact double of Father Gulvenny, the priest of John's teenage years at St. Vigor's. Father Gulvenny would be dead now, of course. The cut along this man's thumb had already been frozen by some kind of fixative; there was no real danger, but John watched anyway as the doctor's delicate mandibles drew the sides of the wound together and bound them with a filmy fluid that would soon change, harden, and become part of the flesh. When the doctor finished, John was still looking at the man's face. Father Gulvenny, he was tempted to say, it really *is* you, isn't it? This wasn't the first time he'd glimpsed people he knew, in the Endless City. There was the witchwoman who, but for the steel eye and the caroni bird on her shoulder, could have been his mother. And there was Annie, standing in a spice souk one night last winter as the snow fell and the lanterns swung, casting light and shadow over her lovely half-turned face. But he hadn't seen Hal yet. He was still looking.

Blinking, half dazed, Father Gulvenny left the clinic, making a surreptitious sign against the evil eye with his damaged hand as he left. There were other patients. A blind man who often came on some pretext or other, hoping that John or the doctor would suddenly offer a cure. And children with bellyaches and sores, muttering *ma, madre*, today worried that they might end up confined to bed and miss the carnival fun. And elderly people, pulling aside baggy elastic to show joints swollen by nothing more than a lifetime's use. Some were past seventy, even eighty, although they seemed grumpy, ungrateful for their fullness of years. But he envied the way life here could begin or end like the turning of these streets, narrowing, widening, opening suddenly into a whole new vista or closing unexpectedly on a dead brick wall.

The final patient came and went. Light billowed in from the open window. Even today there was a breeze. The posters on the wall crackled. "Don't," one of them muttered, the remnant of some long-forgotten health campaign. *"Danna..."* The doctor creaked forward slightly to regard him, a lens focusing in his direction as it absorbed the odd metabolic changes that had taken place in his body, changes it recognized as human yet also alien and beyond its capabilities to heal. Looking down at the screen as he moved his fingers to turn it off, John briefly saw the flashing image of his silver-threaded body.

"I won't be here much longer," he told Nuru, who stood waiting in the doorway. "You know that?"

Nuru nodded and pushed his hands into his pockets. His hair was freshly cut in neat sharp lines across his ears and forehead. His eyes fixed on John's, tracked away, came back again.

"This may be my last day."

"You last?"

"It's a little early. But you know where all the codes and cards are. You know that you can call on Felipe. And there's Kassi, of course. And the people at the Zone."

Nuru nodded.

"And I'll make sure," John said, "that you can keep on working here when someone else arrives in a few days. But you really need a proper salary."

"Salary?"

"Regular money paid by the church instead of cash from that box over there."

Nuru looked at the cashbox, then at John, his face a little pained.

"Well . . ." John leaned back on the desk, spreading his hands to take the strain from his back, feeling the gloves pull and wrinkle, the painful itch of his palms. "Perhaps things work well enough as they are. But, you know, you could run this place on your own . . ."

Nuru nodded, but he still looked pained. He wouldn't want that, either. Without a European and aid from the Zone to keep the doctor going, he'd just be another local healer.

"But thanks, Nuru. Thank you. I'll never forget the help you've given me. And don't worry about Mass this morning—just go and do what you want to do. And there's that bicycle outside—my bike, you know?—I'd like you to have it, as a gift."

"Yes Fatoo." Nuru looked at John thoughtfully, probably calculating whether the machine would be worth more sold in one piece or broken up. "Thank you too . . ."

John left Nuru to lock up. He walked away from the clinic, where his bicycle leaned with its powerlight glowing, across the Plaza Princesa, and up the hill. It felt good to discard things—and the odd sense of lightness that had been with him all morning was even stronger now. This was a different city, strangely quiet under a white haze with the smells of coalsmoke, fresh paint, and wet jelt breaking over him in papery veils. He wandered the climbing alleys and quarrelsomely tangled streets, nearly losing himself, tripping over duckboards and puddles. In this odd, detached silence, he missed all the usual clues. He checked his watch, seeing frozen lines, and jumped as a cat hissed unexpectedly at him from the top of a glass-strewn wall.

He now recognized the big brick-paved square where Sarai and Mo had their tenement. They would be busy with their goat this morning, washing, combing, putting in ribbons, trying to cover up the remains of the foot rot. He looked up at the windows, but they all shone black. His footsteps clipped and echoed in silence as he walked towards the open door of the big warehouse where the carnival floats were stored, expecting noise, the commotion of the last hours before the procession. But even here it was empty. A small girl sat alone, snipping out shapes from paper, her face pale with concentration, her cheeks two angry red spots. She looked up when he came in, and shook out a tumble of people holding hands. He said *gunahana* and pushed his way through the gleaming displays. Close up, they were hard to make out, really just angles and curves, splashes of primary color, but the big spidery float at the back of the warehouse had at last taken shape into something familiar. It was covered with sheets of the thin film that the old man had been sewing, and it had been painted filigree-white and given great ghost wings and spars. John sat down on a crate beside it, looking up. A cloudpicker. It was big, but still far too small, and wrong, he guessed, in every detail. But it was also unmistakably right. The taut membranes shimmered rainbows, popping and straining as if ready to take flight.

There had once been nights, he thought, blinking, his shoulders hunched against some unaccountable pain, when the sea and the sky joined, became one element, when the climate was pure and warm and the rest of the world slept far away. But the summer after Hal's accident, they hadn't gone to Ley; Hal's condition hadn't stabilized yet; although actually, if you looked back, Hal had been stable enough. He was settled and at peace—it was everyone else who hadn't stabilized, who still oscillated wildly from joy to hope to anger to puzzlement and grief at the merest twitch of his eyelids, or at the unexpected stab of a memory or regret. Two years afterwards, they finally went back to Ley. John, his parents, Hal. Technically, moving Hal hadn't been so difficult. A big doctor was rented to lift him up, carry him downstairs to the van that his father had also rented and was even talking of buying. Hey, look at these features, Son. And the machine had stayed by him, monitoring and clicking on the strange and familiar journey to Ley's seagull-wheeling streets, where the process, with some minor difficulty at a sharp turn in the stairs, was repeated in reverse. For all the weeks that they were there, the big doctor squatted self-importantly in the room with Hal, strung to him by silver. John had weird visions of taking the thing out with him with its heraldic head to walk the cliffs or navigate *Omega*—although that year he never quite got around to making her seaworthy. Or even—now that he was too old to do so—imagined sitting with it on Chapel Beach, digging castles and canals in the pale hot sand. The hope, of course, had been that if they reenacted some of the normal rituals of their old summers at Ley, a still functioning part of Hal's consciousness would clear. He'd hear the seawind, feel the soft grit of the sand that John dribbled between his toes. He'd awake to the cry of gulls and the tinkle of spars and say, *Hey, Skiddle.* Or he'd come in the night to the cabin where John lay awake and gazing up at the big sea moon that so often filled his window, waiting, as sometimes happened, for a shape, winged, dark, to pass between him and it...Not that it happened, not that he expected it to happen, even if the sun each morning was as bright as ever, and the sky—well, the sky; he still hadn't worked out a proper word to describe that deep blue that lay over your eyes in those noonday depths. But nothing happened, and they went back to Hemhill when the evenings began to chill. They caught the house and the garden, as always, in green and ragged surprise, and arrived just in time for the festival of harvest, the big carnival, and the night when the long trucks went past and the low deep humming of the compound at the end of the valley rumbled deep between the hills.

John stood up. The cloudpicker squealed and fluttered. He could almost feel the pull of it, like a kite, and now he could also hear voices and the growl of a handtool back at the entrance of the warehouse. He walked out. The people drifting in to prepare for the carnival made a space for him to pass.

Darkness was already rising in the square when John stood above it, swaying on the steps that led back through lost alleyways to the church where he had waited, lost as well, in a timeless moment of empty prayer. The sky was still pale over the rooftops, but dim now, faded as white paper fades. Twilight billowed up, softening the paved square where the people wandered through a mist. Suddenly, now, they were all here, and dragons and hippogriffs unfurled their wings from the big main doors of the warehouse. He walked down the steps as a giggling river of girls dressed in white ran by him. There were cheers when the warehouse disgorged a giant dark-eyed figure, the leering half-solid head emerging through the roof even before the body left the doorway. Then came the cloudpicker, hardly visible, a bubble of light.

Now, the goat was coaxed down the ribboned steps of the tenement, Sarai and Mo leading it. The crowd sighed. Doubtless drugged more heavily than ever, but with its coat a glossy white and its legs apparently fully healed, the creature managed to look regally important as it was coaxed onto the back of a flatbed truck that was now wreathed in rocket cones of pink and yellow hyacinth. A figure, caped and many-jeweled—possibly a witchwoman, although today they were hard to distinguish from the rest of the population—raised a hand that glinted with a vial and proceeded to anoint the goat. Then the engines started. White balloons lifted from the square, the drums commenced their clatter, colored lights played through the smoke, the procession began to move.

John followed at the back, where the small boys scampered. He felt empty-handed, and almost wished that he'd followed Felipe's example and brought the incenser with him. But at least he was in the carnival now. It had lost the intimidating strangeness he'd witnessed looking down at it from the window of the presbytery all those months ago; the demons were mostly papier-mâché, and the faces behind the painted-on skulls usually seemed to be laughing. In many ways, it wasn't that different from the carnival at Hemhill, even if Hemhill's was confined to a field. The occasional talk there of a procession down High Street always came to nothing, because people were too busy with the harvest to get things organized, or they were away on holiday like his parents. Lifted up in Hal's arms in the days when he was small, he'd often watched the trucks arriving on the empty field, the big rigs and the gaunt, scary shapes of the self-propelled gantries.

People lurched around him, bearing monolithic heads on their shoulders, barely able to see where they were going through the eye slits in the mouths. One, either weary or drunk, staggered into him. The looming face, he saw, was unmistakably one of the stone kings on the cliff face of Hettie's cave near Ifri Gotal. Then something stuck John hard on the back. When he looked around, he saw a black-robed woman at the side of the road. She was bending down to the mud to scoop up more.

He was borne in the river of the procession now. The sky was fully dark, and the buildings flickered with lights, screens, and lanterns. Looking over the bobbing heads at the Pandera presbytery, he saw the open window of the top room where

Felipe would be sitting. He shouted out the old priest's name as a tinkling keyboard rang in his ears, but the crowd surged on and, looking back, he couldn't even be sure that he'd seen the right building. But he knew that everyone was here. The image in his head was of this carnival procession running like a glittering snake east to west for all the thousands of kilometers of the Endless City, as far as Mizraim and over the wreckage of Jerusalem to the domes of the albino people, the clifftop dwellings, the ash deserts of the tundra. All joining together under a dark-white sky.

He looked ahead for the goat now as the procession spilled out into the Plaza El-Halili and the purposeful movement of the crowd grew turbulent and air filled with the sound of arguments and the smell of spice, fried onion, sour manure, fresh popcorn. Parents grabbed anxious hands, and he heard the wailing pull of children's voices. *Madre, ossar. Ah protho...* He wandered the lines of stalls, finding his way easily past bats fluttering in cages, crabs scuttling through mazes and urged on by cheering crowds, and, everywhere, balloons squealing. Some stalls, it seemed to him, contained monstrous clawing shadows, and there was an edgy sense that it would be easy to step sideways from here into the darkness that underlies every kind of carnival, to take a wrong turn where feathers and blood trickled in the gutter beside him. But by the stage and the brightly lit Kasbah wall, the local bands were playing music while people clapped and danced and nodded their heads and held babies and camera screens up to see. He was hit by the bass and the heat, the thrump of many generators, the dizzy lights that swept the sky. *Ah, fatoo, gunafana...* Fireworks and rockets clattered over the stage, and he shivered, looking up and losing his sense of horizon as the fire-threaded black poured over him. Whoosh.

Bang. *Nach.* Ahhhh. He stumbled out of the crowd towards the steps of an empty alley, vomited quickly and discreetly in a gap between the buildings, then sat down on the slick paving to nurse his dizziness and watch the show.

It was easier here, anyway—just watching, being apart. That autumn after they returned from the Annie-less summer in Ley, he'd gone down through the carnival turnstiles at Hemhill when the grass was still wet and the rides were scarcely open. He'd wanted to catch the day off-guard, and in a way—in a wrong way—he'd succeeded. For the first time he found himself looking at the back of things, the way the tents were pegged, the screens supported, the rides powered and anchored; looking at the hot juddering cables and the chipped corners and the flaking paint, the half-broken crabs that climbed and tended the great wheel that he'd broken his promise again last year to ride. This year Hal had been too absorbed with departure to extract the same promise from him.

It already had the feeling of a last carnival, and John wondered if Hal would even find the time to come. He hadn't seen him that morning. Hal would probably be in his room packing now, or off somewhere with Annie, or saying farewell to one or another of his secret haunts. This was, after all, his last day before London. But John really wasn't that bothered. He was glad, for once, to be back in Hemhill. At Ley this year, his brother had pottered around like some mournful ghost, getting in the way. And things went wrong, were misarranged. *Omega* hadn't been serviced, John had to do it himself, and even a lazy afternoon on the beach had been polluted by the atrocity of that seagull. Although he knew it wasn't fair, John blamed Hal for that as well.

It was still too early for any sign of his own friends at the carnival, or for anything really to happen. He walked into the beer tent, wondering if he'd be stopped this year as he'd been every other. But no one noticed; the invisible barrier that had always separated him from this dim and green-lit adult world, where he'd once peered under the flaps and seen old Father Virat staggering drunk, had dissolved. He walked past the largely empty lines of trestles. He asked for a beer at the counter and looked for a place to sit after the machine served him.

And there was Hal, sitting alone with a beerglass in his hand and a corral of empty ones around him. He looked up without smiling when John sat down beside him.

John took a sip of his beer. It was cold, slimy. "I was thinking," he said, "that this year, I'll go on the great wheel. I won't run like I did last year, you know."

Hal nodded, a half-moon of foam drying on his upper lip and a popped blisterpack of soberups lying by his elbow. He wasn't even bothering to get drunk. "Yes," he said. "I know."

"I mean, I don't expect you to pay, Hal. Not after wasting your money last year."

Hal looked mournful and bilious in this greenish light. Music began to crunch outside, then stopped as suddenly as it had started.

"Did you hear the truck last night, Skiddle?"

"Truck? No."

"I thought..." Hal looked pained. "I went down there this morning, before I came here. There was dew on the shockwire, and the compound was alive. They were everywhere."

John nodded, wondering what the point was in staring at people you couldn't understand or even touch.

"Oh, there are stories," Hal said, gazing down into his glass. "But I expect you know that."

"Well, Hal, I..."

"A few years back, you know, one of them went missing. One of the Gogs. A girl—she was kidnapped. It never really came out what had happened, but I heard it was some Hemhill lads. You know—my age. Or yours...Or only a little older. They tied her up in the back of an agripede and took her down to the ruins around the old cathedral. There's an old building that's kept its roof. It was once a pub called the Orange Tree, and the sign still sticks out into the street. They dragged her into a room with wet plaster falling off the walls. Ripped the lydrin implant out of her arm, raped her, held her, pissed on her, spat on her. Made her eat..." Hal squeezed his eyes shut and rubbed them hard with his fist. "You know, for the viruses. Just to see what would happen. Of course, she died."

"That's horrible."

"Yeah." Hal took his blisterpack and popped another soberup tablet. "So why do I keep thinking about it?"

"These things are—"

"Thinking about it even when I'm with Annie. Pretending in my head that I'm...That she's..."

John stared at him, feeling an odd, disconnected anger, something that blazed and passed through without finding a focus. You, my brother, he thought, waiting for something else to come into his head. But he was simply glad that Hal would be going to London tomorrow, that Hal wouldn't be coming into his bedroom again as he'd done on recent nights, overwrought with the world and the prospect of things to come and the souring of his once golden relationship with the sweet and lovely Annie. John was sick of Hal opening the door and breaking through the clean silence just as John was falling into sleep.

"Well..." Too quickly, John finished his beer. He stood up,

feeling his gut clench and ache. "See you later, Hal." He walked out of the tent into the light of the carnival, and stood looking up at the great wheel. The sun was glinting through the spokes, spilling the warmth of what would be—what always was, for the carnival—a hot day. He no longer felt afraid, but the cost of the ride was exorbitant and the queue was slow and long. You wasted a small fortune and half your afternoon simply waiting to get on. He already knew that with or without Hal, this year or any other year, he wouldn't be going on the great wheel. It wasn't a question of fear. It was simply a matter of giving up . . .

"*Skiddle?*"

John started and turned, looking up the enclosed Magulf alley behind him, then down through the steam and smoke across the stalls and the dancing, shifting people. But the sound had come only from his own head. Wincing, he clambered to his feet and wandered back through and into the carnival. He saw a woman's face as she turned and laughed—looking startlingly like Laurie for a moment. It was getting late, and the crowds were both thinner and more frantic, the competing lights, attractions, sounds, and the generators that powered them had all been turned up. He watched a carousel spin, a dragon roar, and a shooting gallery where the targets burst and spouted blood; the split wreckage of what might have been a cloudpicker or the wings of a dead insect blown in on a counterwind from Europe; and a wrestling machine oiled with the sweat of a hundred competitors—it now lay slumped in a corner, in flickering light, its screen blind and its mandibles dislocated. Gazing down at its smeared and dented golden dome, John thought it was familiar. But everything was familiar in this place.

Crowing laughter and fistfights. A stale, hot wind. The snap and clatter of empty cans and tubes, snakes of vomit and urine and the weak fizzing of chemlights trapped in puddles. The half-laughing, half-protesting cries of a woman, as a man, his voice thick with all the pressures of the night, leaned against her. Everything was lost and waiting on a still wind. Everything banged and clanged. His gloves were red from fingertip to wrist now, and the color had even spread inside, with the angry burning of his palms. There were nights, he thought, looking up at the glinting white lace of interference lines in the sky, and the turning, beckoning wheel of the stars. There were nights...

Shadows flickered from a fire over the pink Kasbah wall. Voices crackled, rags of clothing swept back like ash from the flames, throwing furrows across the silently gathering crowd. Walking the tightrope line of space that opened around him, John pushed on towards the front, looking for faces he knew, for Sarai and Mo, Juanita, Nuru, Kassi, for Martínez, for Father Gulvenny, looking even for Hettie and the witchwoman he'd seen on the night of the spring carnival at Banori's tenement. But the faces all drew back into the shadows that flowed and opened towards the space where the figures flew upward, caught on the sweep of this wild and hallucinogenic wind.

The goat was tethered to a post now in the middle of a madly dancing circle that thinned like smoke as John reached to join hands. He looked at its wise white head, pulling off his gloves as he did so and seeing the red fluid that dribbled out from them and the deep gashes that had somehow appeared in his palms. His fingers left streaks on the goat's coat, drawing the fur into beaded clumps. He felt a gasp ripple through the crowd like the wind that tousled the green cloud-racing hills where once he had stopped to talk to creatures almost like this, looking up at the mystery of their slotted eyes, feeling the waiting melancholy of the backrooms to which—*here, Father, and he seemed so bright and chipper in the summer*—he was later taken. And the goat's eyes, he saw, were each a different color. One was brown and the other silver.

The crowd gasped again. A thrilling tension ran through him—that he should be here where the flames danced on the walls, with the cold emerald light of the fire and the drip-tap of drums and the swaying, scurrying witchwomen who were fingering their honeycombed moonrock and drinking their Venusian vials, and that the crowd should be with him, touching without touching, sighing with the wind, pushing him on. A black shape scuttled up to him. Something silver flashed from the sky. It touched his hand, and his fingers slipped, almost dropping the metal. The knife handle was cold and smooth, and he watched a red line dribble out along the curved and shining blade from his hand, watched the droplet that formed at the tip and grew and hung there. A white wind poured around him. This, he thought, as the bead of blood finally broke from the knife and dropped slowly towards the paving, as the goat tried to raise its tethered head and clattered its hooves, this is my blood, my covenant, my rainbow, my promise to a ravaged world. His raised his hand, and brought the knife down in a red blur. Once, and then again, feeling something break, feeling something crumple, feeling the gasp of life and a hot spray like the salt of the ocean and the pull of the tide washing over him.

He dropped the knife, looked down at the still-kicking, half-butchered animal, then turned, dazed, his feet sticking in the spreading pool, his eyelids glued with blood, and stumbled back through the parting crowd. There were faces he recognized now, people he had seen, and they were more afraid of him than ever, the *fatoo baraka* who was madder than the witch-women, than *chicahta*. At least the witchwomen believed only in the whirl of this planet through the stars...

"Skiddle?"

John spun around. But he saw only Borderer faces and carnival light. He stumbled on, kicking over brimming chemical buckets and clattering through a stall, staggering up the slope and away to the dark and hidden streets, falling against doors and walls beneath the churning sky, leaving a bloody trail behind him, smearing hieroglyphs and symbols, swirls and crosses. He had no idea where to go.

He began to slow as he ran from the carnival, lost in these empty ways, his breath rasping, hearing the beat of music echoing far off. He stumbled through a courtyard and along an unlit corridor past the communal wastebarrels and water butts, up the creaking steps to a landing and a door that rocked back with the swaying imprint of his hands. But there was no one inside—this was the wrong room. He looked around and saw fresh white walls, screens and bowls of flowers and cheap but newly gleaming furniture, and he smelled kelpbread and Borderer flesh. It wasn't Banori's room. Not any longer. A cheap, decently placed apartment, it would have been taken and rearranged within a few days of his death. John wandered, bumping into things, his fingers sticking and skidding. He worked a drawer out along its glides. Inside were a few cracked disks, a large dead beetle, some dried-out tubes—and a postcard. It glowed up through the smears of his fingers as he lifted it out, and it formed the image of a wide, empty shore where the waves were white-tipped, rolling high, breaking green over blue, freezing to ice, then breaking again. He heard the hissing of shingle; smelled, too, the clear tang of the River Ocean; saw the grass that covered the dunes at his back bowing in the wind, and the pantiled roofs along the sandy road where graceful birds circled like flecks of foam. Then the sound of the sea ended, and he heard—

"Skiddle?"

Dropping the postcard, he turned and saw, as the light flashed and faded over the smeared walls, that a figure stood in the doorway.

She blinked at him with pebble eyes and beckoned amid the sway and glitter of her beads, jingling a forest of silver.

"Come with me, Skiddle," she said. "Come this way..."

Almost immediately, the witchwoman retreated into the dark. He stumbled from the room to follow her. She was shifting and indeterminate now along the corridor and down the stairs, past the black mouth of the courtyard then out into the streets, where she seemed to scuttle and slide over the wet roads, splashing through puddles, her black image thrown back at him and across the mottled walls. On this night, when even the carnival now lay silent, he could hear her muttering, the tinkle of the ribboned clothing that would suddenly flash scatters of sparks. She was in no hurry—humming, picking things up from the gutter, tasting them, even, spitting them out—yet he felt slow, thick, clumsy as he followed her past the loneliness of black windows, along turns and alleys that unfolded into wide, vacant squares. These streets were unfamiliar to him now, and the silence was huge and strange, amplified, it seemed, by a deep humming. But he recognized the lines of shockwire and the empty warehouses and the wide sweeps of concrete, shot through now, as his breath grew ragged, by white lines and shimmers of pain.

There. She was fluttering across Kushiel's gleaming concrete, pausing, hopping, tumbling beneath the pylons and gantries that leaned and bowed. Dark whiteness seemed to be flooding up from the earth, enclosing him as he struggled to follow. Something clattered, and a spray of sparks scattered around him, raising the matted hair of his head and neck.

"Skiddle."

There was a rusted ladder before him now. On it, the shape of rags was crawling towards the sky. Feeling the earth crackle with static at his feet, he began to climb after her. Metal swayed and clanged. Dust rained down on him. His hands glowed. He could see the wires that were threaded beneath the flesh, the stuff that made him. He was weary as he climbed, but he willed another part of him to take over, those strong silver threads, and clambered finally over the sharp edge of a girder and stood swaying as stars and sparks fell around him on the wide slope of a long, high roof.

Far ahead, the large black bird-thing leaped and flapped. He skidded down and across the mossy tiles. The stickiness of his hands and body were a help now, giving him adhesion, and even the gashes in his palms were useful. When he slipped over into space, a wound in his flailing hand caught on the bracket of a broken gutter and stopped his fall. He hauled himself back up towards the sky. I'm climbing, he thought, crawling on his knees now, shaking his head in a wet spray, even though the power here in Kushiel surely lay below, in the earth. But beyond the last flock of scattering tiles there was a doorway. And the humming was louder. And with it came the promise of light. He pushed through a frost of glass and crawled inside.

"Skiddle..."

There was a long corridor, and the stiff crackling of an electric wind. Filaments and cables curled out from shattered housings, twisting in sparks and flashes of quaternary lines.

His feet crunched over a snowfall of cards. They were bigger and thicker, he saw as they stuck to his face and hands, than cards were now, fountaining out from cabinets and drawers and billowing around him. Probably at least fifty years old. And many were broken, trailing a wet lace of nerve tissue, corrupted and yet reactivated in this wild storm, muttering the garbled syllables of voices long dead.

"Skiddle . . ."

Hal's voice was still there on the crackling wind as John saw a stairwell on his left and a bobbing, leering face that could have been real or a trick of the spinning light, or a carnival balloon.

A last turn, and he saw the doorway that he knew. Half open already, with the light fanning out over the familiar landing. And Hal sitting there amid the disorder of his life with the cases that he was supposed to be packing open and empty, the palettes and books and games on the bed and the floor all around him. And on the desk, in a weird geometry, there were lights, wires, screens, the tiny, humming city of whatever strange and new project he was currently working on. And the semeny hot smell of nerve tissue, the humming and the charged scent of electricity, of armpits and whisky, of the bright cruel sea.

"Skiddle . . ."

Hal turned to him and beckoned. "Come on, Skiddle," he said, holding out his hand. "I have something to show you."

John hesitated, then reached for the room, the doorway. As he touched, interference lines crackled running through this ancient and abandoned screen somewhere in Kushiel. And the image of Hal froze, flattened, then gained depth again.

Hal beckoned. "Come on, Skiddle." He held out his hand. "I have something to show you."

This time John pushed straight through. White fire shot around him and he felt something hard, then soft and giving. He hovered for a moment in black, open space. The darkness where the net was unwritten and lacy nebulae hung far above and below him.

"Skiddle..."

Floating, spinning, he looked.

The sound came through the blackness. And other voices, too. The endless babble of lives. People talking, exchanging. The music of cloud formations and crop codes, of bodies embraced by machines, of a Borderer couple in their room saying *anything, whatever,* and the scent of the koiyl leaves was there too, and the wind in the Northern Mountains, and even, faintly, the voice of Laurie's answerer, the smell of antiseptic and flowers, the far-off click-sigh of mechanical breathing.

John began to fall, swimming towards a growing cluster of quaternary light. There was Hal's voice again.

"Skiddle. Come on, Skiddle. I've been going through my things before I go..."

He saw the shadowy figure in the bedroom, explaining through a snow of lines of how he'd done this, how he'd done that, how he'd found some long-forgotten high-level port into the net, routed through it and accessed the codes to his own implants, his own cpu.

AACGCATAGTCCCTCGGTAGAAATCGGGGTCGATT

"See, Skiddle. We're in."

John looked and saw the pulse of blood, the whole turbulent angry river of life.

"Will you look at that? Would you believe?"

The voice faded as lines shot out and through, as the white lattice became a cage and fell away into bright points. And there was Hal again. Real and living for once and surrounded by the whole mess of a life he couldn't find it in him to discard. He was holding out his hands.

"It's all ready now, Skiddle. The virus that I've made. All it takes is a final link to make it combine. Just a seed, a ripple in the ether..."

The palms of Hal's outstretched hands, John saw, were hollow, pooled with spinning white.

"Touch me, Skiddle. Here—take my hands. I'm full of the charge. Just touch me—make it happen..."

He could smell Hal's body, hear him breathing, and see his eyes shining, his hair sticking up at the crown, feel him radiating into that moment all his love and life and hope and energy. Wanting to hold, to touch, to share and understand, John reached out for his brother, and fell endlessly through into whiteness.

BLACK LINES SLID by when he looked up. Jagged branches scrawled against a clear and open sky, the branches of a forest emptied by winter or burnt out by the sun. A breathless voice was muttering, pausing, muttering, as he was dragged over bumps of fallen shockwire in a handcart. By lifting his head a little and pushing against the sharp line of pain that held him down, John could just see the witchwoman's bobbing shoulders and the beaded snakes of her hair, and the warm reddish brick of the empty warehouses.

He knew where he was, even if he couldn't find a name or a reason for his knowledge. His hands seemed to have swollen into useless clubs. And that sky. When the last of the powerlines slid away, he looked up, and the sun flooded over the tenement rooftops beyond. That sky, warm and open as far as the stars, which were still spinning somewhere in the heart of the pure black-blue.

The cart stopped. He blinked and shivered as the witch-woman's tinkling, pebble-eyed face leaned over him, and he felt the heat of her skin, the rank sweetness of her breath. Her face was tilted and watchful. She said something in a rain of spittle that he didn't understand, although he guessed that he'd been talking too, rambling feverishly about the color of the sky while she hauled him along in this cart. He chuckled—he and she must make an odd sight even in this city of odd sights. The witchwoman chuckled too, and from over her shoulders the sky poured blue. She looked down into his eyes and reached in a clatter of bracelets and rings, and he glimpsed the pale-mouthed sores in her palms before her hands dipped from focus and her fingertips probed his face, his mouth, nostrils, eyes.

"What is that?" he croaked. The witchwoman frowned, pushing back a rope of hair and holding a pointed ear close to his mouth. "That sky, that color...There has to be a word..."

The witchwoman pursed her lips and nodded. She stepped back, and once again the cart began to jolt and rumble, and he looked up, falling into the sky.

This was a shadowed place with a curved, cracked ceiling. The darkness flowed with coughing and laughter, snores and moans.

A shape loomed over him. A hand raised his head, and something hot was pressed to his lips. He gagged at the dense aroma. It was drawn away for a moment, then tipped back, the liquid sliding over his swollen tongue, down his throat. The taste was familiar, savory. Soup. Asparagus soup. He fell back, feeling the heat spread through him.

"Skiddle..."

His gummed eyes were closed. He could hear only the scuffle of feet, the drip of water, the breathing of rank air.

But Hal wasn't here. He knew that now. The sound was just the clang of a bucket. The echo of footsteps on stone. Hal wasn't anywhere. What John had seen on that old screen in Kushiel were only ripples from the past, caught in the net from an abandoned project to bring light and heat to the Endless City. Kushiel was probably the lost port that Hal had accessed, a forgotten backdoor into the net's higher levels—but he and it were both history. Gone.

"Skiddle..."

Drip, tap. The rasp of his own breath. The bang of a door.

He remembered bursting into his parents' room in the clarity of that long-ago autumn morning when the birds were singing in the browning trees and carnival litter blew across the park, and the compound in the valley was humming. Bursting in and yelling something. Hal. His brother's name. Something about Hal. And his mother, already frail as she clutched the sleeves of her nightdress and her pale bare feet pattered down the landing. And his father, who yawned and stumbled behind. They pushed open the door to Hal's room, and he was there. Slumped over the desk and half off his chair, the cases empty and open on the bed and his mouth slack and his breath coming in long slow rasps. The wires and screens were all around him, and the soldering crab still moved, clawing pointlessly across Hal's face, squatting to lay another tiny silver egg above his flaccid eyes. The smell in the room was of hot nerve tissue and electricity, of armpits, socks, and semen.

The men and women who came later that day from the big torus at Leominster put on gloves and prodded amid the clever tangle on the desk, which the medical people had so carefully left undisturbed when they took Hal away to Southlands. And they sat and questioned John in the lounge, although it was already obvious that this was some sad and stupid prank. Or an accident. The house's own screens gave proof of that, and there was the evidence of the room, and what had been gathered from the few ravaged clues that Hal left in the net. Sitting with John in the pale light of the lounge with his father's big loud-speakers like sentinels around them, the men and women who came from some branch of Halcycon S.A. told him over and over that Hal had been alone all night. John, you weren't re-sponsible. John. You just walked into his room when it was morning. You saw him slumped there when it was already too late. And of course you ran and told your parents. All the rest has to be a bad dream. Truly understandable, but you mustn't blame yourself. When the pretty silver-eyed woman leaned over and smiled and reached to touch him, he shrank away. The screens and the tests cannot lie, John. There's still a great deal we'd like to know about how Hal created the virus that de-stroyed him, how and from where he managed to get so deep into the net, but even he wouldn't have been able to change the record of everything around him. Not even your big brother Hal could make you disappear from his room all night if you'd really been there. The evidence is plain, John. Hal was alone when it happened. The woman smiled. The silence settled in white folds.

John opened his eyes and managed to turn his head. Bright, then gone, a lantern bobbed by with a rounded figure shuffling behind it. He looked at the ceiling, feeling tacky wetness along his back, pain in his hands, the heat and the cold that surrounded him. He tried to persuade his mind to produce the commands that would tell his body to sit up. Suddenly, he managed it, and saw this tunnel-like room. The man on the pallet beside him was coughing and muttering, plucking feverishly at his vest. A few of the other patients, John saw, were sitting up, inspecting themselves, counting limbs and bruises, rubbing heads, covering torn or exposed parts of their bodies. A bald man with a swollen eye and a luminous snake tattooed on his arm looked over, spat, then shook his head.

"Vi mal ahoara, eh? Ice fa nah judia..."

John nodded. Somewhere to the right, a door banged open, shut again. Bang. And a silver balloon with a demonic, leering face bobbed out from beneath his pallet. The witchwoman had dumped him, he guessed, among the rest of the human detritus washed up at the Cresta Motel after the carnival. People mostly injured through fights, falls, one kind of overindulgence or another. The door in the corridor banged again, and the balloon, caught on a pleasant and oddly fragrant breeze, floated away. It was, he now saw, plain silver, although he couldn't quite believe that the face reflected in it had been his own. Using his teeth and the crusted claws of his hands, he pulled the rags off his sleeve. The screen of his watch was entirely blank.

As the door banged, posters and blinds fluttered along the stained walls. Breathing in the rich cool scent that flowed around him, John felt a sudden strength come into his limbs. Bang. He found that he was standing up almost without willing it. He hobbled between the pallets. The heavy iron door—rusted, apart from the shine of the drawn bolts—was swinging open, banging shut. The soft wind blew through him again. He felt pain as he held the door and limped down the worn stone steps. The door closed behind him. A cold, healing wind pushed at his face. Bang. Sigh. A hissing in his ears, prolonged by some trick of this building. He smelled a fresh and delicious breeze, which brought memories of clouds racing over a high valley and white-flowered bushes trembling where a stream ran clear. The scent of koiyl.

The steps straightened and leveled into a domed subterranean room. It was lit by one halogen lamp and half obscured by a ribboned forest of oddly assorted rocks. Gray clinker, he supposed, from the moon. Crumbling red dirt from Mars. And between, in shadows and swathes, were darker piles of leaves. They were shriveled and uncured, but he could tell simply from the look of them that they were mostly from Lall. Here, at last, was this year's crop. He swayed, feeling sweat beading through the grime of his skin. It was warm in here despite the breeze, and the sweet strong scent that had drawn him came not from these shriveled leaves but from drifts of steam, from a big-bellied pot that bubbled in a corner. Swallowing saliva, he peered over the rim. A black residue was plopping inside. It looked like glue or overdone jam, but on a lined shelf at the back he saw, neat and out of place in this primitive kitchen, tubes and wires, a monitoring screen and a retort, a small set of Halcycon-logoed scales. Some method, he guessed, of refining and distilling, of turning the residue of a harmless narcotic into a poison. Hal would have been at home here.

The pot bubbled, and the breeze blew up and around him. Bang. Then the slide of bolts. Footsteps and the sound of jingling. His heart kicked as he turned from the pot and gazed over the moonrocks through the steam-ribboned room at the figure that emerged at the base of the stairs. Though she was wearing gloves and a mask and struggling to carry a tray of empty vials, he saw at once that it was Kassi Moss. More shocked than he was, she dropped her tray in a silver shower when she saw him.

"*Nach Fatoo,*" she said, pulling back her mask, stumbling in one sentence from Borderer to European, "...your eyes."

F ROM HIGH ON the flat tiled roof of the Cresta Motel, the Endless City gleamed, and the sounds of life that the wind and rain had masked for so long rose with the steam from the sun-warmed streets. There were children shouting, pump engines coughing, people cursing, chickens clucking, dogs barking, couples arguing, music playing, shutters banging, brooms swishing, footsteps squelching in the mud.

As John looked up at the deep blue sky, another sound caught his ear, distant, perhaps only recognizable because his ears were still European, still attuned. The whine of fanjets. He saw a bright speck, then another. Two veetols like scratches of orange paint above the misty rooflines of the Endless City. He saw a third to the south, hovering over its reflection beyond the kelpbeds of the Breathless Ocean. They were still a long way off, but all were leaving the Zone. As he watched, the two inland veetols turned slowly, headed one way, then another. A tiny ballet. He decided they were working some kind of triangulated grid, methodically searching the Endless City for him, although they were still three or four kilometers off. It would be many hours before they got here. But there was no hurry. He could wait.

H<small>E WAS IN</small> an airy suite at the Zone's medical center, propped up and massaged by cooled shifting sheets and a powered mattress. A bright yellow spray of chrysanthemums sat on the console beside him, a gift Felipe had brought from one of the souks. The petals were already falling, but the scent was ripe, almost overpowering. The old priest had gone. But for the spectacle of the hopelessly optimistic spider that was attempting to draw its web between the serrated leaves, John would have called the machine that squatted in the corner and had the flowers removed.

The small screen on his lap was specially configured to respond to the wildly approximate movements of the glossy cocoons that still swathed his hands. He'd spent some time scrolling through the net's great multilayered dictionary, from which his own translat's data had come. There were so many words in so many languages for the word *blue,* and the word *sky,* but the best word—the nearest to the soft, short sound that he was almost sure the witchwoman who'd taken him to the Cresta Motel had uttered—came from the old English-American language that once dominated the world, the language from which much of both the Borderer and European languages were derived. *Blue.* A good word.

He pulled back from the database and paged down through the communications field of the local area of net, calling up the full address—28 All Saints Drive—now that he could get no response to the simple instruction to find Laurie Kalmar.

"Yeah?"

Broad cheeks and dark hair, a fleshy but handsome face. From the man's expression, John guessed that even though the silver iris pigment had almost fully returned, and his eyes were no longer blue, he still looked iller and stranger than he thought. Or perhaps it was just the background that he hadn't bothered to blank out. The humming sheets, the hospital smell.

"Have you been here long?"

"Here?" The man's eyes darted up to the cursor to check who John was, then back again.

"I mean in the Zone."

The man raised his shoulders in a lopsided shrug. "Just a few days, Father. I'm settling in. Why?"

"Do you know anything about the previous tenant? Where she went? Whether there's still a port to access her anywhere?"

"Wait..." The man looked down, his hands rippling the screen. "No. I don't think so. Not at this end."

"Did you see her?"

The man shook his head.

"But I suppose the place must have needed a lot of clearing up," John said. "All that dust, mess...Life..."

"Someone said she was a Borderer, so I guess. But look, Father, if there's a problem, if you want to—"

"No. It's okay," John said, feeling white waves of tiredness begin to descend on him again. "It's okay. And I hope you enjoy your time here."

He faded the screen. When he looked up, he saw that Tim Purdoe was standing in the doorway.

The barrier flickered as Tim walked in and leaned down to inspect the monitor screens, hands on his knees, the sleeves riding up on his old tweed jacket and that ridiculous fringe of his thinning hair in need of a trim once more.

John said, "I couldn't get Laurie."

Tim sat down on the bed, his shoulders stiff and the steepled tips of his fingers whitening as he pressed them together.

"And you know, Tim, I really did think you were responsible for copying the cards about the leaf. I thought at first that it was Laurie, then I thought it was you. I never imagined that there was a port into the net at Kushiel."

"Whoever closed up the plant probably thought they'd be coming back in a few weeks. Anyway, someone sent a veetol over. It's been closed now."

"What about the geothermal root? All that power in the ground?"

"There's hardly any power in the ground, John." Tim was looking down at the sheets now, holding himself oddly.

"I thought—"

"It wasn't Kushiel that damaged you, John. Don't you think they make you strong enough to stand a few electric shocks, a magnetic field? It was just some virus you picked up." Tim glanced up at him, then down again. "Actually, it's not quite like anything we've seen before, otherwise your recombinants would have dealt with it. But I did a search on the net, and there it was, not in the medical sectors at all but in the Magulf environmental stuff. A suggested code for the infection that might cause the, ah...disturbance of the witchwomen. I don't suppose that their and our paths cross that often, which would explain..." Tim smiled briefly. "So it's really a bit of a discovery, John. A new virus that could hurt us Europeans. But then that's one of the main reasons we're here, to catch anything bad before it reaches Europe. So we could both be minor celebrities for this, although I guess that's not either of our styles." Tim clenched and unclenched his hands. "Look, I—"

"And the leaf. You know, Tim, the leaf from Lall. I found out where the year's crop went. It was Kassi Moss."

Tim nodded. Even now, John thought, he's not interested. But then his recollection of the times they talked before in this room was hazed by the drugs the doctor had pushed into him. Perhaps he'd said all this before.

"...and she uses the refined leaf on her patients, Tim, to kill them when there's nothing else left that she can do. To bring an end. I remember how you said that if you distilled it and strung the molecules up, it would become a poison. And that's what she was doing. She says she bought the Lall leaf because a witchwoman once told her it was close to a place of death. I guess Kassi's a little mad herself, a little that way. But then, who isn't?"

"Yes," Tim said.

"But it's not an answer."

"Maybe not. But what is?"

411

"Kassi doesn't need that much of the leaf. It's become an obsession with her. But it'll stop. And people are still dying, Tim. Even now, some of the polluted leaf is still reaching the streets. And there will be more of it in a few years, unless something is done."

Tim nodded. "You know that place—the Cresta Motel. I should really call in there. See what I can..." As Tim looked out through the window at the green lawns, the racing skies, the ducks on the chilly, wind-ripped lake, John studied his profile, the way he was holding his mouth, wondering what was bothering him.

"About Agouna, Tim. I have no right to—"

"Look, John." Tim turned back to him and placed his bare hands over the shiny lumps of John's own. "I have some bad news about your family. It happened three days ago, but I've been holding it until I was sure you were mending. I hope you'll forgive me. It had to happen soon anyway, and there was nothing you could have done."

John stared at him, waiting.

"Your mother's dead, John," Tim said. "I'm terribly sorry."

THIS TIME, HE PAID extra and hired a personal veetol for the flight back to Hemhill from the shuttleport on the Thames. It was a cloudy day, but for a while the craft stayed low, and he could make out the glassy walls and pipelines that kept the more precious architectural relics safe from the tides. But the Tower of London, he saw, was now a crumbling island. The riverside gardens were flooded. The great dome of Wren's Abbey was moated by greenish scum. Looking down at a stretch of jagged ruins in the moment before the net routed him higher and the clouds closed in, he was reminded of the Endless City.

The stubby-winged machine rose into sunlight. He was alone with blue skies and the passing leviathan of a freighter before the veetol dived back down and the clouds parted for him over the valley of Hemhill. From the Magulf to Bab Mensor, from the rim of space to London, from blue skies to here, all in a few hours. He saw the neat line of High Street, the toy squares and the toy people, the spreading ordered grid of houses, and the wide acres of the processing compound and the fields beyond, mostly fallow at this late season: blank, resting, unwritten. And there, whorled and ravaged as if by subterranean heat, was the carnival field. The screen made no objection when he steered the veetol towards it. It was common land, a throwback to the time when his ancestors grazed their cattle there and feared the uncertain sky.

The veetol settled. John stepped out and felt the unfamiliar give of soil beneath his feet. As the craft rose again, he stood and watched, shading his face from the hot oily wind when the veetol pitched sideways, skimming the rim of the trees, then climbed almost vertically. He saw it swoop, spin, flip over, and disappear into the clouds—free to do as it liked now that it no longer held vulnerable human cargo.

John walked across the field, at first making for the gap in the fence through which he used to climb. But his bag was heavy, and he was conscious of the freshly knitted wheal that ran like a double tramline parallel to the scar of his recombinant, then veered left across his shoulderblade towards the new powerpack in his armpit. The gap in the fence would have been fixed long ago anyway.

The gate swung open at his approach, and he walked the smooth gray road past the last of the fields and into the first of the houses. He felt hot and breathless even in this fresh autumnal air, but still he was glad that he'd arranged to walk the last mile of his return. This gave him a final moment to believe what lay ahead.

The trees were shedding. Dry leaves tumbled in flocks along the gutters. The shops and the houses looked the same. Everything came back to him—like going through old photographs

—people and places fitting in with memories he didn't even know he had. He was conscious that he was being stared at, and was sure that an old man—familiar but unplaceable, with a face that had once been young—crossed to the other side of the road when he saw him.

John turned away from the shops and went past the gateway to the park with the public toilets by it. He heard the familiar stutter of his breath as he went along the railings, and, looking through, he saw the spinning machines and the brown-limbed figures still playing on the tennis courts in the specially warmed air. The season for competitions was over, but you had to keep your hand in if you ever wanted to win anything. Tennis was a game where the body and instinct counted for more than the mind, and in the middle of all that sweaty effort was this magical area that Hal once described—walking back along this same street, exuding new sweat and joy at a local quarter-final victory. For most of that last set, Skiddle, he'd said, I wasn't actually there. I was just reactions and muscles. This, John knew, was what all the serious players strove to achieve. The place that was known, oddly enough, as the zone, where everything clicked and body and mind and emotion became one. The place that had to be endlessly worked towards, that could never be taken for granted even by players at the highest level, that was always beckoning at the start of every match, waiting out there somewhere to be attained. There...

The house seemed the same, even to the cat-and-mint smell of the biannually flowering bush by the front doorstep and to the waft of air as the door opened for him. His father was sitting in the lounge, poised, it seemed, from the rigid set of his body, between finishing one thing and starting another. But the room was clear and overtidy. And there was no music.

They said each other's names. The chair helped his father up, and the two men regarded each other for a moment. Then there was a rough, ill-arranged embrace, and they sat down facing each other.

John felt weak, dried out, dry-eyed.

"Dad, I missed the funeral," he said. "I wish I'd—"

"It couldn't be helped, Son. Your being ill. When I heard, I..." His father shook his head at the thought of some impossible eventuality, and the wattles beneath his cheeks creased and uncreased. "But you look okay."

"There was never any real danger. I just wish I'd been here with you, Dad."

"To be honest, Son, this place has been like a hotel, and I was glad to send them all away this morning when I knew you were coming. Glad to be alone. And when it happened, I didn't know how I was going to tell you. It's something you worry about when it happens. Who to call, what to do, whether there's enough food in the kitchen. It's never anything big..."

The room became quiet and still. John blinked as it seemed to fill with a gas, with the clouds that he'd ascended through and looked down on. He realized that he was listening for the sound of his mother's voice, for the clatter in the kitchen as she and the cleaner competed to get things done, for those singsong, semi-internal conversations where questions unraveled into answers that became questions again. He took a breath and looked down at the scarred palms of his hands. His father sat rigid. The smell of his tubes, John realized, was also missing.

"I kept thinking," John said, "when I was stuck in the Zone, about how you'd be managing with Hal."

"*That's* been no problem." His father looked affronted. "I

can manage with Hal. After all, there's very little to it, and anyway I could have got in a doctor. Remember that machine we took with us once to Ley?" He smiled as if at some fond memory—and John supposed that in a sense it was.

"I'm sorry, Dad. I guess I'm just feeling guilty for not being here."

"And you'll be wanting to see him now?"

See him? John nodded, feeling as though he was drifting again, breaking through an endless series of paper-thin walls.

He stood up.

"But he hasn't changed," his father called through the doorway as John began to climb the stairs. "Everything's the same."

Later, the two men ate dinner together in the brightly lit kitchen. John picked at the geometrically presented food, wondering if he should add salt to make it come alive, wondering exactly what flavor it was he was missing. He could see his own pale face and his father's hunched, birdlike shoulders reflected in the blackened window.

"I don't," he said, "have any immediate commitments."

"No, Son. I'm glad."

"I'm not even sure if I . . ."

His father looked up at him, the tip of his fork trembling in his hand. There were many decisions for them to make about life, about the future, about Hal. But the silver of his father's eyes seemed detached now, like separate lenses, nothing to do with the bloodshot and whitish-brown orbs that surrounded them. He said, "You do what you want to do, Son."

"I thought I'd stay here with you for a while. The bishop's given me permission to . . . take a break."

"It'll be good to have you around. As long as you know that you don't have to. That I can manage."

After the cleaner removed and destroyed the uneaten remains of their meal, they sat and drank whisky between the silent loudspeakers in the lounge. His father went up to see Hal once, when a screen bleeped, and came down again within a few minutes. His mother, John remembered, had never gone up there for less than an hour.

"I don't know how much you've heard," his father said, sitting and studying the planes of his glass and the golden fluid that glittered in his eyes. "People expected me to be shocked—but of course I knew. Sarah and I used to talk about it, when we could still make a joke of it, when we were young. How she was older, how she'd be the first to go. And I knew that she'd always hated Southlands. We used to talk about that, too. Until . . ." He shook his head. "But she'd seen too much of it with Hal. She'd had her fill. So when that new implant they fitted above her watch started acting up, I knew it was a sign. A bad sign. I didn't *think* it, Son," he said, gazing levelly at John, "I knew it. So when it happened, it was like feeling something snap that was already pretty much broken. It was no surprise."

"She didn't say anything?"

"It was me really, Son. It was what I said. We were sitting at the breakfast table eating—I don't know why, but she always gave me cold cereal after we retired, even though I like something cooked—and I saw this red spot on her wrist, and I pointed and said, That'll be Hal. And she looked down at it and tutted, and I saw that it was actually a spot of blood soaking up through the sleeve of her cardigan. She said something—I think it was just, Oh dear—and put her hand on my shoulder and squeezed as she went out to the stairs, which wasn't like her, not at breakfast anyway. I just sat there and waited. Stared at the table and my bowl of flakes. And everything went quiet and I could hear this humming and then I remembered that yesterday had been the day of the carnival. Not that we'd gone, but you could see the litter blowing over the park, and that big Ferris wheel had been up in the afternoon sky while I was listening to *Turandot*. It made me think that, well, this is really a kind of anniversary. Not the precise date that Hal's accident happened—that was the week before—but still, with the carnival, a kind of anniversary. And that humming from the compound where the Gogs work seemed to get louder and part of me started thinking, This is it, the end, while the rest of me was saying, Oh, this is silly, Sarah's dabbing the wound and changing her cardigan, or she probably went to see Hal. That would explain it—you know how long she spends in there. But after a while, when she still didn't come down, I started to cry. It's the first time I cried in years, apart from when I'm listening to music. And that doesn't really count, does it?"

"I don't know, Dad." John closed his eyes and opened them again, trying to block the image of his mother lying on the bed with the implant trailing from her wrist and blood on the bedsheets, blood in wild sweeps and scrawls across the walls. But his mother was a neat and orderly woman. It wouldn't have been like that. "You don't think it was some change in Hal that finally made it happen?"

"What happened, Son, was that nothing changed. Nothing ever changed. That was what happened."

A little later, John and his father both went to bed. John lay all night, his head fizzy with the whisky. Staring at the closed door that led to the landing. Listening to the sound of humming.

The rooks were circling the hill, and the long churchyard grass had turned a greenish gray that swept down into the valley below, softening to ember blacks and reddish browns in the wooded hills.

"I always thought this would be her last place," his father said, holding the brass-plated box in his hands. "She never said, of course. But we used to come up here, long ago, in the summer dusk."

John nodded. He knew that his father was telling him that this was where he wanted his own dust to be cast when the time came.

"They ask you about the extra stuff," his father said. "All the bumps and the wires. They don't burn in the furnace like we do, but there's another machine afterward, and they'll grind them up and give them back to you in much the same kind of powder. But you know that, Son, don't you? I said no anyway, keep them, you can reuse the metal—it's made in space, isn't it? Expensive." He nodded at the box, then looked at John. "And the Gog—the Borderers. What do they...?"

"It isn't that much different, Dad."

"Couldn't be really, could it?" His father looked around at the huddle of gravestones: cracked and weathered, nameless. "Not like this lot. No room left under there now—they've crowded us out. But it's a nice thought. To think that so many are waiting for us."

From the valley a wind was pouring across the brown rooftops of Hemhill, the tall trees in the park, the scarred field of the carnival. John watched as his father, ever practical, licked his finger and held it up to determine the direction.

"I'm glad it's just us here, Son," he said, taking a few steps down the slope towards the ha-ha. "We don't need Father Leon, that priest. I mean, I know you're a priest too. But you're my son. All the rest—it's just badges we put on, isn't it? Things we try to do."

They stood together, each holding the open box with one hand where the soft lip of the land fell away. In the moment that the ash fell, the air seemed to rise and take it all from them, lifting it across the valley, bearing it high into the gauzy light, carrying it on some stray thermal. A little more grit in the wind.

Later that afternoon, John got around to emptying the bag he brought with him from the Endless City. Bella had cleaned everything in it before he left, but the bag still smelled of dust, smoke, and dysol, and his clothes felt pleasantly damp when he held them to his skin. At the bottom were scattered the few ancient music disks he'd noticed in the souks and bought occasionally for his father. Leaning over the bed to pick them out from the koiyl that was there also, feeling the scar along his back tighten, he wondered what he had planned to bring back home for his mother. He took the leaves out individually, turning them over, running a finger along the indented stems. In all, he'd brought a dozen home with him, and every one of them was from Lall. But when he scratched their oily surfaces and held them close to his face, the scent was surprisingly weak, drowned out, really, by this Hemhill room. They just looked like shriveled leaves. The physical longing he once felt for them was gone too. There, he thought, another lesson: they're not truly addictive—unless Tim and his doctor switched off the relevant synapses when they opened me in the Zone. And here, last of all, tucked beneath a sealed flap, was the tiny vial of the leaf-based poison that Kassi Moss had given him. He lifted it to the light and turned it over, gazing at the sticky fluid, wondering if he was ready to open it yet.

Next morning, he borrowed his father's car. It took him to Southlands along a well-remembered route. He stepped out in front of the big facade where the wind rattled the trees across the lawns, pulling at the clouds, a reminder that he would have to buy warmer clothes if he stayed here for the winter. Up the steps and inside the echoing entrance hall, he sent a machine off to find Eliot Farrar and stood and waited.

Farrar arrived soon enough. John had made an appointment, after all. They shook hands and went to Farrar's office, going by corridors and across a courtyard that avoided the wards and recreation rooms, the whispering voices, the sad clutching hands. Farrar probably felt he'd made the point he'd wanted to make to John, last time.

When the office door closed, John took a seat in the leather-backed chair facing Farrar's desk. "Well, here I am," he said.

"This has all been very sad," Farrar began. "I had a strong affection, a great respect..."

As Farrar spoke, John's eyes were drawn to the pale dots that drifted on the screen behind him. All this talk of sadness, regret: as if things could be different. But he knew from experience the replies you were supposed to give, the slow dance you had to do in times of bereavement. He waited. In due course, Farrar would steer things back to the specifics of the situation. How his father was coping—and Hal. But John wasn't ready to talk about Hal yet.

John took a card from his top pocket and placed it on the desk in front of Farrar. He hadn't brought any of the koiyl leaves with him today, but the card contained all the necessary information. It would be a start, a way forward. That, at least, was what he was allowing himself to hope. Farrar's eyebrows went up, and his silver eyes turned blanker than ever when he took the card in his hands. Tapping it with his well-manicured fingers, he promised with a trace of weariness that yes, of course, he would take a look at the possibilities.

He spent the days mostly walking, dutifully exercising as Tim Purdoe had said he should, climbing the hills and looking out over the familiar countryside. He walked the high-hedged lanes that briefly dripped with birdsong and wild fruits before the flashing galleons once more threaded the skies, spiraling a pale wake that frosted the rucked earth to iron. And in the days after, when the weather grew warm again and a pale sun shone over the bare trees, the big machines moved into the fields, automated hippos that wallowed in mud and churned and ex- posed the soil. The air stank of clay, and the roads were lumped with the clods. The mist that filled the hollows was torn away when the wind came up with the stars. He stood gazing through the shockwire where the lights of the compound shone and the Borderers shouted in strange accents and scurried, working their last few days to make targets and meet deadlines. He walked into the village past the railings where the white figures on the tennis courts were still playing. Even as the door of the house closed and he went up the stairs, he could hear the pock of balls and the faint humming.

He often sat at Hal's bedside in the evenings, the way Hal had once sat at his. John sat in silence, unwilling to break the antiseptic air with the sound of his voice. What, anyway, could he say? Mother's dead, Hal. Ma. Mum. *Madre.* And I found that port in Kushiel you accessed. And I killed a goat. And the sky is *blue.*

Late autumn hardened to winter. The freshly turned fields grew livid green with late high-nitrogen clover and gave off a strange acid tang. Then something seemed to lift from the air one morning, and as he walked by the shockwire of the compound, he saw empty spaces and that the warehouse doors were closed. Though he hadn't heard them going, the Borderers had left. He turned and walked back through the streets and up a hardened track at the far side of the valley, through a swing gate leading into the forest. The cold air was still filled with the sharp oily smell of chloroethane sap, but the tree-tappers had settled in the branches, curled until spring into hard silver lumps like ice. Sitting on a fallen log on a hilltop to catch his breath, he could see the green ruins of the city that had been Hereford jutting from the trees below.

The streets, when he walked down into them, were pitted, caved in, distorted by rearing sewerpipes or blocked by the rusty deadfalls of what was once traffic. He remembered someone saying you could still find corpses in some of the roofless houses. Yet he felt at home in the wrecked, ivied buildings, in the snap of his footsteps in the tumbling empty squares around the fallen cathedral, in the brown and furtive animals that lived and died here—excluded from Hemhill's fertile valley by bitter saps, predatory insects, and shockwire. Although he looked, he

couldn't find the pub with the sign THE ORANGE TREE sticking
out into the street, where an atrocity was once committed by
Hemhill lads on a Borderer girl.

There were cars parked outside the house when he returned
from the woodland that evening, and people filled the hallway
and the lounge, taking drinks from the hired machines and the
cleaner, propping themselves against the table in the kitchen.
Music was playing for the first time since he'd come home,
although it wasn't the sort his father would have chosen. It
had a beat, da-de-da de-de-de dum-dum. Felipe would have
loved it.

John, the people said, *Father* John, you must meet... Laying hands on his shoulder, steering him this way and that. His
father, now red-faced, seemed genuinely cheerful amid these
neighbors, relatives, and cronies. This, he said, seeing John
standing alone in a corner in the moment before someone else
came over to ask him about the Gogs, is the life. John smiled.
He'd noticed how rarely anyone went upstairs, except quickly
and furtively when the downstairs toilet was occupied, with
glances along the darkened landing. Later, as he stood wedged
in a corner while one of the junior Youngsons told him about
his plans to marry a girl he'd met on a training course in Car-
dington, Bedfordshire, John found himself thinking of Hal lying upstairs with the sound of the party and the smell of
European bodies and buffet food seeping through the molecular
barrier. He understood now why his mother had put that extra
monitor into her wrist. Perhaps he should have the same thing
done himself.

It was snowing when the people finally left—the first proper
flakes of the year—and they all looked up with their hands held
out to the darkly spiraling sky. The snow continued all night,

and in the morning the whole world was transformed. Even the tennis courts beyond the white-shouldered trees and the railings in the park were finally empty.

John went down to the lounge through the mess that the cleaner had vainly attempted to clear. He powered a chair over to the house's main screen and called up Tim Purdoe in the Zone. He saw from the image that Tim's bungalow was much like Laurie's, although he'd never visited it, and he realized from the crumpled look of Tim's face that Tim had probably been asleep. Here or there it was still early, but John was touched to think that Tim had arranged for his answerer to awaken him if John happened to call.

They talked for a while about John's health, then about news from the Zone, although half the names Tim mentioned were unfamiliar.

"How's Felipe?"

"Oh, he's fine. He came to a big performance of Mozart's *Requiem* that Father Orteau put on at All Saints—snored and farted all the way through."

John smiled. "And the new priest?"

"I don't see as much of him as I did of you. But he's doing okay."

"I used to think it was terrible—the way posts change hands without people having a chance to meet."

Tim nodded.

"I was determined that I'd get in touch with whoever replaced me at the presbytery. Maybe even go back for a few days, or at least speak to the person on a decent-sized screen. But I think I understand now why the Church does things this way. All I could give would be preconceptions."

Tim nodded again and smiled.

"And there's no point in bothering Felipe, dragging him all the way down the corridor to the airwave on those legs. And I never did know what to say to Bella."

"No."

"Anyway, I . . ."

"Yes."

"I was wondering if you'd heard anything about Laurie."

Tim shook his head. "Nothing's changed, John. She's disappeared, left the Zone—quit her job without what I believe they used to call a forwarding address. Still, I did check as you asked me to, and she's not with her mother in Mokifa either. I spoke to her mother."

"You went there?"

"It's along Gran Vía, John. I *do* know the way. Mrs. Kalmar politely told me that it was none of my business. Of course, I tried mentioning you, but that didn't help much. She said Laurie would get in touch if and when she wanted to. I'm sorry, John— but it's not like Europe. In the Magulf, you can't just call people up on a screen." Tim stifled a yawn. "Apart from me, that is."

John nodded. Laurie. The Magulf. Mokifa. Gran Vía. He heard the cleaner knock something over in the kitchen. Outside, a white labyrinth of snow was falling. "Anyway," he said, drawing a breath, "about the leaf—"

Tim waved a hand. "Christ, John, I'm sorry. I'll chase it up for you. I'll have a word with Cal."

"Don't worry, Tim. Something may be happening here."

"Look, if you want—"

"No, really. It's okay. I mean it."

"John, is that snow outside? *White* snow?"

"It's white."

Tim shook his head. "It really is another world."

They smiled at each other for a moment. But there was nothing left to say now, except *gonenanh*, goodbye.

Paging back out of the Zone from Tim, John saw that a message flag was flashing for him. His heart began to pound, but then he realized it was from Eliot Farrar's answerer at Southlands. The answerer said that Farrar had copied the card John gave him about what Farrar called "the foreign analgesic"; he'd sent it down the net to a big Halcycon-funded project in London, and that they were as excited as he was by it. It was clearly vital for them to meet and discuss tactics at the earliest possible date—so could they link datebooks and suggest a time? John got up and went over to the window. Gazing out at the falling white, his shoulders began to shake. He realized after a while that he was laughing.

White streets in moonlight, the snow piled into mountain ridges by the machines that had been brought down specially from Carlisle. Even then, the car moved with a skidding sigh. It snowed every night, although Halcycon kept making assurances that it wouldn't. Even the children had grown tired of snowball fights and toboggan sliding. But to John, still an onlooker in Hemhill's affairs, everything felt as it should. It was the last night of the year, still the Christmas season: it was right that there should be snow.

Colored lights glittered in the windows and dimly through the white-furred trees. John heard a familiar rustle and snap and saw in the dashboard's glow that his father was breaking open and inhaling a tube. John smiled as he breathed the scent and the headlights plowed on out of the village past the fields and through the whiteness.

Radway Farm shone like a lantern with its huge lighted doorways. Tonight it was filled with parked cars, the steam of baked potatoes, hot punch, the thump of music. The tall tree in the main barn glittered with phosphorescent tinsel and a million tiny ornaments. John left his father with friends and pushed his way through the crowd to cup one of the globes in his hand where it drooped glowing from the boughs in a haze of green scent. There, inside the intricate hand-made glass, Mary sat nodding and murmuring to the baby in her arms, surrounded by kingly men and plump unengineered cattle. They all had wise and slightly quizzical expressions, no particular shade to their eyes. In one corner, if you held the globe just right, you could read the words MADE IN THE MAGULF.

When he looked up, Annie was standing beside him.

"I should have come over to Hemhill," she said, "when I heard what happened. But you know how it is." She gestured, slopping her punch. The lights of the tree glittered, and John felt the falling needles tickle his back and hands. "The kids, the farm, Bill ... How's your Dad managing? I remember how mine was—picking around all day at the traces. Taking stuff out from the chests and shelves and cupboards, then putting it all back again."

"There really aren't that many traces of Mum, Annie. She was like me, neat and tidy most of the time."

Annie nodded. She was wearing a long green dress, low cut at the shoulders, showing the divide of her breasts.

"Anyway," he said. "Here I am."

"Here you are." She smiled, already a little drunk, and looking, it seemed to him, quite marvelously pretty. "So. It's the New Year." She drew him away as a shouting group closed in on them. "What are your plans now?"

He shrugged.

"Someone said you were going to quit being a priest."

"I've thought of it. But I need to find something else to do with my life."

"Don't look so glum." She nudged his side. "It's still a big world, it's just Hemhill that makes it..." She chuckled and sipped her drink. "But why am I telling you this? You're the wanderer, John, the pilgrim. Not me."

"All you change when you go to another place is the sky."

"Who said that?"

"I think it was the old priest I shared the presbytery with in the Endless City. Anyway, I've had some discussions with Eliot Farrar at Southlands recently."

She nodded, drawing her top teeth over her bottom lip.

"He...seems genuinely interested in a project that I started in the Endless City. There's a leaf, a drug, that could help people here. The ill, the old—it would allow them to exercise a kind of control over their minds. A way of getting rid of anxiety and suffering without the need for painkillers."

"We could all do with some of that."

They looked at each other. It was getting close to midnight, and the band on the stage beyond the buffet had struck up. The roof, he now saw, had dissolved into stars, story-bright stars overlaid on a sky of black velvet. And it was hot in here.

"Come on," she shouted. "I need to see how Harry's doing."

"Harry?"

"My baby, John. Remember? You saw him in the summer."

Outside, through the big doors and the barrier that kept in most of the heat, a tracked machine was scouring safe pathways across the ice, marking them with a fluorescent dye.

"It didn't seem fair to ask anyone to sit with him tonight," Annie said. "But I really don't like leaving him with a machine."

"Aren't you cold?"

She had her hands clasped tight around her bare arms, and her breath came in clouds, but she shook her head. The farmhouse lay between the powerlines and brightly lit buildings. Inside, it was all still so antique. She had to finger a switch to turn on a light. And there were frost flowers on the windows.

"Don't you worry," he asked, "about this hard winter?"

"It's the same for everyone."

"I thought you farmers were always complaining."

She shrugged, her silver eyes shining. A cat shot by. "What is there to complain about?"

He watched the sway of her body as she climbed the creaking stairs ahead of him, and the freckles that dotted her shoulders, the pale scar on her back, the gray in her hair.

In the nursery, the dancing-elephant wallpaper was peeling, and there were familiar odors of dust and mildew. The baby was asleep. It, too, had a familiar smell. Of soap, a whiff of shit, and, even now that its first implants had stabilized, of a different kind of humanity. Of Borderer. The padded machine that squatted by the cot blinked its cartoon face and looked up at them.

"He's grown so quickly," John said.

Annie chuckled and brushed at a wisp of the baby's golden hair. "They do." Laid out on the coverlet, the screen of a tiny watch now shimmered on the plump curve of the baby's wrist.

"What made you call him Harry?"

She raised her shoulders. "I didn't even think. Of course, Bill wouldn't have made the connection—and for a long time, even after Harry was born, it didn't occur to me either. I mean, no one ever called Hal Harry, did they? He was always just Hal."

"No."

"And I'll always call my Harry Harry."

He nodded, gazing at Annie. "You know, I—"

"But it seems right, now, doesn't it, John? Calling him Harry. We're older, and we've changed. And it was all such a long time ago."

They walked back down the stairs and across the hallway, where a grandfather clock began to chime just as Annie turned the handle and began work the front door open. Bong.

"There..." She stopped, leaning against the frame, tilting her head, goose bumps on her arms. "Listen."

Bong...

The clock whirred and clunked through the year's last moments. And outside in the darkness and over the rooftops, John could hear cheers and shouts, the ironic drum-thump of the band.

"We've missed it," Annie said. "But no one ever takes these things seriously, do they? Happy new year, John."

"Happy new year."

Half in and half out of the cold, Annie pressed herself against him, and they kissed.

He sat in a London restaurant with Eliot Farrar. They'd taken a seat by the window, and the world outside was crystalline, the passersby hunched and encased in plumes of breath even though it was early afternoon. A long black car slid by, a new model that John didn't know. Something in its engine was squealing.

"Well." Farrar raised a glass. "Looks like we have a success."

John clinked his glass against Farrar's rim. He was getting used to the feel of these places, to the softness of the carpet, the rippling pools of conversation, the eager and accommodating chairs, the glinting warmth—and to the meetings: Cal Edmead, Bevis Headley, the Zone's steering committees hadn't even been close to what went on here.

"Of course," Farrar said with a grin, "it's all come quicker than I expected. To get something through channels this fast is quite a miracle. I needed the help of a man of God."

"Will they use Southlands for the tests?"

Farrar shook his head. "At least, not at first. They'll do a triple-blind. People like me won't have any idea what's happening until the results come out."

"Do you think they'll actually use the leaf? Allow people to chew it?"

Farrar smiled. "It's a nice thought. But no, I don't think so."

The waiter came up with a pen and pad. He had a small dimplelike scar on his jaw and black eyebrows that met above his brown eyes. John said *gunafana* to him when they ordered, but the waiter didn't blink, didn't even glance up from his pad.

"I guess you're tired of it," Farrar said later, when they walked out into the street.

"Of what?"

"People asking you what you're going to do." Farrar puffed out his cheeks, wrapped his scarf around his neck, and pulled on his gloves. John, bare-handed, shoved his arms deep into the pockets of the big old coat that his father had insisted on lending him. They walked on for a while, vaguely in the direction of the rental site and the veetol that would take them back to Hemhill. Neither man was in a hurry.

"Oddly enough," John said, "people don't ask. Not in a way that expects an answer."

"I suppose you've leaned farther over the edge than most of us have. Even me, doing what I do at Southlands... You know, I had this image of you, John." He chuckled, looked down a long street at the white, yellow-lit buildings and the frozen river. "But my problem is that when I get to know people, I start to realize that I should never give them advice."

"So you don't think I should let Hal go now?"

Farrar sighed, his feet crunching the frosted ground. A muttering male figure ran out towards them across the street, waving his hands. It seemed for a moment that he was going to ask for money.

"John," Farrar said, "I really don't think it matters now."

John's father was sitting in the lounge when John got home that night. Smoking tubes and listening to the slow movement of Mahler's Fifth, his father was resting a hand on the warm top plate of the cleaner squatted beside him. There was a trace of what might have been tears on his cheeks.

"How did it go?" he asked, lowering the music.

"Pretty well," John said, struggling with the coat's torn inner sleeves and the ragged sense of domesticity that surrounded him. His dinner, he knew, would be dried up on the server in the kitchen; a mute rebuke for his returning a little later than he'd said. And later it would be his turn to see to Hal before he went to bed and dropped into the black pit of sleep that always seemed to be waiting.

"Did you know," his father said, "that Mahler was forever trying to recreate a moment that happened when he was a child?

434

His mother was near death from this terrible fever, and outside through the open window in the street he could hear a hurdy-gurdy playing this jolly song..."

"Do you still input that stuff into Hal's monitor?"

"Stuff?"

"The music."

"No." His father shook his head. "Not since I started listening again. It seemed wrong...To keep pushing."

John reached down and took his father's hand. It was an odd feeling; the pale scars on his palms—he'd insisted they be left as they were—gave only an intermittent sense of touch. But although his father and he had never really become close after sharing the house for all these months, they kept their hands pressed together, John at his father's side and the music in the background still whispering about tragedy and loss. At some point, they both started to cry, quietly. It was suddenly clear to both of them that Hal had died long ago.

John called Eliot Farrar at Southlands the next morning through the net. The answerer paged Farrar, and Farrar said he'd come to the house straightaway, but John told him there was no hurry. This evening would be soon enough. He and his father sat together afterward in the kitchen, eating the large breakfast for which, after their decision, they both felt suddenly and shamefully hungry. When the cleaner removed the plates, they went upstairs. Hal's door opened for them, and the molecular barrier that John had ceased to notice suddenly seemed strong again. A last wall. Stepping in, he checked, as always, the monitors that would have called for aid anyway if there had been the slightest disturbance to the smooth flow of his brother's vital signs.

Now, he thought—couldn't help thinking—now is your last chance. Sit up and say *Hey, Skiddle, what's been happening?* But Hal's face was placid and his flesh was smooth and clear. His hair was a little more ragged now that his mother wasn't there to see to it, and more of the gray had frosted the temples. John heard a rasp behind him, and looked around to see his father stooped in his awkward old man's gait, pulling a drawer and tipping out the contents across the clinically dust-free floor.

Although they hadn't intended to do so, they spent most of the day going through Hal's things. Part of it felt wrong—almost like the wild-eyed relatives whom John had seen descending on houses in Yorkshire even before the final decision for death was made—but they were soon caught in the past, and moved with slow and half-conscious absorption even as Hal's body lay with them. John unfolded boxes and had the cleaner take down to the garage all the things they were sure they didn't want. The ridiculously unfashionable clothing. Little screens that had leaked gummy pools. And the boots, the running shoes, the tennis shoes, the trainers. Those empty receptacles that smelled of nothing but old leather.

"Isn't there somewhere we can send all this?" his father asked. "Some charity for the Borderers?"

"Dad, you called them Borderers."

His father blinked at him, a broken dodger ball tinkling in his hands. "What do you mean? What else should I call them?"

"No, I don't think there is a place where we could send all this. We just have to get rid of it."

Occasionally a car or van went past, wheels and fans sighing and crackling over the snow. And Hal lay there breathing in his bed as they moved quietly through his possessions. Even now they were expecting, John supposed, some final shock, some great revelation. But there was nothing. Just memories. And the memories seemed less than real. Only once, when his father opened a tall narrow cupboard by the window, was there any sense of surprise when a tide of cups, plaques, and rosettes clattered across the floor.

"I thought we had them all out," his father muttered, regarding the display of trophies that filled the shelves beside the door. John picked up a shallow brass bowl from the floor. One of the ribbons, faded with age, broke off when he touched it. He read the engraving.

RUNNER-UP

BECKFORD CHAMPION'S CUP

2152

Then a plaque.

HARRY ALSTON

JUDGES' COMMENDATION

SUMMER 2149

After looking at a few more, he understood why these had been hidden. None were first prizes.

"Aren't you supposed to hand them back after you've kept them for a year?" his father asked, holding up a big-handled loving cup of tarnished pewter.

"I doubt if anyone wanted to come and ask, Dad."

They packed the trophies away. For a while, with the dust billowing too quickly for the filters to handle it and with Hal's things spread across the floor, the room looked almost as it had when he was alive. There was no sign, of course, of the equipment that he'd used to destroy himself—that had been taken away by the people from Halcycon S.A. in Leominster. But the suitcases he'd never got around to packing, they were still pushed above the wardrobe. His father couldn't reach. John took them down and left them open and empty on the floor until he turned and saw them lying there, and the mess of life that was all around them, and felt his spine ache and his heart grow weary. *I've been going through my things, Skiddle. Clearing out... That was how it started anyway.* John closed the cases and looked around. But there was nothing, just the click and sigh, his father's unhurried movements, the lime trees guarding the tennis courts, and the grainy whiteness of the world.

They were listening to music in the lounge when Eliot Farrar finally came. John supposed that these last hours should have been a time of prayer, but the music—a solo piano, pleasant, though he couldn't place it—and their exhaustion from the work of clearing had taken over, filling them both with an almost comfortable melancholy. It felt for a while as if they'd done the right thing with the day. John heard the sounds in the driveway and opened the door and saw the vans, cars, machines, and assistants, the lights blazing and circling. He realized that he'd forgotten just how much effort was needed. Father Leon Hardimann was there, he saw. The presence of a priest was desirable on such occasions—and after all that had happened, John could hardly perform that role today.

They filed in, businesslike. Even the people that he knew were strangers. He should have spent more time alone with Hal, shared a last and final word. He wanted to grab an arm or shoulder as they went past and say, Look, I know I called, but I didn't mean *now.* This is a little early. Can't you wait?

They'd already turned up the heat and the light in Hal's room when John got there, and they'd brought the powdery smell of snow and European sweat in with them. It was tidy here again, with a just a few extra boxes piled beneath Hal's desk in the corner. A new machine, bigger and mobile, squatted beside Hal's monitors now. John saw that Farrar had added some extra wires to the ones that ran into Hal's nose. It was all swiftly and discreetly done. The procedure was familiar to everyone, though it was not something you ever got quite used to. John and his father touched the icons in the screen they were given, to signify their consent, which was witnessed in turn by Eliot Farrar and Father Leon, and then by the net. John watched as the priest unscrewed the little vial and with his hands dripped holy water on Hal's chest and brow.

> *In the name of God the almighty Father who created you,*
> *In the name of Jesus Christ, Son of the living God, who*
> *suffered for you,*
> *In the name of the Holy Spirit, who was poured out upon*
> *you,*
> *Go forth, faithful Christian.*

Outside the window, pushed by a sudden wind, flakes of snow began to tunnel and fall. Then the final moment came. John took hold of Hal's left hand and his father took hold of the right, and Farrar did something with the screen. The breather went click, sigh, click, sigh, *click,* and white silence flowed through the room. John waited for the sound to come again, for something to break, for something to happen. Then, as he looked down at Hal's face, there was a slight but definite ripple of movement. The eyes and mouth tensed and, for the first time in years, John felt his brother's hand briefly tighten in his own.

W OULDN'T IT BE GOOD, *Skiddle, to be up there?*

There was a sunflash in the white sky as John walked out from the church, a hint of blue. At last the bushes were dripping and the ground was softening. Soon, no matter what the machines did, the whole of Hemhill would be a quagmire. But it was to be welcomed, even if this thaw was too frail and early to be called spring.

Annie had come to the funeral with her husband and baby Harry, who mewed and chuckled all the way through the service, trying to squirm from her arms. Coming out afterward into the churchyard, she took Harry over to John's father. The baby laughed at the old man's face and grabbed his knobbly, arthritic fingers. John smiled, watching them and the other people who milled by. Their silver eyes averted, they muttered thanks for the words he'd said at the service. His address had been short and unrehearsed. Even now he couldn't remember exactly what he'd said—just that Hal had been his brother, that he'd loved him, and that the time had come, not to give up but to let go.

Letting go...There was, it seemed to him now, as he looked up at the clearing, shifting air, a difference. And the moment of prayer he'd entered into as he sat at the back of the church; that had been unplanned too, unthinking. With his head bowed and the smell of the old beams and the flowers, with the waiting silence of the people in their best clothes and slush-sodden shoes surrounding him, he'd just prayed that there would be no more death for a while. And for once, now that he had almost given up hoping, the whiteness and the silence seemed to brighten, and a warmth gathered at his back. It might have been only his scar, but it felt like something more.

Letting go...

"I thought you'd like to see this," Eliot Farrar said, calling him at home on the net a few days later. "Come around to Southlands this afternoon and take a look. I have a bigger screen."

So John drove out in his father's car, seeing the patches of brownish green, which were starting to appear around the village and above the valley, reflected in the flooded fields with the pale blue sky. At Southlands, Farrar took him into an office that was like Laurie's in the Zone: one entire wall filled with screen.

"Any news," John asked, "about the—foreign analgesic?"

"Relax, sit down."

Farrar paged through the Halcyon logo. The room blackened, until suddenly they were looking down at the tumbling streets of the Endless City agleam with grayish snow, patched with fires, smudged with smoke. John searched for the broad stripe of Gran Vía, for Santa Cristina's stubby tower, and sniffed for the kelpbeds on the wind, but the view was already shifting as the veetol they were in rose and turned and the heat from the fanjets made everything shimmer. The rooftops shrank and blurred, turning to scatters and a few jagged stretches of brown, then to ice-dusted desert and the fuzzy lights of the phosphate mines.

The Northern Mountains began to loom, white and truly majestic at this time of year, and before the veetol entered the wide upward sweep of a valley, John glimpsed a walled settlement that could only be Tiir. The village of Lall soon lay below amid the snow, caught in a spiderweb of trails and footpaths. Figures came running out as the veetol turned in to land. When the engines stilled, the roar of the wind strengthened, and with it came a bitter chill, the tinkling of bells as sheep stirred in their winter pens, the barking of dogs, the smell of burning dung, and humanity.

Even through the net, and although the villagers were wrapped in furs against the cold, John recognized the faces of many. They were smiling at the veetol's arrival as they had smiled at him, speaking a softly accented *gunahana*. They watched as the machines the Europeans had brought with them scurried in and out of the drifts beyond the village, clearing ice and snow, erecting the domed and tunneled buildings where these gloved and hooded *Outers* would stay for the next few seasons. John listened to the explanations and negotiations that night in the main hut's dingy firelight, and struggled, even as these Halcyon specialists with their barking translats struggled, to make sense of what was said. But there was no hostility, and no real surprise—word must have gone ahead. These villagers knew the prospect of aid and money when they saw it.

So, John reflected, Laurie had been right: this had all ended with veetols landing in Lall, even if they'd come to study rather than destroy. But the hills would be penned with shockwire to keep out the wild animals and sheep, and little of the koiyl crop would find its way down to the markets for Kassi Moss or anyone else to buy. And the veetols would be back next year to put right the things that they were bound to get wrong in this initial study. Perhaps they might even have the sense to bring a human interpreter with them. The people of Lall would become used to the *cassan* and the screens and new jelt roofs and generators, and they would be envied and ostracized by the other growers and traders. Within a few years, there would be nothing left of Lall but the machine-guarded stump of some Halcyon project beside the abandoned village, a place to be stumbled on and puzzled over in the future, just as John had puzzled over Kushiel. But the Borderers who lived in the village would at least have time to make new lives, to change and re-adjust. Borderers always changed and readjusted.

Driving back through the darkness from Southlands to Hemhill, John wondered how much of this had been inevitable since that day he arrived at Lall with Laurie and Hettie. Was there any way he could have made contact with these people without destroying their lives? He hadn't thought that the Halcyon-financed study would settle on Lall as a base—Lall was, after all, inaccessible and radioactively polluted—but the specialists had been too wrapped up in clinical questions to consider whether there might not be a better site. John knew Lall would be changed and eventually destroyed when someone in a meeting joked about how convenient it was that the foreign analgesic came ready-tagged with an isotope for tracking its progress through the bodies of the experimental subjects.

When John got home, he found his father sitting in the lounge smoking a tube, smiling, and close to tears as he listened to one of his favorite slow movements. That was almost always the case now. Nor was it unusual for the old man to have a screen on his lap, but this evening he wasn't using it to change some aspect of the music. He seemed oddly relaxed, his shoulders less hunched. He seemed almost jolly.

"Will you look at this?" he said, holding up the screen and prodding it. John leaned over. He heard the screech of gulls, smelled salt, and saw sunlight and bobbing boats: the harbor-front dwellings of Ley. "You know that cottage with the yellow windows that we always walked past on our way to the harbor? There was a stepped alley ..."

John nodded, remembering the sway in his hands of the buckets and spades, the warm breeze sweeping up from the glittering bay. The sound of Hal's voice as they walked together. *Did you know, Skiddle? Just think* ... The sense of the whole day and nothing but sea and sunlight and laughter ahead.

"Well, it's come up for sale." John's father looked up at him, his face happy, uncertain, eager. "And I was thinking. I was thinking that ..."

AS THE WEATHER warmed, his father went to Ley one day to sort out the handover of the cottage with the yellow windows, and for the first time in his life John spent the night alone in Hemhill. The house seemed empty, each room solid like a cube of glass, though there were no barriers left in any of the doorways. He listened to his father's music, he stared at the polished wooden box engraved with Hal's name and the dates of Hal's life that lay on the mantelpiece, then at the blank and meaningless screens. He lay on his bed fully dressed and watched the occasional light flow across the ceiling when the valley grew silent. He got up and pulled his case down from the wardrobe, breathing in as he opened it, although no trace remained of the Magulf air. The lights of a car went by, catching the glint of the vial that Kassi Moss had given him. I'm still waiting, he thought, his fingers gripping the thin glass stem, for something to give, something to snap, something to break. Hal's dead, but I'm alive.

He went into his brother's room, wondering without looking down at the new screen of his watch what time of night it was—somewhere in the uncertain middle hours, when it was too late for sleep, too early to get up, the time when sperm met egg and life began and dreams were formed, when the sky was at its darkest, hope ended, and hearts stopped beating. Hal's room remained as they'd left it on the night when Eliot Farrar and Father Leon came to take his life. A temple, abandoned, smelling for the first time in years simply of empty air. The breathers and monitors were gone, leaving their indentations on the special floor, and the bed had been powered down. It looked just like a bed now. The sheets sagged and slumped when John touched them.

Neither he nor his father had thought to reprogram the cleaner to come and do its usual tasks in here. The bowls and trophies on the shelves by the door had become tarnished. He took down the biggest cup, pewter and long-handled. It rattled as he did so, and he unscrewed the lid. Inside, there was a smooth stone—no, a piece of glass. Red, sea-corroded driftglass. He wet it with saliva and held it up to his eye, seeing how his brother's room changed, how the shadows grayed and the ceiling softened and swelled. The night sky outside the window lightened to mottled red-pink, glowing, forever strange.

He put on his father's old coat and went out, gazing at the houses and through the railings of the park. Everything was newly revealed, yet everything was the same. He walked by the shockwire of the compound where the snow still lay in patches beyond. He went up High Street, where a machine whizzed by in a clicking of blue lights. He walked along the road to the field that had once contained the carnival. He looked up at the hills as dawn whiteness began to appear at the edge of the sky. Finally, on his way back into the village, he stooped by a gutter and took Kassi's vial from his pocket. He crushed it through the grating with the heel of his shoe. Then he walked home, and found his father arriving from Ley, still half asleep as he climbed from his car but excited with the prospect of change and carrying with him the scent, John was sure, of sea and sand and far away.

Father and son stood watching on the pavement as the house at Hemhill was finally cleared. Machines scuttled in and out, singly and in twos and threes, carrying things into the spring morning, chairs and tables and ornaments that waited on the pavement, looking naked and out of place before they were put into the vans. The cottage with the yellow windows at Ley was too small to take more than a little of this furniture. John's father had even come to accept that he'd have to change his loudspeakers for something smaller. But that was just another challenge.

A few days before, the Youngsons had switched on their pool. John could see the top of its steaming bubble over the edge of the fence. He'd watched earlier from a back window as a granddaughter, her hair slicked along the scar of her spine, splashed about in the shallow end. And the tennis players were back out practicing in the park, swiping at balls and bemoaning their lack of timing. *Pock. Fuckit.* Life went on.

"You know, Annie called when you were out one day," his father said. He was dressed in his best suit. His shoes shone. His hair was parted. "We sat and talked about some of the old times. She said I should get a dog for myself when I move to Ley."

"It's not such a bad idea, Dad."

"I don't fancy those collars, though. Snap your fingers, and the creature whines. She says they get used to it, but what kind of life is that?"

A chair went by, then a mirror, then a rolled carpet. John remembered how after Hal's accident he'd sometimes look out of his bedroom window as the local kids, in an elaborate mime, put their fingers to their lips as they tiptoed by on the street.

"I've got happy memories of here, Son. Me and your mother and Hal used to sit and play cards a lot when you were younger. The three of us eating crackers and drinking fizz after you went upstairs. I'd sometimes look in on you, sit by your bed. You liked to have the screen from whatever story you were watching left running. Have the bubble images float around you. You seemed to be able to tell if I turned it off, even when you were sleeping."

John nodded. They studied the cracked skirt at the rear of the big van they were standing by. In the gutter, bright as tinsel, a thin last thread of frost still lingered in its shadow. The machines were spinning a protective web of shockwire around the house, now that its shell was almost empty and the major work could begin. One of the bigger machines had already climbed up on the roof and was starting to pull away the jelt. The cable-entwined ribs of the joists emerged. Then they, too, disappeared.

As the task continued, John and his father went and had lunch in the village. They sat at the bar of the café that had once been Tilly's. By the time they got back, the vans were fully loaded and the site was empty. Even most of the garden had been stripped: his father had decided to take only the codes of a few of the most precious plants with him for the window-box he'd keep at Ley.

"You know it'll be different, don't you, Dad?" John said. "We only went to Ley for a few months in the summer."

"Different." His father nodded. "You *will* come and visit, won't you, Son? When you've seen the bishop, in a few days. I mean, that room at the back is small, but—"

"It's okay, Dad. It'll be good to see Ley again."

But they looked at each other, suddenly aware that this was more than the temporary parting they'd planned. John opened his mouth to say something, but at that moment one of the brown-eyed Borderer workers who'd supervised the removal came over and handed his father the house's last screen. There, glowing in the warm spring air, were all the rooms and all the history, all the changes and adjustments they'd made. His father moved his hand to erase the house forever, then paused and held it out towards John.

"I can't."

John took it without looking, feeling the quaternary pressure on his fingertips.

"And you'll know what to do about Hal, Son? Something that's right?"

John nodded.

"I'd better be going. It's a long way."

They embraced.

"Goodbye."

"Goodbye."

His father opened the doors of his car, half-lifted the cleaner into the front passenger seat, then got in himself. John heard the plangent trumpets of Mahler's Fifth fading as his father drove off. He stood watching the car until it vanished down the familiar street where the lime trees were starting to bud. Then he realized that he still held the house's last screen in his hand. As he raised it and prepared to bring an end, he saw that one final message had come through.

THE SHUTTLE WAS quite different from the ones he'd taken before in his life. The floor was tilted even before takeoff, and the seats were crammed close together, up against the thick and tiny portholes. The food, as he juggled elbows with the other passengers during the wait of some technical delay, was clearly expensive, as was the wine, and the screen in front of him offered to take him far away. He supposed it was all an effort to justify the cost of the tickets, although when the engines finally thundered and flames flickered at the edge of the porthole and his flesh seemed to slide from his bones, it was obvious where the money was actually going.

He'd dressed as a priest today, and as a result the other passengers seemed more inclined to talk to him when the bellow of the engines finally settled down, and to smile nervously and nod. Most were like him, on their first orbital flight.

The Earth still looked beautiful from high in the blackness: blue, brown, and green marbled with white—there was barely any red or gray—and surrounded by a loose necklace of satellites that turned and flashed in the light of a rising moon. There were glimpses in the distance of dark wings that trapped the sun, and of something else large and closer, distorted to a glowing oval at the edge of the porthole as the shuttle turned to dock with the barrel-bodied silver insect to which several other similar craft already clung.

The chair released John, and he drifted with the other passengers through the irised doorway into a concourse that, despite all he'd expected, had walls, a floor, a ceiling: an up and a down. He guessed it was for the benefit of novices like himself who feared that they would bob up like corks if they let go of the handholds or kicked wrongly with their adhesive shoes. It was easy enough, as long as he kept his eyes ahead of him and concentrated on moving his legs and arms and stilling the airy balloon that floated in his belly. Then he was occupied in a dispute with a Halcycon-logoed screen about the small cargo he'd brought with him. Yes, the screen said, not deigning, here, to give itself a human face, yes, it had dealt with such requests before. But it was customary to apply some time in advance. You must understand, Father John, it added, that more is involved than simply opening an airlock and pushing out your brother's remains. Special canisters are required. Machine, human, and online time must be set aside. John nodded, waited. Arguing with a screen wasn't like arguing with a human. If it was going to say no, it would have said no already. Yet it was with a sense of vague anger, diffuse regret, that he lowered the weightless wooden box into the drawer that finally presented itself. Once more, his last moments with Hal had been snatched away.

He drifted along the handrails into a moving tunnel and through the surprisingly strong wall of a molecular barrier. I'm here, he thought, and yet, even when he saw her waiting, her dark midlength hair fanning out around her like seaweed in clear water, he still didn't believe. But there she was. Her green eyes. Smiling. He drifted to her. His heart, he realized, was hammering. His throat ached.

Laurie said, "I wasn't sure you'd come."

He lifted his shoulders in a shrug and felt his whole body start to sink with the motion. "I had another thing to do here."

She placed a hand on his arm. "Hal's dead, isn't he? And your mother? I heard, John. I'm so sorry..." Her hair billowed, and her eyes glinted in the sourceless light. Her hands, he saw, were gloved.

"We call this docking satellite the Median," she said, leading him into a large sphere where people floated, talked, drank, and ate on the walls, floor, ceiling. "It's the place where down there and up here meet."

Down There. Up Here. He nodded, watching her fingers unseal a tube. She snatched at the wrapping as it started to twist away. Her gloves had colorless spines along their backs. It was hard to tell in this light whether they were glowing. She chuckled. "I'm really not used to pure free fall," she said. "The Median is pretty strange to me, too. Out there, it's different."

"You look great."

Unself-consciously, she nodded. But it was true. She was wearing the kind of unfussy coverall that he'd always imagined people wore in places like this. It was pale green and blue, silver-buttoned, clean and new and neat. He caught a waft of the gas from her tube, and her Laurie-scent as she turned her head and her hair swayed around him. The memories

453

tumbled in. "And you look better, John," she said, studying him. "Healthier."

"It's sometimes that way, after you've been ill." He chuckled. "I'd never expected to be ill."

"How bad was it?"

"I don't know. Ask me in twenty years. If I'm still here."

"But I thought..." She stopped and narrowed her eyes.

"I really don't know how long it'll be, Laurie. They had to rip the old recombinant out, put a new one in."

She nodded, unsure whether this new uncertainty was good or bad. But how could she know, when he didn't know himself?

He looked around again. All he could hear was the murmur of voices. "It's so quiet here. I'd imagined..."

"We regulate the sounds and vibrations. Tune them to the right pitch and recycle them through the oxygen vats as heat. Nothing's wasted. In space, a lot of things are more straightforward, once you get used to the difficulties."

He nodded.

"It's a small self-contained environment," she said. "That's where my own experience came in. The net, the kelpbeds, recycling. If you're going to live up here, it all has to be done."

"It's funny," he said, "that the technology of the Endless City should—"

"John, are you going to stay a priest?"

"It's what I always was, wasn't it? We found that out. And the mystery, the loss, the whiteness..."

"Whiteness?"

"Didn't I ever tell you? It was as though I was looking through into emptiness—blazing white. Seeing that beyond everything there was nothing."

"Do you feel the same way now?"

"I'm still looking," he said. "I've realized that that's what I'm here for. To look." He gazed at her. Even the gas from her tube behaved differently here, spread and tugged into ripples by the silent air. "So I've stopped pretending that I was owed some great insight. It's just a journey, isn't it? A journey for all of us, no matter what we think. And I have to go where my heart leads, which is still towards God, even if I may never find Him. I'm not giving up."

"You'll never give up, John. That isn't how you are."

"I learned that too. What's—"

"John, I . . ."

They looked at each other, feeling the barriers falling momentarily, opening into other worlds, other times, other ways. Places where they might never have met, or might have stayed apart, or remained together and in love.

She lowered the stub of her tube. A receptacle opened like a mouth to take it.

"I'd like to show you something."

He followed her as she swam and tumbled across the sphere. Here was Laurie upside down—or was it him? And here was a vertiginous glimpse, as if of a great wellshaft, all the way down through the Median's main central tunnel. A plump machine fluttered by them, flapping silver wings in pursuit of a stray glob of litter.

She caught his hand and pulled him through a doorway; out, it seemed, into the bright darkness of space itself.

"Over there," she said, hovering by him inside the huge transparent dome, pointing across Earth's nightside curve towards the great space station that turned nearby. "That's where I live."

"Does it have a name?"

She chuckled. "Several."

He turned slowly to look at her. He saw her smiling, outlined against the stars.

"Will you stay for a while, John? Will you come over there with me?"

"I can't just go across, though, can I?"

"It's only a couple of days here in Median for quarantine, and then a few more to let your recombinants subside. And these gloves—" She drew a slow, bright curve. "I hate them. These rules. But it's the price you pay. There's always a price, isn't there?"

"Then it's really true, that on the satellites it doesn't matter?"

"It's what I told you, John. It's a controlled environment. The dangers aren't the ones you get down there...unless someone carries them up. Recombinants are hardly needed, and it doesn't matter what color your eyes are. In fact, there are quite a lot of my people up here. There"—a smile—"you see! I still think of them as my people. But I'm glad we're here. All of us. It's the best chance we have. I remember when we ran out in the streets under those skies, and the witchwomen, the starmaps, the moonstones..." She blinked. Her eyes were shining. "One day, this'll be about more than just tending the climate, John. One day, we'll..." Laurie shook her head, gazing out at the turning wheel of the great station. "I wish I could show you."

"I really can't go over there, Laurie. I have to return to Rome. I have an appointment with the bishop tomorrow, and the last reentry's—when?" He looked at his watch. When he touched it with his fingers, it told him that he had less than an hour.

"Okay," she said. "It's not as though we're..."

"No."

"...never going to see each other again. I mean, I just wanted to settle, John. To get used to being *here*. You do understand that?"

"It was what I needed too."

"But if you really are...if you're going back on the reentry. I need to go back myself. It's where I live, and I have a shift tonight."

"What you do, does it have anything to do with structural communication?"

"Structural what?"

"It was just a thought."

Laurie floated in the starry darkness, her shining hands outstretched. He took them and felt the warmth of her flesh through the thin gloves.

He said, "I'll stay here alone for a while."

"You brought Hal's remains with you, didn't you?"

He nodded.

"Maybe we could..." She let go of him as she pondered something, then shook her head and waved a hand. The motion made her begin to drift away, and at their backs the space station she called home rolled on and on over Earth's darkside. "Over there, it makes you dizzy at first, although they've never quite worked out why. Something called the Coriolis force."

He said, "*Gunafana*, Laurie," as she drifted, before she could pull herself back to him.

He saw her grin.

"You just said good evening," she said. "Even here, John, it isn't evening."

"Goodbye, then."

Her face flashed out of the moon's light. She became a thinning silhouette as she waved to him from the tunnel leading from the dome, then there was nothing at all.

He looked out into space, where time poured from the darkness and where, so close, the endless lights of the space station turned. She'd be there again soon, tumbling over and over in that great wheel where all hands were joined. Or that, anyway, was how he'd like to leave it. That was what he'd like to think.

He looked at the Earth's gleaming darkside curve. Even with all the wonders of up here, down there was still more wonderful, and vast. He gazed at his planet for a timeless moment, feeling the glint of stars and satellites all around him, breathing Laurie's scent as it faded in the silent air, knowing that he was truly here, and watching as the hidden but rising sun broke a silver crescent on the gleaming rim of the River Ocean. Just as the sun began to throw filaments of light into his eyes, he saw something else flash below in the near-darkness, a silver capsule breaking the surface of the atmosphere like an arrow, a pointing finger, a line of fire where all elements were joined. Blue and black and white. It was the last of Hal. A shooting star.

Father John turned away and floated back towards the lighted tunnel.